REBEL RAPTURE

Leanna leaped to her feet and ran frantically. She could hear Major Clayton's footsteps, but she dared not break her stride to look behind.

Jeff lurched forward and grabbed her around the waist. They both fell unceremoniously to the ground, their fall cushioned by the soft grass. Leanna shrieked and struggled wildly. Grasping her wrists with one hand, Jeff held her arms over her head.

"You rebellious little hellcat!" he raged. "Must I put you in chains to keep you from escaping?"

"What's wrong, Major?" she taunted, panting. "Does it bother you that it is so easy for a Southerner to outsmart you?"

She began to struggle anew, but her provocative moves only brought a glitter to the major's eyes.

"Leanna . . ." he said, and then his mouth was pressing demandingly against hers. For a moment, Leanna lay perfectly still. But as a feeling of ecstasy floated gloriously through her entire being, she parted her lips in wonderful abandonment.

He released her trapped wrists, and her arms went about his neck. Her better judgment told her to push him away before it was too late. But for one rapturous moment she wanted to forget the war that made them bitter enemies, forget that she was his prisoner, and give herself up to searing passion. . . .

MORE CAPTIVATING HISTORICAL ROMANCES!

SURRENDER TO DESIRE   (1503, $3.75)
by Catherine Creel

Raven-haired Marianna came to the Alaskan frontier expecting adventure and fortune and was outraged to learn she was to marry a stranger. But once handsome Donovan clasped her to his hard frame and she felt his enticing kisses, she found herself saying things she didn't mean, making promises she couldn't keep.

TEXAS FLAME   (1530, $3.50)
by Catherine Creel

Amanda's journey west through an uncivilized haven of outlaws and Indians leads her to handsome Luke Cameron, as wild and untamed as the land itself, whose burning passion would consume her own!

TEXAS BRIDE   (1050, $3.50)
by Catherine Creel

Ravishing Sarah, alone in Wildcat City and unsafe without a man's protection, has no choice but to wed Adam MacShane—in name only. Then Adam, who gave his word of honor not to touch his Yankee wife, swears an oath of passion to claim his TEXAS BRIDE.

SAVAGE ABANDON   (1505, $3.95)
by Rochelle Wayne

Chestnut-haired Shelaine, saved by the handsome savage from certain death in the raging river, knew but one way to show her thanks. Though she'd never before known the embrace of a man, one glance at the Indian's rippling muscles made her shiver with a primitive longing, with wild SAVAGE ABANDON.

SURRENDER TO ECSTASY   (1307, $3.95)
by Rochelle Wayne

From the moment the soft-voiced stranger entered Amelia's bed all she could think about was the ecstasy of his ardent kisses and the tenderness of his caress. Longing to see his face and learn his name, she had no idea that he hid his identity because the truth could destroy their love!

Available wherever paperbacks are sold, or order direct from the Publisher. Send cover price plus 50¢ per copy for mailing and handling to Zebra Books, Dept. 1601, 475 Park Avenue South, New York, N.Y. 10016. DO NOT SEND CASH.

RECKLESS PASSION

BY ROCHELLE WAYNE

ZEBRA BOOKS
KENSINGTON PUBLISHING CORP.

ZEBRA BOOKS

are published by

Kensington Publishing Corp.
475 Park Avenue South
New York, NY 10016

First printing: May 1985

Printed in the United States of America

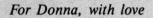

For Donna, with love

Part One

The Pines

Chapter One

Leanna Weston watched the red-and-white bobber float buoyantly on the rippling waves of the water. She held her fishing pole loosely in her hands, but as the Georgian sun continued to beat down on her, she switched the pole to one hand so she could use the other to wipe her perspiring brow. Because of the intense heat, she knew it would have been more pleasant to wait until late afternoon to go fishing, but by then it would have been too late to cook the fish for supper. Meat had become scarce for Leanna and her family. They had six hens and one rooster, but they needed the hens for eggs. Until recently, they'd had scores of chickens and three pigs, one of the pigs had been the right size for butchering and would have provided the Westons and their servants with pork through the upcoming winter months.

Leanna's pretty face puckered into a frown. "Damned stealing, Yankees!" she muttered. Angrily, she thought about the afternoon two weeks ago when Union troops had ridden brazenly onto her plantation, The Pines, destroying things at will and stealing whatever they wished.

It was the first time Leanna had actually seen a Yankee, and she hoped she'd never have to see one again. They had taken the meat stored in her smokehouse, plus most of the livestock. Then they had actually disgraced her house with their hated presence as they had ransacked every room in the large, columned mansion. Breaking into the pantry, they had helped themselves to the stored dry goods, vegetables, and shelf after shelf of canned food.

As the bobber continued to drift undisturbed on the top of the water, Leanna began to feel discouraged. Wasn't she going to get so much as one bite? She had never fished before in her life, and she was completely at a loss as to how long it took to get any results.

Leanna Weston was twenty-three years old. She was very lovely, although dressed as she was now, she looked more like a boy than a young woman. She had borrowed her straw fishing hat from the house servant Jackson to protect her face from the hot sun. Leanna had her long, light ash-colored hair tucked up beneath the wide-brimmed hat, and she had donned a pair of her brother's old breeches, which she had cut off at the knees so that they would be more comfortable and cooler to wear in the scorching summer temperature. She also wore a shirt that had once belonged to her brother. It was much too large, and she had rolled up the full sleeves, but the shirttail was so long that it hung past her hips. Her feet were bare, and edging closer to the riverbank, she stuck her toes into the water. The refreshing wetness felt so good that she was tempted to forget fishing and go swimming instead.

Smiling a little wickedly, Leanna envisioned herself stripping away her clothes and skinny-dipping as her brother Brad and his boyfriends had done during their youth. But thinking of her brother caused her smile to vanish, and sudden tears came to Leanna's large blue eyes. Brad had been dead now for almost a year; she still couldn't quite believe that she'd never see him again. He had fallen heroically in battle, fighting for his homeland and the Confederacy.

Leanna's father, Frank Weston, had been ailing when they had received word of Brad's death. The tragedy had sapped what little strength he'd had left, and on the same day Leanna had learned that her brother was dead, her father had died of a heart attack.

Suddenly, the bobber dipped beneath the water, and the tip of Leanna's pole followed. Reacting alertly, she gave the pole a short jerk, and as she pulled it up she could feel a fighting weight squirming at the end of her line.

Getting to her feet, she drew in her catch, a flapping, good-sized perch. Taking hold of the line, she brought the fish in closer. Looking down at what she hoped would not be the only piece of meat at dinner, her brow furrowed with mild bewilderment. How does one go about removing the hook from a fish? she wondered. A look of determination crossed her face. If she could actually touch a slimy worm and put it on a fishhook, then taking a hook out of a fish's mouth was, at least, less disgusting by comparison.

Leanna wrapped her fingers around the still lively perch. He wiggled and, instantly, she released him. "Don't be a ninny!" she told herself firmly. "He's only a little fish, and he can't hurt you!"

Once again, she grasped the active perch, but this time when he flipped his tail, she only gripped him more securely. Sitting, she placed the pole at her side; then with careful precision, she pulled the hook from the fish's mouth and dropped her catch into the large bucket half filled with water.

Proud of herself, she grabbed the can of worms, and as though she were now an experienced fisherman, she quickly baited the hook, then flung the line back into the water. The bobber was resting on the surface, and she watched it intently for the first sign of a nibble.

Hearing a fallen twig snap in the woods behind her, Leanna turned swiftly to glance over her shoulder. Seeing the house servant Jackson approaching, she smiled.

"How's it goin', Miz Anna?" he asked, grinning fondly at The Pines young mistress. He had never dreamed he'd see the day that Miss Leanna Weston would be fishing attired in boy's clothing. But then the war was bringing many changes that he had never imagined would come about.

"Jackson!" she said with excitement. "I caught a fish!"

Walking to her side, he looked down at the fish swimming in the bucket. "A fine-sized perch," he replied.

Leanna sighed discontently, "But he isn't big enough to feed all of us. I certainly hope he isn't my

12

only catch for the day."

Sitting beside her, he explained, "Fishin' takes patience, Miz Anna. But if you want, I'll take over for you."

"Did you finish repairing the door to the chicken house that the Yankees destroyed in their selfish haste to steal our hens?"

"No, ma'am, not yet. I thought I ought to come down here and check on you. I don't like you bein' this far from the house. It ain't safe with them Yankees and deserters from both sides ramblin' round the countryside."

Jackson was a strongly built man in his middle forties. His mother had been a Negro slave, but his father had been a white overseer. Leanna smiled at him with affection. She had known Jackson all her life. He had been her father's personal servant before she was born, and when Leanna was ten years old, Jackson had married the Westons' cook Matilda. The couple had had one child, Louise, who was now eleven years old.

Soon after Frank Weston's death, many of the slaves had disappeared, some running away in large groups, while others wandered off alone or in twos and threes. Then last month Confederate troops, on their way to Atlanta, had ridden to The Pines and taken all the able-bodied male slaves that remained to dig trenches to help defend the city of Atlanta. The slaves' families soon followed the menfolk. Although, at the time, Leanna had resented their leaving, now she was grateful that they were gone. She didn't know how she was going to feed eight people, and she was glad she didn't have over a hundred slaves to worry about as well.

Eight of us! she thought glumly as she returned to watching the bobber, mentally willing it to dip beneath the water. She had herself, her mother Mary, her sister-in-law Jennifer, her two nephews Bradley Junior and Matthew, plus Jackson and his family to try to furnish with fish for dinner. And, so far, all she had was one lonely perch!

Leanna's brow furrowed with worry. Her family's survival weighed heavily on her narrow shoulders. If only she had someone stronger and wiser than herself to ask for help. But there was no one. Her mother's health was failing, and since her husband's and son's deaths, her mind wandered continually into the past. Jennifer, Brad's widow, spent her time taking care of her children, never bothering to help Leanna with her numerous chores. Although Jackson and Matilda worked as strenuously as Leanna, they were slaves and were unaccustomed to making decisions, so all the responsibilities fell on Leanna.

"Miz Anna! . . . Miz Anna!" Jackson's daughter Louise called, her shrill voice suddenly piercing the quietness.

Placing her fishing pole on the ground, Leanna and Jackson stood together and, turning, they watched as she emerged hastily from the wooded area behind them.

Rushing up to them, Louise was breathing so heavily that she couldn't find her voice.

"Louise!" Leanna said sternly. "Calm down!"

Gasping, the eleven-year-old child cried, "Oh, Miz Anna! . . . Miz Anna!"

Frightened that something might have happened to

14

a member of her family, Leanna grabbed the girl's shoulders and shook her firmly. "Louise, what is wrong?" she demanded.

Making an attempt to control herself, Louise said between rapid gasps, "Yankees! . . . Oh Lord, Miz Anna, de Yankees is here! . . . It ain't like the last time dey was here . . . this time, there be more of 'em! There be over a hundred of 'em, Miz Anna."

"A hundred Yankees!" Leanna cried incredulously.

"Yes'm," Louise assured her. "Miz Anna, there is bunches of dem Yankees up at the house!"

Leanna released her firm hold on Louise, and as the little food left on the plantation fleetingly crossed her mind, she fumed, "The damned scavengers! They're like vultures returning to pick our bones clean!"

Taking long, angry strides, she began heading in the direction of the house as she swore resentfully, "Well, if they steal from us this time, it'll be over my dead body!"

"Miz Anna!" Jackson called after her with concern. "You stay away from them Yankees!" He knew the Weston temper flowed strongly in Leanna and he feared what would happen if it flared in front of the Union soldiers. He hurried after her, telling Louise to stay close behind him. "Miz Anna, you come back here!" he yelled.

Hearing Jackson's steps drawing closer, and worried that he would try to restrain her, Leanna hastened her strides; but in doing so, she tripped over a protruding tree root. She took a hard tumble and blocked her fall by holding out her arms and letting her hands hit palms down onto the red Georgian clay.

15

Because of recent rains the dirt was still moist and it clung to her fingers.

Jackson reached Leanna, and chastening her as he helped her to her feet, he grumbled, "You ain't got no business goin' after no Yankees! You stay here with Louise, and I'll go see what they want."

"Oh, I know what they want!" she blurted testily. "They want anything and everything on this plantation that might serve a useful purpose!" Her fall had caused her hat to slide sideways on her head, and strands of Leanna's long hair streamed across her face. Haphazardly, she tucked her loosened tresses back under the straw hat, but as she did, she smeared some of the dirt on her hands across her face.

Swerving brusquely, she continued her march up to the house. Realizing he couldn't talk Leanna into staying, Jackson followed close behind while mumbling under his breath.

Hurrying down the dirt path, Leanna could envision these Yankees invading her home, stealing and plundering at will. Dear God, they would most likely take what was left of her food and livestock! What would she do then! How could she conceivably feed eight people if the Yankees completely wiped out her meager supply?

It took Leanna nearly fifteen minutes to get close enough to the house for it to come within her view. Her determined strides faltered as she was confronted by the sight of an entire Union battalion covering the large, sloping lawn that surrounded the white, six-columned home.

"Good Lord!" she gasped. When Louise had told her that at least a hundred soldiers had arrived,

Leanna had not quite grasped how huge the number would appear when she actually saw it broken down into Yankees. As her initial shock passed, she began running toward her home. Anxious to reach her family, she fled past the mounted soldiers, maneuvering her way through their close formation.

She could see her mother and Jennifer standing on the large porch at the top of the long flight of steps that led up to the house. Two officers, a lieutenant and a major, were mounted on their horses. The major was speaking to Mary Weston and Jennifer when Leanna suddenly made her unexpected appearance. Pausing at the bottom of the stairs, her eyes reflected her hatred as she looked up toward the two officers.

Giving Leanna's presence little thought, the major continued speaking, "I am hereby informing you that your land has been confiscated by the U.S. Government. My troops and I will be staying here temporarily. I will need the use of your home."

Mary Weston was a timid woman, and Jennifer always prided herself on behaving as a proper lady, so they did not openly display their dislike for the Yankees. The two ladies merely responded to the major with cold silence.

But Leanna was too spirited to remain quiet, and the Weston temper she had inherited from her father exploded, "Why you dirty, stealing Yankees! . . ." But, suddenly, Jackson and Louise showed up, and Jackson silenced her with a solid nudge to her side with his elbow.

The major gave Leanna only a passing glance, due to her clothes mistakenly taking her for a boy. Re-

17

turning his attention to Mary Weston, he introduced the man mounted at his side, "Madam, this is Lieutenant Buehler."

Standing rigidly, Mary gave the lieutenant a stiff nod.

Sweeping his hat from his head, the major continued, "And I am Major Clayton. I hope our intrusion will not prove to be too much of an inconvenience for you and your family."

For a fleeting moment, Leanna saw the major as a man and not as a hated Yankee. His thick head of hair was curly and coal black, the temples tinged with attractive streaks of premature gray that gave him an aura of distinction. His lips were full and sensual, shadowed by a well-trimmed mustache. His eyes were a deep brown, and even from a distance, Leanna could see how his long, dark lashes curled up at the ends. She had never seen a gentleman so handsome, but becoming perturbed with herself for admiring a man who was her enemy, she quickly reminded herself of all the reasons why she despised him and all his kind.

As he was replacing his hat, Leanna recalled the words he had spoken to her mother, and she spat out resentfully, "Major Clayton, your presence is already an inconvenience! I want you off this property immediately. You Yankees are worse than the plague!"

His arrogant indifference aroused her anger even more, causing her ranting to continue, "I'll die fighting before I let you scum steal from us again!"

The major and the lieutenant started to dismount, but Leanna halted them by yelling angrily, "Get off our land! You . . . you . . ." She wished she knew a

18

word worse than "damn" to better express how she felt, but she couldn't think of one. "You . . . you damned Yankees!"

Jackson's large hand clutched her arm, but turning to him, she jerked free. Annoyed, she looked up at him, her cheeks were still smeared with red Georgian dirt. Due to her anger, she had forgotten how she was dressed, or even that she was shamefully barefooted, until she spun on her heels to continue her verbal abuse. A small rock dug painfully into the bottom of her foot, making her conscious of what a sight she must be presenting. If Leanna had known there was a large smudge of dirt on her face, she would have been mortified.

The major dismounted with ease, but he hadn't had any sleep for over twenty-four hours and was extremely fatigued. Glancing at Leanna, he said tediously, "I am tired, and in no mood to listen to any more insults from a scrawny little boy."

Boy! How dare he call me a boy! She seethed inwardly. Her temper running amuck, she shouted, "You Yankees are not only thieves and murderers, but you're also blind!" In one swift move, she took off her fishing hat, and her long blond hair fell gracefully past her shoulders.

Major Clayton was astounded, but he kept his surprise well masked. As he studied Leanna from head to toe, his experienced eye told him that beneath her loose fitting clothes lurked a very lovely woman.

Moving smoothly, the major stepped over to her side. Leanna was tall for a woman, but she had to look up to meet his eyes. Her expression was obsti-

19

nate, and her chin was held defiantly. She felt she had proven this Yankee a fool!

"Well?" she taunted flippantly, when he didn't speak. "Aren't you going to say anything, or are you at a loss for words?"

"No, ma'am," he replied. "I have something to say that you might be interested in knowing." His dark eyes sparkled with amusement, and, smiling, he told her calmly, "Your face is dirty."

Leaving her blushing with embarrassment, he hurried up the flight of steps and Mary Weston reluctantly showed him into the house.

Leanna entered the house by way of the back door. Storming into the spacious kitchen, she flung her hat down on the square wooden table. Stalking over to the wash basin, she quickly scrubbed her face as her thoughts churned turbulently. Oh, that Major Clayton has his nerve! How dare he speak to me so rudely! Informing me that my face was dirty as though I were a . . . a child!

Standing in front of the large cast-iron stove, Matilda inquired breathlessly, "Miz Anna, what do dem Yankees want?"

"They have confiscated our property!" Leanna spat, drying her face with a towel.

Unlike her husband Jackson, Matilda had absolutely no education and she asked, "What dat word mean?"

"Confiscate?" Leanna specified, raising her eyebrows questioningly.

"Yes'm," Matilda nodded, folding her arms beneath her heavy bosom. She was a tall, large-boned woman.

Walking to the table, Leanna sat on one of the kitchen chairs. "Confiscate is the word Yankees use when they intend to take something that doesn't belong to them," she answered sarcastically, her eyes darting angry sparks.

"How long do dem Yankees plan to stay here?" Matilda asked urgently.

Leanna shrugged her narrow shoulders, and Matilda noticed that she suddenly looked very tired. The older woman's heart went out to her young mistress. The young woman worked so hard, and she was too delicate for such strenuous labor. Matilda knew Leanna had taken it upon herself to tackle many chores that should have been done by someone much sturdier. She tried to help Leanna as much as she possibly could, but her own chores kept her busy from sunup to sundown, and Jackson was so overworked that sometimes he was still busy hours after sunset. Louise was only a child and too young to be of much assistance. Miss Mary was no help at all, but she was ailing and Matilda feared she'd soon be joining her husband and son in the good Lord's heaven. As for Miss Jennifer, she had her hands full taking care of her sons, the four-year-old Bradley and the two-year-old Matthew.

Sighing heavily, Leanna explained, "Major Clayton said that he and his troops will be staying here temporarily."

"What's Major Clayton like?"

His handsome face flashed across Leanna's mind very briefly before she was able to force herself to envision him only as a disgusting Yankee. Her emotions confused her, causing her to speak as though she were trying to convince herself as well as Matilda. "He's a rude, boorish . . . scoundrel!"

"A rude, boorish scoundrel?" a deep voice suddenly sounded from the open doorway that led from the kitchen into the dining room.

Startled, Leanna tensed, and jerking her head awkwardly, she saw Major Clayton watching her. He appeared to be not in the least annoyed by her insults, but Leanna detected an intensity in his dark eyes that made her wonder if he was truly as composed as he wanted her to believe.

Without waiting to be invited, he stepped into the room followed by two soldiers, who immediately began searching the kitchen.

Springing to her feet, Leanna asked them harshly, "What do you think you are doing?"

"What does it look like they are doing?" the major replied. "The entire house is being searched."

"Are they searching for something to steal?" she asked angrily. "Well, there isn't much left for you vultures to take. More of your kind have already been here!"

"I can assure you that nothing will be stolen." An amused smile flickered across his face as he added, "Confiscated perhaps, but not stolen."

Oh, the man was insufferable, and Leanna told herself that she despised him.

"Miss Weston . . ." he began, but looking at her questioningly he added, "You are a Weston, aren't you?"

Lifting her chin haughtily, she spat, "Of course, I am!"

Clearly, his eyes took in her bedraggled appearance as he replied, "Well, you look somewhat different from the other ladies of the Southern gentry that I have met."

She tried desperately not to blush, but against her will, she could feel her cheeks grow warm. The major noticed her embarrassment, and knowing he had evened the score with this spirited little rebel, he decided to stop teasing her.

"Miss Weston," he began evenly, "hereafter the study will be off limits to you and your family."

"Why?" she demanded.

"It will be my temporary office," he explained.

Finishing their search, the two troopers informed the major that they had found no lethal weapons in the kitchen, except for the customary knives. He told his men to let the knives remain and then dismissed them.

Leanna now knew the reason behind the search, and she revealed, "There are only two rifles left in the house, and we need them for hunting game."

"They will be returned to you when we leave," the major assured her.

Before she could tell him how much she resented his authority, Lieutenant Buehler came into the kitchen and announced, "The supply wagons have arrived."

"Good," the major responded. "Give orders for the men to bivouac a few yards from the house and have the mess tent erected. I'm sure that everyone is tired and hungry."

As the lieutenant marched out of the room, Major Clayton turned back to Leanna. "As I said earlier, I

hope our stay will not be too much of an inconvenience."

Standing proudly, she replied, "And as I said
earlier, you are already an inconvenience."

"Miss Weston," he said tolerantly, "there is a war
raging between your people and mine, must we also
have a personal war between ourselves? Isn't one war
quite enough?"

No! She wouldn't call a truce with this arrogant
intruder who wore the colors of the Union! "Major
Clayton, you and your men are not welcome on my
property, and I will hate every minute that you are
here!" Swerving sharply, she turned her back to him.
Agitated, she began to breathe rapidly as she folded
her arms beneath her breasts.

"Miz Anna, is you all right?" Matilda asked.

"I will be as soon as this Yankee removes himself
from this room!" she answered irritably.

Staring at Leanna's turned back, Major Clayton
said patiently, "Miss Weston, my troops and I will be
staying here for an indefinite period of time. May I
point out that it would be in your best interest to
accept our visit with a certain degree of civility."

"I'll never be civil to a Yankee!" she fumed, keeping her back turned. "And you are not visiting,
Major Clayton, you are intruding!"

Admiring her spunk, he smiled, and before leaving
the kitchen, he said cordially, "Good day, Miss Weston."

Major Jeff Clayton sat at Frank Weston's desk in
the privacy of the study, nursing his brandy. He
hadn't seen Leanna since their confrontation in the

kitchen. That had taken place earlier in the day and it was now dusk. Relaxing, he leaned back in the comfortable leather-bound chair. Thinking about the spirited Miss Weston, he chuckled softly. Although she had been dressed in ragged boys' clothing, he had still found her enticing. He wished she weren't quite so hostile, he would enjoy getting to know her. Toying with his half-filled glass of brandy, he shook his head slightly. There was little chance of that happening. He doubted she would let down her guard long enough for him to engage her in polite conversation. But Jeff Clayton was not a man to be easily discouraged, and he made the decision to become better acquainted with the lovely and vivacious Miss Weston.

Standing, he pushed back the chair, and placing his glass on the desk, he walked across the room to gaze out the window that faced the front lawn. He could see the flickering glows of the campfires around which his men were assembled. He wondered how long he would have to remain on this plantation before General Sherman arrived to give him his next set of orders.

At the age of thirty-four, Jeff Clayton was one of Sherman's youngest majors. His intelligence and superior military leadership had led to his rise in rank from lieutenant to major.

Still gazing out the window, Jeff sighed deeply as his thoughts continued. He knew Sherman's goal was to take Atlanta, and Jeff could not foresee General Hood's troops stopping Sherman's army. Sherman then planned to march onward to the sea where Jeff was sure Savannah would also fall to the Union's better equipped army. He wondered how many Confederates would give their lives protecting the two cities, and how many Union soldiers would die besieging them. He was sure the deaths would number in the thousands, and the tragedy of it all fell heavily on his shoulders. Jeff hated this war, but he believed it was necessary. He didn't want the country to be separated, and he intended to fight to keep it united.

Moving away from the window, he returned to the desk. He reached for his glass of brandy, but his fatigue was so great that he realized he was on the verge of becoming intoxicated. Remembering that he'd had one of his men deliver a bag of coffee to the Westons' kitchen, he decided to ask Matilda to make a pot of strong, black coffee.

Leanna helped Matilda lift the last huge bucket of water from the stove, then pour the water into the bathtub placed in the middle of the kitchen floor. It had taken several buckets to fill the tub, and Leanna was relieved the chore was over. Before the war, she would never have considered taking a bath anywhere except in the privacy of her bedroom. But then there had been servant girls to carry the water-filled buckets upstairs. Now, it was much easier to simply bathe in the kitchen and save herself and Matilda all the numerous trips up the stairs to her bedroom to fill a bathtub.

Leanna wanted to pamper herself, so she poured the last of her bath oil into the water, and the tub was suddenly filled with perfumed bubbles.

Dipping her hand into the sudsy water, Leanna said decisively, "The temperature is just right." Unbuttoning her shirt, she continued sounding fatigued, "Oh, Matilda, I'm so tired that I feel as though I could relax in the tub for hours." Suddenly, Leanna remembered her robe. "I forgot my wrapper. Will you please go to my room and get it for me Matilda. And take your time, for I intend to bathe leisurely."

"Yes'm," Matilda replied and, deciding to use the servants' back stairway, left the kitchen by the rear entrance.

Anticipating a relaxing bath, Leanna quickly shed her clothes. She knew Jackson had been told that she was bathing, and she didn't have to worry that he might barge into the kitchen; that Major Clayton might be in the house had slipped her mind entirely.

Leanna had only one foot in the large marble tub when the kitchen door unexpectedly swung open. Gaping, her eyes flew to the now unbarred doorway. Coming face to face with Major Clayton, her shock rendered her incapable of moving.

The major's steps halted brusquely, and the sight of Leanna's bared beauty took his breath away. During the moments it took for Leanna to recover from her shock, his eyes trailed boldly over her, admiring her firm ivory breasts and her slim but feminine hips. As his vision fell upon the delectable golden mound between her thighs, he could feel his loins responding.

Leaping into the tub, Leanna slid down into the sudsy water until it was up to her chin. Glaring at the major, she snapped, "How dare you! Get out of this room immediately!" She had never been so embarrassed. Good Lord, this man had actually seen her completely unclothed!

Instead of leaving, he astounded Leanna by ambling farther into the kitchen.

"If you don't leave this instant, I'll scream!" she threatened.

"I wouldn't, if I were you," he advised insouciantly. "You scream and you might very well find yourself surrounded by dozens of Union soldiers investigating the reason for all the disturbance." His half-smile was cocky. "But if you insist on screaming, go right ahead. I'm sure my men will be appreciative."

Deciding screaming was not the solution to her dilemma, Leanna's eyes flashed with rage as she spat, "Don't you dare come one step closer!"

Her order did not deter his strides, and reaching the bathtub, he leaned over it, placing a hand on each side. Gazing down into her flushed face, he said sensually, "Miss Weston, your enchanting eyes are bluer than your Georgian sky."

Dumbfounded, she responded simply by staring at him. But as he lowered his face closer to hers, the intense stimulation his presence was sending through her entire being, frightened her.

"Miss Weston," he began, but, pausing, he questioned, "It is . . . Miss Weston, isn't it?" She nodded stiffly. Continuing, he asked, "May I take the liberty of kissing your sweet lips?"

Oh, this man had his nerve! "No, you may not kiss me!" she said furiously.

Standing straight, he shrugged his strong shoulders as though her refusal was nothing more than a mild disappointment. Spotting the coffeepot on the stove, and smelling the aroma, he stepped to the cupboard and helped himself to a cup. Filling it with coffee, he said calmly, "I will leave you to your bath, Miss Anna Weston."

"Leanna!" she promptly corrected.

"But Matilda called you Anna."

"The servants have always called me Anna."

"Servants?" he questioned cynically. "Don't you mean slaves?"

"You're not only a disgusting Yankee, but apparently, you are also an abolitionist," she retorted. Oh, if only she hadn't told Matilda to take her time. Desperately, she wished for Matilda's return so this arrogant devil would leave.

"Well, I don't believe in slavery. Does that make me an abolitionist?"

Evasively, she remarked, "If the shoe fits . . ."

Taking a sip of his coffee, he studied her over the rim of his cup. God, she was beautiful! He longed to kiss her, and he wished he had tasted her lips moments before when he'd had the opportunity. Placing his cup on the table, he grinned slyly as he told her, "Miss Weston, if the shoe fits is only one of many clichés. There is also one that says, if you don't succeed the first time, try, try again."

"Succeed at what?" she asked smugly.

"Getting your permission to kiss you," he said, taking an empty pan from the kitchen counter. Stepping to the tub, he dipped the pan into the sudsy water, then emptied it into one of the buckets that Leanna and Matilda had used to heat water in. Once again, he dipped the pan into the bath water.

"What are you doing?" she exclaimed angrily.

Pouring the water into the bucket, he answered

flatly, "I'm emptying your bathtub."

"Stop it this instant!" she snapped, slapping at his hand. Without a filled tub, she would have no way to hide her nudity from this . . . this black-hearted scoundrel!

Grinning roguishly, he baited her. "Not until you give me a kiss."

"You're insufferable!" she cried.

"Determined." He came back to her side.

Feeling the water beginning to recede, Leanna surrendered, "All right! Kiss me, and then get out of here!"

Putting down the pan, he once again leaned over the tub, balancing himself by placing a hand on each side of it. She raised her face to his. Let him have his way! she thought. I certainly won't respond to his dreadful kiss!

Understanding her obstinate, but delightful expression, he chuckled inwardly. This enticing little rebel was definitely a challenge. He leaned in closer, and Leanna closed her eyes, but the image of his handsome face lingered in her mind.

The initial touch of his lips was so gentle that Leanna was able to keep her resolution not to respond. The pressure of his mouth slowly deepened on hers, and, unconsciously, Leanna clenched her hands into fists as she tried to fight against the warm feeling that was starting to flow through her. Tenderly, he urged her lips open beneath his, and she began losing herself in their passion-building kiss. If Matilda hadn't chosen that moment to return, Leanna's resolutions would have crumbled, and she would have wantonly responded.

"Miz Anna!" Matilda gasped.

Quickly, the major stepped back from the tub. Blushing visibly, Leanna looked up at him, but if he was disturbed by Matilda's sudden presence, she couldn't tell by his casual manner. Taking his time, he walked to the stove and lifted the coffeepot, then picking up his cup, he moved back to the side of the bathtub.

Gazing steadily down into Leanna's eyes, he smiled charmingly. "Miss Weston, thank you very much for your Southern hospitality." He gave her an affectionate wink, then nodded cordially to Matilda and, turning swiftly, left the kitchen.

Wide-eyed, Leanna watched his departing back. She wondered why she hadn't answered his last remark with a retaliatory quip.

"Miz Anna!" Matilda began reproachfully. "Why was you kissin' that man?" Not giving her a chance to reply, she continued rapidly, "And shame on you for lettin' him in here while you is takin' a bath! What if your mama had walked in here and found you actin' like poor white trash?"

Remembering how nice it had felt to have the major's lips touching hers, Leanna sighed with exasperation, "Oh, if only he weren't a damned Yankee!"

Chapter Two

The next morning, Leanna slept later than usual and was awakened by her two nephews barging into her bedroom.

"Aunt Leanna!" the four-year-old Bradley called, jumping onto her bed. Matthew, only a few days past his second birthday, tried to follow his brother's example and made an effort to pounce upon Leanna's bed, but his legs were too short so his attempt only succeeded in frustrating him.

Sitting up, Leanna reached for Matthew and lifted him to her side. Looking at Bradley, she asked cheerfully, "Who gave you boys permission to come in here and wake me up?"

"Jackson said it's time for the shootin' lessons," Bradley answered.

Glancing at the bedroom window, Leanna became aware of how high the sun had climbed into the sky. "My goodness!" she exclaimed. "I overslept! And I have so many things to do!"

"I wanna learn to shoot too. Can I go with you

and Jackson?" Bradley asked hopefully.

"Honey, you're still too young," she replied gently. He frowned with disappointment, and studying his face, his resemblance to his father brought Brad to her mind. At times her brother's death could still hit her acutely, as at that moment when the pain of losing him once again struck her sharply. She drew both boys into her embrace. Oh, damn this war! she thought bitterly. Damn this war that takes fathers from their children . . . fathers who will never return!

Entering the bedroom, Jennifer said reproachfully, "Shame on you boys for waking up your Aunt Leanna."

"Jackson said we could," Bradley explained quickly.

Releasing her nephews, Leanna swung her legs over the side of the bed. "Don't fuss at them, Jennifer. I really shouldn't have slept so late."

"You work too hard." Jennifer chastened her concernedly.

It was on the tip of Leanna's tongue to tell her that if she didn't work endlessly from sunup to sundown none of them would survive, but she held back the retort. She knew Jennifer meant well. Neither her sister-in-law, nor her mother, could face the bitter truth. They thought they could see this war through without change, still living by the old ways and customs.

Jennifer Weston was a pretty woman, the same age as Leanna, and they had been friends since childhood. When they had matured into young ladies, many Georgians had claimed they were the two

34

prettiest belles in the county. Jennifer's dark hair did contrast beautifully with her light complexion, and her jade green eyes had once been sparkling. But since Brad's death, the sparkle had gone out of her eyes and the expression in them now was one of despair.

Walking to the bedroom window, and looking outside, Jennifer said indignantly, "Yankees camping on The Pines! Oh, Leanna, it just breaks my heart to see the enemy intruding on Brad's home. He loved this plantation so much!"

Jennifer's talk of Yankees made Leanna think of Major Clayton, and remembering the kiss they had shared, she suddenly flushed. Purposely dismissing the handsome Union officer from her mind, she said briskly, "You boys run along so that I can get dressed."

As the children scampered from the room, Leanna walked over to her wardrobe. Within were several pairs of Brad's old breeches and she started to pick up one of them, but remembering her home had been invaded by scores of Yankees, she decided to slip into one of her old gowns. Dressing like a boy was all right when only her family was on the plantation, but she would not dress so in the presence of others.

Rummaging through her gowns, she decided on a simple calico dress. She didn't go to her bureau for petticoats; it was too hot to be bothered with them.

Moving away from the window, Jennifer offered, "I'll go downstairs and tell Matilda to fix you some breakfast."

As Jennifer was crossing the room, Leanna asked hesitantly, "Is . . . is Major Clayton in the house?"

"He's in the study," Jennifer answered, her tone revealing how bitterly she resented his presence. Her steps halting abruptly, she whirled and faced Leanna. "How long do you think those Yankees will stay?"

"I don't know. But I'm sure it won't be for very long," Leanna stammered, suddenly realizing that she wasn't looking forward to Major Clayton's departure. She felt guilty, for she knew she should despise him. He was the enemy! But Leanna had no control over the emotions the attractive Union major had stirred within her heart. She felt like a traitor to her family and the Confederacy, and her betrayal weighed heavily on her conscience.

Leanna knew the major had confiscated her rifles and it would be necessary to go to him and ask his permission to use the guns. So immediately following breakfast, she hurried to the study, where she was confronted by a young sentry. When she told him she needed to see the major, he announced her presence. Receiving permission to enter, she stepped into the room.

Major Clayton was standing beside the desk, and as she moved gracefully into the study, his eyes took in her obvious beauty, noticing the way her dress clung to her lovely bosom and feminine hips. It was apparent that she wasn't wearing stuffy petticoats, and for the first time since he had ridden into Georgia, Jeff found a reason to be grateful for Georgia's scorching summers.

"Major Clayton," she began, trying to keep her composure, but she had seen the way his penetrating eyes had looked at her as though they could see right through her clothes.

"What can I do for you, Miss Weston?" he asked. His expression, as usual, was cocky.

"I need the rifles you took from my home," she replied, hoping she sounded totally collected.

"They are still in your home," he answered, gesturing toward the two rifles propped in the corner of the room. His eyes twinkling, he asked, "Why do you need weapons? Are you expecting Yankees?"

Leanna tried to look annoyed, but she couldn't hold back the tiny smile that teased her lips. "For the past month," she began explaining, "Jackson and I have been going into the woods twice a week for shooting lessons. The lessons have been going quite well, and I prefer that they not be interrupted." When he didn't give his consent, she continued short-temperedly, "For goodness sake, Major Clayton. We can't very well shoot at least a hundred Yankees with only two rifles."

"One rifle," he corrected. "You have my permission to take one of them." Ambling toward the weapons, he asked, "Which one do you prefer?"

"It doesn't matter," she sighed.

As he picked up one of the guns, an idea suddenly occurred to him, and returning to her side, he said, "I don't think it would be wise to allow you or Jackson the freedom of having a loaded weapon in your possession without being thoroughly supervised. So, Miss Weston, I will escort you into the woods and give you your shooting lesson." He wanted very much to be alone with her and was glad he had grasped the opportunity. He wasn't exactly sure why he wanted to be in Leanna's company; he

37

only knew that for some reason he found her more attractive than any woman he had ever met.

Wide-eyed, Leanna breathed, "You are going to give me a? . . ." But, of course, this man was a Yankee, and he had no way of knowing that slaves were never allowed to shoot firearms. Naturally, he would presume it was Jackson teaching her to shoot instead of the other way around. Leanna was a perfect shot, and suppressing a smile, she replied, "Very well. If you insist, then you may give me a lesson."

Returning the gun to the corner of the room, he decided, "We'll take my rifle, it's newer and in better condition."

Looking at him with feigned innocence, she said a little timidly, "Whatever you think is best. I can't tell one rifle from another, and they do frighten me, so you will be a patient teacher, won't you?"

He studied her questioningly. Something was not quite right, but he couldn't put his finger on what it was. Noting his distrust, Leanna feared she may have overplayed her role, and not giving him time to dwell on his thoughts, she said briskly, "Are you ready to leave? I don't have all day."

Hiking into the woods with Leanna at his side, Jeff decided to keep their conversation casual and to avoid any mention of the war that stood like a wall between them.

"Miss Weston," he began insouciantly, "tell me about yourself."

"What do you want to know?" she asked.

"Why don't you tell me what your plans are for the

future?"

"I plan to live on my plantation if you Yankees don't completely destroy it," she remarked, her voice tinged with bitterness.

Jeff grimaced. How could he have thought the war would be a topic he could avoid between himself and this spirited little rebel?

"But surely you don't intend to live here for the rest of your life," he replied. "Don't you suppose that someday you'll marry and live elsewhere?"

"Maybe," she mumbled evasively. Tentatively, she broached the subject that had been plaguing her thoughts. "Major Clayton, how long will you and your troops stay here?"

"I don't know," he answered truthfully. "I'm waiting for orders."

"Orders from whom?" she queried.

"General Sherman," he revealed.

"Sherman!" she exclaimed irritably, despising Georgia's most hated enemy. "I hope he doesn't plan to deliver your orders in person. The mere thought of that horrible man on my property makes me so angry that I could . . . I could . . ."

"You could what?" he coaxed.

"I could just spit!" she blurted, using one of her favorite expressions from childhood.

Jeff laughed boisterously, his laughter full and deep. Leanna blushed, wishing she hadn't spoken so unbecomingly.

"Leanna Weston," Jeff said jubilantly, "you are totally delightful!"

Leanna wasn't sure if he had given her a compliment or was only teasing. "I'm delightful?" she pressed, wanting him to define exactly what he meant.

Gazing down into her face, he answered, "Beautifully so."

Leanna gleamed. He thought she was beautiful! Although she was perfectly aware that she shouldn't care whether he found her beautiful or not, she couldn't repress the wonderful thrill that flowed through her.

They reached the area Leanna had chosen as the ideal spot for Jackson's lessons, and pointing at a large oak, she said, "There are some cans stacked under that tree." Years ago, her father had kept pigs penned on this part of his land, and pieces of the old corral were still intact. "Line up a few of the cans on the fence," she instructed.

Handing her his rifle, which Leanna knew was loaded, he turned his back to her as he walked over to get the cans. He picked up four and placed them on top of the dilapidated fence that had once kept the Westons' livestock securely penned.

Glancing at the loaded rifle, Leanna admired the major's courage. They were enemies, and yet he trusted her enough to place his life in her hands. She watched him intently as he carefully placed the cans on top of the wooden fence. Studying his tall, lean frame as he walked back to her, Leanna was acutely aware of his overwhelming masculinity. He looked so handsome in his well-tailored uniform, and lowering her intense gaze, she noticed the way his trousers fit tightly across his slim hips. Becoming aware of the male bulge at his crotch, Leanna suddenly flushed and sensed a longing spreading downward between

40

her legs. Flustered by these strange and wonderful feelings that his presence incited, she quickly raised her gaze. As he reached her side, her thoughts cried desperately, If only his uniform were gray instead of blue!

Looking back at the line of cans, he said doubtfully, "They won't be a very easy target for a beginner like yourself. Don't you think you should aim at something larger?"

"Oh, the cans aren't for me," she answered promptly. "I thought you might like to show me how well you shoot." When he didn't respond, she taunted, "You can hit those little cans, can't you, Major?"

He grinned, and she noticed that his smile brought a bright twinkle into his brown eyes. She handed him his rifle, and he turned to face his intended targets.

Stepping back, she watched as he fired, sending the first can flying into the air before it plunged back to the earth. He didn't stop until he had shot all the targets without missing one.

"Very good, Major Clayton!" she acclaimed. "You are quite a marksman!"

He reloaded the rifle, then handed it to Leanna. "There are more cans under the tree. Would you like me to build them into a pyramid? That way they will make a larger target."

"No, I don't think so," she said a little uncertainly. "Why don't you line them up in a single row? I watched you very closely when you were shooting, and I think I might be able to hit at least one of them."

He did as she requested; then when he returned to

her side, she took careful aim and hit the last can in the row. As he had done earlier, she did not stop until she had shot all the targets. Proud that she hadn't missed, she handed him his rifle, stating casually, "I think we should find a smaller target, don't you?"

When Leanna had struck the can on her first shot, Jeff had believed it was pure luck, but when she continued to hit her marks, he realized she had very cleverly tricked him. Bowing gallantly, he remarked, "Touché, Miss Weston, and hereafter, I will never again take you for granted. Speaking of a smaller target, I am seriously considering the spot between your beautiful blue eyes."

"Don't be a poor sport, Major," she said pertly. "You shouldn't have taken it for granted that Jackson was the teacher and I the student. My father never allowed his slaves to shoot firearms."

"I'm sure he didn't, for fear that they might turn about and use them against him," he replied mockingly.

"Slave uprisings were not uncommon."

"I can't quite picture Jackson turning against the Westons."

"Jackson was a house slave. There was no reason for him to learn to use a weapon."

"Was a slave?" he questioned. "Have you set him free?"

Why had she spoken as though Jackson were no longer a slave? But then she seldom thought of him in that way. He and Matilda were like members of her family and she loved them dearly. "Maybe Jackson doesn't want to be free," she retorted.

"Have you ever asked him?"

42

"No," she replied reluctantly.

He shook his head in disbelief. "You arrogant Southerners astound me. You reign majestically over your slaves and never once question their rights as human beings."

"The Westons were kind to their slaves," she said, sticking up for her family.

"So kind that all your slaves, except for Jackson and his family, deserted you at the first opportunity."

"Major Clayton," she began, annoyed, "this conversation is leading us absolutely nowhere, and to continue it is a waste of time."

Stepping over to a nearby tree, he propped his rifle against it. Moving back to Leanna, he agreed, "You're right, Miss Weston, we are wasting our time together; and we have so little to waste."

"Time together?" she queried.

Placing his hands on her shoulders, he answered, "I'll be leaving soon, and I may never see you again. Leanna, let's make the most of these next few days."

Stepping back from his touch, because she seemed to have no defense against it, she stammered, "Major Clayton, you are too forward."

He moved toward her, and afraid he intended to embrace her, she turned away to head back for the house. Lurching, he grasped her arm and pulled her against him.

Gazing down into her face, he said sincerely, "Leanna, I've never met a woman like you. If things were different . . . if there was no war . . ." Her face so close to his was a temptation he couldn't refuse, and his lips swiftly sought hers.

His exciting and demanding kiss made Leanna's

43

knees weaken, and she fell against him as his arms encircled her, drawing her even closer. She didn't want to respond to the warm mouth on hers, but how could she conceivably fight the burning stimulation his kiss was arousing through her entire being? Sliding her arms about his neck, she parted her lips so that his tongue could savor the inside of her mouth. Their passionate kiss aroused Jeff, and Leanna could feel his solid hardness against her soft thighs. His hand moved upward to caress her breasts, and his intimate touch sent her mind swirling with an awakened desire so powerful that she completely lost touch with reality. She was aware only of this beautiful moment in which she found bliss in the arms of a Union major.

Suddenly, Jackson's voice sounded nearby. "Miz Anna! . . . Miz Anna!"

Jeff released her unwillingly, and still overcome by his kiss, Leanna tottered precariously. "Are you all right?" he asked urgently.

Regaining her composure, she breathed, "Yes . . . yes, I'm fine."

Emerging from the thicket, Jackson said rapidly, "Miz Anna, are we gonna have our lesson?"

Jeff eyed the man knowingly. He was sure it hadn't been Jackson's desire for a shooting lesson that had sent him in search of Leanna, but rather his concern for her virtue.

"I'll leave my rifle and ammunition for your use," Jeff announced.

"But I thought you didn't trust Jackson or me with a weapon," she reminded him.

"As you pointed out earlier, it would be quite

44

impossible for the two of you to take on a full battalion." Touching the brim of his hat, he said cordially, "Good day, Miss Weston."

She watched the major as his long strides carried him away. She wondered a little nervously what would have happened between herself and the major if Jackson hadn't shown up. Afraid she would shamelessly give herself to this handsome Union officer if the opportunity should arise, she faithfully promised herself that she would never again be alone with him.

When Leanna returned to the house she headed straight for the kitchen, searching for Louise. Finding her, she informed the child that she was to work beside her for the rest of the day. Louise was surprised by Leanna's request, but she enjoyed her mistress' company, so she accepted her decision without argument. Leanna had decided the only way to avoid being alone with Major Clayton was to make sure she had Louise in her presence at all times.

Leanna and Louise were working in the vegetable garden when Matilda came to inform Leanna that her mother wished to see her in her sitting room.

Telling Louise to wait for her, Leanna hurried into the house, up the stairs, and to her mother's quarters. She knocked lightly on the closed door before opening it. Entering the room, she saw her mother resting on the chaise longue that Frank Weston had given her on their tenth wedding anniversary, having imported it from France.

"Did you want to see me, Mama?" she asked, moving across the room.

45

Mary Weston gestured toward the chair placed close to the chaise lounge. "Sit down, Leanna," she said softly. Mary was a small and very delicate woman. Leanna had inherited her ash-colored hair from her mother, and as Leanna sat on the chair, she noticed the gray that had come into her mother's tresses since Frank Weston's death.

"Leanna," Mary began upbraidingly, "this morning I was standing by my window, and I saw you walking away from the house with that Major Clayton." Drawing her mouth into a thin, disapproving line, she asked sternly, "Why? Why were you with that deplorable Yankee?"

Guiltily, Leanna stammered, "He insisted on giving me a shooting lesson."

Mary was surprised by her daughter's answer. "Leanna Weston, your brother taught you to be a perfect shot! Stop fibbing to me, young lady!" Five years ago, when Mary had found out that Brad was teaching Leanna to shoot, she had been mortified. She had tried to put a stop to the lessons, telling her husband that learning to use a rifle was unbecoming for a lady. But Frank Weston had known how much the lessons meant to Leanna, and to his wife's dismay, he hadn't ordered them stopped.

Mary continued harshly, "I insist that you explain why you were in the company of a Yankee!"

Hesitantly, Leanna revealed what had happened between herself and Major Clayton in the study.

"That is no excuse!" Mary seethed. "You should have told the major the truth, and then if he had still insisted on giving the lesson, he would have given it to Jackson."

46

Leanna knew her mother was right. She should have been honest with the major, but she had wanted to go into the woods with him. What is wrong with me? she thought wretchedly. How can I be so disloyal to my own kind?

Sitting up, Mary eyed her daughter severely, "Leanna, I forbid you to speak to that horrible Yankee!"

Suddenly, impatient with her mother for treating her as though she were a child, Leanna replied firmly, "Mama, he is staying in this house. I can't very well avoid talking to him."

"Then I must insist that you go to your room and stay there until these Yankees have left our property!" Mary ordered determinedly.

Leanna stared incredulously at her mother. If she stayed in her room, who was going to tend to all her chores? Didn't her mother realize how much work there was on this plantation, and that there were only three people to take care of everything that must be done? Testily, she replied, "I can't stay closed up in my room! There are vegetables to be picked, and then I must help Matilda can them so we'll have food for this winter. The chickens have to be fed, and their grain is running low, which means I will have to go out to the cornfields and see if there is any corn left to be picked. Hopefully, I will find enough to grind up for the chickens—"

Interrupting, Mary chastened, "Leanna, that is no kind of work for a lady. You leave those chores for Matilda and Jackson."

Standing, Leanna explained, "I'm sorry, Mama, but if we are going to survive this war, then it is

47

necessary that I work alongside Matilda and Jackson."

Conceding reluctantly, Mary replied, "You are a grown woman, and I can't force you to obey me."

"Mama, I'm not disobeying you, I'm merely trying to keep us all alive."

"Perhaps," Mary said shortly, "but I don't think that means it is necessary for you to socialize with a Union major." Her voice breaking with anguish, she pleaded, "Leanna, the Yankees killed your brother!"

"I know!" Leanna cried, guilt piercing her. She knew she must try to avoid Major Clayton and keep Louise with her at all times.

Covering her face with her hands, Mary began crying heartbrokenly for her son, and kneeling beside her, Leanna took her into her arms.

Chapter Three

Plagued with guilt, and frightened by her feelings for Major Clayton, Leanna kept Louise at her side for the remainder of the day. Keeping Louise as a constant companion had been unnecessary, because Jeff did not try to approach her. Instead, he had spent the day in the study or else in the presence of his soldiers.

The next morning, Leanna awoke early, and following breakfast, she decided to go fishing before the day grew too hot. Taking Louise with her, she gathered up her pole and the can of worms, as well as a bucket to hold the fish she hoped to catch.

Trudging into the woods with Louise following, Leanna found her long dress a nuisance and was tempted to return to the house and slip into a pair of trousers. Noticing Louise was falling behind, she glanced over her shoulder and said sternly, "Louise, don't lag."

Louise was carrying the empty bucket, and letting it slap against her leg, she replied slothfully, "I's comin', Miz Anna."

"Honestly, Louise," Leanna complained, "you've been acting strange ever since I told you we were going fishing."

Making a halfhearted attempt to keep up with Leanna's sturdy strides, she mumbled, "I hates to go fishin', Miz Anna."

Pausing, Leanna turned to face her. "Why?" she asked.

Nearing her mistress, the child puckered her face into a frown. "Fishin' is too borin'. I gets tired just sittin' and doin' nothin'."

Leanna sighed impatiently, but she couldn't really blame Louise. Fishing could be a very tedious and drawn-out affair. She supposed it would be quite difficult for an eleven-year-old child to sit idly for an hour or longer. Deciding Major Clayton would not find her at the river, she held out her hand for the bucket that Louise carried. "Very well, Louise. You may go back to the house."

Smiling brightly, the girl gave Leanna the bucket. "Thank you, Miz Anna!" Louise said quickly, and turning, she scurried back down the dirt path; but when the house came within her view, she stopped running and began skipping. She was sure glad Miss Anna hadn't made her stay with her while she tried to catch fish for dinner, she would much rather find Bradley and see if he wanted to play a game of hide-and-seek.

Louise's thoughts were so concentrated on the game to come that when Jeff stepped in front of her she was startled and opened her mouth to scream, but recognizing him, she gasped, "Major, you done scared the daylights out of me."

"I'm sorry, Louise," Jeff apologized. "But earlier I

saw you and Miss Weston leave the house. Where were you two going?"

"Miz Anna's gone fishin', but she told me I could come back to the house."

"Where is she fishing?" he asked.

Pointing at the dirt path, Louise replied, "Just follow that trail, it'll take you to the river where Miz Anna be."

Heading in the right direction, he said quickly, "Thank you, Louise."

As he walked briskly to find Leanna, Jeff wondered if she was aware of how dangerous it was for her to be so far from the house. Didn't she realize this area was full of deserters?

Sitting on the riverbank, Leanna baited her hook, then flung the line into the water. Her mind on fishing, she didn't detect the two men slipping up behind her.

Steathily, they crept closer until they were so near to Leanna that one of them could place his hand over her mouth. Kneeling, he pulled her down onto the ground. Leering at her, a lustful smile spread across his bearded face.

Terrified, Leanna tried to struggle, but the other man grabbed her arms and held them over her head.

Keeping his hand over her mouth, the bearded attacker pulled a handkerchief from his pocket and used it to gag her. The gag was stretched so tight that it cut deeply into the corners of her mouth, and Leanna winced with pain.

Staring cruelly into her frightened eyes, he sneered, "It's been a long time, since I had me a woman."

"Hurry up, Duke," the other man warned. "I don't like bein' this close to all them Yankees that are in these

51

here parts. Let's stick it to her, then get the hell out of here."

Southern deserters! Leanna thought angrily, and, for a moment, she hated them more for deserting the army than for their personal attack on her. The bearded deserter placed his hand on her breast, squeezing her painfully. Squirming wildly, she began fighting against the man restraining her arms.

Laughing viciously, the bearded attacker clutched at her long skirt and was about to pull it upward, when Jeff stepped out of the wooded area behind them.

Swiftly, Jeff unsnapped the flap on his holster, and drawing his pistol, he shot the man grabbing at Leanna's skirt. The bullet lodged in the man's shoulder, and the impact sent the deserter, sprawling backward. The other man released Leanna. Turning, his hand lurched for the gun strapped to his hip, but Jeff's deadly warning halted him, "If you draw your gun, it'll be the last move you make in your life."

Sitting up, Leanna removed the gag from her mouth as Jeff held his pistol on the deserters. Getting to her feet, she moved away from the men and stood at the riverbank.

The pistol shot had carried to the house, and within moments, Lieutenant Buehler and six soldiers had arrived upon the scene. Jeff ordered the lieutenant to take the deserters away and place them under arrest.

Jeff waited until he and Leanna were alone before going to her side. He started to take her into his arms, but she quickly stepped back from him. She wanted to go into his embrace. She longed to be close to him, but she knew she must be strong and resist the wonderful haven she would find in his comforting arms.

"Are you all right?" Jeff asked, wishing she hadn't moved away from him.

"Yes, I think so," she answered shakily.

Gesturing toward the rowboat tied up at the water's edge, he asked, "Is it in good condition?"

"Yes," she nodded.

He took her hand, and leading her to the boat, he helped her inside. He went back for her fishing gear, and returning, he placed it at her feet. He untied the rope that bound the boat, then giving it a gentle push he stepped aboard, sat down, and lifted the oars.

As he rowed them into deeper water, he didn't try to engage Leanna in conversation, he wanted to give her a little more time to recover from her shock. When they were some distance from the bank, he pulled in the oars and dropped the small anchor. Taking the pole, he adjusted the weight on the line, saying casually, "We'll fish shallow, and if we catch a perch we can use him for bait, then fish a little deeper. This river should be full of bass and catfish."

His pacifying presence had calmed her nerves, and smiling faintly, she said earnestly, "Thank you, Major. If you hadn't shown up . . ." A shiver ran down her spine as she imagined what would have happened to her if he hadn't come down to the river. She was quiet for a moment before stating bitterly, "They were Southern deserters!"

"This countryside is full of deserters from both sides," Jeff replied. "There is danger everywhere; so the next time you decide to fish, take Jackson with you. And bring a rifle."

"Major, you have confiscated my rifles," she reminded him, but her tone was devoid of anger.

"I'll give them back to you," he answered.

"Do you really trust me that much?" she asked, surprised that he planned to return her weapons.

"Yes, I do," he answered seriously.

"Why?" she inquired curiously.

"I don't know why," he admitted. He started to say more, but the bobber suddenly dipped beneath the water. Pulling in a perch, he removed the hook from the fish's mouth and, using this catch for bait, lowered the weight and flung the line back into the water. "Tell Jackson to string a trotline across here. It'll save you all the hours you spend down here fishing."

"Are you a fisherman?" she asked.

Jeff shook his head, answering, "I haven't fished since I was a boy.

"Where did you fish?"

"On the Missouri River."

"Are you from Missouri?"

"I was raised in St. Louis, but I had a grandfather who lived in St. Charles. When I was a boy, I visited him every summer, and he always took me fishing."

"Do you have family in St. Louis?"

"My parents are dead, but I have an uncle. He's been taking care of our business since I joined the army."

"What kind of business?"

"Mostly real estate."

"Then you don't have a wife waiting for you to come home?" she questioned, wondering why she had been relieved when he had only mentioned an uncle. She would have no future with him, so why should she be happy to know he wasn't married?

"I don't have a wife, but I do have a fiancée," he revealed, deciding to be totally honest with her.

Leanna's elation was quickly shattered, and to cover her hurt, she replied, "I also have a fiancé." Leanna hadn't spoken the complete truth. She and David Farnsworth were not officially engaged, but it had always been taken for granted by both families that someday she and David would marry. Leanna was sure if the war had not intervened they would have married by now.

"Is he in the army?" Jeff asked, finding himself envying this man who would be Leanna's husband.

"Yes," she replied. "His name is David Farnsworth, and his plantation is a few miles north of here."

"The Farnsworth plantation. Yes, I know where it is. We rode by it before coming here."

"Did you meet David's parents and sister?"

"Well, I don't know if meet would be the correct term. But, yes, I saw them. They are moving to Savannah."

"But why?" she asked, surprised that the Farnsworths would leave their home.

"Their home was burned, and so were the slave cabins, and the overseer's house," he answered reluctantly, knowing the effect his news would have on her.

Astonished, she demanded, "Did you order their plantation burned?"

Jeff nodded. "It wasn't exclusively my order."

"Oh, how could you do that?" she exclaimed angrily. "Their home was so beautiful!"

"Sherman plans to destroy everything in his path, and the Farnsworth plantation is only one of many that will be burned."

Suddenly, Jeff's blue uniform stood out blatantly, and Leanna's dislike for Yankees became uppermost in her mind. How could she have believed that he wasn't her enemy? Envisioning the Farnsworths' columned home consumed by flames, she said irritably, "Row back to the bank."

Looking at her questioningly, he asked, "Why?"

"I don't want to be with you," she replied coldly.

He studied her for a moment, reading her thoughts. Pulling in the fishing line, he consented, "All right." He released the still lively perch and threw him back into the river. Quickly, he raised the anchor, then rowed them back to the shore.

As he was securing the boat, Leanna stepped to the bank. She attempted to brush past him, but, alertly, he took hold of her arm and drew her against his strong frame. "Don't act like a foolish child. There is a war taking place between your people and mine. Any military command I give is going to go against what you want."

Feeling herself responding to his masculine nearness, she pulled free and demanded, "Don't touch me!" Taking a step backward she regained her composure, and lifting her chin proudly, she continued, "What you say is true, Major Clayton. There is a war raging, and we are on opposite sides, and we were both mistaken to think for one minute that we could be friends."

Turning, she retreated quickly, and this time Jeff did not try to stop her from leaving.

Returning to the house, Leanna went straight to her bedroom where she paced back and forth, battling with her conscience. Major Clayton was the enemy! A hated Yankee! Yet she was more drawn to him than she had ever been to any man. Oh, if only she could repress these intense feelings that his presence stirred within her! Even though he had saved her from those two deserters, she must force herself to think of him indifferently.

A sudden knock on the door interrupted her thoughts, and believing the caller to be a member of her family or one of the servants, she opened the door without hesitation. The sight of Jeff standing in the hall caught her off guard, and, stammering, she gasped, "Wh . . . what do you want?"

"Leanna, may I talk to you?" he asked pleasantly.

Her better judgment warned her to turn him away before she became so helplessly enamored with him that she lost the little will power she still had. "Major Clayton," she said, trying desperately to sound composed, "we have nothing to discuss."

"Yes, we do," he replied with an air of assurance, stepping uninvited into the room.

Leaving the door standing open, Leanna turned and faced him. "Major Clayton, you have confiscated my property, and my father's study. Do you now plan to confiscate my bedroom?" she asked irritably, convincing herself that she was perturbed by the intrusion.

Jeff took a quick glance about the bedroom as though he were considering taking it over; then grinning wryly, he replied, "Confiscating your bedroom is an idea that hadn't occurred to me, but now that you have brought it to my attention, I have one question to ask. Do you go with the bedroom?"

"Don't be impertinent!" she spat testily.

Chuckling, he answered, "Miss Weston, you may keep your sanctuary, I do not plan to move into your bedroom. I came here to inform you that I'll be using the spare room next door."

"But you can't use that room!" she blurted.

Cocking an eyebrow, he queried, "Why not?"

Pointing at the closed door beside her bureau, she explained, "The bedroom next door adjoins this one. When the house was originally built, these two rooms were used by my grandparents. Then, later, Papa built onto the house, and he and Mama took the new rooms."

Stepping to the closed door, Jeff gave it a fleeting appraisal. His brown eyes twinkling with amusement, he noticed, "There's no lock on this door."

"You must stay elsewhere!" Leanna insisted. She could already imagine spending sleepless nights knowing that Major Clayton would be completely free to enter her bedroom whenever he wished. Was she afraid that he'd take advantage of the situation, or was she afraid that he wouldn't? Oh, what is wrong with me? Leanna wondered frantically.

Studying Leanna with a discerning look, Jeff moved to her side, and entranced by his gaze, she raised her face. "Are there any extra locks in the house?" he asked.

"I don't know. You'll have to ask Jackson," she replied, noticing once again the way Jeff's long eyelashes curled up at the ends.

Tearing herself away from his disturbing gaze, and turning her back to him, she said matter-of-factly, "I have a lot of work to do in the vegetable garden, so why don't you locate Jackson and tell him to come into my room and install the lock."

"Your room?" he questioned, suppressing a smile. "But I'm planning to order the lock put on my side of the door."

Whirling about, Leanna gaped, "What?" This Yankee was impossible! He was insufferable! "You have your nerve!" she exclaimed furiously.

Walking out of the bedroom and stepping into the hallway, Jeff paused to look back at her. "I am on enemy territory, Miss Weston, and I don't relish waking up in the middle of the night to find a hostile rebel standing over my bed."

"Are you implying that I would? . . ." She breathed angrily.

Jeff shrugged. "It's better to be safe than sorry."

"But what about my side of the door?" Leanna demanded. "How do I know you won't slip into my room in the middle of the night?"

"You don't," he grinned boldly. Not giving Leanna a chance to continue her objections, he closed the subject, departing with curt abruptness.

It was close to dusk before Leanna and Louise finished their work in the vegetable garden and returned to the house. When they entered the kitchen, Matilda was busy cooking dinner. Standing at the stove, she stirred the stew which was simmering in a large, cast-iron dutch oven. Placing the long-handled spoon on the counter, she turned to watch Leanna and Louise come wearily into the kitchen.

"Miz Anna!" Matilda exclaimed, obviously disturbed. "Dat Major Clayton is plannin' to sleep in the bedroom next to yours, and he done ordered Jackson to put a lock on his side of the door!"

"Yes, I know," Leanna sighed, her fatigue causing her to practically drop into one of the kitchen chairs.

"Louise, fetch a couple of blankets and a pillow,"

59

Matilda ordered. "Then make yourself a pallet at the foot of Miz Anna's bed. You will be sleepin' in Miz Anna's room 'til dat Yankee major is gone from dis house."

"Yes, Mama," Louise complied, leaving to carry out her mother's instructions.

Folding her arms beneath her heavy breasts, Matilda fumed, "You ain't gonna sleep alone in a room next to dat Major Clayton. I don't trust dem Yankees. Imagine him orderin' Jackson to put a lock on his side of de door! Why when your Mama heard 'bout it, she was so upset that she took to her bed!"

"Is Mama all right?" Leanna asked anxiously.

Nodding, Matilda answered, "When I tol' Miz Mary that I aims to let Louise sleep in your room, she calmed down considerably."

Starting to rise from her chair, Leanna decided, "I had better go up and check on her."

Waving her back down, Matilda told her, "Miz Anna, you just sit where you are and rest for a spell. I'll go look in on your mama."

The temperature inside the kitchen was extremely warm and for comfort, Leanna stretched out her long legs, hiking her skirt up to her hips. "Would you mind opening the back door before you go upstairs?"

Doing as her mistress requested, Matilda propped open the door, allowing air to circulate through the stuffy kitchen, then, using the rear stairway, she left to check on Leanna's mother.

The mild breeze floating through the room felt refreshing on Leanna's bared legs, and undoing the buttons on the bodice of her dress, she leaned her head against the back of the chair. Sighing wearily, she closed her eyes, enjoying her moment of complete rest.

Dozing, Leanna didn't hear Jeff enter the kitchen through the door that led from the dining room. From Jeff's angle, he could only see Leanna from one side, but he was well aware of her raised skirt and opened bodice. He carried Leanna's two rifles, and quietly, he leaned them against the wall. He knew he should behave as a gentleman would and make his presence known, but he'd be damned if he'd let chivalry cause him to miss savoring such a beautiful vision.

Moving soundlessly, Jeff maneuvered his way through the room until he was standing in front of the sleeping Leanna. Leisurely, he allowed his eyes to linger on her face, studying her prominent cheekbones and delectable lips. Slowly, his appreciative gaze moved downward, to where her soft breasts were partially revealed. He noticed the way her nipples pressed against the confining material as she breathed. His adoration increased as he looked at the lovely shape of her long, slender legs.

Leanna was merely dozing, and when consciousness slowly returned, her eyelids opened drowsily. Suddenly aware of Jeff's presence, she came fully awake with a start. Bounding to her feet, her skirt fell back down over her legs, and fastening her bodice, she exclaimed peevishly, "How dare you!"

His smile cocky, Jeff drawled, "The last couple of times I've come into this kitchen, I have found you either unclothed or else seductively disheveled. I must make a point of visiting this room more often."

Reacting impulsively, Leanna drew back her arm to slap him, but he caught her wrist in midflight. "Don't you realize that violence leads to violence?" he challenged.

"Are you threatening me?" she asked indignantly.

"Let's just say, I'm warning you," he answered evenly, relinquishing her wrist.

Ranting, she spurted, "You are an impudent, intolerable Yankee! And I wish . . . I wish . . ."

Brusquely she spun away, but placing his hands on her shoulders, he turned her so that she was again facing him. Surprised to see a trace of tears in her eyes, he asked tenderly, "What do you wish?"

"I wish you had never come into my life," she admitted, forcing herself not to give in to her pressing need to be in his embrace, not to plead with him to hold her as she cried. Leanna was terribly confused. She didn't understand why she longed to feel his arms about her, or even why she wanted to cry.

Leanna's eyes were now downcast, and placing his hand beneath her chin, Jeff tilted her face upward. "Why do you wish I had never come into your life?"

"I don't exactly know why," she answered truthfully.

Understanding, he queried gently, "Leanna, do I make you feel guilty?"

Her resolutions to remain aloof in Jeff's presence crumbling, Leanna decided to terminate their conversation. "Of course you don't make me feel guilty," she said unconvincingly and started to move away from him to leave the kitchen.

Reaching out, he touched her arm and slowed her retreat. "You don't have to run out of the room to avoid me. I came here looking for you so that I could return your rifles." He nodded toward the open doorway, where he had propped her weapons against the wall.

Remembering he had promised to give them back,

she mumbled hesitantly, "Thank you."

Ambling out of the kitchen, he continued quite calmly, "Both guns are loaded, and the ammunition is in the gun cabinet." Halting, he looked back and added with a half-grin, "If it'll make you feel safe from my possible advances, you can always sleep with one of the rifles next to your bed."

"That won't be necessary," she told him, now successful in her attempt to appear composed. "Louise will be sharing my bedroom."

He studied her for a moment, his expression indiscernible. "Miss Weston, don't forget that you and your family are now under my military jurisdiction."

"Which means?" she pressed.

Smiling, he replied, "Which means you are totally in my charge and I will decide where people will sleep and what they will do. It so happens I don't care if you have Louise and a loaded rifle in your room, I shall do exactly as I please." His even tone revealed nothing, and Leanna wasn't sure if he was serious or not. But as he walked out of the kitchen, she had a distinct feeling that Major Clayton's words were not to be taken lightly.

Leanna awoke early the next morning, and when she finished eating breakfast, she offered to help Matilda can the vegetables that she and Louise had picked the day before.

After Leanna and Matilda had been working steadily for over an hour, Matilda realized there weren't enough jars in the kitchen to hold all the food that they were canning. Telling the servant to attend to the steaming vegetables, Leanna hurried down the back stairway to the cellar where the extra jars were stored.

Leanna had scarcely left the kitchen, when Jeff came into the room searching for her. Seeing Matilda, he inquired, "Where's Miss Weston?"

Gesturing toward the rear stairway, the woman answered, "Miz Anna's fetchin' some jars."

"In the cellar?" Jeff asked.

Nodding, she mumbled, "That where she be." Jeff moved swiftly toward the stairs, but his long strides were halted momentarily by Matilda's strong objection, "Major Clayton, you got no right a-followin' Miz Anna down into that cellar."

Resuming his steps, Jeff said casually, "She might need help carrying up the jars."

Watching him disappear down the narrow flight of stairs, Matilda huffed, "Miz Anna don't need no help, and dat man know she don't!" Clucking her tongue against the roof of her mouth, she fussed, "Dat Yankee major, he up to no good. Oh Lawdy, I sure hopes Miz Anna don't go a fallin' in love with no Yankee!"

The murking light in the basement filtered through the windows and the open cellar door, making the murky interior to be shadowy. Standing on the bottom step, Jeff spotted Leanna taking empty jars from a shelf and placing them in a basket.

"Leanna?" he called softly, not wanting to startle her.

But Jeff's unexpected voice caused her to drop the jar she was holding, and hitting the floor, it shattered into pieces. Whirling, Leanna watched Jeff as he hurried to her side. Oh, why had he come down here? Couldn't he leave her alone? Didn't he realize why she was trying to avoid him?

"Are you all right?" he asked urgently.

Stepping back from the broken glass, she muttered,

64

"I'm fine." Wishing his presence wasn't causing her heart to pound rapidly, she stammered, "W-why are you here?"

"I wanted to see you."

"Why?" she breathed.

"I need the floor plans to your house."

"Floor plans?" she repeated vaguely, trying to concentrate on what he was saying instead of wondering how he could be so flawlessly handsome.

"The house was thoroughly searched, but this place is mammoth, and there could be secret rooms that I'm not aware of."

"Why are you concerned about secret rooms?" she pondered.

"You could be hiding Confederate soldiers."

"Well, I don't know where Papa kept the floor plans. In fact, I don't even know if the drawings still exist. But I can assure you that there are no secret rooms, nor am I harboring Confederate soldiers."

"Do I have your word, Miss Weston?"

"Yes, you do," she replied. "Is that the only reason you wanted to see me?"

"Yes," he answered, wondering why he had found it necessary to look for Leanna to question her about something that could have waited until a more convenient time. Was he so captivated with this enticing little rebel that he was actually seeking opportunities to be in her presence?

Bending, Leanna reached down for the filled basket, but reacting alertly, Jeff picked it up. "I'll carry it for you," he offered.

Leanna led the way, and Jeff followed her up to the stairs and into the kitchen. Seeing her mother standing beside Matilda and awaiting their return, Leanna dreaded the unpleasant scene that was sure to occur.

Placing the basket on the kitchen table, Jeff asked, "Mrs. Weston, where are the floor plans to this house?"

"I don't know," she answered icily.

Aware of her contempt, he quipped, "Would you lie to a Yankee, Mrs. Weston?"

Raising her chin defiantly, she remarked, "Of course, I would."

Bowing graciously, Jeff replied with a charming smile. "Touché, Mrs. Weston."

The moment he left the kitchen, Mary turned on Leanna, once again chiding her for keeping company with a Yankee officer. Sinking into a chair, Leanna listened guiltily to her mother's upbraiding.

Chapter Four

As always, Leanna arose early, and finding Jackson, she told him to go hunting while she ran the trot lines he had strung across the river. Anxious to start on her chores, Leanna hurried through breakfast. Still wanting to keep Louise in her presence, she planned to take the child with her to the river, but when Matilda informed her that Louise was still asleep, Leanna decided not to bother her.

Taking her rifle with her, Leanna left the house. The morning air was refreshing, but Leanna knew that as soon as the sun climbed a little higher, its rays would be scorchingly hot. As she walked down the dirt path that led to the river, she listened to the musical chirping of the birds as they welcomed a new day.

Nearing the river, Leanna suddenly detected splashing, and, cautiously, she stepped into the bordering shrubbery. Grasping her rifle firmly, she knelt behind a thick bush, parting it enough so that she could see through to the other side.

The unexpected sight of Jeff stepping out of the water completely unclothed made Leanna to inhale deeply. Apparently, he had decided to bathe in the river, certain that no one would be about so early in the morning. Entranced with his masculine build, Leanna couldn't turn away. She had never before seen a man nude, and her eyes boldly examined every inch of his strong physique. She was fascinated by his maleness and speculative thoughts flashed through her mind. She continued watching as Jeff picked up a towel from the bank and began to vigorously dry himself. Oh, he was indeed a handsome man, and his lean body was flawless.

Worried that he might catch her spying, Leanna quickly decided to slip back into the woods. She planned to stay close to the ground until she was a safe distance away, but as she turned to leave, she noticed that her skirt was caught on the prickly shrubbery. Trying not to rustle the bush, she made a desperate effort to unsnag her dress, but she couldn't pull it loose.

Hastily, Jeff finished dressing, and, as he was strapping on his holster, he detected a rustling sound in the nearby shrubbery. Removing his pistol, he edged his way toward the thicket.

Giving her skirt one hard tug, Leanna finally pulled free. She was about to make a swift retreat when a threatening rattle sounded from beneath the heavy bush. Just as Leanna bounded to her feet, the strike rattlesnake's deadly fangs sank into her bared ankle. Falling to the ground, she screamed and grabbed the fresh wound.

Jeff arrived as the snake was recoiling. Aiming his

pistol, he shot the reptile; then, slipping the gun into its holster, he knelt beside Leanna. Helping her to lie down, he asked anxiously, "Were you bit?"

"Yes," she cried, already feeling the intense pain.

Pushing aside her skirt, Jeff saw the swelling puncture marks on her ankle. Moving quickly, he removed his belt and made a loose tourniquet above her knee. Then reaching into his pocket, he brought out a knife. "I'll have to make a small incision so that I can suck out the poison," he explained.

Leanna nodded, feeling too weak to speak. She could hear a roar in her ears, and black spots were darting before her eyes. She knew she was on the verge of passing out.

Placing the blade of the knife against Leanna's ankle, Jeff made the incision across the wound. Bending, he sucked out the venomous poison, spitting it onto the ground. Finishing, he turned to speak to Leanna, but gazing down into her pale face, he saw that she was now unconscious. Replacing the knife, he removed his belt and put it back on. He lifted Leanna and, holding her against his chest, hastily carried her down the path toward the house.

Catching sight of Lieutenant Buehler strolling across the front lawn, Jeff ordered the lieutenant to find the medic and bring him to the house.

Jennifer and Matilda were in the kitchen when Jeff carried the unconscious Leanna into the rear of the house.

"Oh Lawdy!" Matilda cried, turning away from the stove. "What done happened to Miz Anna?"

Jennifer had been sitting at the table, and leaping to her feet, she gasped, "Good Lord!"

"Leanna was bitten by a rattlesnake," Jeff explained, his tone heavy with worry.

"Carry her to her room," Jennifer commanded, leading the way.

As Jeff was taking her up the back stairway, Leanna began to fret uneasily. Holding her close to his wide chest, Jeff whispered soothingly, "You'll be all right, Leanna."

Opening her eyes, Leanna studied Jeff's handsome face as he carried her down the hall and into her bedroom. She could see his grave concern, and she was a little surprised, but also pleased that he apparently cared a great deal about her.

Taking her to the bed, Jeff gently laid her down. Noticing that she was fully conscious and watching him, Jeff smiled warmly. "I sent for the medic, he'll be here in a few minutes. But, Leanna, I'm sure you're in no danger."

Although her ankle ached severely, Leanna had seen enough snake bites in her lifetime to know that she wasn't dying. The slaves on the plantation had often been bitten by rattlers, and she knew if the wound was tended to immediately, it was rare for the victim not to survive.

Leanna meant to thank Jeff for saving her life, but before she could, Jennifer pushed him aside, ordering firmly, "Major Clayton, you may leave. I'll take care of Leanna."

Reluctantly, Jeff stepped away from the bed. Leanna's sister-in-law was right, he wasn't needed, so he might as well leave. As he walked into the hall, the medic was hurrying toward Leanna's room, Matilda ushering him in the right direction. The man saluted

Jeff, then entered the room and closed the door.

Worried, Jeff began pacing back and forth in front of Leanna's bedroom. He had assured her that she was in no danger, but now he felt the need to reassure himself. Surely he had gotten most of the poison from the wound before it could spread through her system. But how much venom would it take to be fatal to a woman as delicate as Leanna?

The door suddenly opened, and halting his pacing, Jeff watched as Jennifer emerged. Casting a cold glance upon Jeff, she started to move past him, but he clutched her arm.

"How is Leanna?" he asked pressingly.

Shoving his hand aside, she responded frigidly, "I don't know. The medic is still tending to her. If you'll excuse me, Major Clayton, I must go to Leanna's mother and let her know what has happened."

"Didn't the medic say anything?" he insisted.

"No," she replied firmly. She took a step away, but changing her mind, she questioned warily, "Major Clayton, why were you down at the river with my sister-in-law?"

"I wasn't at the river with her," he explained. "I was already there when she arrived."

"But why were you there so early in the morning?"

"I was taking a bath," he said flatly.

Gaping, Jennifer stammered, "Did Leanna . . . did Leanna see? . . ."

Cocking an eyebrow, he grinned, "Did she see what, Mrs. Weston?"

Blushing, Jennifer left in a flurry.

Jeff continued his pacing, and when Jennifer returned with Mary, he said nothing to the ladies and they, in turn, ignored his presence as they entered Leanna's bedroom.

Finally, the medic stepped into the hall, and closing the door to Leanna's room, he reported, "Miss Weston is doing very well."

"She's in no danger?" Jeff questioned anxiously.

The medic shook his head. "No, sir. But she is running a low-grade fever. I gave her some laudanum, and she'll sleep for the next few hours. I'll return this afternoon and check on her condition."

Jeff dismissed the medic, and for a moment, he stared at the closed bedroom door. Suppressing the urge to barge into the room and see for himself that Leanna was all right, Jeff turned sharply and headed downstairs.

It had been a trying day for everyone, but for Jeff Clayton it was more so. Patience had never been one of his stronger points, but he'd had to ask Leanna's family or the medic about her recovery. He wanted to see her, and it took a lot of self-control to stay away from her room.

Sitting behind the desk in the study, and sipping a glass of brandy, Jeff watched the open doorway. He had ordered the sentry stationed outside the study to let the door stand open. From where Jeff was seated he couldn't see the staircase leading upstairs, but he could hear anyone go up or descend. Whenever he detected a presence, he never failed to hurry into the foyer to ask about Leanna.

Once again hearing footsteps crossing the uncarpeted foyer, Jeff placed his glass on the desktop and got to his feet. Going into the foyer, he saw Matilda

72

carrying a covered dinner tray.

"Is Miss Weston feeling well enough to eat?" Jeff asked Matilda.

Smiling broadly, she answered, "Yes, sir, Major Clayton. Miz Anna, she feelin' just fine." The Union officer's grave concern for her young mistress had surprised Matilda, and his deep compassion had changed her opinion of him, weakening her hostility considerably.

Reacting impulsively, Jeff stepped to Matilda and took the tray from her hands. "I'll take this to Miss Weston," he announced.

"B . . . but, Major Clayton," Matilda stuttered, knowing it was not proper for a man to enter a lady's bedroom.

Holding the tray, Jeff hurried up the stairs, leaving Matilda staring at his departing back. Going to Leanna's room, he knocked on the door.

"Come in," he heard her call.

Balancing the tray in one hand, he turned the knob, and leaving the door ajar, he entered. Leanna was sitting up in bed, pillows propped behind her as she leaned back against the huge headboard. The sheet was pulled up only as far as her waist, revealing the top of her flimsy blue nightgown. Approaching the bed, Jeff's roving eyes fell to her full breasts which were seductively silhouetted beneath the soft material of her gown.

His presence startled Leanna. She could just imagine the scene that would occur if her mother were to learn that Major Clayton was in her bedroom.

Reaching the bed, Jeff carefully placed the tray on Leanna's lap. Forcing himself to look away from the

73

tempting sight of her lovely bosom, he gazed down into her face. Smiling, he asked, "How do you feel?"

"I . . . I'm fine," she stammered, his presence making her feel uneasy.

Pulling up a narrow-backed chair, he sat down, and removing the silver-plated cover from the tray, he coaxed, "Eat your dinner."

Dinner! How could she possibly have an appetite with him sitting beside her? Didn't he realize what a temptation he was to her? Suddenly, remembering him stepping unclothed out of the river, Leanna's cheeks reddened. Flustered, she said hastily, "Please cover the tray and put it on the night stand. I'll eat later."

He did as she requested, hoping her lack of appetite wasn't a sign that her condition had worsened.

"Major Clayton—" she began.

Interrupting, he said, "Please, call me Jeff."

"Jeff," she began again, "I want to thank you for helping me." She added fervently, "You saved my life."

As though his deed was of little importance, he muttered, "You don't owe me thanks. I'm just grateful that I was there to help you."

"Your medic said I must stay in bed for three more days," Leanna frowned.

"You need the rest," he replied.

"Rest!" she scoffed. "There's too much work on this plantation for me to rest. Now so much of it will fall to Jackson."

"I'll tell Jackson if he needs any help to let me know. I have over a hundred soldiers, who at the present, have very little to do to keep them busy."

Studying Jeff, Leanna wondered how she could have been so biased about Yankees. Were they truly so different from Southerners?

A strained silence fell between them, causing Leanna to fret. Was he thinking about this morning, recalling how she had hidden in the shrubbery to watch him?

Reading her turbulent thoughts, Jeff was tempted to tease her about the incident, but he had a feeling Leanna would be too embarrassed. So he decided to leave the topic alone.

"Major Clayton!" Mary's voice suddenly shrieked.

Looking quickly toward the open doorway, and seeing Leanna's mother, Jeff hastily rose to his feet. "Mrs. Weston." He nodded courteously, watching her storm into the room.

Pausing at the foot of Leanna's bed, Mary raged, "How dare you come into my daughter's bedroom!"

"Mama," Leanna spoke up, "Major Clayton was nice enough to bring me my dinner tray and ask about my health."

"Cover yourself!" Mary chastened, her eyes taking in Leanna's flimsy nightgown. She waited until Leanna drew up the sheet before turning her attention back to Jeff. "Major Clayton, I want you to know that I am very grateful to you for saving my daughter. But, sir, that does not mean that I like your presence in my home, nor do I approve of you being in my daughter's bedroom. I insist that you leave immediately!"

Obligingly, Jeff walked swiftly across the room. As he was leaving he made a point of telling Leanna that he'd see her when she was recovered.

"That Yankee has absolutely no manners!" Mary spat angrily.

"Mama, that isn't true," Leanna said.

"Leanna, don't you dare defend that deplorable Yankee! It was men like Major Clayton who killed your brother and caused your father's death!"

As Mary continued her ranting, Leanna rolled onto her side and buried her face in one of the feather-filled pillows. Why? Why? she asked herself for at least the hundreth time. Why couldn't Jeff have been a Confederate instead of a Yankee?

Chapter Five

Obeying the medic's advice, Leanna stayed in bed for three days, during which time she did not see Jeff. On the morning after the third day, she awoke refreshed and determined to get out of her confining bedroom, and she was terribly anxious to see Jeff again. While she had been impatiently convalescing, she'd had more than ample time to give a lot of thought to Jeff. She knew their relationship was precarious, and perhaps on her side even a little treacherous; nonetheless, she had no intentions of terminating their friendship. Although Jeff easily ruffled her feathers and aroused her temper, he had always been kind to her when she had needed his understanding. Also, he had twice saved her life, and she was deeply grateful to him. He would be leaving soon, and she'd probably never see him again, so what harm was there in accepting him on a cordial basis? Here on the plantation, which was practically isolated from the war, there was little chance that their split loyalties could destroy their mutual respect for each other.

Slipping into one of her mended gowns, Leanna stepped to her dressing table where she brushed her hair with brisk strokes. Hearing a soft knock on her door, she called, "Who is it?"

"Jackson, Miz Anna," came the muffled reply.

Crossing over to the door, she opened it and asked, "Is anything wrong?"

Secretively, Jackson mumbled, "Miz Anna, I gots to talk to you in private."

Puzzled, she questioned, "My goodness, Jackson, why are you behaving so strangely?"

Keeping his voice lowered, he said urgently, "This is serious, Miz Anna."

She stepped back. "Come in, Jackson." Closing the door behind his hesitant entrance, she pressed him, "What has happened?"

"This mornin' while I was huntin' in the woods, I was approached by Confederate soldiers."

"Confederates!" she breathed. "But there aren't supposed to be any Confederate soldiers left in these parts."

Nodding vigorously, Jackson agreed, "Yes'm, I know, but these soldiers were prisoners of war and they done escaped. They was bein' taken to the train depot to be sent North, when they broke themselves free."

"How many men are there?" Leanna asked.

"There's six of 'em, Miz Anna. They wants to get to Atlanta and join General Hood's Army."

"Is the Union searching for these men?"

"They are quite sure Union troops are a-chasin' 'em because . . . because . . ." He hesitated.

"Because why?" she demanded.

"When they were escapin', they killed four Yankee soldiers."

"Oh no!" Leanna gasped. "But why did they approach you?"

"They wanted to know if there was anyone livin' here who could help 'em. Miz Anna, they don't have no food, guns, or horses. They been on the run for four straight days and nights."

Clutching Jackson's arm without conscious thought, Leanna said intensely, "You must take them some food, but be very careful that you aren't followed."

Shuffling his feet, and uncertain of his young mistress' reaction, he said cautiously, "Uh, Miz Anna, ma'am, one of them soldiers is seriously wounded, and they wants you to come and take a look at him."

"But what can I do?" she exclaimed. "I know nothing about nursing."

"But, Miz Anna," Jackson pleaded, "the wounded soldier ain't much older than sixteen. Can't you try to help him?"

"Of course, I'll try," Leanna agreed, although she didn't know what she could possibly do to help the young man. Briskly, she instructed, "Jackson, tell Matilda to pack a basket of food and ask her to find something that we can use as a bandage. Mama has a small medical kit; I'll sneak it from her room before coming downstairs. We'll take both rifles with us, and if Major Clayton or one of his men ask about the food in the basket, we'll tell them that we plan to hunt all morning and the basket is our lunch."

"Yes'm," Jackson replied, leaving hastily to carry out her orders.

Feeling apprehensive, Leanna paced across the floor. Only moments before she had told herself that here on her plantation there was little chance that split loyalties could destroy her friendship with Jeff. But now, with the escaped Confederates on her land, her home was no longer isolated from the war.

Two of the Confederate soldiers walked out to greet Leanna and Jackson when they were still several yards from where the soldiers were holing up in the thick woods.

Tipping his cap, the oldest of the two men spoke to Leanna, "I'm Corporal Donaldson, ma'am, and I'm mighty beholden to you for comin' out here to help young Mike."

"Mike?" Leanna repeated. "Is he the wounded soldier?"

"Yes, ma'am," he answered somberly. "And it grieves me to tell you that it's too late for anyone to help him. He died 'bout an hour ago."

"I'm sorry," Leanna murmured.

"Miss? . . ." he raised his eyebrows.

"Weston," she told him.

"Miss Weston, if you'll send your servant back with a shovel, we'll dig a grave for Mike."

Leanna nodded, a sudden lump in her throat choking back words. The young soldier would rest for an eternity in an unmarked grave.

Gesturing toward the basket Leanna carried, the corporal said cheerfully, "Ma'am, I sure hope there's food in that basket."

Handing it to him, she smiled, "Yes. It's not fancy but very filling."

Giving the basket to his companion, the corporal ordered, "Take this back to the men, and don't forget to save some food for me."

As his man was walking swiftly away, Corporal Donaldson asked Leanna, "Miss Weston, I hate to impose on you or place your safety in jeopardy, but is there any way you can help us get to Atlanta?"

"Didn't my servant tell you that my home has been confiscated by Yankee soldiers?"

"Yes, ma'am, he told me, but he said none of you are under guard. Miss Weston, I have a plan and I'd like to explain it to you. But if you should decide not to get involved, I'll understand."

Leanna had a sinking feeling that she was about to become entangled in this war. But these men were her own kind, they were fighting for her homeland, and if she could help them in any way, she would do so willingly. Jeff's face flashed briefly in her mind; but, quickly, she cleared him from her thoughts.

"What is your plan?" she asked the corporal.

"Do you have a wagon and a horse?" he inquired.

"Yes, I do," she replied.

"Will the officer in charge give you and your servant permission to ride into town?"

"Atlanta?" she gasped. "No, I'm sure he wouldn't."

"No, ma'am, you can't tell him you're goin' to Atlanta. Tell him you need to ride into Marietta. It's now controlled by the Union. The main fork in the road to town is 'bout three miles north of these woods. We'll meet you there, then you can give us the wagon, and we'll try to make it on our own to

81

Atlanta."

"But what will I say when I return home without the wagon and horse?"

"Tell the officer in charge that your wagon and horse were taken by deserters."

"Deserters!" Leanna repeated, remembering the men who had attacked her. With so much danger lurking about, she knew Jeff would never give her permission to leave. She would have to find a way to slip the wagon and horse from the house. But how? How? With a certainty she was far from feeling, she assured the corporal, "I don't know for sure how I'll manage it, but I'll bring you the wagon and horse. But I must warn you that the horse is quite old and he won't be very fast."

Sighing heavily, the corporal answered, "Miss Weston, he'll be better than no horse at all."

"I'll send my servant Jackson back with a shovel. What time do you want us to meet you on the road?"

"Any time after dark. We'll wait for you in the woods alongside the road." Then he pressed her further. "Miss Weston, is there any way you could possibly get us some weapons?"

She shook her head. "No, I'm sorry. But I own two rifles, and you can have one of them." She looked at Jackson, who gave the corporal one of the weapons. "Tonight I'll bring you extra ammunition."

Accepting the rifle, Corporal Donaldson praised her. "Miss Weston, it's gallant ladies like yourself who give us men the initiative to continue fighting for our beloved South." He bowed elegantly, then taking her hand, he placed a kiss upon it.

Leanna couldn't believe her luck when, upon returning to the house, she learned from Matilda that Major Clayton and thirty of his men had left on military business. Leanna promptly asked how long he would be gone, but Matilda said she didn't know. Five Union soldiers had ridden up to the house, and after meeting with them in the study, Jeff and his men had left. With Jeff out of the way, Leanna was sure she could convince Lieutenant Buehler to let her ride with Jackson into Marietta. She would tell him that she needed to visit the family doctor and pick up some medicine for her mother.

In carrying out her plans, everything went smoothly, and by late afternoon, she and Jackson were on the road heading for a rendezvous with the Confederate soldiers. They were early, so Leanna allowed the old horse to walk at a leisurely pace, and by the time they reached the fork in the road, dusk had fallen. Pulling up the horse, Leanna looked cautiously about, hoping to spot the corporal and his men.

The night was eerily quiet, and an uneasy feeling came over her. Because she was a better shot than Jackson, she took the loaded rifle from his hands.

"Miz Anna," he whispered, "where are them soldiers?"

"I'm sure they'll be here at any moment," she replied, unable to control the trembling in her voice.

Suddenly, hearing a twig snap in the surrounding woods, Leanna and Jackson tensed.

"Miss Weston?" her name was called from the dark thicket.

Recognizing Corporal Donaldson's voice, she

called softly, "Yes, I'm here."

Walking out of the woods, the corporal and his men came within sight. Leanna and Jackson stood, intending to get down from the wagon so that the soldiers could have it when, all at once, the sounds of horses' hoofs completely surrounded them.

"Damn!" Corporal Donaldson cursed. He wasn't surprised that they had been caught. He had known for the last hour that he and his men were being closely pursued.

"Drop your weapons and raise your hands," a deep, menacing voice warned from the black background.

"You'd better do as he says," Corporal Donaldson told Leanna as he dropped the rifle she had given him earlier.

Leanna's hands were shaking so badly that her rifle slipped from her grip of its own accord. It wasn't fright that was making Leanna tremble but dread. She knew the voice that had ordered them to drop their weapons. Jeff! Apparently, he had left the plantation house to search for the escaped Confederates. Sinking to the wagon seat, Leanna moaned deeply. He had not only found the Confederate soldiers, but had also found her aiding and abetting them!

As the Union troops advanced, Leanna kept her eyes lowered, postponing the moment when she'd have to face Jeff. Listening, she heard him order a group of his men to place the Confederates under arrest and take them to Marietta.

Leanna was very aware of Jeff's stallion walking up to her side of the wagon, but stubbornly, she kept

84

her eyes downcast.

"Good evening, Miss Weston," Jeff said lightly, but Leanna could detect an edge of anger in his voice. He's barely controlling his temper, she thought, and at any moment it's liable to explode.

"Major, sir," Jackson spoke up, "none of this is Miz Anna's fault. I talked her into it. I swear I did. Punish me, Major, but let Miz Anna be."

"You talked her into it?" the major asked skeptically.

Nodding vigorously, Jackson answered, "Yes, sir!"

Smiling cynically, Jeff replied, "I can't quite picture anyone talking Miss Weston into doing something that she wasn't willing to do in the first place." Gritting his teeth, he added hoarsely, "Miss Weston is too damned stubborn and too damned defiant!"

Her short-fused temper firing, Leanna looked up sharply into Jeff's condemning eyes. "Go to the devil, you . . . you disgusting Yankee!"

"I don't deny that I'm a Yankee, but I resent the term disgusting."

"All you Yankees are disgusting!" she blurted, her Southern patriotism surging.

"And all you rebels are untrustworthy!" he retorted.

"Good Lord!" Leanna cried desperately. "Surely you didn't expect me to turn my back on my own kind!"

Her reasoning hit Jeff profoundly. What she said was true. Had it really been wrong for her to assist Confederate soldiers? Strangely, Jeff could feel his anger toward Leanna becoming mixed with admiration.

Deciding to end their bantering, he jerked his horse's reins, and riding past Sergeant O'Malley, he ordered, "Escort Miss Weston and her servant back to the house."

Chapter Six

Leanna's long dressing gown flared about her ankles as she made a sharp turn to once again pace across her bedroom floor. Curled up on the pallet at the foot of Leanna's bed, Louise slept soundly through her mistress' restless pacing. As soon as Leanna and Jackson had returned home, Jackson had gone to the servants' quarters, and Leanna had headed straight for her bedroom.

Wringing her hands apprehensively, Leanna's thoughts were in a turmoil. She was sorry that Jeff had been so upset with her, but she knew if she had it to do over again, she'd still try to aid the Confederate soldiers.

Deciding worrying wasn't helping matters, she went to the bed, slipped out of her dressing gown, turned off the lamp, and lay down. If Jeff wanted to remain angry, then there was nothing she could do about it. She certainly had no intention of apologizing; in her mind she had done nothing wrong!

Holding back her rising tears, Leanna wondered

gravely what would happen to Corporal Donaldson and the others. Would they be transported to prison, or would they be executed? "I hate this war!" she moaned aloud, doubling her hands into fists.

Hearing the door opening in the bedroom next to hers, Leanna tensed. When she saw Jeff in the morning, what would he say to her? Did he intend to punish her and Jackson for abetting the Confederate soldiers? Would she and Jackson be placed under arrest? If they were taken away by the Union, how would the rest of her family survive? Knowing the others couldn't possibly make it without Jackson or herself, Leanna was suddenly confronted with horrible possibilities. She imagined all kinds of tribulations befalling her loved ones.

She knew she couldn't possibly sleep with her family's uncertain fate on her mind, so she sat up and swung her legs over the side of the bed. She'd go to Jeff and demand that he tell her if he planned to take her and Jackson away. She would beg him to let Jackson remain. Surely he wouldn't leave three women and three children helpless without a man to take care of them.

Putting on her dressing gown, and taking a deep breath, Leanna marched determinedly to the door that adjoined the two bedrooms. She knocked on it quickly before her courage could falter.

Faintly, she could hear Jeff's footsteps approaching, then pausing in front of the door as he swung it open. He was wearing his uniform, but the buttons on his shirt were undone, revealing the dark hairs on his chest. It was apparent to Leanna that she had interrupted him as he was undressing because his shirttail was hanging over his trousers, and he was minus his boots. His brown eyes bore darkly into hers, and she wondered if he was still extremely upset. She had hoped that by now his anger might have mellowed.

"Jeff," she began shakily, "I need to talk to you."

He took a couple of steps backward so that he could see her better. The burning lamp in his room cast a soft glow through Leanna's night clothes, silhouetting her rounded curves. He wondered if she had any idea how beautifully tempting she was.

Glancing over Leanna's shoulder, Jeff could see Louise sleeping on the pallet, and he said softly, "We'll talk in my room, so the child won't be awakened."

Leanna was wary about entering his bedroom. She wasn't sure if she wanted to be so intimately alone with him. What if he should try to kiss her? Would she be strong enough to resist him? She doubted it; nonetheless, she found herself accepting his invitation. When she heard him close the door behind her, she felt as though she had willingly walked into a trap, a trap from which she might never want to be set free.

"What do you want to talk to me about?" Jeff asked, moving around to stand in front of her.

He smelled strongly of brandy, and Leanna wondered if he had been drinking heavily; and if he had, was it because of her?

"I need to talk to you about what happened tonight," she replied tentatively.

"There's no reason to discuss it," he broke in. "It's over and done with."

"But what will happen to Jackson and me?" she questioned, holding her breath.

"Nothing," he answered flatly.

"Nothing?" she was amazed.

Unexpectedly, a small smile flickered across his sensual lips. "Did you think I was going to send you and Jackson to the gallows?"

"Of course not," she replied firmly, puzzled as to why he always seemed to tease her. "But I was worried that we might be punished in one way or another."

"For instance?" he coaxed, his smile broadening.

"I didn't know," she shrugged, feeling slightly flustered. "I was afraid that you would arrest us and take us away, and there would be no one here to take care of my mother and the others."

"You can rest easy, Leanna. You and Jackson are not in trouble with me or the Union."

Sighing with relief, she murmured, "Thank you."

"Will you join me for a nightcap?" asked Jeff, his request taking Leanna off guard.

"Wh-what?" she stammered, immediately perturbed at herself for losing her composure. A man as debonair as Jeff was probably used to sophisticated women, and here she was acting like a country bumpkin.

Taking her hand, he led her over to his dresser, where there was a decanter of brandy, plus two glasses.

Seeing two glasses instead of one, Leanna asked saucily, "Were you expecting company?"

Pouring the brandy, Jeff grinned. "Let's say, I was hoping I'd have company. But if you hadn't come to me, I had planned to talk to you first thing in the morning."

"Why?" she queried, accepting the glass Jeff placed in her hand.

"I owe you an apology. When I caught you helping the Confederates, I came down on you a little hard." Winking, and raising his glass, he said with an air of casualness, "But, then, we are at war, aren't we?"

She nodded, "Yes, Jeff, I suppose we are."

Touching his glass to hers, he toasted, "May this damnable war end soon."

Clinking glasses, Leanna replied with an enticing smile, "Salute!" Putting the glass to her lips, she took a generous swallow, and the burning liquid searing her throat took Leanna by surprise. It was her first taste of hard liquor, and holding back a pressing need to cough, Leanna looked up into Jeff's face, unaware that her watery eyes betrayed her attempt to appear unaffected.

"Is this the first time you have had brandy?" Jeff asked, watching her closely.

"No, of course not," she answered, feigning nonchalance. She wasn't about to tell him that her parents had forbidden her to partake of hard liquor; then he would certainly think her immature and unsophisticated. Quickly, she helped herself to another drink, relieved that this one seemed to burn her throat a little less than the first one had.

She wasn't fooling Jeff, but not letting on that he was wise, he warned, "Well, if you aren't used to brandy, then you'd better drink only a small amount. It's a potent liquor."

"Nonsense," she remarked, hoping she sounded

quite experienced. "I've always been able to hold my liquor quite well." Her expression daring him to think otherwise, she tipped the glass to her lips and drank the remainder.

She handed him the empty glass, and taking it, he asked with an inward smile, "Would you like another?"

"Another?" she repeated, wondering why the room was suddenly so unbearably warm. She knew she should refuse, but, after all where was the harm in having only one more? And, besides, it gave her an excuse to remain in his company. "Yes, thank you," she replied.

Filling her glass, he gave it back to Leanna. Noticing he hadn't finished his brandy, she asked pertly, "Aren't you going to join me?"

Lifting his glass, he said cheerfully, "Bottoms up!"

Wide-eyed, Leanna queried, "What?"

"An experienced drinker like yourself should have no problem downing her brandy." Once again raising his glass, he repeated, "Bottoms up, Miss Weston."

Following Jeff's example, Leanna finished her drink in one swallow, and when she handed her empty glass back to Jeff, her legs suddenly weakened.

Swaying precariously, Leanna leaned toward Jeff. Moving quickly, he placed the glasses on the dresser, then reached for Leanna and took her into his arms.

He was about to help her back to her room, but she raised her face to look up at him, and her sweet lips, so close, were a temptation he couldn't refuse. Bending his head, he brought his lips down to hers.

Leanna fell against him, and sliding one arm

tightly about her waist, Jeff pressed her thighs to his.

Jeff's exciting kiss sent Leanna's mind swirling, and she wrapped her arms around his neck as her lips parted beneath his. In response, Jeff's tongue darted between her teeth, deepening their kiss.

His lips still on hers, Jeff swept her into his arms and carried her to his bed. Placing her on the soft mattress, Jeff's lean frame covered hers, and, instinctively, Leanna parted her legs so that his hardness could rest between her delicate thighs.

"Leanna," he whispered thickly, sending light kisses over her face and down to the hollow of her throat.

Her mind muddled by brandy, and Jeff's ardent advances, Leanna murmured invitingly, "Love me, Jeff . . . I need you . . . I need you so very much."

For a moment Jeff contemplated taking her to her room. He knew she was feeling the brandy, and it was wrong for him to take advantage of her vulnerability. But when Leanna suddenly pressed her lips to his, and arched her delectable body, Jeff's thoughts of guilt fled.

Moving to lie at her side, Jeff started to help her out of her night clothes, but, modestly, Leanna pleaded, "Please put out the lamp."

Jeff hesitated. The heavy bedroom drapes were drawn, and if he turned off the lamp, the room would be totally dark. He was eager to see once again Leanna's seductive beauty. He had not forgotten the night he had caught her stepping into the bathtub. Her full breasts, tiny waist, and rounded hips had been the most tempting sight he had ever seen.

"Jeff, the light," she pleaded again.

With much reluctance, Jeff leaned across the bed and turned down the wick of the lamp which was on the small night table. Fuming inwardly, he then helped Leanna remove her clothes, wishing fervently that she hadn't insisted on modesty.

Stretching out his long frame beside hers, Jeff's lips again relished Leanna's as a hand traveled to her breasts, cupping one and then the other. Bending his head, his warm mouth suckled her nipples, the gentle stimulation sending delightful chills up Leanna's spine.

Entwining her fingers into his thick hair, she purred throatily, "Oh, Jeff . . . Jeff . . ."

Bringing his lips back to hers, Jeff moved his hand downward to find her soft womanhood. His intimate touch caused Leanna to tense, but he soothed her fears by murmuring tenderly, "Relax, sweetheart, and let me love you. Leanna, you are so desirable, and I want you more than I have ever wanted any woman."

Pleased by his confession, she whispered hopefully, "More than any woman?"

"Yes," he groaned sincerely.

Giving herself over completely to the desire Jeff had aroused in her, Leanna parted her legs so that he could satisfy her need for fulfillment.

When, unexpectedly, he drew away to remove his clothes, she felt as though all the warmth in her life had suddenly been taken away. Her arms actually ached as she waited for him to return to her embrace, and her entire being craved his body next to hers.

He lay back over her, and, instantly, she gathered him close. Leanna was not sexually uninformed; her mother had explained marital relations to her, and she knew there would be a moment of pain. But, strangely, she was not afraid. Jeff Clayton had stolen her heart, and she wanted to belong to him so desperately that she'd have been willing to suffer immense pain to do so.

Carefully, he slipped his arm around her waist, lifting her thighs to his. Placing his lips on hers, Jeff kissed her passionately as his arousal found the entry to her ecstatic warmth. He had no doubt that Leanna was a virgin, and not wanting to prolong her pain, he penetrated her suddenly and swiftly.

As he achieved complete entry, Leanna's soft cry was muffled beneath his loving kiss. Waiting for her discomfort to subside, he continued to kiss her without moving his hips.

"Leanna, my sweetheart," he whispered in her ear, "are you all right?"

"Yes," she moaned tremulously, as a glorious feeling began flowing through her entire being.

He moved against her, slowly at first, until he felt her beginning to respond. Then, finding it terribly difficult to hold his passion in check, he urged her legs across his back.

His deeper penetration aroused Leanna, and losing herself in their exciting union, she began to arch her hips rhythmically.

Jeff was now driven by desire, and Leanna equaled Jeff's passion in every movement of their thrilling union.

Jeff's climax came to him powerfully and uncontrollably, causing his strong frame to tremble as he released his seed deep inside her.

Breathing heavily, he whispered tenderly, "Leanna,

you are wonderful." Moving to lie at her side, he drew her into his arms.

Nestling close, Leanna was mystified as to why sudden tears had come to her eyes. Why did she feel an urge to cry? Their togetherness had been beautiful, and she had found only pleasure in Jeff's intimate embrace. So why did she feel sad? She should be ecstatically happy! Sighing, Leanna reluctantly admitted the truth to herself. Jeff would soon leave her. His departure was inevitable, and she didn't want him to go away.

"Leanna?" he coaxed gently, worried over her strange silence. "Is something bothering you?"

She wondered if she should confess her true feelings. Deciding to be totally honest with him, she sat up and was about to reveal her deepest thoughts when she heard Louise calling for her.

"Oh no!" Leanna gasped, bolting from the bed. Due to the darkness, it was difficult to find her clothes, but, somehow, she managed to dress.

Jeff rose to help her, but before he could offer his assistance, she had on her night clothes and was heading for the door that led into the hallway.

"Leanna," he called in a hushed tone, "I'll see you in the morning."

Mumbling a hasty good-night, she darted out of his room. Sitting on the edge of his bed, Jeff lit the lamp. Staring at the closed door, he wished Leanna hadn't had to leave so abruptly. She had surrendered herself to him so sweetly that he longed to hold her in his arms, to tell her how much she meant to him. He knew Sherman would be arriving with his orders sometime within the next forty-eight hours, and then he and his troops would be leaving the Weston plantation for good. There were so many things he needed to tell Leanna before he left. Well, he would see her in the morning, and, when he did, he'd hold her close and let her know how much he cared.

Leanna entered her bedroom by the hall door, and hoping she didn't appear too disheveled she asked Louise, who was lighting the lamp next to the bed, "Did I hear you calling me?"

"Yes, Miz Anna. I was wonderin' where you was," the girl answered drowsily.

"I went down to the kitchen for a bite to eat," Leanna replied. Going to her bed, she added, "Go back to sleep, Louise."

Complying, the child went to her pallet and lay down. Slipping out of her dressing gown, Leanna turned off the lamp. Snuggling into bed, she gave a soft sigh of relief. Thank goodness no one else had heard Louise calling her. She could only imagine what would have happened if her mother had caught her with Jeff. Finding the thought too terrifying, she pushed it from her mind, deciding to give Jeff her full concentration. And with dreams of Jeff Clayton filling her mind, as well as her heart, Leanna drifted into sleep.

Chapter Seven

Sitting at her vanity table, Leanna looked into the mirror, studying her reflection. She knew when her family saw her this morning, she would appear to be the same. But she wasn't, she had changed drastically. She was no longer an innocent girl; last night Jeff had made her a woman. Peering closer at her reflection, Leanna was sure the change was not an outward one, but inwardly, she felt as though she had matured.

Knowing she'd soon be seeing Jeff made Leanna feel apprehensive. How would he act, and, most importantly, how should she behave?

Wanting to look especially nice, Leanna rose from her dressing stool and slipped hastily out of her night clothes. Going to her large mahogany wardrobe, she rummaged through her dresses, deciding on a gown that was the palest of pinks, with a full bow attached to each shoulder. Placing the gown on her bed, she then went to her bureau, and taking out a voluminous petticoat, she quickly donned it. Stepping to her bed, she picked up the elegant gown, admiring it for a moment before putting it on.

Returning to her vanity table, Leanna adjusted the mirror so that she could see her full reflection. The gown was designed to be worn off the shoulders, and it seductively revealed her deep cleavage. Suddenly, realizing this dress was much too elaborate for a day gown, Leanna laughed gaily.

I'll wear it tonight, she decided. I'll ask Jeff to meet me in the study after everyone else has gone to bed. Still studying her reflection, she wondered if Jeff would find her especially pretty. Scrutinizing herself intently, she wondered whether tonight she should wear her hair down. Deciding to see how she'd look with her long hair worn up in a formal fashion, she sat down on the dressing stool.

Looking for her hair pins, Leanna opened the dresser drawer, and, as she reached inside, her hand brushed against a small stack of letters tied together with a ribbon. Leanna's heart warned her to overlook the letters, pick up the hairpins, close the drawer and keep her thoughts exclusively on Jeff. But, against her will, her fingers encircled the letters, taking them from the drawer.

Leanna's gaiety vanished, and as she placed the letters from her brother on her lap, tears came to her eyes and trickled down her cheeks. The top letter was the last one that Brad had written to her. Her hand trembling, Leanna removed it from the stack. Don't open it! she thought desperately. It'll only make you feel guilty, and, dear God, reading your brother's last words will only be a painful reminder that he was killed by Yankees! Yankees! And Jeff is a Yankee!

Guilt overwhelming her, Leanna clutched her brother's letter to her breasts as uncontrollable sobs racked her body. Oh, it was so wrong for her to care about Jeff! How could she have allowed herself to betray her family as well as the Confederacy? Had she no moral values at all? With tears streaming down her face, Leanna bowed her head and cried heartbrokenly.

Leanna was crying so hard that she didn't hear Jennifer's soft knock, nor was she aware that Jennifer entered her bedroom.

Seeing Leanna sitting at her dressing table, weeping pathetically, Jennifer hurried to her sister-in-law and knelt beside her. Noticing the letters on Leanna's lap, and the one she held to her breasts, Jennifer pleaded with heartfelt sympathy, "Leanna, darling, don't cry. We must remember Brad with happiness not with tears. He wouldn't want us to be sad."

Her voice quivering piteously, Leanna sobbed, "I loved Brad, Jennifer. Truly, I did!"

"Of course you loved him," Jennifer replied soothingly. "And Brad loved you. He loved you very much." Gently, Jennifer took the letter from Leanna's hand, placing it and the others on the vanity table. Still kneeling at Leanna's feet, she asked tenderly, "Darling, are you all right?"

Controlling her tears, Leanna whispered, "Yes, I think so."

Standing, Jennifer questioned carefully, "Why were you reading Brad's letters?"

"I wasn't reading them, I just happened to come across them."

"Are they the reason you are upset, or did some-

101

thing else happen to disturb you?"

"No, nothing else happened," Leanna lied, despising herself for not telling the truth. Her relationship with Jeff had made her a deceitful person, as well as a traitor.

Taking note of Leanna's dress, Jennifer continued her questioning, "Why are you wearing an evening gown?"

Avoiding her sister-in-law's prying, Leanna rose and, walking toward the bed, said casually, "I was just trying it on. It's been so long since I wore a pretty gown that I put it on just for the fun of it. I was being very foolish."

Jennifer wasn't sure if she believed Leanna, but deciding to let the subject drop, she said, "I'm going downstairs for breakfast. Are you coming?"

Turning to face her, Leanna replied, "I think I'll skip breakfast this morning." If she went downstairs, she might run into Jeff, and she wasn't ready to see him. Not yet. First, she must get her thoughts into perspective.

"All right," Jennifer answered, wishing she knew what was so obviously upsetting Leanna.

The moment Jennifer left the room, Leanna's tears returned. What was she going to do about her feelings for Jeff? There was only one sensible solution to her dilemma. She must leave the plantation. As long as she was in the same house with Jeff, where they could be together, she'd never have the strength to resist him. As soon as she was in control of her emotions, she must go to Jeff and ask his permission to travel to Marietta. She would stay with Dr. Simons and his wife until Jeff and his troops left

The Pines. Dr. Simons was the family physician and a good friend; she knew that he and his wife would let her stay temporarily with them.

As Jennifer was descending the stairs, Jeff was climbing them on his way to his bedroom. He had been in the study, waiting impatiently for Leanna to come downstairs. Finally, he had decided to go to his room and contact her through their adjoining door.

Passing him on the stairway, Jennifer gave him a frigid look, but not even Jennifer's hostility could put a damper on Jeff's good spirits. Smiling widely, he greeted her. "Good morning, Mrs. Weston."

Lifting her chin haughtily, Jennifer responded with cold silence.

His long strides carrying him quickly to the top of the staircase, Jeff went into his bedroom, heading straight for the adjoining door. He was anxious to see Leanna. He could hardly wait to hold her in his arms, and tell her how much she meant to him.

Rapping twice on the door, he called, "Leanna?"

Leanna was standing in the center of the room when Jeff called to her, and, startled, she whirled toward the closed door.

"Leanna?" he said again. "Sweetheart, I need to talk to you."

What should she do? She wasn't ready for him. Not yet! She needed more time to emotionally prepare herself. "Jeff, please leave me alone," she pleaded.

Her answer surprised Jeff, he hadn't expected to be turned away. "Leanna, if you don't open this door, I'm coming in."

She knew he meant what he said, and realizing

103

their confrontation was about to take place, she forced herself to suppress her true feelings. Thinking only of her family and the Confederacy, she answered smugly, "There is no lock on this side of the door to prevent your intrusion, Major Clayton."

As Jeff entered the room, Leanna turned her back, trying to gain complete power over her emotions before facing him. He moved soundlessly, but she could sense his closeness before he placed his hands on her shoulders.

His touch made her long to whirl around and fling herself into his strong arms. She had so little will power with him, he had only to touch her to melt her resolutions. Knowing she must avoid personal contact between them, she moved away and took a few steps before turning to confront him. Now, with a safe distance separating them, surely she could keep her emotions in check. "Jeff," she began, her voice unsteady, "I was planning to talk to you as soon as I came downstairs."

He was hurt by her aloofness, but keeping his feelings well masked, he merely watched her questioningly.

"I . . . I wanted to ask your permission to move temporarily to Marietta," she stammered, wishing he wasn't so excitingly handsome. Just the sight of him made her heart pound rapidly.

"Move to Marietta?" he snapped, his abrupt anger alarming Leanna. "Why in the hell do you want to leave?"

"Because I don't want to stay here!" she cried out hastily, surprised that he was so upset.

"You're running away because of what happened

between us last night, aren't you?" he demanded.

"Partly," she mumbled.

"Partly, Leanna?" he questioned sharply.

Nervously, she tried to explain, "Jeff, I don't want to be in the same house with you, and the only way I can avoid that is to stay elsewhere."

"It's not necessary for you to take such drastic measures, Leanna. I'm expecting my orders today or tomorrow at the latest, so I'll be leaving myself within the next day or two. I'm sure if you set your stubborn mind to it, you can successfully manage to avoid me for the rest of my short stay here."

He turned brusquely to leave the room, but Leanna halted him by asking, "Why did you want to talk to me?"

"It doesn't matter anymore," he grumbled.

"I don't understand," she replied, wishing she knew what he was thinking.

"Don't you?" he quipped, pausing at the open door. "It's too bad that you can't understand me, for I can read you perfectly. You have decided that your loyalties are with the Confederacy and to hell with us. Your patriotism is admirable; one's loyalty to one's country must come first." Cocking an eyebrow, he grinned roguishly as his eyes examined her elegant gown. "By the way, Miss Weston, you look very lovely." Stepping into his room, he shut the door behind him.

Jeff was in the Westons' study, sitting behind the desk, when the young sentry opened the door and took a step into the room, announcing, "There is a Dr. Simons here to see Mrs. Weston."

Standing, he replied, "Show him in."

The soldier moved aside, allowing the doctor to enter. Dr. Simons was an elderly man, and as he removed his hat, he revealed a head full of gray hair.

Moving out from behind the desk, Jeff said cordially, "Dr. Simons."

Not trying to conceal his hostility, the doctor's eyes glared into Jeff's. "I came here to call on Mary Weston, not to talk to Yankees."

"Why do you need to see Mrs. Weston?"

"She's ill and has been under my care for the past year."

"Did you come from Marietta?"

"Yes, I did," he answered stiffly. "And the town is filled with you Yankees."

Walking to the door, Jeff opened it and ordered the soldier to search the doctor and then allow him to go upstairs.

Dr. Simons found the personal search humiliating, and with his dignity severely wounded, he swore under his breath as he climbed the stairs to Mary's quarters. The door to her sitting room was closed, but he knocked firmly.

It was opened by Jennifer. "Why, Dr. Simons!" she exclaimed. "What a pleasant surprise."

Mary was lying on her chaise longue, and, at the doctor's entrance, she started to rise, but he quickly waved her back down. "Don't get up, Mary." Leanna was sitting in a chair close to her mother, and glancing at her, he continued, "Leanna dear, I hope you are well."

"I'm fine, thank you," she replied, smiling.

"Is something wrong, Phillip?" Mary asked, using

the doctor's first name. "This isn't the day you usually come out to see me."

Jennifer was still standing by the closed door, and he motioned her over to join them.

"General Sherman has besieged Marietta," he revealed, keeping his voice lowered. "He is now on his way to this plantation."

Terrified, Mary gasped, "Oh, Phillip, are you sure?"

"Relatively so," he answered. "That's why I'm here. I was sure the general's presence would frighten you. But I will stay here until he leaves."

"But why is he coming here?" Mary wanted to know.

"I imagine he is bringing orders for the major. I could be wrong, but I believe those orders will be very vital." His voice filled with frustration, he added, "I wish there were some way I could overhear those orders, because I could get word of them to the Confederacy." Shaking his head, he sighed, "Well, that is a hopeless wish."

Pulling up a chair, the doctor began asking Mary about her health. Neither paid any mind to Leanna as she rose and walked over to the sitting-room window. As she stared vacantly out of the window, Leanna's thoughts were running fluidly and dangerously. Her relationship with Jeff had made her feel like a traitor to the Confederacy, but if she could find a way to overhear Sherman's military plans, that would give her a chance to make amends. Her mind in a turmoil, Leanna was surprised to find herself seriously considering spying on Jeff and his comrades. But, then, hadn't he once told her himself that any military command he gave would go against what she wanted? Well, perhaps she wasn't in the military, but she was a Confederate; and as he had pointed out, there was a war taking place between her people and his. Hadn't he said himself that one's loyalty to one's country must come first?

She was sure Sherman would hold his conference in the study, which meant she must find a way to slip into the room when it was unoccupied. If she hid herself, she could overhear the Union's military tactics. But I'll need help, she thought. I can't do it alone! There is a guard at the study door, and he will have to be distracted so that I can sneak into the room.

Turning away from the window, her eyes fell upon Jennifer. Could she convince her sister-in-law to be a part of her conspiracy? Determined to talk her into it one way or another, Leanna asked, "Jennifer, will you come with me to my bedroom?"

Glancing at Leanna, her sister-in-law replied, "Yes, of course."

"You will excuse us, won't you, Doctor?" Leanna said politely.

Simons nodded, giving their departure little thought, so, moving quickly, Leanna ushered Jennifer into the hall and down to her bedroom.

Closing the door behind them, Leanna said secretly, "I think General Sherman will use Papa's study to meet with his officers. Jennifer, you must help me get into that study so that I can overhear his orders."

"You can't be serious!" Jennifer exclaimed.

"I've never been more serious," Leanna replied

impatiently. "When the major leaves the house to greet the general, I will sneak into the study and hide."

"But there is a guard at the study door," Jennifer pointed out.

"You must find a way to distract him," Leanna stated.

"And while I am distracting him, you plan to slip into the study?" Jennifer asked.

"Yes," she answered breathlessly.

"Do you realize what you are doing? Spying is very serious, and if you are caught—"

"I know," Leanna said gravely. "I could be executed."

"No!" Jennifer adamantly refused to help. "The answer is no. I won't let you take such a perilous chance."

"Jennifer, we must help the Confederate Army!" Leanna pleaded.

Jennifer's loyalty to the Confederacy weakened her convictions and she asked warily, "But how would I distract the sentry?"

"When the major leaves the house to greet Sherman, I will slip down the back stairway as you walk down the front staircase. I'll enter the foyer from the back of the house. When you are almost to the bottom of the steps, you'll pretend to faint. When the guard goes to your side, you can recover weakly from your swoon and ask him to help you into the parlor. While he is assisting you, I'll sneak into the study."

"Oh Leanna!" Jennifer cried, exasperated. "How can this possibly succeed? You are making all these plans on the spur of the moment."

"It'll work!" Leanna assured her as though she herself had no doubts about the plan, but she was actually trying to convince herself as well as Jennifer.

"When the conference is over, how do you plan to leave the study without being seen?"

"You'll get me out the same way you got me in. When the major and the others leave, walk slowly into the foyer and once again pretend to faint. The guard will assist you back into the parlor."

"But, Leanna," Jennifer began, "you have no guarantee that Major Clayton will leave the study with Sherman and the other officers."

Reassuringly, Leanna replied, "If the major leaves the study to greet Sherman, then he will most likely escort him back outside."

Jennifer said raspingly, "Oh, Leanna, I'm so afraid you'll get caught!"

Leanna's nerve almost faltered, but determined to help the Confederacy and to ease her conscience, she said briskly, "I'll tell Dr. Simons everything that I overheard, then he can get the information to the army."

Turning, Leanna began walking across the room, and Jennifer asked, "Where are you going?"

"To the window to watch for General Sherman," Leanna replied with a calmness that she was far from feeling.

Chapter Eight

Looking across the front lawn from her bedroom window, Leanna became aware of a cloud of dust materializing at the end of the long drive that led up to the house. She watched with amazement as the massed army of Union troops advanced upon her property. Their horses' hoofs stirred up the loose dirt and sent it swirling into the still air. The procession drew steadily closer as hundreds of animals and numerous wagons sent clouds of Georgian dirt across the landscape.

Hearing the soldiers arriving, Jennifer hastened to Leanna's side and looked out the window. "Sherman!" she sneered, her expression revealing her loathing for the Union general.

Taking Jennifer's arm, Leanna urged her away from the window and across the room. Escorting her toward the door, Leanna said hastily, "I'll slip down the back stairs. You watch the study door from the front staircase. If the major leaves the house, we'll go through with our plans."

Jennifer's fear for Leanna's safety caused her to have second thoughts, but noticing her indecision, Leanna reminded her, "Think about Brad who died for the Confederacy, and David who is at this very moment fighting for the cause! We must do this for them!"

Reluctantly, Jennifer conceded, "All right."

Quietly, Leanna opened the door, and the two women stepped into the hall. Giving Jennifer a quick hug, Leanna turned and hurried toward the stairs that had been built for the servants to use.

Cautiously, Jennifer moved toward the huge, marble staircase. When she paused on the landing, she could see the sentry standing in front of the study. Secretly, she watched as the study door was opened wide and Major Clayton stepped into the foyer. He held his hat in his hand, but as he moved quickly to the front door, he placed it on his head.

As soon as the major left the house, Jennifer took a deep breath and began descending the flight of stairs.

The young sentry heard her approaching and glanced up. He tried to make his admiration of her beauty less obvious.

Nearing the bottom of the steps, Jennifer placed her hand to her brow and tottered insecurely.

"Are you ill, ma'am," the sentry called with concern.

Taking another step down the stairway, she moaned weakly, "I . . . I feel as though . . . I'm going to faint."

Jennifer collapsed gracefully, clutching the banister to break her fall before she dropped gently to the

112

floor. Hurrying to her side, the sentry knelt beside her.

Her eyelids fluttering open, Jennifer pleaded sweetly, "Please help me into the study."

"I'm sorry, ma'am, but I'm not supposed to leave my post," the soldier explained apologetically.

"Very well," she sighed, her voice sounding terribly weak. "I will try to manage alone." She made a feeble attempt to rise, but placing her hand to her forehead, she moaned, "I'm so dizzy."

Reacting chivalrously, the soldier slipped the sling on his rifle over his shoulder. Bending over Jennifer, he lifted her with ease and carried her into the parlor.

Watching the scene from the back of the foyer, Leanna hurried toward the study door, thankful that her soft-soled slippers made no noise as she sped across the bare floor. As quietly as possible, she opened the door and darted into the room. Closing it behind her, she stood uncertainly as she glanced about the large room. Where should she hide? She wished she hadn't thought of a place to conceal herself before she had entered the study. She considered the chair placed in one corner of the study. Was it large enough to cover her if she knelt behind it? No!

Suddenly, she heard the major and the others entering the house. Holding back a scream of panic, her eyes turned to the floor-length velvet drapes that covered the side window. She ran across the room. She knew there was a guard stationed outside by the window, but the curtains were much wider than the glass pane, and her back would be against the wall. Reaching the drapes, she pulled back the heavy

113

material and slipped behind them.

The sentry, thankful that he was back at his post, saluted the six officers before opening the study door for them. He stepped aside as they strode briskly into the room. Major Clayton was the last one in line, and as he passed the sentry, he glanced into the parlor. Seeing Jennifer lying on the sofa, he halted his steps. Nodding toward her, he asked the sentry, "Is something wrong with Mrs. Weston?"

"I think . . . I think the lady is ill, sir," the man stammered, knowing he could never tell the major that he had left his station.

"Make sure she stays away from the study until the meeting is over," he commanded.

"Yes, sir," the soldier said clearly.

Walking into the study, Jeff closed the door behind him. General Sherman was sitting at the polished mahogany desk, and looking at Lieutenant Buehler, he ordered, "Close both windows." Glancing quickly at his fellow officers, he apologized, "I realize it will be very stuffy and unbearably hot in here, but it is imperative that we are not overheard."

When the lieutenant closed the window where Leanna was hiding, she dared not breathe until she heard his footsteps retreat. As she let out her breath very quietly, she could feel her heart beating rapidly, and wondered if her trembling legs would continue to support her.

"Considering the heat," General Sherman continued, "I will make this as short as possible."

The five officers gathered around the desk, waiting for their commander to give them their orders. Pushing back his chair, the general stood, and reaching into his pocket, he removed a map. Spreading it out on the desk, he spoke to Jeff, "We must cross the Chattahoochee River, but the Confederates have all the best fords covered. Major, you and Colonel Andrews will rendezvous at the river, where you will engage the enemy in battle. It will appear as though this ford is being cleared for the rest of us to follow. The Confederate Army is spread sparsely along the Chattahoochee, and it will be necessary that they send for reinforcements. That will weaken their lines even more, and we will take full advantage of their weakness to cross farther down the river while you keep the majority of their army engaged in battle. When we have crossed the Chattahoochee, we will circle back and attack their flank."

Leanna listened closely as the general continued his instructions, and as he began naming exact locations, times, and dates, she tried to commit them to memory. But the heat behind the heavy, velvet drapes was becoming unbearable, and she was beginning to find it difficult to breathe. The curtains kept the little air in the room completely blocked off, and the lack of oxygen drove her to the verge of passing out.

When the general finally finished his orders and decided that the windows could be reopened, Leanna wanted to sigh with thankfulness, but she knew even a weak sigh might be overheard.

Lieutenant Buehler walked to the front window, and Jeff decided to open the side one, where Leanna was safely hidden behind behind the drapes. Jeff had approached the window when General Sherman's voice announced strongly, "In the morning before you move out, I want this plantation house burned to the ground."

The impact of his words struck Leanna so severely that she gasped involuntarily. Reaching toward the closed window, Jeff detected her low gasp, and his eyes flew to the full drapes. His instincts told him the soft cry had come from Leanna, and cautiously, he turned to look back at the others, but they apparently were unaware of Leanna's presence. Swerving back to the window, he raised it quickly, and a refreshing breeze drifted immediately into the stuffy room.

"Major Clayton," the general began impatiently, "did you hear what I said? I want this house burned."

Moving across the room to rejoin his comrades, Jeff answered, "Yes, sir." Hesitantly, he made an attempt to save Leanna's home, "General, there are only three women, two children, and three slaves living in this house. Is it really necessary that we destroy their home?"

Sternly, the general reprimanded him. "Major, this time I will be lenient and forget what you said. But if you should ever again question my orders, I will have you stripped of your rank! I don't give a damn who lives in this house! I'm not a bleeding Samaritan, I'm a Union officer fighting a war that I intend to win . . . at any cost!"

"Yes, sir!" Jeff conceded respectfully.

The general liked Major Clayton, and as his temper cooled, he smiled. "Jeff," he explained informally, "I don't take pleasure in leaving women and children homeless, but if enough of them are left destitute, perhaps their men will give up their lost cause and return home to take care of their families. I am willing to give any order and to make any decision that will inevitably hasten the end of this war."

The general offered Clayton his hand, and Jeff shook it firmly.

Picking up the map, General Sherman folded it and slipped it back into his pocket. Their conference over, the six officers left the room in single file, Jeff at the rear of the line and his lieutenant walking in front of him. Touching Lieutenant Buehler on the shoulder, Jeff said in a lowered voice, "See the general outside. I have some urgent business to take care of in the study."

Sitting in the parlor, Jennifer watched with consternation as Major Clayton left his fellow officers to return to the study. "Oh no!" she moaned faintly, feeling pangs of remorse. Spying on General Sherman had been foolhardy, and now Leanna would pay the price. Crying softly, Jennifer began to pray, asking God to please not let Major Clayton order Leanna before a firing squad.

Leanna had remained behind the drapes, giving Jennifer time to once again distract the sentry. The heavy curtains prevented the fresh air drifting through the open windows from reaching her, and she longed to leave her hiding place, but she decided it would be best to stay where she was until she judged it safe to leave the room.

Jeff entered the study quietly, and Leanna was unaware that he had returned until the drapes were suddenly pushed aside. As his eyes glared into hers

117

with intense fury, her hand flew to her mouth to hold back a cry of alarm.

Clutching her arm, he jerked her away from the curtains and shoved her to the middle of the room. His rough treatment caused her to lose her footing, and for a moment, she swayed precariously before regaining her balance.

Going to the windows, Jeff slammed them shut to insure privacy, then returning to Leanna, he grabbed her shoulders and shook her violently. "You little fool!" he raged. "Do you realize what you have done?"

Trying desperately to free herself from his painful grip, she replied firmly, "Of course, I realize what I have done! I overheard your military plans. I suppose that makes me a Confederate spy!"

Digging his fingers even deeper into her flesh, he answered hoarsely, "Spy is the key word, but do you know what it means?"

Jerking away from his tenacious hold, she asked flippantly, "One who obtains secret military information from the enemy?"

Crossing his arms over his chest, he eyed her menacingly, "Very good, Leanna. Do you also know what happens to spies when they are caught?"

She raised her chin bravely, although inwardly she had never been more frightened. "They are executed?" she questioned a little shakily.

"Executed?" he repeated, smiling slightly. "It's one sensible solution, but the Union also has a prison camp where they send Southern ladies who become involved in this war. From what I hear, it is guarded by the scum of the army, and the only way an attractive woman like yourself can survive is to , . . Well, to speak as a gentleman, she must be very agreeable where the guards are concerned."

Her blue eyes reflecting her distaste, Leanna snapped, "In that case, I'd rather face a firing squad!"

He didn't respond to her choice, he merely continued to stare darkly into her face. "How did you get in here?" he suddenly demanded.

Afraid Jennifer would also be punished if Jeff learned that she had participated, she refused to answer.

Storming across the room, Jeff opened the door. Speaking to the sentry, he commanded, "Soldier, did you leave your post?"

Standing in the open doorway, the young soldier caught sight of Leanna in the study, and, all at once, he realized he had been cleverly deceived.

"Answer me, soldier!" Jeff ordered harshly.

"Yes, sir," he admitted reluctantly. Gesturing toward Jennifer, he explained, "The lady fainted, and I carried her to the sofa. I'm sorry, sir. I should have known it was a trick."

Seeing Lieutenant Buehler entering the house, the major asked him, "Has General Sherman left?" As he nodded affirmatively, Jeff commanded sharply, "Get Sergeant O'Malley, and tell him to bring ten men and report to me on the double!"

"Yes, sir!" he replied, hurrying back outdoors.

Turning his attention to the sentry, Jeff said severely, "If Mrs. Weston tries to leave the parlor, I want her placed under arrest!" Stepping back into the study, he slammed the door closed behind him, and

Leanna could see a terrible rage in his eyes as he returned swiftly to her side.

"How could you order that soldier to arrest Jennifer? Good Lord, she's a mother with two small children!"

"When women forget their sex and involve themselves in a man's war, they must face the consequences. The Code of War doesn't have two sets of rules, one for women and one for men."

"Code of War!" Leanna smirked. "You disgusting Yankees live by whatever code suits you!"

"Damn it, Leanna!" he raved, and his furious anger startled her. "If you call Yankees disgusting one more time, I'm going to make it very difficult for you to say another word!"

"Are you threatening to strike me?" she asked, astounded.

"I strongly advise you not to tempt me!" he bellowed, and the hardness on his face convinced her that he was not bluffing.

Anxiously awaiting the lieutenant's return, Jeff began pacing across the room. He owned Leanna no explanations, but seeing the worry on her face, he told her calmly, "Your sister-in-law will not try to flee with a soldier standing guard over her. But, hopefully, I have put the fear of God into her, and she'll never again try anything so foolish."

A firm rap sounded on the door, and Jeff called gruffly, "Come in!"

Lieutenant Buehler strode into the room, followed by Sergeant O'Malley, who told his men to wait in the foyer.

"Sergeant," Jeff ordered, "post two guards at the

120

study door, two outside Miss Weston's bedroom windows and two more outside her bedroom door. I also want two men posted at Mary Weston's quarters and two more at her daughter-in-law's. None of the ladies are allowed to leave their rooms. Is that understood?"

"Yes, sir!" the sergeant replied.

When he made no move to obey, Jeff shouted testily, "I want this order carried out immediately!"

The sergeant, a middle-aged and stockily built man with a distinct Irish brogue, answered, "Sir, exactly where are each of the ladies' bedrooms?"

Striding to the open doorway, Jeff could see that Jennifer had heard his orders, and he told her, "Mrs. Weston, show the sergeant and his men upstairs and to the correct rooms."

Responding with cold silence, Jennifer walked elegantly toward the staircase as the sergeant and the intended guards followed close behind.

"Lieutenant Buehler," Jeff continued, gesturing toward the sentry who had carried Jennifer into the parlor, "place this soldier on detention for leaving his assigned post."

Returning to the study, Jeff once again slammed the door closed. Leanna was wary of his violent anger, but she could feel a part of her responding to his dominance. She had never before been so acutely aware of his male magnetism.

"Major, are you always so hot tempered?" she asked.

"Only when a woman has made a fool of me!" he grumbled. His dark eyes flickering dangerously, he crossed the room to stand in front of her. "I wonder if you truly realize what you have done and how grave the outcome could be."

"Major," she began, the extreme heat in the room making her irritable, "surely one woman cannot be that much of a threat to the powerful Union Army."

"You are no threat to the Union, you are a threat to yourself."

Moving away from him, she took a couple of steps as she wiped at her perspiring brow. If only she could have some fresh air! She was starting to feel as though she couldn't breathe. Turning to face him, she was about to ask him to please open the windows, when the room began to tilt and dark spots darted before her eyes.

Noting her sudden paleness, Jeff approached her quickly, and as he reached for her, Leanna's knees buckled. Fainting, she fell against him, and catching her, he lifted her into his arms. As he was carrying her to the door, Sergeant O'Malley's firm knock announced his presence.

"Come in," Jeff called.

Opening the door, the sergeant was surprised to see the major holding Miss Weston. "What happened to the pretty lass?" he asked.

Jeff's stern expression softened as he gazed down into Leanna's face. "It seems our rebel spy is not quite as strong as she thinks she is." Holding Leanna closely, Jeff carried her up the stairs. The door to her bedroom was standing open, with a guard stationed on each side of the doorway. As he entered the room, Jeff ordered one of the soldiers to close the door. Taking Leanna to her large, canopied bed, he laid her down gently. Stepping to the washstand, he lifted a pitcher and poured water into the basin. Grabbing a washcloth, he soaked it in the water then wrung it out. Returning to Leanna, he sat on the edge of the bed and placed the wet cloth on her warm forehead.

When Leanna's eyes fluttered open, she was startled to find herself on her bed with Jeff sitting beside her. "Wh . . . what happened?" she stammered.

"You fainted," he answered, smiling tenderly.

"But I've never fainted in my life!" she exclaimed.

"Well," he drawled, "you've had a very exciting day. Taking it upon yourself to spy against General Sherman was very brave and very dangerous. I suppose you earned yourself a good swoon."

"Don't be ridiculous!" she spat tartly. "It wasn't the danger that made me faint but the heat!"

"Why did you do it, Leanna?" he asked suddenly, his face serious.

"Do what?" she asked evasively, knowing exactly what he was referring to.

"Damn it, Leanna, don't play games with me!"

Bristling, she retorted, "I did it for the Confederacy and . . . for my brother."

"Do you have any idea what would have happened to you if you had been caught by Sherman instead of me?" he asked testily.

"Honestly, Jeff," she began impatiently, wishing he'd let the subject rest. "It's over and done with, and although I'm not sorry about what I did, I would appreciate it very much if you'd stop reprimanding me as though I were a child."

Standing, Jeff said evenly, "There are two guards beneath your bedroom window and two more outside this door. I have given strict orders that you are not to leave this room."

"But I must see my mother, and let her know I'm all right," Leanna insisted.

"You are forbidden to speak to any member of this household," he replied inflexibly.

"My mother and Dr. Simons had nothing to do with this. And Jennifer is not really to blame. I talked her into helping me. She assisted me reluctantly."

"Nothing will happen to your mother or sister-in-law, and Dr. Simons will be sent back to Marietta." He paused for a moment, before continuing, "I'll talk to you later, after I have decided what I'm going to do with you."

She watched him as his sturdy strides carried him across the room and to the door. "Jeff," she called hesitantly.

He turned to face her.

"Yes?"

"Did you know I was in the study when General Sherman was there?"

"Yes, I did," he admitted.

"Why did you protect me? Why didn't you turn me over to the general?"

She saw a look of anger in his eyes as he explained testily, "You're my responsibility, not his!" Opening the door, he walked out of the room.

Chapter Nine

Matilda had brought up a dinner tray for Leanna, and one of the guards had carried it into her bedroom. Now, one hour later, the tray sat, untouched, on the table beside her bed. Remembering Sherman's strategic plans to cross the Chattahoochee River, Leanna's grave concern for the Confederacy caused her to have no appetite. How could she eat when she knew hundreds of Confederate soldiers would die protecting the wrong ford at the river? If only she could find some way to get word of Sherman's plans to Dr. Simons. She knew if she could manage to slip away, Jeff would realize that she had taken her information to Marietta and that from there it would be delivered to the Confederacy. He would then be compelled to inform Sherman that they would have to find another way to cross the Chattahoochee. She could totally destroy Sherman's military operation, if she could only find a way to escape!

Leanna was resting on the bed, and growing restless, she swung her legs to the side. Rising, she began to pace the room, desperate to think of a way to flee the plantation and ride to Marietta. But how could she conceivably escape when there were two guards outside her door and two more beneath her window? There was no way to leave this room without being seen.

Leanna's pacing halted brusquely as, suddenly, she thought of a solution. Fleetingly, she wondered why it had taken her so long to remember that she had a perfect route for escape. But that didn't matter. Even if she had thought of it earlier, she couldn't possibly have left until dark. Now it was nighttime, and she must move — fast.

Standing in the middle of her bedroom floor, Leanna looked upward and studied the trap door in the ceiling that led into the attic. A triumphant smile spread across her face as she thought victoriously, Jeff only thinks he has me safely confined!

Continuing to look up at the trap door, she tried to think of a way to reach it without a ladder. Concentrating, she glanced around the room for a piece of furniture that was light enough for her to move and decided on her vanity table. Grasping one end of it, she moved it forward a couple of inches. It would be fairly easy to push that table across the room and place it beneath the trap door.

She hadn't forgotten that Jeff had said that he would talk to her later. For a moment, she thought it might be wiser to wait for his visit before leaving. But, no, she mustn't dally, it would be best to escape now before anything happened to ruin her plans.

Hurrying to her door, she opened it, and sounding quite fatigued, she said to the guards, "I'm retiring for the night, so when Matilda comes for my dinner tray, tell her she can get it in the morning." She turned as if to leave; then acting as though she had had an insignificant afterthought, she added tediously, "If Major Clayton wishes to see me, tell him I have gone to bed, and I do not want to be disturbed."

"Yes, ma'am," the soldiers assured her.

Closing the door, she hastened back to the vanity table. Carefully, she began sliding it across the uncarpeted floor, moving it inch by inch so there would be as little noise as possible. When the table was positioned beneath the trap door, she started to stand on it to see if she could reach the ceiling, but she found her long dress a hindrance. Impatiently, she discarded the gown and grabbed a pair of trousers and a shirt from her wardrobe. Slipping quickly into the clothes, she put on her riding boots, tucking the long pants legs inside the high-topped boots. She realized it would be pitch dark in the attic so she stuck a candle and a match in her back pocket.

Stepping up on the vanity table, she reached for the trap door, easing it open. It scraped against the attic floor, and for a few tense moments, Leanna froze. She waited fearfully for one of the guards to open her bedroom door, but when it remained closed, she sighed thankfully. Cautiously, she pushed the trap door aside and, grasping the sides of the opening, hoisted herself into the attic.

Sitting on the attic floor, she held the candle in one hand while with the other she struck the match and lit it. After blowing out the match, she got hastily to her feet. With the candle lighting the way, she crossed the attic and reached the door that led to the rear stairway. Praying it wouldn't be locked from the other side, Leanna turned the knob gingerly. She sighed with relief when the door opened.

Furtively, she crept down the stairs, which ended in two exits at the rear of the house. One exit led into the kitchen and the other onto the back porch. The door to the outside was locked. Carefully, Leanna slid back the bolt. Opening the door, she stepped outside, and keeping to the shadows, she hurried to the stables.

Because the Westons' horse was old and in poor condition, Leanna decided to take the major's chestnut stallion. She didn't waste valuable time with a saddle, she simply slipped on his bridle and guided him out of the stable.

Because the soldiers were camped on the front lawn, Leanna led the stallion into the woods, deciding to walk her mount down to the riverbank and follow it until she was far beyond the house; then she would ride to the main road and stay on it until she reached Marietta. She knew the detour would cost her vital time, but she had no other choice.

Enjoying a glass of brandy, Jeff sat casually at the desk in the study. Leaning back in the leather-bound chair, he stretched out his long legs, crossing his ankles. Reaching into his shirt pocket, he withdrew a cheroot and, taking a match from the box on the desk, lit the small cigar. He inhaled deeply, and for a moment, he felt content as he appreciated a good smoke and a glass of warm brandy. He wasn't sure how Sherman managed to accomplish it, but he always kept his officers supplied with expensive cigars and fine liquor.

But as Jeff's thoughts turned to Leanna, his brief feeling of contentment departed. What was he going to do with her? He was sure Sherman would have placed her under arrest and sent her to the women's prison camp. Jeff's handsome face hardened with anger as he pictured Leanna in such a place, totally at the mercy of guards who would have no qualms about forcing themselves on her. He sure as hell wasn't about to send her to prison, so he supposed the only logical solution was to take her with him when he and his troops moved out.

Remembering the way he had lashed out at her, Jeff began to feel a little guilty. How could he really blame her for spying, if it had been the other way around, wouldn't he have done the same thing?

Twice now, he had caught Leanna trying to help the Confederacy, and both times he had judged her too harshly. But Jeff Clayton had a hair-triggered temper, and he had never learned to control it.

Thinking back, he began to wonder if his anger had actually been caused by Leanna's spying. Perhaps his concern for her safety had set off his violent temper. If Sherman had caught her hiding in the study, Jeff knew he could have done nothing to protect her.

Putting down his glass and crushing the cigar in the ashtray, Jeff decided to go upstairs and talk to Leanna. Now that his temper had cooled, perhaps they could communicate civilly; nevertheless, he must make her aware of the seriousness of this situation.

Leaving the study, he hurried up the stairs and to

Leanna's room. He raised his hand to knock on the door, but one of the guards informed him, "Sir, Miss Weston has retired and she asked that she not be disturbed."

Letting his hand drop, Jeff nodded, "Thank you, soldier." He turned sharply and began moving down the hall toward the stairway, but an inexplicable feeling that something wasn't right caused him to pause. Uncertain, he stood for a moment, shifting his weight from one foot to the other. The feeling wouldn't go away, and Jeff returned hastily to Leanna's door. He knocked firmly and, receiving no answer, rapped on it twice more. "Leanna!" he called loudly. When he didn't get a response, he swung open the door. Seeing the vanity table moved to the center of the room, he glanced upward and was confronted by the sight of the open trap door.

His temper again aroused, he cursed angrily, "Damn it!" Swerving, he ran down the hall and descended the stairway. Spotting Sergeant O'Malley entering the house, he ordered, "Get me a saddled horse!" When the sergeant didn't move fast enough, he bellowed, "Now!"

Rushing into the study, Jeff strapped on his holster; then grabbing his hat, he hastened to the front porch, where the sergeant was waiting with a horse.

Taking the long flight of steps in three great strides, Jeff took the bridle reins from the sergeant and mounted the horse.

"Major, do you need some men?" he asked.

"No!" he replied testily. "I'll take care of this myself!"

"Sir," the sergeant began tentatively, "may I ask

130

where you're going?"

"Toward Marietta," he answered. "Tell Lieutenant Buehler I'll be back later. This shouldn't take too long."

"What shouldn't take too long, sir?" O'Malley questioned, confused.

"To catch a rebel spy," Jeff replied before turning his horse and riding speedily away from the house.

Leanna had been on the main road to Marietta for about five minutes when she heard a horse swiftly approaching. She glanced over her shoulder, but due to the darkness of the night, she could barely make out a lone rider dangerously near. Leaning over the stallion's neck, Leanna urged him into a run, and his powerful legs moved so quickly that he began to leave the trailing horse far behind.

Pursuing Leanna, Jeff had recognized the stallion she was riding, and he knew there was no way the horse he was on could possibly catch her mount. Realizing there was now only one way to stop Leanna, and hoping she wouldn't be injured in the process, he slowed down his mount and whistled loudly.

Jeff's stallion was well trained, and hearing his master's whistle, commanding him to stop, he pulled up so brusquely that he was forced to lean back on his haunches to come to a complete halt. The horse's unexpected stop took Leanna by surprise. Losing her balance, she slid from his bare back and fell heavily to the ground. The hard jolt knocked the breath from her, and for a few moments, she was stunned.

Pulling up his horse, Jeff dismounted swiftly and

hurried to where she had fallen. Kneeling beside her, he called her name anxiously, "Leanna!"

Recovering, Leanna breathed in deeply, filling her lungs with life-giving air. She was lying face down, but she had recognized Jeff's voice, and realizing her frantic attempt to help the Confederacy was now spoiled, tears of exasperation stung her eyes before trickling down her cheeks. If only she hadn't had to make that detour, by now she could have been half-way to Marietta! But Leanna was not one to give up easily, and she knew if she could slip into the sur-rounding woods, she might be able to elude Jeff and still reach Marietta.

"Leanna?" Jeff called again, reaching for her.

Moving carefully, Leanna dug her fingers into the loose dirt, filling her hand with red Georgian clay. As Jeff touched her shoulder to turn her over, she bolted up and flung the dirt into his face.

Taken by surprise, he turned away from her as he rubbed at the particles stinging his eyes. Leaping to her feet, Leanna ran off the dirt road and into the grassy area bordering the woods. She fled frantically, hoping she could reach the dense thicket before he could catch up to her.

Although she could hear Jeff's approaching foot-steps quickly shortening the distance between them, she dared not break her strides to look behind her.

Having covered the ground between them, Jeff lurched, and grabbing Leanna around the waist, he tackled her. The soft grass cushioned their fall. Leanna struggled fruitlessly against his superior strength, but restraining her with comparative ease, Jeff jerked her over so that she was lying on her back. Grasping her wrists with one hand, he held her arms over her head. She kicked out at him, but his strong frame covered hers, pinning her beneath him.

Jeff's temper was simmering hotly. Removing the hat that had fallen forward onto his brow, he threw it to the ground. "You rebellious little hellcat," he raged. "Must I put you in chains to keep you from escaping?"

"Is it my fault that you were too foolish to search my room for a means of escape?" Her eyes slanting shrewdly, she taunted him. "What's wrong, Major? Did I wound your Yankee ego? Does it really bother you that much when a Southerner outsmarts you?"

His anger boiling, he gripped her wrists so tightly that she winced. "By God, maybe I'll not only chain you, I'll also gag and silence your sharp tongue!"

Finding his weight uncomfortable, she arched her thighs to push him aside, but as she did, he inadvertently shifted his frame so that he was lying between her legs.

Feeling his manhood pressed against her, Leanna gasped. Once again, she began arching her hips to try to shove him away. Her provocative moves stimulated Jeff, and his maleness responded immediately to her soft body thrusting beneath his.

Aware of his hardness, Leanna ceased to struggle, and becoming more and more conscious of his firm arousal, a warm longing spread downward in her, coming to rest between her legs where she could feel him pressed against her.

He pushed his hips to hers, making her even more aware of his hard maleness. Responding, she opened her legs wider, wanting to feel his manhood touching

133

her so intimately.

She gazed into his dark eyes, and in the glowing moonlight, she could see the depth of his passion. "Leanna," he murmured sensually.

Trying desperately to regain her senses, she protested feebly, "Jeff, please let me up."

"I want you, Leanna," he told her hoarsely.

Struggling, she made another attempt to free herself. She must not make love with him again! She must remain strong and refuse his advances, because if she didn't, this time, she'd forever lose her heart to this handsome Union major who would probably vanish from her life as unexpectedly as he had appeared!

Ignoring her weak struggles, Jeff moved his free hand to her breasts, caressing her gently before finding her lips with his. His mouth pressed against hers demandingly, and as a feeling of ecstasy floated gloriously through her entire being, she parted her lips so that he could deepen their kiss. When his tongue darted between her teeth, she opened her mouth wider, accepting his probing tongue with wonderful abandonment.

He released her trapped wrists, and her arms went about his neck. Her better judgment told her to push him away before it was too late, but how could she refuse him! She loved his dominance, his strength. She had never known a man who could stir her desire merely by his male presence.

His mouth still relishing hers, Jeff slid a hand down to stroke her inner thigh. Smoothly, he shifted so that he lay at her side, but when she started to turn toward him, he grasped her hip firmly, keeping her on her back. As he removed his lips from hers, he placed one hand at the joining of her legs, and the sensation caused Leanna to moan with pleasure. Suddenly, his lips were again on hers, kissing her aggressively. Meanwhile his fingers sought the buttons on her trousers, and adeptly undid them. Slowly, he slipped his hand beneath her cotton underwear, his palm running warmly over her stomach and down to her womanhood.

"Leanna . . . Leanna," he groaned, sending fleeting kisses over her neck.

"Jeff," she responded tremulously.

He gazed down into her flushed face, and she could feel his strong, lean frame tremble with longing as he gasped gruffly, "Oh God, how much I want to love you!"

His vulnerability touched Leanna's heart, bringing tears to her eyes. "Oh Jeff!" she cried desperately. "I wish you had never come into my life!"

"Don't say that, sweetheart," he pleaded gently.

"But it's true! . . . It's true!" she moaned, her voice quivering.

"You don't mean that, Leanna," he murmured, his lips brushing her forehead, her cheeks, before moving down to the hollow of her throat.

She wanted to cry out to him that she didn't want him in her life because she knew he'd leave her, and his leaving would break her heart! But Leanna kept her feelings to herself, afraid if she revealed them to Jeff, he'd not understand and think her a child.

When Jeff knelt at her side, and slipped off her boots, she didn't try to stop him. Frantically, she wished she understood the power he had over her;

but she didn't, she only knew that she wanted him. He reached for her trousers, and she raised her hips so that he could remove them.

Jeff wished he could totally undress her, but there was no guarantee that someone might not travel down the road that was only a few yards from them, and he wouldn't have time to completely dress her before being discovered.

Placing her trousers beside them, he quickly removed her undergarment. The soft moonlight shone down on her, and Jeff's eyes trailed leisurely over her long slender legs, her full sensual hips, and the golden vee between her thighs. The sight of her caused him to catch his breath, and bending his head, he touched his lips to her tempting womanhood.

Leanna cried out with surprise, she had never imagined that a man could love a woman so intimately. His lips moved slowly in an exquisite rhythm that drew Leanna into a rapturous whirlpool of feeling.

Easing his body upward, his lips sought hers as he undid the buttons of her shirt and then slipped a hand beneath her chemise to fondle her bare breasts.

Taking his lips from hers, he whispered in her ear, "Leanna, I want you so badly that I can't wait any longer."

"Oh yes, Jeff!" she murmured intensely. "I want you too!"

"My sweet darling," he crooned lovingly.

"Love me, Jeff," she invited seductively.

Sitting up, he unbuckled his holster and placed it at his side; then he quickly took off his boots.

Impatiently he unfastened his trousers and, removing them, knelt between her spread legs. Leaning over her, he encircled one arm around her small waist, and brought her thighs up to his.

His mouth came down on hers, and she wrapped her arms about his neck. Wanting him inside her, she lifted herself to him, making it easy for Jeff to slide into her warmness.

Placing his cheek next to hers, he whispered, "Leanna, you feel so wonderful."

"So do you," she sighed, turning her face to kiss his ear lobe.

The feel of her warm breath sent a delightful chill down his spine, and holding her tightly, he entered her even deeper. The first time he'd made love to Leanna, knowing she was a virgin, Jeff had taken her with extreme gentleness. But, now, as her inciting heat engulfed him, his passion soared, and using his knee, he spread her legs farther apart so that he could thrust against her freely and powerfully.

Clinging to him, Leanna began matching his demanding rhythm. Suddenly he grasped her legs, placing them over his back. Leanna began to experience a feeling so intensely exciting that she moaned aloud. Fully aroused, she locked her ankles and pushed her thighs to his time and time again. In Jeff's bedroom, she had thoroughly enjoyed their union, but this time it was excitingly different!

Her fervent response, thrilled Jeff. Thrusting against her vigorously, he uttered, "Yes, Leanna . . . Oh darling, you're driving me crazy."

Wanting him even deeper, she scooted her body downward, as she moved her legs farther up his back.

He was now so far inside that she felt as though he were an inseparable part of her.

"Oh Jeff . . . Jeff darling," she cried ecstatically, every fiber of her being on fire with need for him.

"Leanna . . . Leanna," he moaned hoarsely, before kissing her so demandingly that she responded by slipping her tongue between his teeth to explore the inside of his mouth. Her boldness aroused him beyond reason, and in the heat of their kiss, he placed his hands beneath her hips to hold her thighs flush to his.

Rising to his knees, he plunged into her deeply. Her hand on the back of his neck, she pressed his mouth to hers. Their tongues met, and their kiss became wildly passionate.

Grasping her securely, he rolled over so that she was on top. "Sit up straight," he directed, urging her into the position he wanted.

She complied, and he placed his strong hands on her waist, lifting her up and down over his hard manhood. Catching his motion, she began to ride him with a smooth and exciting rhythm.

Shoving her thighs to his, and feeling him slide farther inside her, she leaned over and devoured his mouth with hers as she swiveled her hips, letting her warmth completely consume him.

Once again, he turned them. Then, kneeling over her, he placed his hands behind her knees and, spreading her legs, held them up as he drove into her rapidly.

Lowering her eyes, Leanna could actually see his male hardness moving in and out of her, and the sight caused her to tremble with longing.

His craving for fulfillment building, Jeff urged her legs across his back, and gathering her into his embrace, he moved demandingly against her. His aggressiveness sent tremors through her body, and clutching him, she shoved her thighs against his. Her need for Jeff now all consuming, Leanna found total completeness as, together, they reached love's highest peak.

Jeff kissed her tenderly, then slowly withdrew to lie at her side and clasp her in his arms.

They fell silent, each waiting for the other to speak. Finally, it was Leanna who broke the strained silence. "Jeff," she whispered hesitantly, "what will happen to us?"

"What do you mean?" he asked gently.

"You'll leave me, won't you?" she asked, the question passing her lips before she could suppress it.

"Eventually, I'll have no other choice. I'm a soldier fighting a war."

Raising herself, she looked down at him, and deciding she might as well throw her pride to the wind, she pleaded, "After the war, will you come back to me?"

"Is that what you want?" he asked.

"Please don't answer my question with a question," she said impatiently.

"Leanna," he began, trying to be reasonable, "this isn't the time to talk about the future. We must think about the present, and at present you are a rebel spy with very vital information for the Confederacy."

"Oh Jeff!" she said heavily, sighing. "What does that have to do with us?"

"Leanna, if I walk back to get the horses, will you

give me your word that you won't sneak into the woods while I am gone?"

Her first impulse was to promise him faithfully that she would not run away, but her love for the Confederacy came to mind and she murmured, "No, I couldn't give you my word. I'd do anything, take any chance, to stop the battle at the Chattahoochee River."

"Why?" he asked softly.

"Because the Confederacy is destined to lose."

"Yes, they are," he agreed. "And, Leanna, I will be involved in that battle. Confederate soldiers will die, some by my own gun. Keeping that in mind, do you still want me to promise that I'll come back to you after the war?"

Confused, she stammered, "I . . . I don't know."

Reaching for his pants, he stood and slipped them on. "Leanna, let's not make any promises." Helping her to her feet, he handed Leanna her clothes. "Get dressed, we need to get back to the house before Lieutenant Buehler sends out a search party."

Hastily, she put on her clothes, and as they were stepping into their boots, she asked warily, "When you and your troops ride out in the morning, what happens to me? How do you intend to keep me from letting the Confederacy know of Sherman's plans?"

Putting on his hat, he turned to face her, and eying her closely, he answered, "I only have two logical choices."

"What are they?" she asked, holding her breath.

"I can have you executed, or I can take you with me," he answered.

Knowing he wouldn't have her killed, she exclaimed, "Take me with you! But you're going into battle!"

Grinning, he replied, "That's quite true, my little rebel spy. You shouldn't have hidden in the study and stuck your pretty nose into this war if you weren't willing to become involved."

"But I never dreamed my involvement would mean that I'd be riding with the Union Army!" she cried incredulously.

Grasping her shoulders, he pulled her close, and looking deep into her eyes, he asked, "Would you rather face a firing squad? If you insist, it can be arranged."

Pushing away from him, she blurted testily, "Oh, why am I so attracted to you? You're so arrogant and . . . and . . ."

"A damned Yankee?" he concluded. Chuckling, he drew her back into his embrace, and placing his hand beneath her chin, he tilted her face upward. He pressed his lips to hers, and his kiss sent her thoughts fleeing. "Leanna," he whispered, "we may be enemies in war, but we'll never be enemies in love."

Chapter Ten

Leanna was awakened by the rays of the morning sun filtering through her open bedroom window and falling warmly across her face. Lying on her side, she turned away from the glaring light and snuggled into the feather-filled pillow. She was still sleepy, but in a few minutes her drowsiness had diminished. Her legs were cramped so she straightened them and turned onto her back. Placing her arms over her head, she was about to ease her body into a relaxing stretch, when the tenderness between her thighs brought her wide awake. Remembering how passionately she had responded to Jeff caused her to blush.

Rolling onto her side, and clutching the pillow to her breasts, she murmured dreamily, "My goodness, I never imagined making love with a man could be so heavenly." No, not any man! she thought. I could never respond so fully to any man but Jeff!

Realizing she'd soon have to face Jeff, her cheeks darkened to a shade of scarlet. What would he say to her, and what should she say to him?

As she turned to lie on her back, keeping the pillow in her clutches, memories of last night flooded back to her in vivid detail. Why did Jeff hold such power over her, and why did just thinking about him make her want him so badly?

She wondered what they would have talked about last night on the way back to the house if they hadn't been met by the soldiers Lieutenant Buehler had sent to search for the major. On the ride to the plantation, she had hoped they'd have some time alone, but as soon as they'd entered the house, Jeff had sent her to her room. Then he had ordered the trap door to the attic nailed closed.

A solid rap on her door broke into Leanna's reverie, and she responded.

"Yes?"

"Miss Weston," a soldier called from the other side of the door, "Major Clayton requests your presence in the study."

"Tell the major I'll be there in about an hour," she answered, deciding it would take that long to make herself presentable since she wanted to look especially nice for Jeff. Although she was apprehensive about seeing him, the thought of doing so sent her pulse racing.

"The major insists you come immediately," the soldier informed her.

Frowning, Leanna mumbled to herself, "I've never met a man with so little patience." A secret smile played across her face as she added, "But that's one of the reasons why he fascinates me. He has such an aura of strength."

Swinging her legs over the side of the bed, she told

144

the soldier, "I'll have to get dressed."

"The major said for me to wait for you, ma'am."

"Very well," she called. "I'll dress as quickly as I can."

After tending to her morning ministrations, Leanna slipped into a simply cut gown that was the exact color of her sky blue eyes. Standing at her vanity table, she picked up a brush. She didn't have time to arrange her hair, so she brushed briskly at her long tresses before using a blue ribbon to hold her hair away from her face. Stepping into a pair of dainty slippers, she walked over and opened the door.

The young soldier in the hall turned toward her, and the admiring look on his face told Leanna that he thought she provided a pretty picture. She could only hope that Jeff would also find her attractive.

Placing his hand on her elbow, the soldier escorted her downstairs to the study. He knocked on the closed door.

"Come in," Leanna heard Jeff say from inside the room. The mere sound of his deep voice made Leanna feel light-headed, and once again, she questioned the strange but wonderful power that Major Clayton had over her.

Opening the door, the soldier stepped aside for Leanna to enter. Jeff was standing in the center of the room, but before she had time to let her eyes trail completely over the masculine physique that she knew so intimately, she suddenly became aware that her mother and Jennifer were also in the room.

Stepping swiftly to her side, Mary placed her arm over her daughter's shoulders in a protective fashion. "Leanna," she said, her voice filled with anguish, "Major Clayton has just informed me that you are under arrest, and he intends to take you with him!"

Clasping her mother's hand, Leanna squeezed it gently, saying reassuringly, "Yes, Mama, I know. But please don't worry about me. I'm sure I'll be perfectly safe."

Releasing Leanna, Mary placed her hands over her face as she sobbed hysterically, "I'll never see you again! This Yankee plans to have you executed! That's why he's taking you away, so your family won't witness your murder!"

Making an attempt to control his patience, Jeff said with as much tolerance as he could manage, "Mrs. Weston, I do not plan to execute your daughter."

"It would probably be more merciful than the fate you have in mind for her!" Jennifer suddenly shrieked. She was standing in front of the unlit fireplace, and they turned to look at her.

His patience wearing thin, Jeff asked curtly, "Exactly what do I have in mind, madam?"

Drawing her dark eyebrows together into a frown, Jennifer eyed him with a look of unmistakable revulsion. "I know what happens to Southern ladies who are abducted by you depraved Yankees!"

On the verge of losing his temper, Jeff replied irritably, "Madam, I give you my word that Miss Weston will be safe from sexual assault!"

"And do you think I would take the word of a Yankee?" was the scathing response.

Suddenly, while crying convulsively, Mary began to plead hysterically, "Oh God, Major Clayton, I implore you not to let your men abuse my daughter! . . . Oh please! . . . Please!"

Flustered, and becoming extremely agitated, Jeff

146

bellowed, "Didn't I just give my word that your daughter wouldn't be violated?"

"But you're a Yankee!" Mary shouted desperately. "And Yankees are not gentlemen; so, Major, I cannot take your word! I insist that you allow me to accompany my daughter!"

"No, Mama!" Leanna protested. "You aren't well, and the trip would be too exhausting for you." She wished she could convince her mother that Jeff would never let any harm come to her. She didn't know how she knew he'd keep her safe, but there was not one shred of doubt in her mind.

"No one is accompanying Miss Weston!" Jeff answered inflexibly. "One woman on this mission is quite enough." Going to the desk, he leaned back against it, and folding his arms across his chest, he stole a glance at Leanna. God, she was beautiful, and the expression in her eyes when she met his gaze was one of tenderness. Remember that look of total sweetness, Jeff told himself, because in a minute she'll probably be glaring at you with hate.

Forcing himself to turn away from Leanna's trusting face, he gave Mary and Jennifer his full attention. "You ladies have exactly one hour to take your most needed and treasured possessions from this home and move them to the overseer's house."

The overseer's house was quite roomy, and Jeff knew there would be ample space for all of them. The house had been vacant since the beginning of the war when the Westons' overseer had left the plantation to join the Confederacy.

"But . . . but why?" Mary stammered. "Why do you want us to leave our home?"

"This house will be burned," Jeff answered bluntly.

"No!" Mary cried frantically.

For a moment Leanna froze as she remembered Sherman's order to burn her home. Surely Jeff didn't really intend to carry out the order. After all they had been to each other, he couldn't possibly hurt her this way!

"You can't be serious!" Leanna choked.

Jeff longed to be gentle and to plead with Leanna to try to understand his position, but this wasn't the right time. Perhaps later he could find a way to reason with her.

"I am very serious, Miss Weston," he replied with an aloofness he was far from feeling.

He could see angry sparks darting in her blue eyes, and he looked away, recalling sadly the love that had been in them only moments before.

"Why you contemptible, heartless Yankee!" Leanna snapped, but before she could continue her insults, Jeff moved quickly to the door. Opening it, he spoke to the soldier who had escorted Leanna to the study. "Take Miss Weston to her room," he ordered.

"Yes, sir," the man replied quickly.

Facing Leanna, Jeff said briskly, "Pack a small bag and don't change into trousers. If we should be ambushed by Confederates, I don't want them to shoot you because they have mistaken you for a man."

"Only a Yankee could be that big a fool!" she retorted, remembering their first meeting when he had mistaken her for a boy. Then, giving him a frigid look, she brushed past him and left the room.

He watched her go up the stairs with the guard; then, turning to one of the soldiers stationed outside the study, he said, "Tell Sergeant O'Malley to bring some men in the house to assist the ladies with whatever they need moved."

Stepping back into the room, Jeff said authoritatively, "Ladies, you have exactly one hour to vacate the premises, so I suggest you start packing."

Alone in her room, Leanna finished packing in an amazingly short time. She was anxious about her mother. She could only imagine how upset Mary Weston must be. She purposely avoided thinking about Jeff because she considered his order to destroy her home a personal betrayal.

Opening the door, she started to leave, but the soldier who had taken her upstairs was outside her room. Apologetically, he said, "I'm sorry, ma'am, but Major Clayton sent orders that you are to remain in your quarters."

"What!" she stormed. "Does he intend to burn down the house over my head!"

"Of course not, ma'am," the soldier replied tentatively, wary of Leanna's sudden temper.

"I want to see my mother!" she insisted.

Gently, he nudged her back into the room, and closing the door, he mumbled, "I'm sorry, Miss Weston."

Fuming, Leanna spent the next hour pacing her room, thinking of all the angry words she intended to fling into Jeff's face if she was ever again alone with him.

When, finally, she heard a knock on her door, she spat testily, "Come in!"

Upon entering, the soldier who had apparently become her personal guard, told her, "Ma'am, it's time to leave . . . if you'll come with me please."

She started to pick up her packed bag, but he took it for her. Holding her arm with his free hand, he ushered her from the room and down the stairs.

The study door opened, and Jeff stepped into the foyer. "Take Miss Weston outside," he ordered the soldier.

"Yes, sir," the guard replied, and grasping Leanna's arm more firmly, he began leading her to the front door.

Looking up at the soldier, she pleaded, "I need to see my mother!"

Pausing, he said tenderly, "Wait here. I'll ask the major."

Jeff had moved to the bottom of the staircase where he was in a deep conversation with Lieutenant Buehler.

"Sir," Leanna could hear the soldier say, "Miss Weston requests to see her mother."

Abruptly, Jeff replied, "Her request is denied."

Her temper rising, Leanna marched across the foyer, and reaching his side, she seethed, "How dare you refuse to let me see my mother!"

"Captured spies are not given permission to converse with the enemy," he answered sharply.

"But she's my mother!" Leanna exclaimed.

Looking at the soldier, Jeff commanded impatiently, "Take her outside and see that she is on her horse and ready to leave."

The soldier attempted to grasp her arm, but she stepped swiftly out of his reach. Shouting at Jeff, she demanded, "Where are my family? What have you done with them?"

"They have been taken to the overseer's house," he

answered. Speaking to Leanna's guard, he said ill-temperedly, "Soldier, if you cannot handle your charge, I will send for reinforcements."

His ego wounded, the soldier assured the major, "I do not need help, sir."

Raising his eyebrows, Jeff questioned, "Well?"

"Well what, sir?" he asked.

"Take her outside!" Major Clayton persisted.

"Yes, sir!" The soldier snapped to attention. He reached for Leanna, but this time when she tried to move away, he grabbed her arm in a tenacious hold. As he was forcing her to the front door, Leanna made a desperate effort to look around at the interior of the house, realizing she was seeing it for the last time. Soon the Westons' majestic, columned house would be destroyed—the home where she had been born and raised would be consumed in the midst of towering flames.

I won't watch! she thought frantically. Dear God, I can't bear to watch it burn!

Stepping out to the front porch, Leanna paused to stare at the Union troops who were now mounted and ready to move out. Catching a movement out of the corner of her eye, she saw a group of soldiers gathered at the far side of the house. Seeing unlit torches in their hands, she gasped involuntarily.

Tugging lightly at her arm, her guard coaxed, "Come on, Miss Weston."

Submissively, she allowed him to guide her down the steps and over to the saddled horse that was awaiting her. Sergeant O'Malley held the reins, and mounted on one side of her horse was the soldier who had carried Jennifer into the parlor. Her present guard attached her packed bag to her saddle, then turned and mounted his own horse.

"Miss Weston," the sergeant explained, "these two soldiers have been assigned to take care of you."

"Take care of me?" she scowled. "Don't you mean they have been ordered to guard me?"

Letting her remark pass, the sergeant gestured toward the soldier who had helped Jennifer. "Ma'am, this is Jerry." Pointing to the other one, he added, "And this is Paul."

The two soldiers tipped their caps and smiled cordially; then the sergeant helped her mount. The men noticed that as she swung into the saddle her hiked skirt revealed her ankles and shapely calves. She was just taking the reins into her hands when Jeff and the lieutenant walked out of the house. Moving to his horse, Jeff nodded to the men waiting to light the torches, "Carry out your orders, soldiers."

Mounting his chestnut stallion, Jeff told the lieutenant, "I want everyone moved farther back from the house."

Lieutenant Buehler gave that command, and riding between her two guards, Leanna was thankful that her house was behind her so she couldn't see the flames as they destroyed the home she loved so dearly. However, suddenly the troops were ordered to halt, and they all turned around to watch the burning inferno.

Keeping her gaze forward, Leanna murmured over and over, "I won't look back . . . I won't look back."

Even at a distance, she could hear the crackling of the flames as they spread and consumed the structure. Indeed, she could actually feel the warmth from the huge fire. I must get farther away! she thought desperately. I don't want to hear my home burning, or to suffer the horrible heat from the flames engulfing it!

Taking Jerry and Paul off guard, Leanna sent her horse into a run. Hoping the major hadn't seen her escape them so easily, they immediately pursued her.

Leanna had ridden halfway down the lane before they caught up to her. Grabbing her horse's harness, Jerry pulled the animal to a stop.

Glancing over his shoulder, Paul said regretfully, "The major is watching us."

"Damn!" Jerry cursed, but quickly apologized, "Excuse my language, ma'am."

"I'm sorry if my actions have gotten you both into trouble," Leanna murmured. Tears swimming in her large blue eyes, she explained, "But I just couldn't bear to hear my home burning."

Instantly sympathetic to her tears, they both assured her that everything was all right and that she hadn't caused them any problems.

Wanting to think about anything except her burning home, Leanna said to Jerry, "I thought the major would have put you on detention for leaving your post yesterday."

"He did," Jerry admitted.

"Is guarding me your punishment for disobeying?" she asked, her voice tinged with indignation.

"Yes, ma'am," he replied quietly.

Facing Paul now, she asked, "And I suppose you are also being disciplined?"

Nodding, he mumbled, "I got caught while drinking on duty."

"So the major considers guarding me a punishment, does he?" She was piqued.

Hesitantly, Jerry explained, "Well, ma'am, staying

153

safely behind the lines guarding a woman when others are fighting isn't exactly the kind of deed a man can brag about."

Hearing a horse's hoofs, they turned to see Jeff advancing rapidly. Pulling up alongside them, he said demandingly, "I had better not see you two let this woman escape again!"

Her temper exploding, Leanna taunted, "How can you have the audacity to reprimand these men? If I remember correctly, Major Clayton, I very easily escaped from you!"

"Are you referring to the attic door?" he questioned, his expression cocky. "Because if you aren't, then, Miss Weston, you most assuredly did not escape. Surrender would be a more adequate definition."

Enraged, she said harshly, "My first impression of you was right! You're a rude, boorish scoundrel!" Her words provoked no response, and seething inwardly, she said between clenched teeth, "I'll never forgive you for burning my home!"

She thought she saw a flicker of pain in his eyes, but the moment was gone so quickly that she couldn't be sure. "Whether you forgive me or not, Miss Weston, is beside the point. And if you care about the welfare of these two men, for their sakes, you will not try to escape again."

Leanna started to tell him that she wasn't escaping, she only wanted to put more distance between herself and her burning home, but before she could explain her actions, he had turned his horse and ridden away.

Chapter Eleven

The hot sun shone down steadily on Leanna and the soldiers as they rode leisurely toward the Chatta-hoochee River. Wishing for shade, Leanna silently cursed herself for not remembering to bring a wide-brimmed bonnet. She was sure by the end of the day, her face would be sunburned. "How could I have been so forgetful?" she unconsciously said out loud.

She was riding between Jerry and Paul, and hearing her complaint, Jerry asked, "What did you forget, Miss Weston?"

"A bonnet to shade my face," she replied, turning her head to look at him.

Noticing that she was beginning to burn, Jerry frowned concernedly, but suddenly his expression lightened. He jerked on the bridle reins, and his horse did a turnabout. Riding away, he called over his shoulder, "I'll be right back."

"I wonder where he's goin'?" Paul pondered. Arching his neck so that he could view Jeff who was traveling at the front of the procession, he continued,

"I sure hope the major doesn't look back and see that Jerry isn't riding with us."

"Does he consider me so dangerous that I must have two guards?" Leanna asked sharply, still perturbed with Jeff.

"Well, Miss Weston," Paul explained a little unwillingly, "it's not that he thinks you're dangerous. He told Jerry and me . . . he told us . . ."

He hesitated, and Leanna demanded testily, "What did he tell you?"

"You got to understand, ma'am, that I'm merely quoting the major, and he said that Jerry and I have to keep a close eye on you because you're sneaky."

"Sneaky!" Leanna shouted, her anger surging.

"Please, Miss Weston," Paul said hastily, "keep your voice down, we don't want to draw Major Clayton's attention. If he sees that Jerry's not here, then Jerry's gonna be in a heap of trouble."

Seething, but keeping her voice lowered, Leanna replied, "Major Clayton is the one in a heap of trouble. How dare he say that I'm sneaky! Oh, just wait until I talk to him again! Will I ever give him a piece of my mind!" The Weston temper flowing hotly, she whispered resentfully, "Sneaky, am I?"

Leanna's anger was very apparent, and Paul certainly didn't envy the major who would be confronted by the hot-tempered Miss Weston.

Hearing a horse approaching, they glanced behind them and saw Jerry advancing with a wide-brimmed straw hat in his hand. Bringing his mount up alongside Leanna's, he gave her the tattered hat.

"It's not in very good condition, but it'll protect your face," Jerry told her.

Holding the hat, Leanna asked incredulously, "Where in the world did you find it?"

"It belongs to the cook. He keeps it in his wagon and wears it when we're camped someplace where he can go fishing. He said to tell you that you're more than welcome to borrow it."

"When you see him again, please thank him for me," she answered, placing the weather-worn hat on her head. It was much too large for her, and its wide brim fell past her forehead, covering her eyes. Laughing, Leanna pushed it back until she could once again see. She glanced at Jerry and then at Paul, giggling, "Well, it's more attractive than a sunburned face, don't you think?"

Smiling, and quite taken with Miss Weston's charms, they wholeheartedly agreed with her.

Studying her two guards, Leanna decided that she liked them very much, even if they were Yankees. They were handsome young men. Jerry was tall and slim, whereas Paul was short and stockily built. Enjoying their company, Leanna kept up an easy chatter as they continued their journey toward the Chattahoochee River. When the five soldiers riding as lookouts returned to the column and reported immediately to Jeff, Leanna paid little attention, and when, unexpectedly, Jeff changed their course, she didn't connect his order with the lookouts until Jerry surmised, "There must be Johnny Rebs in the area."

"Why do you think that?" Leanna quizzed.

"The men scouting probably ran across Confederates," he explained.

Leaving the main road, the Union troops and Leanna headed into the bordering woods, where the dense thicket quickly hid their presence.

Jeff gave the preparatory command to dismount, and as soon as Sergeant O'Malley passed it down to the troopers, the men swung down from their mounts. Stepping to Leanna's horse, Jerry helped her to the ground.

"Why are we stopping?" she asked, puzzled.

Jerry shrugged. "I don't know. But I'm sure the sergeant will tell us."

Standing beside Paul and Jerry, Leanna looked on as Sergeant O'Malley and Lieutenant Buehler moved through the soldiers giving hushed commands. When the sergeant walked up to Leanna and her guards, he said, "Excuse me, Miss Weston, but the major wants to see you immediately." Stepping to Leanna and touching her arm, he continued, "If you'll come with me, please."

As the sergeant escorted her to Jeff, who was engrossed in a conversation with one of his men, Leanna was mystified as to why some of the soldiers were busy taking the horses and wagons farther into the woods, while others began seeking shelter behind the thick shrubbery.

At Leanna's approach, the soldier conversing with Jeff moved away, and delivering her to the major's side, Sergeant O'Malley left the pair alone.

Lifting her chin, and looking Jeff straight in the eyes, Leanna pretended indifference as she waited for him to speak. But his closeness did send her pulse racing. Actually she was very aware of his presence.

Folding his arms across his chest, he eyed her as though he were studying a naughty child. "Leanna," he began, "there are Confederate soldiers in the

158

vicinity, and they will pass by here in a few minutes. If you'll give me your word that you'll remain silent, I won't be forced to gag you."

Thinking about the Union soldiers hidden behind the shrubbery, Leanna remarked irritably, "Surely, you don't expect me to be silent so that you can ambush Confederates!"

"I do not plan to ambush them. My orders are not to engage the enemy in battle until I have reached the Chattahoochee River. But, Leanna, my men outnumber these Confederates three to one, and if they become aware of our presence, they will stop to fight. If they do, it will be a massacre, with the Confederates the losers. Now, I will ask you again, do I have your word that you'll remain silent?"

"You have them outnumbered?" she insisted warily.

"Three to one," he told her again.

Leanna certainly didn't want to cause a massacre and she promised, "I'll stay quiet."

A soldier on horseback suddenly broke into the woods. Riding to Jeff and Leanna, he pulled up his mount and reported, "Major, the Confederates will be here in about two minutes."

Hastily, Jeff gave the order for everyone to stay hidden, then taking Leanna's hand, he led her behind a thick bush. Telling her to sit down, he knelt beside her, but noticing that her hat was higher than the bush, he ordered testily, "Take off that ridiculous hat and get down."

Jerking it off, Leanna lowered herself as she mumbled peevishly, "This . . . ridiculous . . . hat, happens to be all I have to shade my face from the hot sun under which you are forcing me to travel!"

Glancing at the tattered hat, he questioned curiously, "Where did you get it?"

"Your cook loaned it to me," she said shortly. Noticing that Jeff was smiling, she snapped, "I'm tempted to ask you what you are thinking about, but I've decided that I don't care anymore what you think or what you do!"

"Of course, you care," he replied, still grinning. "And I was thinking about the first time I saw you. That day you were also wearing a ridiculous-looking hat."

She started to remind him that he had actually been foolish enough to mistake her for a boy, but Jeff detected the advancing Confederate soldiers and warned, "Shh . . . shh. Be perfectly still and quiet."

As the sounds of horses' hoofs and the steady creaking of wagon wheels drew closer, Leanna made a small slit in the heavy bush so she could see the road that was only a few yards away.

Leanna watched intensely as the slow procession passed before her eyes. The sight of gray uniforms caused her Southern loyalties to become uppermost in her thoughts. Brad had returned home twice on leave, and she had found him dashingly handsome in his lieutenant's uniform. Now, seeing these men dressed in the colors of the Confederacy, her brother came painfully to mind.

When, finally, the Confederate soldiers had traveled out of sight, Jeff sighed with relief as he stopped kneeling to sit beside Leanna. Glancing at her, he was concerned to see tears in her eyes. But he didn't question her until he had told Lieutenant

Buehler that the troops would remain where they were for a fifteen-minute rest. The moment the lieutenant left to relay his command, Jeff turned his full concentration to Leanna and asked tenderly, "Why are you crying?"

Blinking and wiping away the last trace of tears, she denied it. "I'm not crying."

Reaching over, and taking her hand, he gently squeezed it. "Leanna, I know this is all very difficult for you."

Because she was perfectly aware that she had no defense against his touch, she pulled her hand free. "I don't need your sympathy, Jeff Clayton!" she said stubbornly.

"Leanna, can't we be friends?" he asked softly.

Fighting her desire to be in his embrace, she covered her frustrations by questioning him tartly. "Do you really expect me to be friends with the man who not only burned my home, but who forced me to travel with . . . with damned Yankees?" Her resentment flowing, she blurted, "Besides, why would you want a friend who is sneaky?"

Jeff chuckled. He had tried not to, but he couldn't help himself, "Aren't most spies sneaky? I'm sure it goes with the profession."

"Will you please stop referring to me as a spy?" she snapped.

"Isn't that what you are?" he asked with a cocky grin.

"No, not really," she stammered.

"Oh?" he raised an eyebrow. "Then what were you doing in the study behind the drapes? Were you dusting the panels?"

161

Bristling, she reminded him, "A study and drapes that no longer exist, thanks to you!"

Her accusation hurt Jeff, but he didn't let on. He longed to apologize for the burning of her home. He wanted her to understand that he had had no alternative but to carry out Sherman's order. But this wasn't the time or the place to try to reason with her.

Getting to her feet, and haphazardly placing the hat on her head, she said sharply, "If I have your permission, I'd like to return to my two guards. I much prefer their company to yours!"

Standing, Jeff complied, "Permission granted, Miss Weston." His eyes followed her as she walked away to rejoin Jerry and Paul. Admiringly, he noticed how proudly she moved.

At dusk, Jeff decided to set up camp for the night. He planned to arrive at the Chattahoochee River the next morning.

Using a blanket attached to four stakes, Jerry and Paul prepared a shelter, set apart from the troops, for Leanna.

Leanna was standing a short distance from her makeshift tent, when Paul moved over to talk to her. "Miss Weston?"

"Yes?" she asked.

Shuffling his feet and bowing his head self-consciously, he said in as gentlemanly a way as possible, "Ma'am, if you need privacy, you can step into the bushes."

Noting his boyish embarrassment, she smiled fondly, "Thank you, Paul."

She turned to walk into the surrounding bushes,

but he halted her by saying hesitantly, "Uh, Miss Weston . . . uh, ma'am . . . I'm gonna have to wait for you at the edge of the bushes. . . . And, ma'am, you're supposed to talk to me the entire time you're in the bushes."

Seeing her sudden anger, he explained hastily, "That's the major's orders, Miss Weston. He told the sergeant, and the sergeant passed it down to Jerry and me."

"I've never been so humiliated in my life!" she fumed, placing her hands on her hips. "Why must you follow me, and why for goodness' sake, must I constantly talk to you?"

"Well, ma'am," he replied, stammering, "if I can hear you . . . then I'll know you aren't escaping. The major said if you become silent, Jerry and I are supposed to go into the bushes after you."

"I refuse to make a spectacle out of myself by chatting endlessly while I . . . while I . . ." Embarrassed Leanna blushed blatantly.

Neither of them had heard Jeff approaching, and he startled them when he suddenly asked, "What seems to be the problem?"

"You're the problem!" Leanna lashed out. "How dare you order these men to . . . to . . ."

"To what?" he coaxed, a faint smile touching his lips.

Explaining, Paul answered, "Sir, the lady is greatly opposed to Jerry or me standing at the edge of the bushes while she's seeking privacy. Also, sir, she doesn't want to keep talking."

"She doesn't, does she?" the major queried, raising an eyebrow.

"Stop talking about me as though I weren't here!" Leanna snapped.

"Miss Weston," said Jeff, holding back the desire to smile, "you will do as I have ordered, or else you will stay in the open; and as your needs grow more urgent, you will no doubt become quite uncomfortable."

Stomping her foot to emphasize her anger, Leanna blurted, "You are the most arrogant devil I've ever had the misfortune to meet!"

Gesturing toward the bushes at her back, he suppressed his amusement and replied evenly, "Miss Weston, you are excused. And if you promise to speak loudly, it won't be necessary for one of your guards to follow, they will be able to hear you from here."

"I have nothing to say to them or to you!" she blurted out irritably.

"Then try singing," Jeff suggested, a bright twinkle in his dark eyes. He had never seen a woman who could be so enticing when she was angry.

"Singing?" she repeated, as a mischievous expression came over her face. "Thanks for the suggestion, Major."

She pivoted smoothly, and as she headed for the shrubbery, Jeff called after her, "Miss Weston, be sure that you sing quite loudly."

"Oh, I will, Major!" she assured him, darting into the bushes and out of sight.

Jeff and Paul waited for a minute, but when Leanna remained silent, they both took a quick step toward the shrubbery when, all at once, Leanna began singing so loudly that her song could be heard throughout the camp. "In Dixie land where was born early on a frosty mornin', look away, look away, look away, Dixie land. . . ."

Paul turned sharply to Jeff, expecting him to explode with rage, but instead he roared with laughter as he walked away briskly to rejoin his troops.

Leanna wasn't sure what had awakened her. She had been sleeping soundly in her makeshift tent when, for some reason, she awoke with a start. Sitting up on her bedroll, she looked about, expecting to find someone sneaking into her flimsy shelter. It was still dark, but the night wasn't overcast so she had no difficulty seeing. Relieved to find that she was alone, Leanna lay back down. She decided that sleeping in strange surroundings had caused her to awaken unexpectedly and snuggled beneath her blanket, hoping to drift back into sleep. But now that she was wide awake, slumber eluded her, so after tossing and turning restlessly for a while, she debated whether she should go outside.

Deciding to do so, Leanna threw off the covers, slipped into her dress, and put on her shoes. The shelter was too low for her to stand, so she crawled through the opening in the blanket that sufficed as a tent.

Once outside, she got to her feet. She could make out one guard's form as he lay in his bedroll a short distance from her shelter.

She started to look about for the other, but he was at her side so suddenly that he seemed to appear out of thin air. "Can't you sleep, Miss Weston?" Jerry asked quietly.

"I was sleeping, but I woke up. Now, I can't fall back to sleep."

"Would you like a cup of coffee?" he offered, nodding toward the burning campfire where a pot was placed on the hot coals.

"No, thank you. If I drink coffee, then I'll most assuredly be awake for the rest of the night. By the way, do you have any idea what time it is?"

Checking his pocket watch, Jerry replied, "It's almost midnight."

Simultaneously, Leanna and Jerry caught sight of a figure approaching. Both watched the man. Recognizing Jeff, Leanna was tempted to flee back into the safety of her shelter, but entranced by his mere presence, she stood immobilized as he walked up to them and spoke to Jerry.

"Is anything wrong, trooper?"

"Miss Weston is having difficulty falling asleep."

Jeff turned his gaze on Leanna. "That's too bad. We have a long day ahead of us. You really should try to get a good night's sleep."

"Why don't you try taking your own advice?" she snapped, telling herself that she despised this man who had won her trust only to betray her by destroying her home.

Uncomfortable with their bickering, Jerry mumbled, "I think I'll have a cup of coffee. Excuse me, Miss Weston . . . Major."

As Jerry retreated hastily to the campfire, Jeff kept his eyes on Leanna. "I can manage sufficiently on very little sleep," he told her.

"Most varmits can!" she hissed.

Jeff laughed, which made Leanna angrier. Why

166

didn't he ever take her seriously? Did he think of her only as an amusement?

"So now I'm a varmit, am I?" Jeff questioned, his expression humorous.

"A Yankee varmit," she specified smugly.

Taking her hand, he said smoothly, "Let's take a walk. Maybe it'll help your insomnia." She tried to pull her hand free, but he tightened his grip. "Are you afraid to walk with me?" he taunted.

Lifting her chin, she remarked haughtily, "Afraid? Of course not."

"Then you should have no objection to an evening stroll," he replied.

Because he wasn't expecting the move, she was able to jerk her hand from his. She headed quickly toward the campfire where Jerry was sitting and drinking coffee, and said casually, "An evening stroll sounds marvelous. Jerry, would you mind accompanying me?"

Jerry had overheard their conversation, and knowing Miss Weston was using him to get even with the major, he choked on his coffee before stuttering, "A . . . a walk, Miss Weston?" Dropping his cup and standing, he looked expectantly at Jeff.

Leanna had her back turned to Jeff so she didn't see the anger in his eyes as he said gruffly, "Miss Weston, you are forbidden to take walks with either of your guards!"

Turning and facing Jeff, she replied nonchalantly, "Well, in that case, I'll just stay by the campfire. Besides, it's much safer here. I've always heard that there are varmits in the woods."

Stalking to the campfire, Jeff poured himself a cup

of coffee. He told himself that Leanna Weston was a defiant, unruly little rebel and he should simply clear her from his thoughts. But, damn it, she had been on his mind constantly from the first moment he'd set eyes on her!

"Miss Weston," Jeff began calmly, "you are my prisoner for an indefinite period of time. Don't you think it would be best if we were to call a temporary truce?"

Leanna smiled resentfully. "A truce, Major? If I remembered correctly, I once called a truce with you, and in return you burned my home."

"Damn it, Leanna!" he raged, pouring his coffee on top of the flames and causing them to crackle and dart sparks. Throwing down his empty cup, he moved swiftly to Leanna and lifted her into his arms.

Fighting against him, she demanded, "Put me down!"

Gritting his teeth, he whispered threateningly, "I'll put you down as soon as I take you where we can be alone!"

"Jeff Clayton," she seethed, squirming, "you are a contemptible beast!"

Carrying her away from the campfire and into the surrounding woods, he replied menacingly, "You little wildcat, if it's the last thing I do, I'm going to tame you!"

"Never!" she swore.

"We'll see about that!" he retorted.

Taking her to a billowing oak tree, he knelt and placed her beneath it on a bed of soft grass. Before she could protest, his lips were on hers, kissing her demandingly.

Leanna told herself not to respond, to remain coldly unattached, but as his aggressive kiss continued, her resolution faded into oblivion.

As her arms went about his neck, Leanna wished desperately that she could understand this power that Jeff had over her. Why did she always respond to him? He had only to kiss her, and she was his for the asking.

Placing his lips next to her ear, he murmured, "My little wildcat, you are purring like a kitten."

"Cats have been known to purr before conquering their prey," she retorted.

Leaning on his elbow, he gazed down into her face and smiled. He had most assuredly met his match in this beautiful, defiant little rebel. "I've never known a woman like you," he told her.

"Like me?" she questioned. "What do you mean?"

"You're a challenge, Leanna Weston. And one that I can't refuse. I seriously doubt if I, or any man, could ever completely tame you."

"Do you want me tamed?"

Grinning, he shook his head. "I'll settle for civil."

Sighing deeply, she replied, "As long as we are at war, how can we remain civil to each other? Our split loyalties will always be there to tear us apart."

"We can overcome our differences and forget all that has happened," he stated.

Her burning home flashed briefly before her eyes, causing her to reply bitterly, "Our differences? I didn't destroy your home! And I can't help but wonder just how forgiving you would be if I had!"

Aggravated by her stubbornness, he said testily, "Leanna, it's impossible to reason with you!"

Wanting to return to her tent and leave this man who could so easily wreck her defenses, Leanna started to get up, but forcibly, Jeff pinned her to the ground. Placing his body over hers, he said hoarsely, "Leanna, I'm going to make love to you."

Wishing she wasn't finding the feel of his body on hers thrilling, she asked shakily, "I have nothing to say about it?"

"Nothing," he responded, before pressing his mouth to hers. Gathering her into his strong arms, he continued to kiss her fervently until he could feel her body trembling beneath his. "Leanna, sweetheart, there is no force powerful enough to keep us apart, not even this damnable war."

"Oh Jeff," she cried softly. "I need you. Make love to me."

Raising her long skirt, he slipped off her undergarment. Then undoing his trousers, he placed himself between her opened legs and entered her quickly.

Holding him close, she matched his rhythmical motions as her hips converged with his. Gliding blissfully into paradise, Leanna forgot the war and all it represented as she allowed Jeff to take her away to a Utopian world where there were only the two of them.

Standing, and fully dressing herself, Leanna watched Jeff, who was leaning back against the tree trunk and smoking a cheroot. He had said very little to her since they had made love, and she wondered where his thoughts were.

Sitting beside him, she murmured, "A penny for your thoughts."

"Wh-what?" he stammered vaguely.

"Why are you so preoccupied?" she pressed.

Jeff had been thinking about her home, hoping he could find a way to make her understand that he'd had no choice but to obey General Sherman's order. But before he could bring up the subject, he suddenly heard Jerry calling him nearby. "Major Clayton! . . . Major Clayton, sir!"

Hastily, Jeff got to his feet and, offering Leanna his hand, helped her to a standing position.

"We're over here!" he yelled to Jerry.

Almost immediately Jerry came into view, heading toward them a little hesitantly. He said, "Major, sir, Lieutenant Buehler is looking for you. I told him that you decided to take a walk." Remembering the major had literally carried Miss Weston from camp, he added with embarrassment, "I didn't say anything about Miss Weston accompanying you."

Grateful for Jerry's discretion, Jeff replied, "Thank you, soldier. Will you escort Miss Weston back to her tent?"

"Yes, sir," Jerry answered.

Nodding to Leanna, Jeff said abruptly, "Good night, Miss Weston."

Perturbed at Jeff for his rude departure, which she thought unnecessary, Leanna glared at his retreating back, faithfully promising herself that the next time she was alone with him things would be different. She'd treat him brusquely and with total indifference.

171

Part Two

Sherman's Camp

Chapter Twelve

Recent rains had made the turbid Chattahoochee River rapid and swollen, but the present hot weather, Jeff knew, would level it off. It would be crossable in a couple of days.

Jeff and his troops rendezvoused with Colonel Andrews's army north of the river, while the south side of the Chattahoochee was lined with Confederate soldiers. The two opposing armies began their preparations for the impending battle that would take place when the swift water receded.

The Union troops set up a temporary camp a few yards from the river, but this time Jeff ordered Paul and Jerry to erect a full-size tent for Leanna.

Leanna had been relieved to learn that the Chattahoochee was uncrossable. Although she knew the confrontation between the two armies was inevitable, she welcomed the postponement. She dreaded the awaiting battle in which soldiers from both sides would be wounded or killed.

A narrow army cot had been placed inside Leanna's tent, and she was sitting on the edge of it drinking a cup of coffee when Jeff called to her from outside.

"Leanna, may I come in?"

His unexpected visit startled her, and tensing, she replied, "Yes, of course."

Pushing aside the flap, Jeff had to bend over to pass through the low opening, but once inside he was able to stand erect.

Placing her cup on the ground beside the cot, Leanna glanced up, intending to project an air of aloofness. But as her eyes met his, the pounding of her heart told her she could never feel indifferent while in his manly presence.

Moving lithely, he stepped to the cot, and taking her hands into his, he drew her to her feet. She tried to look away from him, but his intense gaze held her entranced.

"Leanna," he murmured, his sensual tone caressing her name.

Lowering her gaze, and pulling away her hands, she started to move around him; but smoothly, he stepped sideways, blocking her escape.

"Leanna," he said sincerely, "I'm sorry about your home."

She wasn't sure that she believed him, so to cover her confusion, she blurted unfairly, "Is that why you burned it, so that afterward you could be sorry?"

"I burned it because it was a direct order from General Sherman," he replied sternly, impatient with her irrational reaction.

"Sherman!" she smirked with distaste. "I wonder if it even vaguely bothers him to leave women and children homeless."

"I'm sure he receives no personal pleasure from this war," Jeff replied softly. Gingerly, he reached over and placed his hand on her arm. His touch was light, yet she was so conscious of it that her pulse quickened. "I didn't come here to discuss Sherman," he explained. "I came to ask you if you'd like to take a bath." Smiling, he added promptly, "Alone, of course."

"Bath?" she quickly repeated. She had been longing desperately for one. The dusty journey had made her feel unbearably grimy. "I'd love a bath!" she exclaimed happily.

"I found a place in the river that is shallow and calm."

"The river!" she cried. "But I can't bathe in a river!"

"Why not?" he questioned her, grinning.

"I thought you meant I could bathe in a tub, here in the privacy of my tent."

"I'm sorry, Leanna, but the army doesn't issue bathtubs; so it'll have to be the river, or not at all."

Conceding the point, she agreed, "All right." Stepping to her bag, she unpacked one of her summer dresses plus undergarments. She had only brought three changes, and it did not dawn on her until hours after her home was burned that everything left in her bedroom had been destroyed.

Tucking the clothes beneath her arm, she turned to face Jeff. "I'll need a towel and a bar of soap, or doesn't the army issue the small necessities of life?"

"I brought you a towel and soap. I left them outside."

Moving past him, she stepped out of the tent as he followed. Jerry and Paul were cleaning their rifles, and Jeff told them he was taking Leanna to the river. Remembering to pick up her towel and bar of soap, he led her into the woods. They walked a couple of yards before reaching a secluded area on the river-bank.

Handing her the towel and soap, he told her, "The water close to the bank is only about two feet deep, but a little farther out, there is a steep drop. And where it drops off there is also a strong current, so stay in the shallow water."

"How do you know all this?" she asked.

"I took a bath myself before coming to your tent."

"It's only two feet deep?" she questioned warily.

Reading her thoughts, he replied with a smile, "This time you'll have no tub or sudsy water to hide your seductive beauty from my roving eyes." Ambling over to a large oak, and sitting down, he leaned back against the trunk. When she made no move to prepare for her bath, he sighed wearily. "Leanna, I don't have all day. Will you please get on with your bath?"

Incredulous, she gasped, "I don't intend to undress while you are sitting there watching me!"

"Would you rather I stood?" he asked innocently, cocking an eyebrow.

"Jeff Clayton, you're impossible!" she spat, but she couldn't stop the half-smile that touched her lips.

Getting slowly to his feet, he compromised, "Very well, madam, if you insist on modesty I will turn my back. But it's not as though I haven't seen your lovely body before."

178

"Don't turn around," she said firmly as she began removing her dust-stained clothes.

Deciding to enjoy a smoke while she bathed, he took a cheroot from his pocket and lit it. "Leanna," he warned seriously, "don't think you can escape by swimming to the other side of the river. It's too swift, and the current is too strong. Even if you're a good swimmer, you'd most likely drown."

"You needn't worry, Major," she answered, wading into the sun-warmed water. "I won't be trying to cross the river. I am a very poor swimmer."

"But you were raised by a river," he replied. "I should think you'd swim like a fish."

Sudsing herself, she explained, "My mother did not consider swimming in the river proper behavior for a lady. When my brother and I were children, I used to sneak down to the river with him, but he had just begun to teach me to swim when mama found out and very quickly put a stop to the lessons."

The bar of soap slid from her hand, and Leanna grabbed for it, but it sank to the bottom. Putting her hand beneath the water, she tried to retrieve it, but the soap was so slippery she only succeeded in pushing it farther away. Losing sight of it, she stood and, wading, felt for it with her feet.

Forgetting Jeff's order to stay close to the bank, she walked toward the deeper part of the water. The perpendicular slope was so unexpected that she approached it without warning. Suddenly, the water was over her head. Panicking, Leanna flailed her arms wildly. The murky depths pulled her under, but struggling against the tugging force, she fought her way to the surface. She tried to tread water, but the current was like a vaccuum, trying to suck her back down into its deadly grasp.

"Jeff!" she screamed frantically. "Jeff!"

Turning, and seeing Leanna fighting desperately to keep from drowning, he dropped his cheroot and raced to the bank. Quickly removing his holster, he slipped off his boots and ran through the shallow water. As he neared Leanna, the threatening current drew her down into the river and out of his sight. Reaching the place where the river bottom dropped off, he plunged into the swift water. He dove deeply and, finding Leanna, clutched her in a firm hold and took her with him to the surface.

Gasping, Leanna fought for air, and while holding onto her, Jeff swam strongly. When they reached shallow water, he carried her to the bank.

Carefully, he placed her on her feet, and breathing deeply, she filled her lungs with air. She hadn't swallowed any water, and as soon as her knees stopped shaking, she knew she'd be perfectly all right.

Jeff waited until she recovered from her fright before releasing his anger, "Damn it, Leanna! I told you not to try to swim across the river! My God, you'll do anything and take any chance to escape, won't you?"

His vexation surprised her, and, for a moment, she could only stare at him. But as his accusations registered within her consciousness, she tried to explain, "B . . . but Jeff . . . I wasn't —"

Interrupting, he bellowed, "You try to escape again, and so help me, Leanna, I will have you restrained!"

His short-fused temper set off her own anger, and she shouted, "You hard-headed egotistical . . . Yankee!"

Fuming, he reached out and clutched her shoulders. She tried to pull back, but he drew her closer. She fought against his grasp, causing him to press her against his strong frame to prevent her from squirming free.

Her bare flesh was molded to his wet uniform, and there was no way they could not become aware of their bodies now flush together. She could feel him grow hard as her thighs remained pinned tightly against his manhood. The desire that began flowing between her legs was stronger than her anger, and when she gazed up into his face, her blue eyes filled with passion.

His own anger forgotten, Jeff murmured fervently, "Leanna, I want you."

"Yes," she whispered hoarsely, her desire now burning so intensely that she swiveled her hips against his erection, loving, and needing his hardness.

His lips sought hers, and his passionate kiss lifted her into paradise as her clinging body seemed to become a part of his.

"Major Clayton! . . . Major Clayton!" Paul's voice called suddenly from a distance. Stopping their kiss abruptly, Jeff shouted, "Soldier, stay where you are!" Setting Leanna from him, he ordered brusquely, "Get dressed."

Jeff slipped on his boots, and grabbing his holster from where he had dropped it on the ground, he carried it in his hand as he hurried into the wooded area to meet Paul. "What is it?" he asked, approaching the soldier waiting for him.

Trying not to gape at the major's wet uniform, Paul answered, "Sir, Colonel Andrews wants to see you immediately."

Nodding, Jeff replied, "Stay here." He rushed back to the edge of the woods, and waiting where Leanna couldn't see him, he watched until she was fully clothed, then he returned to Paul and told him to take Miss Weston back to her tent.

Lifting the hem of her long dress, Jennifer stepped cautiously over the charred ruins that had once been an elegant and beautiful home. The ashes scattering beneath her feet were soiling her slippers, but she didn't care. The useless devastation sickened her, and it was with an aching heart that she remembered the first time she had seen the columned mansion. It had sat majestically on the top of an incline, overlooking acres and acres of Georgian landscape. She had been a girl of seven, and from the first moment her eyes had beheld its beauty, she had wished that someday she would be its mistress. She had fallen in love with The Pines years before she had fallen in love with Bradley Weston.

Hearing a horse approaching, Jennifer tensed. Frightened, she spun about. The lone rider was at a distance, and she couldn't recognize him, but she could distinguish the color of his uniform. Gray! Thank God, it wasn't blue!

Making her way through the debris, she paused at the top of the steps that had once led grandly to the magnificent, column house, but which now rose grotesquely to a huge mass of destruction and waste.

As the visitor rode closer, Jennifer suddenly recognized him, and smiling happily, she hurried down the flight of steps to greet him.

He reined in his horse and dismounted awkwardly due to a injury. Limping noticeably, he walked to Jennifer and, as she neared him, held out his arms.

Flinging herself into his embrace, Jennifer hugged him tightly. "David!" she cried with disbelief. "Are my eyes deceiving me, or is it really you?"

Reluctantly David Farnsworth released her. He had never before held Jennifer, and he wished he had the right to keep her in his embrace.

"No, your eyes are perfectly all right," he replied, trying to keep his tone jovial. "It's really me. A little worse for wear and tear, but I'm all in one piece."

Aware of his limp, she asked, "How badly are you injured?"

"Well," he drawled casually, as though his injury was nothing more than a mild aggravation, "I'll limp on my left leg for the rest of my life, and the doctor said that on rainy days, it'll ache like the dickens. But at least I still have it, for a while the doctor thought he might have to amputate."

"Thank God, it didn't come to that!" she breathed. "Are you on a medical leave?"

"No, I'm home permanently. I was medically discharged. I just came from my plantation, but there's nothing left." Sighing deeply, he looked around, "I see Sherman has been through here too. He always leaves his calling card, mass destruction."

"Yes, he and his army were here," Jennifer whispered, wondering how she was going to tell him about Leanna. A moment of silence fell between them, and Jennifer tried to study David without being too obvious. She hadn't seen him in over two years, but he looked years older than when they'd last met. Cavernous lines and creases had aged his clean-shaven face, and he was entirely too thin. He was only twenty-five, but he could be mistaken for forty. Nonetheless, Jennifer was sure with rest and nourishment, he would once again become the handsome man he used to be. As David removed his hat and brushed his arm across his perspiring brow, she saw that his brown hair was still full and wavy. She met his gaze and hoped that somewhere behind his vacuous stare lurked the spirit for life that had always sparkled in his hazel eyes.

"I'm sorry about Brad," he mumbled sympathetically. Brad had been his closest friend, and he had loved him like a brother.

"Were you with him when he died?" she asked, her voice breaking.

"Yes," he answered softly. "Brad was a courageous man, Jennifer. You can be proud of him."

Tears brimming, she pleaded piteously, "Please David, let's not talk about Brad. Not now. Maybe later."

"Of course," he assured her gently, wondering if she had any idea how beautiful he was finding her. Although David had loved his friend Brad, that hadn't kept him from also loving Brad's wife. He had been in love with Jennifer years before she had become engaged to Brad, and when she had married, he had tried to stop loving her. But finally he had had to admit that Jennifer was in his heart forever.

He gave up trying to forget her, and simply resigned himself to accept what he could not change.

"Do you know where my parents and sister are?" he asked.

"Leanna heared that they moved to Savannah."

"Savannah," he repeated. "There's no way I can get to Savannah. The Yankees are thick as flies between here and there."

"You must stay here with us," Jennifer insisted. "We're living in the overseer's house, and there is plenty of room."

"I wouldn't want to impose," he replied politely.

"Why, David Farnsworth," she chastened gently, "you could never be an imposition. You are like one of the family. Mary will be thrilled that you're here." Jennifer wondered again why he hadn't asked about Leanna. She knew he and Leanna were not officially engaged, but she had always taken it for granted that they were in love and would marry. Could she have been wrong? Was David not in love with Leanna? As she thought about it, she realized Leanna had never talked about David as though he were the man she loved, only as though he were a very good and dear friend.

"How is Leanna?" he finally inquired, but Jennifer noticed he asked the question casually.

David's injured leg was beginning to pain him, causing him to shift his full weight to the other leg. Noting his discomfort, Jennifer suggested, "Let's sit down on the steps, and then I'll tell you about Leanna."

She took his hand into hers, and her gesture caused him to flinch. He knew she had clasped his hand merely as a good friend, but he couldn't feel her touch without wanting to take her into his arms so he pulled his hand away from hers.

His refusal to hold her hand made Jennifer blush. She had behaved much too brazenly. She hoped he didn't think she was a lonely widow, desperate for a man's advances.

Moving toward the steps with Jennifer at his side, he asked, "What has happened to Leanna?"

Jennifer was deeply worried about Leanna, and she replied gravely, "Oh, David, the Yankees have taken her away, and I'm so afraid we'll never see her again!"

Lying on her cot, Leanna stared up at the canvas ceiling as unanswered questions plagued her. At the riverbank when Jeff had taken her into his arms, why had she given in so easily? If Paul hadn't come searching for them, she knew she would have wantonly surrendered herself to Jeff. She had only known him for a short time, yet, he had become the center of her life, and her thoughts continually revolved around him. Why? Why was she so possessed by this Union major?

The setting sun descended over the far horizon, and as its soft glow faded, dusk began blanketing the landscape. Leanna sat up, and was about to light her kerosene lantern when Jeff's voice outside her tent caused her to halt.

"I'm relieving you men for a couple of hours," she heard him say to Paul and Jerry.

"Yes, sir," they replied simultaneously, glad to leave their prisoner and mingle with the other soldiers.

Without asking Leanna's permission, Jeff entered the tent. Her first impulse was to tell him that she resented his rudeness, but there was something about the stern set of his jaw that cautioned her against starting an altercation.

Going to the cot, he sat down beside her. She waited anxiously for him to speak, but he seemed to need a few moments to get his thoughts in perspective. Finally, sighing heavily, he began, "We won't be able to cross the river until the day after tomorrow. But in the morning, the initial fighting will begin. You will be safe here. We'll be confronting the enemy about a half mile downstream where they are guarding a ford in the river."

Interrupting, Leanna said bitterly, "The ford you want them to believe Sherman intends to cross."

"That's true, Leanna," he agreed, his voice hard. "I have one hundred and twenty-five men, and Colonel Andrews has over three hundred. The Confederates will have to send for reinforcements."

"I already know Sherman's tactics," she reminded him crossly.

His tone edged with impatience, he replied, "I came here to tell you not to be afraid. You'll hear cannons firing and rifle shots, but you will be in no danger."

"Is that supposed to bring me comfort?" she spat sharply.

Losing his patience, he asked brusquely, "Would you rather join in the fighting?"

"And shoot at Confederates?" she scowled. "No, thank you!"

187

"Confederates?" he questioned. "I thought you might enjoy taking the opportunity to shoot me."

Trying not to smile, but failing, she answered lightly, "Don't tempt me." Without realizing it, she reached over and grasped his arm as she pleaded, "Oh Jeff, how many soldiers will die tomorrow? Not only Confederates, but also Yankees? How many young men will lose their lives because of this cruel and useless war?"

"I don't know," he answered, depressed.

"I hate this war!" she cried impulsively, her grasp on his arm tightening.

"So do I," he mumbled quietly.

"You do?" she asked, sounding surprised.

"Do you think I enjoy it?"

Removing her hand from his arm, she sighed, "I don't know. I suppose I never really thought about it." Desperately, she added, "When will this war end?"

"When the Confederates realize they are fighting a lost cause. The South cannot win this war, yet they keep holding on with a resilience that is not only remarkable, but also admirable."

"And yet you are killing men that you admire," she moaned.

"Is it any wonder that I hate this war?" he replied sadly.

The approaching twilight was casting gray shadows, and the inside of the tent was darkening, but Leanna could see Jeff's face clearly. Lovingly, her eyes took in his features, and she became captivated by his good looks. He wasn't wearing a hat, and she studied his coal black hair, finding the streaks of premature gray at his temples extremely attractive. Then, as his brown eyes looked into hers, she noticed once again how his long lashes curled up on the ends. Her gaze shifted to his sensual mouth, to the well-groomed mustache that tapered downward, framing the corners of his full lips.

All at once, she longed to kiss him. She needed to feel his mouth on hers, his arms about her. Maybe, in his strong embrace, she could somehow forget that in the morning there would be bloodshed and death where now there was only tranquillity and peacefulness beside the Chattahoochee River.

"Kiss me, Jeff!" she pleaded. "Please kiss me!"

Instantly he had her in his arms, and his lips came down on hers with demanding force. Jeff, too, desperately needed to forget the doom that morning would bring, and he clung to Leanna with an urgency that aroused Leanna's passion.

She helped him remove her garments, anxious to lie in his arms with nothing to prevent his skin from touching hers. She needed his touch, she longed for it, and as she lay down on the cot and he stretched beside her to cup one of her breasts, she moaned with pleasure.

Kissing her deeply, he ran his hand from her breast over her ribs and stomach, then down between her thighs. She arched her hips, accepting his touch without inhibition.

She writhed under his exciting fondling, and her passionate responses pleased Jeff. Taking his lips from hers, he murmured, "Leanna, when you respond to me as you do now, you arouse me beyond reason."

189

"Oh, Jeff," she purred. "I think I am possessed by you. . . . Love me, darling . . . love me. . . ."

Rising from the cot, he quickly removed his uniform, and the darkness silhouetted his masculine frame as he rejoined her, positioning himself between her legs.

He entered her smoothly, and instantly her legs were over his back, pressing him farther inside her. Her thighs converged with his as his lips sought hers in a long, intimate kiss. Grasping her hips, he pulled her farther down the cot, and Leanna edged her legs higher up his back so that it would be easier for him to push himself into the depths of her warmness.

Tingling sensations permeated Leanna's senses, and she whispered seductively, "Oh Jeff, you are so wonderful." She clutched his wide shoulders. Then, arching her thighs, she slid up and down his hardness, relishing the feel of him moving in and out of her.

Slipping his hands beneath her, he thrust her up against him, pounding into her vigorously. Then, rising to his knees, he pulled her thighs forward and, taking hold of her legs, placed them over his shoulders.

"Jeff . . . Jeff!" she cried tremulously, unsure of this new position.

"Leanna," he murmured soothingly. "Relax, my darling."

She did as he asked, and Jeff's thrilling entry caused Leanna to throw back her head and moan fervently. He thrust into her strongly, and as she equaled his driving force, all thoughts of tomorrow were forgotten; they became totally lost in their need for each other.

Making love with reckless passion, they reached desperately for the wonderful crescendo awaiting them, and when their ultimate climax erupted, it brought them ecstatic satisfaction.

Remaining inside her, Jeff kissed her tenderly before confessing, "Leanna, no woman has ever made me feel this way."

"Oh, Jeff," she replied rapturously, "I never dreamed a man could make me feel the way you do."

He kissed her flushed cheek, then moved to lie at her side. Placing one arm over her shoulders, he drew her closer. Feeling content, Leanna yawned sleepily as she snuggled against him. She wanted to talk to him, but first she would close her eyes and rest for a moment. She wouldn't think about anything except how good it felt to be in Jeff's comforting embrace.

And so Leanna fell into a deep sleep, from which she did not awaken when Jeff left her side to get dressed. She slept so soundly that she didn't stir when he placed a blanket over her, nor was she aware that he kissed her forehead before leaving the tent.

Chapter Thirteen

The loud thunder of cannon fire awakened Leanna, and she sat up on the cot with a sudden movement. She was amazed to see that it was daylight and that she had slept soundly through the night. Immediately, she became perturbed because she had fallen asleep last night instead of talking to Jeff and enjoying his company. She looked at the side of the cot where he had lain beside her, but there was nothing there to remind her that he had shared her bed, only the memory of their beautiful union.

A cannon's ominous rumble once again vibrated across the countryside, and Leanna hurried from the cot. Hastily, she got into her clothes, then darted outside.

Jerry and Paul were standing a short way from the campfire, facing the direction where the battle was raging. The skirmish was too far away for them to see the fighting taking place, but knowing their battalion was participating, they continued to look toward the line of action as if it were within sight.

Joining them, Leanna asked with bated breath, "Is Major Clayton at the battle or is he in camp?"

"He's with his men," Jerry answered, "fighting alongside them, like he always does."

Leanna gasped, and fear for Jeff's safety made her knees weaken. She swayed slightly, and Jerry took hold of her arm to support her. "Ma'am, would you like a cup of coffee?" he asked. "There's a fresh pot on the fire."

Coffee! How could she possibly sit idly by and drink coffee knowing that at any moment Jeff could be wounded or killed? "No, thank you," she replied raspingly; and, as Jerry and Paul had been doing before she interrupted them, she turned to face the direction of the battle as though she could actually see it.

"Miss Weston," Jerry persisted kindly, "you might as well have a cup of coffee. That battle will last 'til nightfall. I'll also fix you some breakfast, it's going to be a long day, and you'll need your strength."

She nodded absent-mindedly, his words registering only vaguely on her mind. Nightfall! she cried inwardly. Oh, please God, keep Jeff safe . . . please! . . . But as the other soldiers fighting came to mind, Leanna silently said a prayer for all of them, and she wished with all her heart that the war would miraculously end.

Leanna managed to drink two cups of coffee, but she merely picked at her breakfast. Her stomach, tied in knots, balked at the small amount of food she had forced herself to consume. She began to feel queasy, and setting aside her plate, she hoped she wouldn't get sick.

Leanna was alone with Jerry, sitting beside the burned-out campfire, when Paul returned from the Union camp to tell them that the wounded were being brought in.

Intending to rush to the camp, Leanna bolted to her feet. She whirled to leave, but, alertly, Paul grasped her wrist. "Miss Weston, you have to stay here."

With a strength that startled Paul, she jerked free of his hold. "No!" she cried desperately. "I must find out if Jeff has been wounded!"

Paul and Jerry were not surprised that she had called the major by his first name. It had become apparent to them that Miss Weston and Major Clayton were involved with each other.

"I'll check on him for you," Paul offered.

"Please let me go with you!" she implored. "If he has been hurt, he'll need me!"

Paul glanced at Jerry, and he nodded his approval. "All right," Paul conceded. "But you stay with Jerry and me."

"I will!" she promised.

Leanna walked to the Union camp between her two guards. Jerry and Paul strode briskly, but they didn't move nearly fast enough to suit Leanna, and she kept tugging at their arms, encouraging them to hurry.

As they entered the camp area, Leanna was so gravely concerned for Jeff's welfare that she could think of nothing else. She barely noticed all the wounded soldiers lying on blankets spread out on the ground around the tent the doctors were using for surgery.

Spotting Doctor Hamilton, Paul told Leanna, "Stay here with Jerry, and I'll ask the doc if he's seen Major Clayton."

Waiting anxiously, Leanna watched as Paul hurried over to Doctor Hamilton. The doctor was kneeling beside a wounded soldier, and squatting next to him, Paul quickly asked him about Jeff.

Her heart pounding rapidly, Leanna held her breath with fear while Paul walked back to her and Jerry.

Looking at Leanna, Paul relayed the information he had learned, "Doctor Hamilton said that Major Clayton was here a few minutes ago, but he's gone back to the river."

"Was he all right?" Leanna cried.

Nodding, Paul assured her, "He was fine."

Relieved, Leanna sighed deeply, relaxing her tense muscles. Thank God, Jeff is all right! she thought. At least for now I know he's alive and well!

Leanna began to look around the camp, and as the wounded soldiers slowly registered on her consciousness, she became aware of their moans. The offensive odor of the blood oozing from their torn flesh assailed her nostrils, and her stomach started churning. Fighting back a feeling of nausea, she turned to go back to her tent, when she noticed the wounded soldier lying only a few feet from where she was standing. Recognizing him as one of the sentries who had been stationed outside her bedroom door at The Pines, she moved over to look down at him. He was extremely young; Leanna knew he couldn't be older than nineteen. His eyes were closed, and he wasn't aware of her presence. The young soldier's hand was resting on his stomach, and blood was flowing through his fingers and rolling down his sides to drip onto the blanket.

Standing beside her, Jerry mumbled, "He's gut shot."

"Wh-what?" Leanna stammered.

"He was shot in the stomach, and a gut shot hurts like hell."

Catching sight of a medic hurrying past them, Leanna reached out and clutched his arm. "Please, this soldier needs medical attention."

"Doctor Hamilton will be right over to check him," the medic said hastily, wishing the lady hadn't halted him. He didn't have time to stand here and discuss one soldier when he had dozens of them to tend to.

"But he's bleeding to death!" Leanna exclaimed.

The medic took a quick glance at the soldier, and his experienced eye told him that the man's wound was probably fatal. Handing Leanna a clean cloth, he told her brusquely, "Press this over his wound, and it'll help blot the flow of blood. I'll tell Doctor Hamilton to hurry."

He darted away, and Leanna stared numbly down at the cloth in her hands.

"I'll do it, ma'am," Paul offered.

She was about to give him the cloth, when a captain called out to Jerry and Paul, ordering them to his side.

"I guess we'd better go see what he wants," Jerry replied.

Holding the cloth with shaking hands, she watched as they hurried over to the captain who was waiting for them. The heat of the day was becoming unbearable, and perspiration beaded Leanna's brow as she turned to look down at the wounded soldier. The odor of the wound had drawn flies in swarms, and seeing the insects hovering above the soldier's gaping abdomen caused bile to rise in Leanna's throat.

While Leanna was grown up on The Pines, Frank and Mary Weston had sheltered her from everything in life that was gruesome or violent, but as Leanna knelt beside the severely wounded soldier, she had no resemblance to the pampered and innocent Southern belle her parents had tried to raise.

She closed her mind to her nausea, willing herself to think of nothing except helping this young man who was bleeding to death before her very eyes.

Gently, she lifted his blood-soaked hand, and placed it at his side. Then she pressed the cloth to the lesion that was bleeding copiously, and increasing the pressure, she held the cloth tightly against the open wound.

The soldier's eyes fluttered open, and regaining consciousness, he recognized Leanna. "Miss Weston," he uttered weakly, "thank you, ma'am, for tryin' to help me. But it's no use . . . I'm gonna die."

Forcing back her tears, she said firmly, "No, you won't die! The doctor will be here soon." Pleadingly, she cried, "Oh, please don't talk about dying!"

In spite of the excruciating pain he was suffering, he smiled feebly and mumbled, "Miss Weston, you're an angel to care about me." His voice fading, he repeated, "You're an angel."

Dr. Hamilton approached so swiftly and soundlessly that she wasn't aware of his presence until he had knelt beside her. He reached toward the blood-soaked cloth, and she quickly removed her hand so that he could push it aside.

"This man needs surgery immediately," he announced professionally, and Leanna wasn't sure whether he was talking to her or to himself.

He glanced around, looking for a medic, but failing to spot one, he faced Leanna as though he hadn't known she was present until now. Dr. Hamilton was a large man in his late fifties, and behind his gruff façade, he was a compassionate, dedicated physician.

"Young lady, have you ever administered chloroform?" His tone demanded an immediate answer.

"No," she replied at once.

"Well, it isn't very difficult," he assured her abruptly. "All the medics are busy, so you'll have to assist me in surgery."

Leanna gasped as she stared at him incredulously. If he heard her gasp, he made no mention of it; he simply ordered two passing soldiers to carry the wounded man into the operating tent.

Grasping her arm with his strong, surgeon's fingers, he drew her to her feet. Keeping a firm hold on her, he began leading her toward the tent used for surgery. When they reached it, he pushed aside the flap, and stepping back for her to enter, he said briskly, "We can wash up inside."

As she entered the tent, the smell of chloroform and blood was so thick that the stench hit her full force, causing her to gag. Through watery eyes, she saw two doctors, each performing surgery, each trying desperately to save the life of his patient.

Dr. Hamilton nudged her toward the corner of the

tent, where clean water-filled basins were placed atop tables.

Moving as though in a trance, she walked at the doctor's side, and when they paused at the basins, she automatically washed her hands, unable to fully grasp what was happening to her.

Handing her a towel, Dr. Hamilton noticed her paleness, and smiling tenderly, he said, "Young lady, if you are not strong enough to bear up, you may leave, but I am usually a good judge of character. The compassion and care you were showing that young soldier proves you care about human life, and I think you also have grit. Those are the only attributes you need to be a good nurse." Raising his thick eyebrows, he asked vigorously, "Well, are you going to help me save that soldier's life?"

"Is there a chance that he might survive?" she queried, wondering how the young man could live after losing so much blood.

"He'll have no chance at all, if we don't operate immediately," the doctor replied hastily, including her as though there was no doubt in his mind that she would agree to assist him.

Taking a deep breath, Leanna answered with a decisiveness she wasn't sure she had the courage to maintain, "Very well, Doctor. I'm ready whenever you are." But silently, she prayed desperately. . . . God, give me strength, and, God, please don't let me fail Dr. Hamilton!

"I just know those Yankees are treating Leanna ruthlessly!" Mary Weston announced wretchedly at breakfast, her eyes glued to David.

200

Glancing across the kitchen table, **David** silently appealed for Jennifer's help in reassuring **Mary** that Leanna was probably safe. Understanding his silent plea, Jennifer said with a conviction she was far from feeling, "Mary, I'm sure Leanna is unharmed and will soon be home."

"Mrs. Weston," David began, offering his own encouragement, "although you may find this hard to believe, there are gentlemen among the Yankees. And from what Jennifer has told me, Major Clayton sounded like a man with integrity. I am sure he will keep Leanna safe."

"I have never met a Yankee who was a gentleman!" Mary huffed, offended by David's remark.

"How many Yankees have you met?" he asked, suppressing a grin.

"Quite a few," Mary revealed. "Before the war, Frank and I visited the North twice, and every Yankee I met was crude and boorish.".

"Mrs. Weston," David tried to explain, "Major Clayton could have justifiably sent Leanna to a prison camp or had her executed. But he did neither one, so, madam, I can't help but believe he is a gentleman. You won't admit I'm right because of your prejudice."

Harshly, she reminded him, "The Yankees killed my son, and were indirectly responsible for Frank's death. Then they burned my home and abducted my daughter. Yes, I'm prejudiced, and I have good reason to be."

David knew Mary wasn't well. Sorry that he had upset her, he answered quickly, "Mrs. Weston, I hope you don't think I was speaking treacherously. God knows, I harbor no love for Yankees."

Her anger mellowing, Mary replied, "David, I love you like a son, and I know there isn't a treacherous drop of blood in your veins." He was seated at her side, so she reached over and clasped his hand, squeezing it affectionately. "I hope you and Leanna marry as soon as she returns. I can't understand why you two have waited so long. You and Leanna should have married years ago."

David nodded as though he agreed, and satisfied that he'd soon be her son-in-law, Mary excused herself, "I think I will go to my room and rest."

"Of course," David replied, rising promptly to assist her from her chair, but the sharp pain that shot through his wounded leg made him wince. Mary didn't notice his pain, but Jennifer did and his discomfort touched her.

When Mary had left the room, and David and Jennifer were alone, Jennifer asked forwardly, "Why haven't you and Leanna married?"

Returning to his chair, David answered evasively, "Well, what with the war and all . . . I guess we just haven't found the right time."

His eyes had avoided hers, and Jennifer strongly suspected that he wasn't being totally honest. He isn't in love with Leanna, she decided, and I seriously doubt if she's in love with him. "When Leanna comes home, do you plan to ask her to marry you?"

David knew everyone expected him to marry Leanna, including Leanna herself, and not one to shirk his duty, he answered, "Yes, I plan to ask her." David did love Leanna as a friend, and he hoped that when she became his wife his love would deepen into one of passion.

Jennifer was tempted to delve deeper into the subject, but deciding she shouldn't interfere, she dropped the topic. Standing, she said, "Louise has the boys outside, and I need to check on them." He started to rise, but knowing his lame leg still pained him, she waved him back down. "Don't get up, David. And finish your breakfast. You need nourishment, you're entirely too thin."

Jennifer was not aware that David's eyes followed her worshipfully as she walked gracefully from the kitchen.

Leanna had never felt so tired, there didn't seem to be a muscle in her body that wasn't sore. Hours of tension had caused the back of her neck to ache, and a sharp pain had lodged itself between her shoulder blades. Worn to the point of exhaustion, she walked lethargically at Dr. Hamilton's side as he escorted her from the operating tent.

Stepping aside to permit her to exit first, the doctor gave Leanna an appreciative glance as she strode past him. Leanna had made quite an impression on Dr. Hamilton. He admired her because she had worked beside him for hours without uttering one complaint. Diligently, she had assisted him through operation after operation, demonstrating a resilience that amazed him. He couldn't remember who had once told him that Southern ladies were all delicate creatures, but whoever it was had been badly mistaken. In Doctor Hamilton's estimation, Miss Weston was a gallant and remarkable woman. She had been forced to watch, helplessly, as men died before her very eyes on the operating table, she had held onto patients' hands, trying to comfort them when it had been necessary to tell them one or more of their limbs had to be amputated; and not once had she visibly weakened, although Doctor Hamilton had observed the grief and pain in her eyes that she had tried so hard to conceal. He recalled their first operation and the patient regaining consciousness as she was preparing to administer the chloroform. Somehow, the soldier had found the strength to reach for her hand and place a kiss on her palm, before murmuring, "Ma'am, you're an angel from Dixie." And Dr. Hamilton wholeheartedly agreed with the young soldier's analysis.

Now, the evening air blew refreshingly across Leanna's perspiring brow, and she welcomed the soothing breeze. She looked around, expecting to find Jerry and Paul, but instead she saw Jeff walking toward her. She was so thankful to see that he was well she completely forgot propriety and ran into his arms.

Embracing her, Jeff whispered tenderly, "Leanna." He held her extremely close for a moment before saying lightly, "Paul and Jerry told me Dr. Hamilton had recruited you for medical duty."

She stepped back and looked closely at him, reassuring herself that he hadn't been injured. Her eyes trailed intently over his lean, strong frame. Studying him adoringly, she realized suddenly and impulsively that she loved him with all her heart and soul. That is the power he holds over me, she thought. I'm in love with him! She longed to tell Jeff how much she cared, but she wasn't sure whether he wanted her to love him, so she suppressed the desire to confess her true feelings.

Joining them, Dr. Hamilton praised Leanna. "Major Clayton, Miss Weston has the makings of a fine nurse. If she agrees, I'd like to have her assist me again tomorrow."

Leanna started to give her consent, but Jeff answered, "I'm sorry, doctor. But Miss Weston must be kept under guard. Nursing isn't her present profession."

"Oh?" Dr. Hamilton questioned. "What is her profession?"

"Miss Weston is a rebel spy," Jeff said, his tone tinged with amusement.

"Spy!" the doctor scoffed. "Well, apparently, she's a better nurse than a spy, otherwise, she wouldn't have gotten caught. I am hereby exercising my right as a commissioned doctor in the U.S. Army to demand that Miss Weston report to me in the morning."

Jeff smiled. He knew as well as Dr. Hamilton that he had no right to order a prisoner to assist him in surgery.

Looking at Leanna, the doctor asked brusquely, "Miss Weston, do you agree to work with me?"

She glanced at Jeff, and he smiled his consent.

"Yes," she answered. "I'll be honored to help you."

Cupping her chin in his hand, the doctor gave her a playful wink. "If you're a spy, then you're the prettiest spy I've ever met." He had seen Leanna run into Jeff's arms, and he added, "If I were about twenty years younger, I'd give the major a run for his money."

As Dr. Hamilton walked away, Jeff touched Leanna's arm, asking with concern, "Are you tired?"

"Yes," she sighed wearily.

"I'll take you to your tent," he offered.

She fell into step beside him, but it was an effort to keep up with his long strides. She kept falling behind. Realizing this, Jeff shortened his strides, but her tired legs still slowed them down so much that he finally lifted her into his arms. Sliding her arms about his neck, she placed her head on his shoulder as he carried her to their destination.

Paul and Jerry were sitting a distance from the campfire, and before entering the tent, Jeff ordered one of them to bring Leanna something to eat. Taking her to the cot, Jeff laid her down with care. When Paul brought in her plate of food and a cup of coffee, Jeff sat on the edge of the cot, and fed her the food spoonful by spoonful, making sure she finished her dinner.

Leanna found his pampering a little embarrassing, but she also reveled in the attention. He must love me, she thought. Otherwise, why would he be so considerate?

Leanna knew he had to be extremely tired himself, yet despite her mild protests, he insisted on sponging her face, arms, and hands with a wet cloth. Then he removed her shoes and dress, and tucked her into bed.

Bending over the cot, he kissed her forehead. "Sweet dreams, my little rebel spy," he whispered warmly.

Leanna responded with a loving smile. Jeff had made no passionate advances, but they hadn't been necessary. His tender ministrations had proven his love more than caresses or words. He might not realize it, Leanna thought, but he loves me. I know he loves me!

Taking his hand, she urged him to sit on the cot at her side; then, reaching up, she wrapped her arms about his neck and, bringing her lips down on hers, kissed him demandingly, almost desperately.

"Leanna," he said thickly, "honey, if you want to fall asleep early tonight, then you better not kiss me like that again."

Smiling, she asked pertly, "What will happen to me if I should ignore your advice and kiss you again?"

"I just might take advantage of you," he grinned.

"What a wonderful idea," she murmured, before kissing him very passionately.

"You little vixen," he said accusingly, pulling her to a sitting position so that he could help her remove her undergarments.

Leaving the cot, Jeff stepped over to the lantern and dimmed the flame. Remembering that Jerry and Paul were stationed outside the tent, he was hesitant about staying. He turned back to remind Leanna of the guards, but her seductive beauty was so striking that, for a moment, he was speechless. The glow from the low-burning lantern shone luminously upon her bare skin. He knew he'd never forget how beautiful she was at this moment as she lay so innocently alluring, waiting for him to make love to her.

Wondering why Jeff hadn't gotten undressed but was only standing and watching her, Leanna was afraid that she had behaved too boldly. Had she been too brazen? Did Jeff resent women who took the initiative? Oh, if only she weren't so naïve about the relationship between a man and a woman! "Jeff, what's wrong?" she asked faintly.

Still amazed by her loveliness, he merely shook his head, unable to find the right words to express how he felt. Slowly, his eyes trailed over her, admiring her flawless beauty.

"Jeff?" she whispered, wishing she knew whether she had done something wrong.

"Leanna," he said hoarsely, "you are so beautiful."

Relieved that he apparently hadn't found fault with her behavior, she invited sensually, "Darling, I thought you were going to take advantage of me."

His thoughts suddenly returning to Jerry and Paul, he reminded her, "What about your guards? If I stay much longer, they're going to become wise."

Raising herself and leaning on an elbow, she turned to her side as she placed one leg partially over the other. Totally unaware that she made an irresistible picture of seduction, she queried saucily, "You're their commanding officer, aren't you? So why don't you command them to go away?"

Chuckling, he commented. "Miss Weston, you have thought of the perfect solution."

Laughing with him, she teased, "Well, we spies didn't get our reputations for being sneaky without good cause."

Moving to the tent flap and stepping outside, Jeff ordered authoritatively, "Troopers Rogan and Lammert, you're dismissed."

"Dismissed, sir?" Paul questioned tentatively. "Dismissed to go where, sir?"

Listening from inside the tent, Leanna was amused and she wondered what Jeff would answer.

Conjuring up an order, Jeff replied, "Report to Lieutenant Buehler and tell him that I said for you two to relieve the guards at the north end of the camp."

"Yes, sir!"

The two men obeyed, picking up their rifles. Jeff waited until they had hurried away before reentering the tent.

"How long do you intend to keep them on watch?" Leanna asked.

Taking off his uniform, Jeff answered, "When I leave, I'll see that they are sent back here."

Entranced with the man she adored, Leanna watched with anticipation as Jeff removed his clothes. How dearly she loved his lean, strong frame.

Lithely, he moved to the cot, and lying at her side, he took her into his embrace. Kissing her, he pressed her soft thighs against his maleness, and Leanna could feel him grow firm with desire.

"Oh, Jeff," she murmured, arching her hips against his hardness, anxious to have him enter her.

He moved over her and, as she parted her legs, slipped into her moist depths. "Sweetheart," he groaned huskily.

Sliding her legs across his back, Leanna clung tightly to him, her heart overflowing with love. Nibbling playfully at his ear lobe, she whispered, "Jeff, I'm so glad you decided to take advantage of me."

"I wanted to make love to you, but I was worried that you might be too fatigued," he replied, her warm breath against his ear sending chills up his spine.

"I could never be too tired for you," she answered.

"Leanna, you're a woman after my heart," he said thickly.

She longed to ask him if she truly had his heart, but afraid that he might think she was pressuring him, she said nothing.

Jeff's lips sought hers as he slipped his hands beneath her hips, bringing her thighs up to his. Losing herself in their exciting union, Leanna's worries vanished as she surrendered ecstatically to the man she loved so deeply.

Chapter Fourteen

Jennifer's bedroom in the overseer's house faced the side yard. Now, standing at the window, she watched David as he chopped wood. He swung the ax unskillfully but with a determination that didn't weaken. She was sure this was the first time in his life that he had tackled such a chore. Chopping wood had been work for slaves; such menial labor was beneath the son of an aristocratic planter.

David was perspiring heavily, and when he removed his shirt, Jennifer noticed that the muscles in his arms and chest were sinewy despite his thinness. Lifting the ax, he grasped it securely and, swinging it over his shoulder, brought it down, striking a large block of wood and splitting it in half.

It had taken him several frustrating tries to get the wood to split, and from her upstairs window, Jennifer saw his smile of achievement.

As though he could feel her eyes on him, he glanced up in her direction. Seeing her watching him, he swiftly grabbed his shirt and put it on. "I'm doing the job awkwardly, but I'm learning!" he yelled up to her.

She smiled, calling back to him, "Why are you chopping wood? Why don't you let Jackson take care of his own chores?"

"Jackson has more work than one man can handle. I don't mind helping. Besides, I want to earn my keep and not live on Weston charity."

"David," she chided gently, "Mary doesn't expect you to work like a slave."

"Jennifer, I honestly don't mind!" he answered, his tone sharp. He looked away from her and continued his chore. He had almost asked her why didn't she pitch in and help Matilda. Jackson had informed him that since Leanna's departure, Matilda's work had doubled. David had always thought Jennifer above reproach, and to learn she wasn't as perfect as he had always imagined disturbed him deeply. But, he thought, maybe he was judging her too harshly. Her upbringing had not prepared her for these times . . . but neither had Leanna's; yet she had adjusted. Jackson had said that she'd worked strenuously from sunup to sundown without complaining.

"David?" Jennifer said softly.

He turned quickly, surprised that she had walked up to him without his hearing her. Jennifer's dark hair was pinned up into a severe bun that was unflattering, and her printed gown was old and had been mended more than once, but David's loving gaze found her extremely beautiful. Lowering the axe so that the blade was resting on the ground, he smiled as he met her eyes.

"Have you seen Matilda?" she asked.

Nodding toward the back yard, he answered, "She's washing clothes."

Jennifer sighed impatiently, "Lunch should've been ready an hour ago, and Mary was wondering why it's so late."

"I suppose Matilda hasn't had time to prepare it," he replied shortly.

A small frown came to Jennifer's face as she wondered why David was acting so curtly. She glanced down at his hands, and becoming aware of the blisters that had formed on them, she reached over and lifted his hands into hers, causing the ax to fall to the ground. "David!" she cried, concerned.

Jerking his hands away, he assured her hastily, "As soon as calluses form, they'll toughen up."

"Come into the house and let me put some medicine on them," she fussed.

"I don't have time," he replied. "As soon as I finish chopping this wood, Jackson and I are going to repair the old corral in the woods."

"Why in the world do you want to repair that old thing?" she asked, surprised.

"The other day, Jackson saw one of my father's slaves. He was on his way to Marietta. He told Jackson that when my father saw the Yankees riding up to the house, he had some of the livestock driven into the woods. There was a sow, two hogs, and a cow. After Jackson and I fix the corral, we're going to try and round up those pigs and pen them. We'll also search for the cow."

"Oh David!" Jennifer exclaimed. "That would mean milk for Bradley and Matthew!"

He smiled tenderly. "I know. One way or another,

213

we'll find that cow. I promise you."

She grasped his arm firmly. "I don't know how to thank you."

Flinching, he drew away, stepping back to avoid contact with her. He couldn't feel her touch without wanting to take her into his arms. "Wh-what happened to all the Westons' livestock?" he stammered, hoping his elusiveness had escaped her notice.

But Jennifer was aware that he had dodged her touch, and once again she believed she had been too forward. Blushing, and assuming she had behaved brazenly, she answered a little breathlessly, "The Confederate Army confiscated almost half of our livestock, and when the slaves ran away, they stole most of what was left. What the army and the slaves didn't take, the Yankees did."

"You should've kept your livestock hidden in the woods. Especially the cows. That's why I intend to keep all the livestock Jackson and I can locate penned in the old corral. I'll also keep the cow hidden safely in the woods."

Jennifer replied, "We didn't have a man to advise us. We only had Jackson, and he had to learn the same way as the rest of us, by trial and error."

"The rest of you?" he asked cynically and without forethought. "Don't you mean Matilda and Leanna?"

"What point are you trying to make?" she asked sharply.

"From what Jackson has told me, all the work has been done by him, Matilda and Leanna. And the entire responsibility for everyone's survival fell on Leanna's shoulders."

214

Jennifer was still not exactly sure of what he was trying to say, but she had heard admiration in his voice when he'd spoken about Leanna. Have I been wrong to believe he isn't in love with her? she wondered, puzzled as to why the thought made her depressed.

David began to feel badly about the way he had talked to Jennifer. Why did he keep finding fault with her? He loved her! No man could love a woman as much as he loved her. Sorry for the way he had treated her, he mumbled apologetically, "I realize you have your hands full taking care of Bradley and Matthew, and I'm sure you'd have offered to help Leanna if it hadn't been for the boys."

Feeling pangs of guilt, Jennifer queried him carefully. "Are you insinuating that I haven't done my part?"

Impulsively, David asked, "Have you considered letting Louise help take care of the boys so you'll have more time?"

"More time for what?" she questioned sharply, flustered.

"To help with all the work!" he replied with a sternness he hadn't intended to use.

Sudden tears came to Jennifer's eyes, and stepping forward, David tentatively pulled her into his embrace. Drawing her close, he murmured, "Forgive me, Jennifer. I have no right to judge you."

Her arms went about his neck, and she placed her head on his shoulder. Her wonderful closeness was almost more than David could bear, and he was tempted to confess his love. Relishing the feel of her in his arms, he envisioned himself tasting her sweet

215

lips, caressing her breasts, then entering the softness between her legs, finding the heaven he had dreamed of for years. His manhood responded to his fantasy, and Jennifer could feel him grow hard against her thighs. For a moment, she pressed herself to him, enjoying his erection that was no so solid she could actually feel, through her clothes, the way it throbbed for relief. Suddenly ashamed because she believed she was behaving like a trollop, Jennifer pushed herself out of his arms. Stepping back and blushing, she said, "David . . . I—"

Interrupting her, he apologized, "I'm sorry, Jennifer. But it's been a long time since I held a woman in my arms."

Against her own volition, Jennifer's gaze dropped to the hardness straining against his trousers. The sight of his arousal made her desire him with an agonizing ache. Abashed by her own feelings, she hastily excused herself and hurried toward the back yard to find Matilda.

Spotting Matilda leaning over a huge washtub, vigorously rubbing a pair of Bradley's trousers against a scrub board, Jennifer asked as she approached, "Matilda, why haven't you prepared lunch?"

Letting the trousers slip from her hands and fall back into the water, Matilda replied with surprise, "Why, Miz Jennifer, I's been so busy with all this washin' that I completely forgot about lunch. Miz Anna always helped me on washday, and I's used to gettin' this laundry done in half the time. I'll tend to lunch just as soon as I finish here."

Remembering her conversation with David, Jennifer replied, "The boys are taking a nap, so I'll help you, Matilda."

The servant looked at her wide-eyed. "What did you say, Miz Jennifer?"

"I said that I'll help you. What do you want me to do?"

Astounded by Jennifer's offer, Matilda said hesitantly, "This basket of laundry needs to be hung on the clothesline."

Stepping to the filled basket, Jennifer lifted it and carried it to the clothesline a few feet away. Placing the basket on the ground, she removed a shirt and two clothespins. Turning, and finding that Matilda was still staring at her with amazement, Jennifer asked, "Do you hang a shirt by the shoulders or the tail?"

Laughing pleasantly, Matilda answered, "It don't really matter, Miz Jennifer. But if you hang it by the shirttail, it'll dry faster, 'cause it's spread out."

Smiling, Jennifer decided, "Then I shall hang it by the tail." Swerving back to the clothesline, she caught sight of David and Jackson heading toward the woods. Jackson was pushing a wheelbarrow loaded with the tools they would need to repair the corral.

Noticing her, David paused to wave, and she could tell by his expression that he was pleased to see she was helping Matilda. His approval gave her a warm feeling, and returning his wave, she called happily, "As soon as Matilda and I finish the laundry, we'll fix lunch, so be back in about an hour."

"We will!" David replied loudly. "And by then we'll be ravenous!"

Going to Jennifer's side, Matilda asked with disbelief, "Miz Jennifer, did you say you was goin' to help me fix lunch?"

"Yes, I did," Jennifer answered determinedly, and recalling David's advice, she added, "Louise can watch the boys."

"Miz Jennifer, is you feelin' all right?" Matilda asked warily.

"I'm just fine, Matilda," replied Jennifer good-humoredly.

Matilda returned to her washing, but she paused to ask, "How long do you think Miz Anna will be gone?"

"I don't know, but I got the distinct impression from Major Clayton that she would be gone only a couple of days."

"Then she should've been home by now," Matilda uttered gravely. "I's worried about Miz Anna. . . . Oh Lawdy, I hope nothin' has happened to her." Sighing heavily, she repeated, "I's awfully worried about her!"

Leanna dipped her hands into the wash basin, scrubbing them thoroughly. She had just finished assisting Dr. Hamilton in surgery, but the patient hadn't been seriously wounded, and Leanna's mood was cheery.

Approaching her quietly, Dr. Hamilton touched her shoulder as he suggested, "Why don't you get some rest? You've been working steadily since early this morning."

Leanna was tired, and she was also longing for a bath. Thinking about the shallow place in the river where Jeff had taken her, she answered gratefully,

"Thank you, Dr. Hamilton." Hastily, she dried her hands, deciding to go to her tent for a change of clothes and the bar of soap and towel. This time she'd be sure not to foolishly wade into deep water.

Anticipating a cool bath, Leanna stepped briskly outside, pausing to breathe in the fresh air. The smell of chloroform that always filled the operating tent still lingered in her nostrils and clung to her dress.

The camp was active. Many soldiers moved about as Leanna walked away from the operating tent, anxious to shed her clothes and enjoy a refreshing bath. The change in the atmosphere didn't register all at once with Leanna; it came to her slowly and vaguely, causing her rapid steps to gradually slow. Halting, she glanced around the campsite, wondering what was different. The reason dawned on her suddenly, making her inhale sharply. The camp area, as always, was busy, in an orderly hubbub, but the sounds of guns firing in the distance had ceased. Thinking back, she realized she hadn't heard any firing for an hour or longer, but she had been so preoccupied assisting Dr. Hamilton that the silence had escaped her notice. Apparently, the battle at the ford of the river was over, and the Union troops would now victoriously cross the Chattahoochee— probably in the morning, Leanna thought, and I will be sent back home. Oh Jeff! . . . Will I ever see you again after tomorrow, or will you vanish from my life?

As Leanna continued on to her tent, a commotion at the edge of the camp caught her attention. Many of the nearby soldiers had begun moving in the direction of the disturbance, and Leanna joined them, wondering if the men who had been fighting were returning. There will probably be wounded among them, she thought, resigning herself to returning immediately to the operating tent to aid Dr. Hamilton. She hoped Jeff would be one of the soldiers coming back to the camp so she could see him before she had to assist the doctor. She also uttered a quick prayer that Jeff wouldn't be one of the wounded or one of the fatalities.

A congested crowd had gathered, but the soldiers stepped aside for Leanna, and she made her way to the front of the large group of spectators.

When Leanna saw the reason why the soldiers were assembling, she couldn't stop the tears that filled her eyes, overflowing and trickling down her cheeks. Trying to clear her vision, she blinked repeatedly as she brushed at the streaming teardrops.

For two days, Leanna had heard the ominous sounds of battle and had assiduously nursed the wounded. But, until this moment, she had managed to mentally avoid picturing the soldiers opposing the Union Army. Attentively, she helped Dr. Hamilton save the lives of his patients, and not once had she let herself think of the patients as her enemy. She had blocked from her mind the fact that their wounds had come from Confederate weapons.

Crying sorrowfully, Leanna could no longer protect her emotions by eluding grim reality. Entering the Union camp under heavy guard were captured Confederate soldiers. They were walking three or four abreast, and the long procession passed slowly before Leanna's eyes. Watching the defeated men through her tears, Leanna's heart broke for her

Southern comrades. These men were fellow Confederates! They had been fighting to save her homeland, to protect her family and other Southern families from the Union invaders. Now, they were prisoners of war and would be sent North. For these brave soldiers the fighting was over, and all that awaited them was the depravity of prison.

Becoming aware of a horseman riding past the prisoners, Leanna turned her eyes away from the Confederates to watch the rider approach. She knew who he was; she had once caught a glimpse of him from her bedroom window and had distinctly heard his voice in the study at The Pines.

Seeing Leanna, he pulled up his horse, and the spirited animal pranced nervously as the man held him on a tight rein. Looking down at her, he tipped his hat and spoke amicably, "Miss Weston, I hope you are well." She was surprised that he knew who she was, and reading her thoughts, he continued, "Major Clayton explained your presence to me." When she didn't offer a response, he proceeded. "In case you aren't aware of who is addressing you, let me introduce myself."

Interrupting, she said, "That won't be necessary." With loathing, she added, "I know who you are. Sherman!"

General Sherman was an imposing figure of a man with a regal appearance. Studying Leanna thoughtfully, he replied, "You speak my name as though it were the plague."

"You are the plague to the state of Georgia!" she stated bitterly, lifting her chin haughtily.

"You Southerners are very arrogant, aren't you?" he

221

baited her. "Too arrogant for your own good. You were so wrapped up in your own arrogance that you believed you could win a war with it."

"You are talking as though the war were over," she replied coldly.

"Figuratively speaking it is over. Only one thing is holding the Confederacy together—arrogance."

"Not arrogance, General Sherman, but pride!" she remarked.

"Pride?" he questioned. "Perhaps, but pride cannot win a war any more than arrogance. It only prolongs it."

"Warmongers, like yourself, are probably, enjoying this extended war."

"Contrary to popular Southern belief, I am not a warmonger, but I did not join this war to win a popularity contest, as you Southerners will find out when Atlanta falls and then Savannah." Once again, he tipped his hat, then, slapping the reins against his horse's neck, he rode away.

For a moment, Leanna glared at his departing back with contempt before turning to watch the Confederate prisoners who were still filing into the Union camp. Her personal grudge against the general made her dislike him immensely. He had ordered her home burned, and for that she would always despise him. There had been no reason to destroy her home, the Westons had no sons or fathers fighting in the Confederacy, and leaving her family homeless would not hasten the end of the war.

The wounded Confederate soldiers were bringing up the rear of the procession, and Leanna's tears returned as she watched the injured men, some of them were struggling into the camp without assistance while others leaned on comrades or were carried on stretchers.

Recognizing one of the soldiers helping to carry a stretcher, Leanna rushed forward. "Charles!" she called excitedly. "Charles Knowlton!"

Halting, the soldier gaped at Leanna, shocked to find her in a Union camp.

Charles was bearing the front part of the stretcher, his hands gripping the two extended poles. His back was facing the wounded soldier, and Leanna could not see the man on the stretcher as she quickly approached Charles.

"Leanna!" he exclaimed. "What in the world are you doing here?"

She smiled fondly at Charles Knowlton. He had been a good friend of her brother's, and she had known Charles and his family all her life. But it had always been Charles's brother, Danny, that Leanna had liked best. She and Danny had been good friends as children, and as they had grown older, their friendship had lasted.

"What are you doing here?" Charles repeated incredibly.

"It's a long story. I've been held captive, but I'll be returning home soon," Leanna said hastily. "Charles, when did you last see Danny and was he well?"

A lump rose to his throat, and swallowing heavily, he answered, "Danny's on the stretcher."

Leanna moved to step around him, but he stopped her by saying gravely, "I don't think Danny's goin' to make it."

"I'll get Doctor Hamilton! He'll help Danny!" she

decided quickly.

Charles shook his head, mumbling, "I'm afraid it's too late for a doctor to save him. I think Danny's dying."

Leanna's legs began to tremble as she moved around Charles to reach the stretcher. Danny's arms were lying at his sides, and placing a hand on one of his, she whispered tearfully, "Oh Danny . . . Danny." His eyes were closed, and when he didn't respond to her touch, she hoped he was only unconscious.

Without warning, Dr. Hamilton appeared at her side, and moving professionally, he checked Danny for vital signs. Sighing deeply, he asked Leanna, "Do you know this soldier?"

"Yes," she answered shakily.

"I'm sorry, my dear, but he's dead," the doctor replied tenderly.

Leanna turned and faced Charles, but he still had his back to the stretcher. She wondered if he'd heard the doctor's words, and she moved to stand in front of him. He was staring straight ahead, apparently at nothing in particular. His expression was devoid of emotion, and only the tears filling his eyes proved to Leanna that he knew his younger brother had died.

She longed to say something to console him; but, dearest God, what could she say that would bring him comfort? Fighting back her own tears, she stepped back to the stretcher, and taking one last look at Danny, she pulled the top blanket up and over his face.

Speaking to the soldier holding the other end of the stretcher, Dr. Hamilton said, "The burial detail is to your right."

Apparently, Charles had also heard the doctor's

directions, because as he began walking, he headed toward his right.

"Miss Weston," Dr. Hamilton began, "General Sherman has informed me that there is only one Confederate doctor with the prisoners, so he asked me to help take care of the wounded. But if you are too upset to assist me, I understand."

"Sherman asked a Union doctor to take care of Confederate soldiers?" she asked with disbelief.

Knowing the reason behind her incredulity, he smiled as he answered, "Miss Weston, General Sherman is a man with compassion, regardless of what you may believe."

Confused, Leanna sighed, "I don't understand this war, nor do I understand the men who are fighting it."

"My dear," he said gently, "if you find the answers, let me know for I am just as perplexed as you are." Looking over the wounded who were still entering the camp in multitudes, he added solemnly, "Americans killing Americans, and brother killing brother! My God, what a waste!" Turning back to Leanna, he set aside his melancholy and asked briskly, "Are you up to helping me?"

Suppressing her own unhappiness, Leanna squared her slender shoulders, and standing tall, she replied, "Yes, of course I'm able to assist you."

Dr. Hamilton gave her an admiring glance before walking over to the wounded. As Leanna followed him her thoughts turned to Jeff. *Where is he? Is he well? Oh, God*, she prayed, *please keep him safe!*

Chapter Fifteen

Leanna was extremely fatigued as she moved list-lessly through the Union camp. She had spent the entire afternoon helping Dr. Hamilton with the wounded prisoners. During the past two days when she had assisted the doctor with the Union soldiers, it had taken great self-control on her part to remain strong and keep her emotions in check; but it had taken twice as much willpower for Leanna to keep her composure when she had aided Dr. Hamilton as he operated on the Confederates who had been seriously wounded. Their deaths and suffering had affected more deeply.

Strolling wearily, Leanna looked about the camp, hoping to spot Jeff. When she failed to catch sight of him, she sighed with disappointment. Hastily, she scanned her surroundings, looking for Paul or Jerry. Perhaps one of them would know where she could find Jeff. But her former guards were not in sight.

The sun was setting, and long shadows were falling across the landscape. If she hurried she could still reach the river and take a quick bath before it grew too dark.

Forcing her tired legs to move faster, Leanna left the Union campsite, and when she arrived at her tent, she gathered up a change of clothes, plus the soap and towel.

Trudging into the woods, she continued to travel as quickly as her weariness would allow. Reaching the place in the river where Jeff had taken her, she placed her articles on the ground. Her tired muscles ached as she slipped out of her clothes, and trying to ease her discomfort, she stretched gracefully before picking up the bar of soap and wading into the refreshing water.

Sitting in the shallows, she began immediately to soap herself. The sun had already descended over the horizon, and dusk was quickly settling. She was wondering if she had time to wash her hair, when out of the corner of her eye she caught sight of a figure emerging from the nearby woods. Frightened, she crossed her arms over her bare breasts as she looked toward the riverbank. Then, releasing the breath she had been holding, she smiled as she watched Jeff ambling to the water's edge.

"Jeff!" she cried. "I've been so worried about you! I haven't seen you all day!"

He had been involved in a skirmish on the south side of the Chattahoochee and farther inland, but the battle was not one he wished to discuss with Leanna. Removing his hat, he placed it on the ground; then he unbuckled his holster. "I thought this was where I might find you." Grinning wryly, he asked, "Mind if I join you?"

Thrilled that he intended to bathe with her, she replied pertly, "Only if you promise to wash my back."

Unbuttoning his shirt, he cocked an eyebrow as he answered, "Miss Weston, it will be my pleasure to wash every inch of your lovely body."

Imagining his hands touching her everywhere, Leanna's pulse quickened with anticipation. Totally entranced with Jeff, she watched boldly as he slipped out of his clothes, and in the approaching twilight, his masculine physique was revealed. Leisurely, she let her eyes trail over his strong frame, admiring the dark curly hair that covered his wide chest and tapered to his flat stomach. Lowering her vision, her gaze centered on his manhood, where she could see that her intense scrutiny was obviously having a stimulating effect on him.

Stepping into the water, he said lightly, "You'll have to excuse my apparent need, but that seems to happen quite often when I'm in your presence." Holding out his hand, he asked, "May I borrow the soap?" She gave it to him, and he waded into deeper water before thoroughly sudsing and rinsing himself. Returning, he pitched the bar of soap onto the bank. Then, taking her hand, he drew her to her feet. "Let's go for a swim," he suggested.

"But what about the current?" she stammered.

"The river isn't swift like it was the other day," he explained.

"I'm not a very good swimmer," she reminded him.

"I'll be with you," he replied. "I won't let you drown."

His presence always made her feel safe so, trustingly, she allowed him to lead her farther into the river. When they approached the steep drop-off, Jeff plunged into the rippling river, then treading water, he offered her his hand. She accepted it, and he easily pulled her into the deep water. Leanna tensed, expecting to feel the strong current trying to pull her down into its depths, but she soon realized that Jeff had been right. The river was now placid and calm.

At first, Leanna's inexperience caused her to swim awkwardly, but with Jeff's guidance, she soon learned to swim smoothly. The cool water was relaxing as it flowed against her bare flesh, and her tired body began to feel rejuvenated.

By the time they decided to return to shallow water, it was completely dark, and the moon was shining.

Wading through the water at her side, Jeff told her, "Stay here."

"But why?" she asked, confused.

"I promised to wash you, remember?"

She started to tell him it wasn't necessary, but before she could, he moved quickly to the bank and retrieved the bar of soap. Returning, he dipped the soap into the water, then rubbed it vigorously between his hands, sudsing them sufficiently. Pitching the bar back onto the bank, he turned to Leanna. Placing his soapy hands on her shoulders, he slid them down her arms and to her finger tips. Moving slowly, he cupped his hands over her full breasts, caressing them gently as his thumbs moved circularly across her nipples.

His sensual movements were heavenly, and Leanna swayed provocatively under his tender but passionately exciting touch.

His hands went to her back, where he let them glide down smoothly to her rounded buttocks, his sudsy hands leaving a thin trail of soap behind them.

Kneeling, he ran his palms softly over her stomach, her thighs, and then down the length of her slender legs. He had intentionally saved the best part of her delectable body for last. To help steady her, he grasped her hip with one hand before placing the other on her womanhood. His initial touch caused Leanna to flinch, but as he continued to caress her feminine mound, a warm longing began flowing through her.

Gripping her wrist, he eased her down into the shallow water. Sitting on the river bottom, he supported her head in the cradle of his arm, and she nestled her face against his shoulder. She stretched out, and he splashed water over her, rinsing away the soap that had lingered on her velvety skin.

Cuddling her to his chest, he gazed down into her face, and bending his head, he placed his lips on hers, kissing her with a passion so intense that Leanna responded by taking one of his hands and moving it to her womanhood, her desire to feel him touching her where her fervent longing was pinpointed overwhelming. She continued to kiss him and moved her lips in perfect rhythm with his stimulating probing.

"Leanna . . . Leanna, my beautiful darling," he murmured ardently before standing and carrying her to the riverbank. Placing her on her feet, he quickly spread out the large towel; then, easing her down onto it, he stretched out at her side.

"Jeff," she began tentatively, "are we safe here? No one will find us?"

"I doubt it," he answered. "But if you'd rather, we can go to your tent."

"No," she decided. "I want to make love here under the stars, and not in my tent on a confining cot."

"My thoughts exactly," he uttered agreeably, leaning over her to press his lips demandingly against hers. His hand returned to her mound, which was already moist with desire for him, and his touch intensified her need for him so that Leanna trembled with ecstasy.

Moving his hand to her thigh, he urged her to lie on her side, then he placed her leg over his waist. She was now open to him, and he slid easily into her warm depths.

His entry sent chills up her spine, and she moaned with pleasure.

Placing his hand against her buttocks, he pressed her closer, causing him to penetrate her deeply. "Leanna," he murmured. "You're so beautiful . . . . God, I could love you like this for an eternity and still want more of you."

He began thrusting strongly against her, and as she felt him moving in and out, Leanna began to float on a cloud of total rapture.

Suddenly, he withdrew, startling her, and eased her onto her back. Kneeling between her spread legs, he grasped her hips and turned her over. Encircling her waist with one arm, he raised her to her knees.

Leanna was shocked by this strange position, but before she could protest, she felt his manhood plunge deeply within her.

Clutching her thighs, he pulled her back against him, causing him to slide so far inside her that Leanna moaned aloud with pleasure.

Resting on his knees, he pounded rapidly into her, and balancing herself on her crossed arms, Leanna pushed her buttocks against him. Moving his hand from her thigh and past her stomach, he found the core of her being. As his finger stimulated her, he continued to thrust his hardness into her female warmness.

Leanna became so intensely aroused that she met his powerful thrusting with a passion that equaled his own.

Totally oblivious to everything but the pleasure they were giving and receiving, Leanna and Jeff reached fulfillment simultaneously experiencing a completeness both satisfying and beautiful.

Breathing heavily, Jeff fell to one side of the towel, and lying flat on his back, he sighed contentedly, "Leanna, you are one hell of a woman."

Stretching out at his side, she asked hopefully, "Do I please you, Jeff?"

He chuckled good-humoredly. "Please me? That's putting it mildly."

He drew her into his arms, and she rested her head against his shoulder. She waited a moment before asking the question that had been plaguing her since the battle had ended at the Chattahoochee River. "Jeff," she began, dreading their separation. "In the morning, are you sending me home?"

She didn't see the small frown that crossed his handsome face. Jeff was sure she was anxious to return to her family, and believing his answer would upset her, he replied hesitantly, "Leanna, I had originally planned to send you home with a military escort. It would be very unsafe for you to travel alone. But, today I received urgent orders from General Sherman, and my troops and I will be moving out at dawn. Because of these orders, I cannot afford men to make up an escort for you." He paused before continuing apologetically, "I'm sorry, Leanna, but you will have to ride with us. It will be impossible for me to send you back home until Atlanta has been taken."

Leanna's initial response was one of happiness because she would be with Jeff, but when her mother came to mind, she said with consternation, "But, Jeff, my mother will be so worried! She isn't well! For her sake, I must return home!"

"You can't go by yourself," he objected. "And I can't give you an escort. I have no alternative but to take you with me."

Thinking about her mother's failing health, Leanna sighed heavily, and Jeff mistook her sigh as one of disappointment because she had to remain with him and the Union Army. He couldn't really blame her for feeling the way she did, it had to be terribly difficult for Leanna to be constantly surrounded by Yankees.

"I talked to Doctor Hamilton before coming here," he began, changing the subject, "and he told me you helped him with the wounded Confederates. He also said that you knew one of the soldiers who died."

Unhappily, she murmured, "His name was Danny Knowlton. I'd known him all my life. His family has a plantation north of Marietta. Or at least they had a plantation. If Sherman rode past it on his way here, I doubt if it's still in existence."

"Speaking of Sherman, he is quite opposed to your presence."

"The feeling is mutual!" she said huffily.

Smiling, he continued, "He ordered me to send you into Atlanta when we neared the city, but I told him that I had faithfully promised your family I'd see that you were safely returned to your home. I think he was about to tell me what I could do with my promise, but Dr. Hamilton was present, and he quickly intervened on your behalf. Not even Sherman can win an argument with Dr. Hamilton."

Leanna laughed lightly. "I think I love Doctor Hamilton. He's a wonderful man, and I admire him very much."

"Should I be jealous?" Jeff asked teasingly. "Is the doctor giving me competition?"

"Since you brought up the subject of jealousy and competition, why don't you tell me about your fiancée?"

"Fiancée?" he said vaguely as though the word were completely foreign.

"You told me you were engaged," she reminded him.

"What do you want to know about her?" he asked unemotionally.

"Anything," she answered nonchalantly, although she was extremely curious about her rival.

"For instance?" he queried.

Impatient with his toying questions, she snapped, "Jeff Clayton, must you behave like a typical man?"

His expression cocky, he queried, "A typical man?

Isn't that how I am supposed to behave? The last time I checked, I'm quite sure I was of the male sex." Raising up on his elbows, and glancing down at his anatomy, he nodded, "Yeah, I'm still a man."

Laughing, she clutched his shoulders and shoved him back down onto the towel. Leaning over him, her curiosity even more aroused, she demanded, "Stop avoiding my question and tell me about your fiancée."

"Well," he began, as though he were bored with the whole idea, "her name is Darlene Whitlock. We became engaged quite suddenly and were planning a hasty marriage, but her father died unexpectedly, so we postponed our wedding. Shortly thereafter, the war broke out, and I joined the army."

When he stopped speaking, she sighed with exasperation, "You didn't tell me anything that I really wanted to know."

"I didn't?" he asked innocently.

Forgetting indiscretion, she asked rapidly, "Is she pretty? Do you love her? Does she love you? Why didn't you marry her before you joined the army?"

Chuckling, he drew her down against him. "I will try to answer your questions in order. Yes, Darlene is very pretty. No, I'm not in love with her. I don't know if she is in love with me. I didn't marry her before I joined the army because I simply had no wish to legally tie the knot."

"But you didn't break off the engagement?" she asked, inwardly thrilled that he wasn't in love with Darlene.

"No," he replied softly. "I should have, but I didn't."

"If you didn't love her, why did you ask her to marry you?"

"I had been dating Darlene, but I didn't want our relationship to be a serious one, although I distinctly got the impression that she hoped we were heading for the altar. One night, I had been drinking with a friend named Darrin Spencer. Well, I had always prided myself on holding my liquor like a gentleman, but for some unexplainable reason that night the liquor hit me like a sledge hammer. I completely blacked out, and when I woke up, I found myself in Darlene's bed with her lying at my side and her father standing over us. Needless to say, I very quickly became engaged and a hasty wedding was on the agenda. The day before we were to be married, Darlene's father suffered a stroke and died. Naturally, the wedding was postponed. When the war started, Darlene was still in mourning. I joined the army, and she tearfully bid me goodbye, promising to write often."

"Does she write often?" Leanna asked.

"No, but neither do I," he mumbled. He paused for a moment before continuing, "Now that you know all about Darlene, why don't you tell me about your fiancé?"

"Fiancé?" she asked, her tone as vague as his had been when she had reminded him that he was engaged.

"David Farnsworth, in case you have forgotten his name." And so he refreshed her memory.

Answering as though her revelation was of little importance, she replied hastily, "David and I were never officially engaged, but our families have always

237

believed that someday we would marry."

"Then you aren't in love with him?" Jeff asked tensely.

"No," she murmured, wanting to tell Jeff that she had fallen hopelessly in love with him, but protecting her emotions, she decided not to confess her true feelings until or if—he told her that he loved her.

Rising, he reached down and, clasping her hand, pulled her to a standing position. "We'd better quit pressing our luck and get dressed before we're discovered."

Agreeing, she swiftly slipped into her clothes as he got into his uniform and then buckled on his holster.

"I'll walk you back; then I'll locate Jerry and Paul and tell them to bed down close to your tent."

"Am I still under guard?" she asked.

"No, they will be there strictly for your protection," he assured her.

"Jeff, how long will it take the Union to seize Atlanta?"

"I don't know, but it may take weeks."

"Weeks!" Leanna repeated. She was elated at the thought of spending so much time with Jeff, but at the same time she was exceedingly worried about her mother. Was her mother's health strong enough to hold up that long?

"Isn't there some way I can get word to my mother?" she inquired.

Aware of her concern, he said regretfully, "No, I'm sorry."

Gently, he took her into his arms, and appreciating his comforting embrace, Leanna held him close. She loved Jeff Clayton with all her heart, and she knew regardless of what might happen to them during these perilous times, she would continue to love him for the rest of her life.

Moving out of Darrin Spencer's arms, and rolling to one side of the bed, Darlene Whitlock stretched sensually. The window was open and the lace curtains were pulled back, allowing the light from the moon to filter into the room and fall across Darlene's naked flesh. Her passionate union with Darrin had left a thin film of perspiration on her skin, and the gentle breeze drifting through the room felt refreshingly cool. Reaching over to the lamp on the table beside her bed, she turned up the wick.

Lying on his side, Darrin rose upon one elbow. He was an extremely handsome man whose dark hair contrasted attractively with his blue eyes, and his body was trim and muscular. His gaze traveled slowly over Darlene's voluptuous curves. Aware that he was studying her, she stretched once again, her moves purposely bringing his attention to those parts of her body of which she was most proud of.

Darrin continued his scrutiny, although he knew her body as well as he knew his own for Darlene Whitlock had the kind of body a man could never grow tired of admiring. He heard a contented moan rise from deep in her throat as she continued her sensuous movements. She always reminded him of a tigress with her slanting green eyes, golden complexion, and raven black hair. Her soft moan sounded like a satisfied purr, and she stretched as lithely as a feline.

"Darling," she said in her husky, provocative voice,

"you should give up being a gambler and become a professional gigolo. You are a perfect lover." Sighing deeply, she embellished her statement. "An unequivocally perfect lover."

His dark eyes glittering with amusement, Darrin replied, "Darling, you should give up being a fortune hunter and become a professional prostitute. You are a perfect whore." Sighing, he added, "An unequivocally perfect whore."

Instantly her green eyes flashed with rage, and bolting straight up, she lashed out at him, trying to rake his face with her long fingernails. But moving quickly, he grabbed her wrists. Gripping her tightly, he said evenly, "Sheathe your claws, my tempestuous tigress. I am not your prey, he's somewhere in Georgia fighting Johnny Rebs."

"Don't you dare call me a whore!" she said between clenched teeth.

Impatient with her cant, he released her wrists and replied testily, "For God's sake, Darlene. I was merely calling the kettle black!"

"If I am a whore then you are a gigolo!" she retorted, springing from the bed with the gracefulness of a cat.

"That's quite true," he agreed, good-humoredly.

"If you are insinuating that you are my kept lover, then I think I should remind you that very soon you will be out of a job for my inheritance is almost gone, and my home is mortgaged to the hilt."

He watched her slip into a sheer dressing gown and walk to her vanity table. "You should've married the very prominent and wealthy Jeff Clayton before he left for the war," he mumbled.

Sitting on her velvet-covered stool and looking into the mirror, she began to brush her long, black hair. "I was in mourning, remember?" she reminded him sharply. "Besides, how was I to know that father wasn't as wealthy as I presumed? I believed I would be a rich heiress, but he only left me moderately well off. My inheritance would've lasted much longer if we hadn't foolishly gambled so much of it away."

"Well, maybe Jeff will be home soon, and if you can still get him to the altar, you will have all the riches you desire. I assume you will share your good fortune with me, naturally."

Catching his eye in the mirror, she asked acidly, "What do you mean, if I can get him to the altar?" And turning to face Darrin, she raised her hand to show him the diamond ring on her third finger. "Jeff and I are officially engaged."

"That was over two years ago," he replied casually. "A lot can happen to make a man change his mind in that amount of time." Leaving the bed, he began slipping into his clothes.

"Are you hinting that he might have fallen in love with someone else?"

Darrin gave her a half-smile, cocking his eyebrows.

"That's utterly ridiculous! He's fighting a war!"

"How do you know he isn't romancing a beautiful Southern belle?" he taunted. Chuckling, he added, "You have heard of Southern hospitality, haven't you?"

Leaping to her feet, Darlene fumed, "You are only saying these things because you love to upset me!"

Sitting on the edge of the bed, he began to put on his shoes. "How long has it been since you last wrote

241

to Jeff?"

Flustered, she stammered, "I don't know . . . but it's been a long time. You know I hate to write letters."

"If you still want to sink your claws into Jeff, then I suggest that you start writing him on a regular basis. Make him believe he has a faithful fiancée awaiting his return."

Pacing, Darlene replied exasperatedly, "Of course I still intend to marry him, and I will take your advice and start writing. This war can't last much longer. I can still manage financially for another year, two at the most, and surely by then those moronic Confederates will have surrendered." Wringing her hands apprehensively, she continued gravely, "Good Lord, I hope Jeff isn't killed; then I'll never have his money!"

"You could always make a play for his uncle," Darrin offered flippantly.

"That stringent old bastard!" she scowled. "I could seduce a priest easier than I could seduce Walter Clayton."

Standing, Darrin stated, "Well, I think that stringent old bastard, as you call him, is getting wise to you."

"Why do you think that?"

He shrugged insouciantly. "Oh, just little hints he's dropped at the club."

"Well, he doesn't know anything for sure," Darlene said firmly. "When Jeff returns, it'll simply be his word against mine, and when I want to, I can be very convincing."

"If I were you, I'd start being more discreet about my illicit affairs," Darrin said as he finished getting

242

dressed.

Moving seductively, she stepped over to him, and sliding her arms about his neck, she murmured innocently, "Affairs? Darling, you know you are the only man who shares my bed."

"That's because I am the only lover you allow in your home. You share hotel beds with the others."

Darlene pouted attractively. "If you asked me to give up my other lovers, I would."

Removing her arms from his neck, he answered calmly, "Darlene, I don't care how many men you fornicate with, so long as you continue to spread your legs for me."

"You contemptible bastard!" she spat shrewishly. "Maybe when I marry Jeff, I won't want to see you any more! Has that possibility crossed your mind?"

Moving speedily, he clutched her shoulders, his grip tightening painfully. "You'll continue to see me for two reasons. One, because I'm the only man who can completely satisfy your sexual desires, so you'll be at my beck and call until I grow tired of you. Two, if you try to dump me after you're Mrs. Jeff Clayton, I'll blackmail you."

"Blackmail!" she said skeptically. "Do you plan to tell Jeff about my lovers? What I do before we are married will not be grounds for an annulment. Besides, he thinks he is the one who took my virginity, and if need be, I will conveniently remind him."

"The night he supposedly slipped into your bedroom and forced himself on you?" he asked.

"Yes," Darlene confirmed smugly.

"If you marry Jeff, then try to stop seeing me, I'll go to him and tell him the truth about that night.

He'll have all the grounds he needs for an annulment, if he doesn't decide to kill you instead."

"You wouldn't dare tell him the truth!" she hissed.

Releasing her, he replied with certainty, "I would most assuredly confess everything. If I can't share in your marital wealth, then I will see to it that you don't get a pittance of his money."

"He might decide to kill you too! Jeff has a violent temper!"

He shrugged unconcernedly. "I'm willing to take my chances." Ambling to the bedroom door, he continued with an air of nonchalance, "I'll be back later tonight. While I'm gone, I strongly suggest that you write your rich fiancé who is off fighting the war, and most likely, fighting it very heroically."

Darrin's threat of blackmail had upset Darlene. She was afraid of Jeff's explosive temper; one night she had seen it burst forth. It hadn't been aimed at her, but she had been present when he'd unleashed it on a man who had worked on one of the riverboats.

She and Jeff had had a date for the theater, but first he'd had a short business meeting with a steamboat captain. Before boarding the boat, he had ordered their public conveyance to wait for them. When Jeff had concluded his business and they had returned to where the carriage was supposed to be waiting, it had been gone. The nearest street was a good distance from the riverbank, and as they walked toward it to hail another cab, Jeff had detected a muffled cry coming from behind a large collection of packed crates that were to be loaded onto one of the boats. Investigating the sound, Jeff had come upon a man attempting rape. Violently, he had pulled the

244

man from his victim, but when Jeff had seen the girl was a child no older than thirteen, his temper had erupted.

Darlene shivered, remembering that Jeff had nearly beaten the man to death before finally backing off and delivering him to the police. Then he had taken the girl home, and when he'd found that she and her family were destitute, he had not only given her father employment but had also advanced him a considerable amount of money. Darlene frowned irritably as she recalled that Jeff had completely forgotten they were supposed to attend the theater. He had spent the evening talking and drinking ale with the girl's father, while she had been forced to sit in a hovel of a home and try to converse with people she considered far below her. Oh, that evening had been so humiliating! How could Jeff have been so inconsiderate of her feelings as to expect her to socialize with her inferiors?

"Jeff's charity and his brotherly attitude!" she said bitterly. "Well, when I marry him, such foolishness will end!" If I marry him, she suddenly thought and then wished Darrin hadn't placed the doubt in her mind. Surely Darrin would never tell Jeff what really happened when Father found us in bed together, she worried. Not even Darrin Spencer could be so reckless as to purposely arouse Jeff's temper!

Chapter Sixteen

When Leanna had first learned that she would continue to ride with Jeff and his troops, she had been thrilled by the prospect of spending more time with Jeff, but she soon learned that his time was taken up with military responsibilities. Their moments together were few and far between.

Once again Jeff's battalion rendezvoused with Colonel Andrews', and they set up a joint camp close to the city of Atlanta. Shortly thereafter, General Sherman and his massive army arrived.

Hospital and operating tents were hastily erected, and Leanna returned to nursing the wounded and assisting Dr. Hamilton. From dawn until dusk, as the Northern invaders attempted to take Atlanta, the sounds of the battle could be heard in the near distance. Like a threatening thunderstorm they rumbled over the Union campsite.

Carrying a water bucket, Leanna walked beside the filled cots in the hospital tent, stopping often to give a thirsty patient a drink.

Pausing beside the soldier who had been her first patient, she put down the bucket, and taking the cup that he kept next to his bed, she rinsed it out, then filled it with water. He was awake and was watching her with unmistakable admiration. Leaning over him, Leanna helped him to sit up, then she held the cup to his dry lips.

The soldier had been seriously injured, and his condition was still critical. Leanna was amazed, but thankful, that he had survived the move from the Chattahoochee River. The wagons used as ambulances had traveled with General Sherman, and although they had moved at a slow pace, the trip had been extremely dangerous for the men who were severely wounded.

Carefully, she eased him back down onto the cot. The temperature inside the tent was becoming unbearably warm, and perspiration beaded his face. Leaving the bucket, Leanna hurried to one end of the tent, where clean cloths and extra basins were stacked on a table. Quickly she filled one of the basins with water; then, taking a cloth, she returned to the young soldier. Placing the basin on the ground, she soaked the cloth with water. Wringing it out, she bent over his cot, and gently sponged his face and arms.

"Miss Weston," he said weakly, "you are an angel from Dixie."

Leanna smiled, he had called her an angel from Dixie so often that the other soldiers had begun to call her Dixie's Angel. The title flattered Leanna, but she also found it a little embarrassing.

She moved to return the basin and cloth, but, feebly, the soldier reached over and caught her hand.

"Miss Weston," he whispered hoarsely, "please stay and talk to me a moment."

She didn't really have time to chat, but unable to resist the plea in his eyes, she conceded tenderly, "All right, but only for a few minutes. There are a lot of thirsty patients waiting."

"I won't keep you for long," the young man promised sincerely. He patted one side of the cot. "Please sit down."

She did as he asked, sitting gently and trying not to cause him any discomfort when her added weight made the cot give a little.

"Miss Weston," he began, and she could tell that it was an effort for him to find the strength to talk. "Would you please do me a favor?"

"Yes, of course," she answered. Leanna and the soldier were unaware of the man who had paused close by to listen to their conversation.

"I don't have any family except for my mother. Major Clayton has her address. Will you ask him for it so that you can write a letter to my mom?"

"Why do you want me to write your mother? Soon you'll be well enough to write her yourself."

He shook his head, mumbling, "No, I'm not goin' to get well. Dr. Hamilton hasn't told me that I'm dyin', but I can see it in his eyes when he looks at me." Suddenly, he began to cough, and the violent spell racked his weakened body. Moving swiftly, Leanna placed an arm behind his shoulders, helping him to sit up. Gasping convulsively, he temporarily cleared his congested lungs.

She assisted him back down; then, once again, she washed his face. Leanna and the soldier were still not aware of the man standing in the background and eavesdropping.

"Miss Weston," he continued raspingly, "Major Clayton will write to mom, but he'll only write that I died with honor and . . . and . . ." He had to rest for a moment before he could continue, "If you write to mom, you'll write to her as a woman. I know you will tell her what she'd really want to know."

Leanna nodded compassionately. Yes, she could write the kind of letter he was referring to, one telling his mother that her son was a fine gentleman and expressing all the sentiments she would want to hear. It wasn't a letter she wanted to write, for she could already imagine how painful the sad task would be. "Yes," she murmured. "I'll write to your mother."

"Promise?" he pleaded desperately.

"I promise," she acquiesced.

"Soldier, you are a quitter!" The authoritative voice came from behind Leanna. Startled, she glanced over her shoulder, and seeing General Sherman, she realized he had been listening to their conversation. Quickly, she rose to her feet.

Stepping closer to the cot and standing at Leanna's side, the imposing general continued briskly, "Only a quitter writes his own epitaph. Young man, you must fight death with a perseverance that befits a good soldier. I don't want to hear any more talk about dying." Turning, General Sherman ordered a passing medic to bring him a chair. He placed his hand on Leanna's arm and his touch made her tense, but if the general was aware of her response, he didn't let on. Urging her to the soldier's cot, he said firmly, "Sit down, Miss Weston."

Complying, she returned to the cot, and she and the soldier looked on with astonishment as the general took the requested chair from the medic, turned it around, straddled it, and folded his arms over the straight back. He looked severely at Leanna, then to the soldier. "Now," he began emphatically, "we will have no more talk of death. We will discuss life!"

Leanna stole a quick glance at the young soldier. She could tell that he was in awe because the famous General Sherman had singled him out, and was actually giving him his time and undivided attention.

"We will begin with you, Miss Weston," the general ordered evenly.

Meeting his inflexible gaze and wishing he wasn't making her feel self-conscious, she stammered, "Wh-what?"

He smiled, but Leanna wasn't sure if it was a mocking smile or merely a friendly response. "Miss Weston, I can't believe you are actually stuttering. The other day, you had no difficulty speaking in my presence. In fact, if my memory is correct, you spoke quite strongly." Tauntingly, he asked, "So why do you now hesitate? Where is your Southern arrogance? Or as you preferred to call it, your Southern pride?"

The soldier admired General Sherman, but to hear him speak unkindly to the gentle Miss Weston angered him. "Sir, in all respect, I must ask you not to speak so rudely to Miss Weston."

As though he were greatly offended, and considered the soldier's remark disrespectful, the general asked demandingly, "Why?"

"Why, sir?" the soldier asked hesitantly.

Impatiently, Sherman insisted, "Why don't you

want me to speak rudely to Miss Weston?"

Stammering, the soldier replied, "Because she is compassionate and a very nice lady."

"Does it anger you to lie there dying, while your angel from Dixie is treated rudely?"

Feeling rage flow through his body and overcome his weakness, he answered, "Yes, sir. It bothers me very much."

"Good!" the general declared. "That means there's still a spark of life somewhere in that body of yours that only a few minutes ago you had resigned to six feet under the ground. Now that I have kindled your anger, which made you forget you were dying, let me revive your passion. Look closely at Miss Weston. Doesn't the sight of a beautiful woman make you long to live?"

"Yes, sir," the young man sighed.

"What is your name, soldier?"

"John Copeland," he replied.

"John, do you have a sweetheart?" the general asked informally.

"Yes, but we aren't engaged. When I return home, I plan to ask her to marry me."

"When you return home?" General Sherman pondered. "Soldier, are you telling me that you'll live to go home?"

He smiled faintly, and a trace of tears came to his eyes as he answered quietly, "Yes, sir, I want to live to go home."

Understanding the general's tactics, Leanna knew he was right. If this soldier was going to survive, he had to fight to live. She and the general must remind him of all the reasons why he shouldn't give up, and

252

his sweetheart was only one of many.

Halting a medic, Leanna asked him to take the water bucket and give the other patients their drinks. Then giving the general and the soldier her full attention, she began talking about the good things in life, things which are always taken for granted.

The general offered many of his own comments, and the conversation inspired the young soldier, but his condition was critical and only through his own determination to live, and by the grace of God, would he survive.

As Leanna and General Sherman were leaving, the general assured the soldier, "As soon as you are well enough the make a long trip, you will be given a medical discharge. Before you know it, you'll be back home proposing to your sweetheart."

"Thank you, sir," he replied, before closing his eyes and drifting into much-needed sleep.

Placing Leanna's hand in the crook of his arm, the general asked, "May I talk to you for a moment?"

"Yes," she consented, allowing him to escort her through the huge tent. As they stepped outside, he released her, and pausing, he apologized, "Forgive me for talking rudely to you earlier."

"You don't need to apologize," she answered reservedly. "I understood your motive."

Noting her coolness, he watched her contemplatively as he asked, "Tell me, Miss Weston, if I were gravely wounded, would you show me the same compassion you show John Copeland and the other soldiers?"

"Yes, I would," she answered truthfully.

"Why?" he queried.

"You would be one of my patients," she replied simply.

He smiled. "A very honest and tactful reply. Miss Weston, are you aware that my men refer to you as the Dixie's Angel?"

"Yes," she murmured, wishing he hadn't mentioned it.

He could see a blush rising to her cheeks. "Does the title embarrass you?"

"A little," she admitted.

"It also makes you feel guilty, does it not?"

"Sometimes I feel like a traitor to the Confederacy," she confessed rashly.

"Don't plague yourself with needless guilt, Miss Weston. It is not treacherous to try to save human life. Are we not our brother's keepers?"

Leanna gave a short bitter laugh. "Our brother's keepers? Brother is killing brother in this merciless and cruel war!"

He offered no comment. What could he say that wouldn't be redundant? He was wholeheartedly in accord with her statement. "As soon as I can afford men to make up an escort you will be returned safely to your home and family."

"Home!" she retorted resentfully, her personal grudge against the general surging forth. "My family is living in the overseer's house. You ordered our home burned to the ground!"

"That's true," he agreed calmly. "But keep in mind, Miss Weston, that I could've also ordered the overseer's house burned." He nodded cordially, "Good day, madam." Then, turning, he left abruptly.

Jennifer sat on the porch steps of the overseer's house and watched the rays from the setting sun cast a golden hue across the landscape. She had worked beside Matilda for the entire day, and she was tired. She sighed with fatigue.

Spotting David and Jackson emerging from the nearby woods and striding toward the house, Jennifer got to her feet so that she could see them better. They had gone into the woods to feed the penned hogs and the cow that had once belonged to the Farnsworths. Jackson carried a bucket at his side, and Jennifer knew it was filled with the nourishing milk her sons' growing bodies needed so desperately.

Seeing her standing on the front steps, David grinned, and his boyish smile was charming. Noticing that his limp was more pronounced than usual, Jennifer wondered if he was working too strenuously.

"Masta David," Jackson said, "I'll take this milk around to the back door and give it to Matilda."

Nodding his consent, David approached Jennifer as Jackson headed toward the rear of the house.

Jennifer usually wore her hair pinned up, but earlier that day she had given it a brisk brushing, and because it was fairly close to bedtime, she hadn't bothered to redo it into a bun.

Nearing the steps, David studied her closely. With her long dark hair falling smoothly over her shoulders, she looked very much as she had when he'd first fallen in love with her. The Westons had given a large barbecue, and Jennifer and her widowed mother had traveled from Macon to attend the function. David hadn't seen Jennifer since they had been children, but on the day of the cookout, she had been fifteen and

255

he had barely passed his seventeenth birthday. He had taken one look at Jennifer's elegant beauty and had fallen hopelessly in love. He had vied for her attention, but so had Brad Weston, and to David's disappointment, it was quickly apparent that Brad was the one she preferred.

"You look very pretty." David complimented Jennifer as he paused at the bottom of the steps to appraise her beauty.

Blushing slightly, Jennifer glanced down at her mended dress, remembering all the beautiful gowns she had once owned and taken for granted. Most of her day dresses had now been worn so often that they were threadbare, and her formal gowns had been destroyed in the fire. Making new clothes was out of the question. Since the Union had successfully blockaded the ports, material was impossible to come by. Looking away from her own apparel, she noticed that David was wearing his uniform trousers and one of Jackson's shirts.

"Oh David!" she cried suddenly and disconsolately. "Three years ago, if someone had told me that someday you and I would be standing at the Westons' overseer's house dressed so poorly, I would have never believed it possible."

"I would have found it quite hard to fathom myself," he chuckled.

"David, how can you take our poverty so lightly?" she asked querulously.

"Jennifer, laughter is the best medicine. If we lose our sense of humor we're doomed, and we'll spend the rest of our lives pining for the past. I don't intend to let that happen to me. And if I can help it, I don't

256

aim to let you drown in self-pity."

Sighing depressingly, she sat down on the top step. "I'm not a survivor like you and Leanna."

Sitting beside her, and letting his lame leg stretch out over the remaining steps, he replied, "You're a fighter, Jennifer. Sometimes you just need a little push in the right direction."

Becoming aware of his closeness, Jennifer tried to ignore the way his presence accelerated her pulse and caused her to feel flushed. He was Leanna's beau, and it was wrong for her to find him so attractive!

Frowning with discomfort, David reached down and began to massage his aching leg. "Damn," he cursed softly, "it pains me considerably."

"You work too hard," she chastened. "You aren't giving your leg time to completely heal."

"I suppose you're right," he responded compliantly. "I'll try to take it easier for a while."

He continued to frown as he rubbed his leg to ease the pain, and his affliction touched Jennifer's heart, bringing tears to her eyes.

Glancing at her, he became aware of her distress and asked urgently, "Jennifer, what's wrong?"

"Oh David!" she cried impulsively. "It grieves me so to see you in pain!"

Her deep sympathy surprised but pleased him. "It really doesn't hurt that badly," he tried to reassure her.

"David Farnsworth, stop fibbing to me!" she chided. "When Doctor Simons comes to visit Mary, I'm going to insist that you let him take a look at your leg. And I also insist that you stop exerting yourself."

"Yes, ma'am," he grinned.

Returning his smile, she replied, "I'm glad you don't intend to argue with me."

"No, ma'am," he said lazily. "I learned a long time ago not to argue with a lady, 'cause there's no way to win the argument."

Playfully, she slapped at his shoulder, and responding, he caught her hand in his. His fingers encircled hers, and, as each became aware of the other's touch, their frolicking mood came to a sudden end. His hand tightening on hers, David whispered pleadingly, "Jennifer, there's so much I need to tell you if only . . ." He didn't finish his sentence because her face was so close to his that he couldn't stop himself from leaning over and kissing her.

Although his lips touched hers gently, they ignited a passion in Jennifer that caused her to press her mouth to his. Aware of her immediate response, David slipped an arm over her shoulders and drew her against him. Fervently, his lips pried hers open, and accepting his ardent kiss, Jennifer placed her arms about his neck.

"Jennifer! David!" Mary Weston exclaimed angrily, stepping out onto the porch.

Instantly, they bolted out of each other's arms and to their feet.

Breathing rapidly, Mary continued harshly, "I have never been so shocked or so disappointed in two people whom I love dearly!" Eying Jennifer severely, she said crossly, "David is Leanna's fiancé! How could you be so deceitful to your own sister-in-law?"

Bursting into tears, Jennifer sobbed miserably, "I'm sorry! . . . Oh Mary, I'm so dreadfully sorry!"

Brushing past her mother-in-law, she rushed into the house.

David made a move to follow her, but Mary stepped in front of him. "I hope what I saw tonight will not happen again," she said sternly. "Because if it does, I will be forced to ask you to leave my home. And I will also forbid you to see Leanna."

It was on the tip of his tongue to tell her that he wasn't in love with Leanna and that he and Leanna were not engaged except in her mind, but David suppressed the impulse. He would wait until Leanna returned, then tell her his true feelings, freeing himself from any obligation that might tie him to her. He didn't believe his revelation would upset Leanna, they had known each other all their lives, and she had never once treated him as anything but a friend. At least, he hoped his news wouldn't distress her.

"Mrs. Weston," David said politely, "please excuse my ungentlemanly conduct."

Mary nodded stiffly. "I will try to erase this incident from my mind." Turning brusquely, she reentered the house.

Moving back to the steps, David sat down. He couldn't repress the pleased smile that touched his lips. Jennifer had actually responded to his kiss! "Is she falling in love with me?" he whispered to himself. After all these years was it possible that he might win the heart of the woman he loved? He didn't know, but for the first time since he had been a young man of seventeen, he had reason to hope.

Chapter Seventeen

In the privacy of her tent, Leanna slipped out of her clothes and took a quick sponge bath before putting on her blue cotton nightgown. She hadn't seen Jeff for three days, and not only did she miss him, she was also terribly worried about him. She knew Sherman had ordered Jeff and his troops to overtake and destroy part of the railroad that was still controlled by the Confederacy, but she didn't know exactly where the skirmish was supposed to take place. She hated to think about the Confederates who would give their lives defending the railroad or of the Union soldiers who would die trying to take it. Leanna's loyalties were still with the South, but she had come to know so many of the soldiers fighting for the Union that her heart was continually being pulled in opposite directions.

When Leanna had been living on the plantation, where the war had touched her only through her brother's death, poverty, and the Yankees who had raided her home, it had been easy for her to feel a strong patriotism for the South and to hate all Yankees. But now that she found herself in the midst of the enemy and had come to know them as individuals, she could no longer despise these men simply because they were Yankees. Leanna hated no one, but she hated the war with a vengeance.

Stepping over to her cloth bag, she removed the pistol that Jeff had given her. For her privacy, Leanna's tent had been set up a short distance from the campsite, and worried about her safety, Jeff had loaned her the gun. She always slept with it close to her cot.

Moving to the kerosene lantern, Leanna placed the pistol next to the cot and then reached over to turn down the wick, but the sound of Jeff's voice outside caused her to whirl about. "Leanna, may I come in?"

"Yes!" she cried happily. As he stepped inside, she rushed into his arms, thankful that he had returned unharmed.

He drew her close, relishing the feel of her clinging body. "Leanna," he whispered, placing his cheek against the top of her head.

"I've been so worried about you," she murmured, unable to stop the flow of tears that were streaming from her eyes. "Oh, thank God, you're all right!" Holding him tightly, she repeated, "Thank God!"

Gently, he moved her so that he could step back and look down into her upturned face. Brushing away her teardrops with his fingertips, he asked, "Why are you crying?"

"I'm so happy that you're alive and well."

"Do you always cry when you're happy?" he questioned tenderly.

Her eyes shone with adoration as she gazed up at him. "No," she replied. "This is the first time it's ever happened to me." But I've never been in love before, she longed to add, and just thinking about how much I love you can bring tears to my eyes.

He released her slowly, and she noticed he moved with fatigue as he stepped over to the cot. He unbuckled his scabbard and holster, placing them beside Leanna's cloth bag. Then, removing his hat, he sat on the edge of the cot. Sighing heavily, he leaned over and, placing his elbows on his knees, rested his head in his hands. Massaging his temples, he uttered gravely, "I just finished filling my report with Sherman. My assignment was successfully carried out." He glanced up at her, and the sorrow and pain she saw in his eyes touched her deeply. "I had ten fatalities and sixteen wounded, and three of the wounded men are critical."

"How are Jerry and Paul?" she asked anxiously, praying they hadn't been injured or killed.

"They're fine," he replied softly.

Greatly relieved that her former guards who had become her friends were all right, Leanna moved to Jeff and knelt in front of him. He drew her between his legs, and sitting on the oval rug that she kept beside her cot, she snuggled next to him. He held her close, and she leaned her head against his chest as she slid her arm around his waist.

"I missed you," he murmured, his quiet confession thrilling Leanna.

"I missed you too," she said intensely. Once again he sighed audibly, and she asked, "Are you extremely tired?"

263

"Exhausted," he mumbled. "My body grows tired, but I can't seem to put my mind to rest. I can never sleep more than a couple of hours at a time."

Understanding, she nodded. Considering all his responsibilities, she marveled that he held up as well as he did. She knew the loss of ten men would weigh heavily on his heart.

"Jeff," she began hesitantly, not sure if she wanted to hear his answer, "how much longer can General Hood hold Atlanta?"

It was a moment before he answered, "I don't know. Another week, maybe two. Leanna, I honestly don't know. You Confederates are a resilient and stubborn breed."

"Will you be with the escort that will take me home?" she asked hopefully.

"No," he mumbled, sounding disappointed. "Sergeant O'Malley will be in command."

"Oh, Jeff," she moaned desperately, "will this damn war ever end?"

He merely shook his head as though there was no answer to her question. She looked into his face, telling herself to memorize his features so that in the future she could reproduce his image in her mind. She realized the Confederate Army was losing Atlanta to Sherman, and General Hood's retreat was certain. Soon Atlanta would fall, and she would be sent back home, away from the man she loved. She wondered if someday Jeff would come back to her, and if he did, would it be months or years before she would see him again? The possibility that he might be killed was so terrifying that she quickly blocked it from her mind. Lovingly, she studied his face; then, rising to her knees, she kissed his handsome features. Placing her hands on each side of his head, she touched her lips to his forehead. He closed his eyes so she could kiss them before kissing his cheeks, and she could feel his mustache tickle her lips as they moved down to his mouth.

Encircling her waist, he pressed her against him, and as her loving kiss aroused his passion, he urged her lips open to intensify their kiss. Wrapping her arms about his neck, Leanna responded ardently, wishing she never had to leave his arms. But their impending separation was inevitable, and, dear God, how was she going to go on living day after day without Jeff? I love him so much! her heart cried. Continuing to return his kiss, tears trickled down her face. I love him . . . oh, God, I love him so dearly!

Aware of her tears, Jeff stood and drew her to her feet. "What's wrong, sweetheart?" he asked tenderly.

How could she tell him she was already grieving over their unavoidable separation when she was here in his arms? This wasn't the time to think about parting, not now when he was here beside her! She mustn't waste their few precious moments together dreading his departure. Love him! her thoughts pleaded. Take him in your arms and love him! You'll have many tomorrows to miss him, but you have only these few remaining days to love him!

Flinging herself into his embrace, she cried with longing, "Jeff, I want you desperately! Please make love to me!"

"Darling," he murmured, wanting her as badly as she wanted him.

Quickly he helped her out of her nightgown,

265

letting it drop at their feet. The light from the lantern shone softly over her bare flesh, and Jeff's eyes trailed over her body, admiring her loveliness.

Placing his hands on her shoulders, he gazed down into her blue eyes for a moment before bending his head to kiss her urgently. "Leanna," he uttered thickly, cupping one of her breasts and kneading it gently.

"Oh Jeff . . . Jeff," she murmured, her breathing quickening with passion.

Sliding his hands down her sides, he knelt in front of her, and when his warm mouth touched her stomach, Leanna moaned with desire. Moving his hands to her buttocks, he pulled her closer as his lips sought her feminine center. Trembling beneath his fiery, sensual advances, she entwined her fingers in his dark hair. He continued to love her in this fashion until her entire being was burning with need for him.

Standing, he lifted her into his arms and placed her on the cot. He dimmed the lantern's flame, then hastily removed his clothes.

She held out her arms to him, and positioning himself between her legs, he went into her loving embrace. His penetration was swift, and as he entered her, Leanna arched her hips, accepting him completely.

Gathering her into his strong arms, he began making love to her fervidly, and loving the feel of him deep inside her, Leanna's passion matched his. Their thighs converged vigorously, her eager response arousing Jeff even more and causing him to make love so forcefully that they both became totally engulfed by their mutual desire and pleasure.

Suddenly Jeff encircled her waist with one arm and, thrusting her up against him, released his seed. Clinging to him, Leanna achieved her own ecstatic fulfillment.

He kissed her deeply before moving to lie at her side. Entering his embrace, she nestled her head upon his shoulder and, snuggling close to him, placed her arm across his chest. He was quiet, and she didn't try to encourage him to talk. She just enjoyed being close to him. Soon she became aware that his breathing had deepened, and moving gently, she raised up on one elbow to look down into his face. Seeing that he had fallen asleep, she smiled as she continued to study him. He needed rest desperately, and not wanting to awaken him, she placed a very light kiss on his cheek before whispering under her breath, "I love you, Jeff Clayton." Carefully, she placed her head back on his shoulder, and lying beside him, she closed her eyes and slowly drifted into sleep.

Sitting on the sofa in the parlor, Jennifer closed the book she had been reading and placed it on the table at her side. She glanced at the clock on the mantle above the fireplace. It was almost midnight. She did not usually stay up so late, but recently she was finding it difficult to fall asleep. Sometimes she tossed and turned on her bed for hours. Tonight she had decided to read before retiring, hoping she would then be so tired that she'd fall asleep quickly. Her recent insomnia had been brought on by thoughts of David and feelings of guilt. She felt that it was morally wrong for her to desire her sister-in-law's fiancé. However, although she was being terribly unfair to Leanna, she couldn't make herself stop longing for David. During the past few days she had often asked herself why she was now drawn to David Farnsworth. She had known him since childhood; however, when they had matured into young adults, it had been Brad who had attracted her.

Leaning back on the sofa and closing her eyes, Jennifer began to think about Brad and David, remembering them the way they had been in their late teens. They had both been extremely handsome, but David had always been quieter and more reserved than Brad. She smiled dreamily, recalling Brad's irresistible charms. Brad had been so dashing and confident that she had fallen hopelessly in love with him. That love had deepened throughout their courtship and engagement, and on her wedding day, she had been ecstatically happy.

Sitting up straight, Jennifer frowned slightly, remembering her wedding night. Brad had been tender and courteous, but he had consummated their marriage quickly and with little emotion. She had hoped he would eventually become more romantic, that he would satisfy the longing his hasty advances had awakened in her. But as their marriage had progressed, she had come to realize that Brad considered her a virtuous lady, and that he had been led to believe a woman like Jennifer considered sex a wifely duty and would merely submit to her husband's needs.

Standing, and walking out of the parlor, Jennifer wondered whether David would be that way if she was his wife, but reminding herself that Leanna was to be David's wife, she once again felt pangs of guilt.

Deciding to check on her sons before going to her bedroom, Jennifer opened their door to peek inside. The boys always slept together on a double bed, but now Bradley was missing. Jennifer hurried inside. Matthew was sleeping soundly, and trying not to disturb him, she looked quickly about, but Bradley was not in the room. Glancing at the chair beside the bed, she saw that his nightshirt was draped across it, and his clothes were gone.

Leaving the room, she checked the kitchen and then the privy out back, but failing to locate him, she hurried into the house. Going to the servants' quarters, she knocked firmly on the closed door. "Jackson!" she called loudly. "Jackson, wake up!"

She could hear the bedsprings squeak as Jackson got to his feet to slip into his trousers. Opening the door, he asked, "What's wrong, Miz Jennifer?"

"Bradley isn't in bed, and I can't find him!" she answered, sounding worried.

Matilda was also awake, and getting out of bed, she put on her robe. "Miz Jennifer, you just calm down. I's sure he's all right. Did you ask Matthew if he knew where he is?"

"No," she replied, turning to rush to her son's room.

"Miz Jennifer," Matilda called, "you stay here. I'll go ask 'im about Bradley. You is so upset, you'll only frighten 'im."

"What's going on?" David asked suddenly, hurrying toward the three of them. He had heard the disturbance and had dressed so hastily that he was still in the process of buttoning his shirt.

269

As Jennifer explained what was happening, Matilda left to wake up Matthew. She was gone only a few minutes before returning.

Talking rapidly, Matilda told them, "Matthew, he tole me that Bradley found a frog this afternoon. He said the frog was injured, and they built a cage for 'im. He thinks Bradley's done gone to check on that frog."

"Where is the cage?" David asked.

"He said it was 'neath the back porch," Matilda explained.

"But I checked out back, and Bradley wasn't there!" Jennifer replied excitedly.

"I'll check again," Jackson offered, rushing toward the rear door, but within moments, they heard him call, "He ain't out here, and there ain't no frog 'neath the porch."

"Where do you suppose he could've taken the frog?" Jennifer cried.

"The river!" David exclaimed. "My God, he probably took him to the river!"

Jennifer and David hurried from the house. David's lame leg made it extremely difficult for him to run, but he managed to move with amazing speed and his long strides soon left Jennifer far behind. David kept to the narrow path, and when he emerged from the woods and onto the open land by the river, he saw Bradley kneeling at the water's edge.

Sighing with relief, David slowed his strides, and moving toward the child, he called his name quietly, "Bradley?"

Startled, the boy turned swiftly to look over his shoulder. "Mister Farnsworth!" he said, surprised that his absence from the house had been discovered.

Going to Brad's side, and kneeling, David asked, "Where's the frog?"

Bradley's face saddened, and he nodded down to where the frog was lying deathly still. "He was awful sick, and I thought maybe he would feel better if I brought him down here and let him hop in and out of the river." Looking up into David's face, he asked piteously, "Is he dead, Mister Farnsworth?"

Jennifer had approached so slowly and soundlessly neither boy nor man was aware of her presence. Watching her son through tears of relief, she silently thanked God that he was safe.

Gently, David picked up the frog, studied him for a moment, then placed him back on the ground. "Yes, I'm afraid he's dead," he answered solemnly.

Moving suddenly, Bradley grabbed the frog and, standing, threw him into the river. "Everybody dies!" he cried angrily. "Why does everybody die?"

"Oh, Bradley, darling!" Jennifer moaned. Becoming aware of her presence, Bradley and David turned to look at her.

Getting to his feet, David reached down and placed his hand on Bradley's shoulder. "When you say everybody, you really mean your father, don't you?"

Fighting back tears, the boy nodded. Bradley didn't really remember his father. He had been only one year old when the war had started, and although Brad had come home twice on leave, Bradley barely remembered the short visits.

But Mary Weston talked constantly to Bradley about his father so the boy felt as though he had actually known him.

Recently Jennifer had begun to worry about Mary's continual talk of Brad. She felt Mary was forcing the boy to worship a father he would never know. Her son was only four years old; he needed to relate to life, not death. This incident with the frog proved that her worries had been well justified, and she vowed to have a serious talk with her mother-in-law.

David brushed his fingertips through Bradley's brown locks, then lifted him into his arms. "Your father was my best friend, you know that, don't you?"

"Yes, I know," he replied.

"No one knew him better than I did, and you can believe me when I tell you that he wouldn't want you to be unhappy."

"I just wish he hadn't died," Bradley pouted.

"So do I," David mumbled sadly. "I lost my best friend, and you lost your father. So, do you know what I think we could do that might make us both feel a lot better?"

"What?" he asked curiously.

"If you'll take your father's place and become my best friend, I'll try to sort of fill in for him and be your father whenever you feel like you need one."

Smiling brightly, Bradley agreed, "All right, Mister Farnsworth!"

Looking quite serious, David said thoughtfully, "A man doesn't call his best friend by his last name, it's too formal."

"Then what should I call you?" Bradley asked earnestly.

Grinning, he answered, "Call me David."

"All right, Mister Farnsworth . . . I mean David."

Putting his arms about David's neck, Bradley hugged him tightly, and returning the child's embrace, David set him on his feet. Clasping David's hand, Bradley led him over to his mother, and gazing up at her, his eyes sparkled happily as he announced, "I'm gonna be David's best friend, and he's gonna be my father when I need one."

Smiling tenderly, she replied, "Yes, I know. I heard everything."

"Is it all right?" they both asked suddenly and simultaneously, causing Jennifer to reply laughingly, "I think it's marvelous."

Hearing Jackson calling to them as he rushed toward the riverbank, David shouted, "We found Bradley, and he's just fine." As Jackson stepped out of the woods, David continued, "Hurry back to the house and ask Matilda to heat some milk, my best friend and I are going to have a glass of warm milk before we turn in for the night."

"That won't be necessary," Jennifer told Jackson. "Tell Matilda to go back to bed. I'll be happy to heat the milk."

"Yes, ma'am," he replied, heading back toward the house.

Bradley, keeping one hand in David's, reached over and also clasped his mother's hand, and as he held onto them, all three began to walk toward the house.

Shyly, Jennifer cast a quick glance at David, and when she saw that he was watching her, she dropped her gaze.

"Jennifer?" David said softly.

"Yes?" she responded, keeping her eyes on the dirt

273

path.

"Leanna and I have never told each other that we are in love."

"David, please. Don't speak of this in front of Bradley," she pleaded, still keeping her gaze turned away from him.

"All right," he conceded. "We won't talk about it now, but soon I must talk to you, and I don't care if Mary Weston approves or not."

"But, David —" she began, looking at him.

Interrupting, he said firmly, "Don't argue with me, Jennifer. Soon I must speak to you seriously because there's something I've wanted to tell you since I was seventeen years old, and after all these years, I'm finally going to say it."

Chapter Eighteen

Leanna dressed hastily, she had slept later than usual and did not want to take time to cook breakfast. She settled for a strip of jerky and a cup of water. Although it was still morning, the day was becoming extremely warm, and as she hurried toward the camp, she could already feel perspiration accumulating on her brow. She headed in the direction of the hospital tent, feeling quite sure she would be spending all her spare time today giving patients drinks and sponging their bodies in an effort to bring them a little relief from this scorching summer heat.

Seeing Dr. Hamilton standing beside one of the wagons used as an ambulance, Leanna moved away from the hospital tent to walk over and speak to him. He was busy overseeing the loading of medical supplies, stretchers, and blankets.

Looking away from the soldiers piling the articles into the rear of the canvas-topped wagon and seeing Leanna approaching, he smiled warmly. "Good morning, Miss Weston."

"Good morning, Dr. Hamilton," she replied, pausing to stand at his side. "Have the wounded been brought in?"

"An ambulance is expected at any moment," he answered.

"Will you be needing me to assist you in surgery?"

"No, not this morning. But one of the other doctors might need you," he said, and noticing the soldiers had finished their packing, he told them it was time to leave.

Leanna looked on as the two soldiers climbed onto the wagon seat, one of them picking up the reins. Turning back to the doctor, she saw that he was glancing about as though he were searching for someone.

"Where is that medic?" he mumbled to himself. "I guess I'll have to leave without him."

Believing the ambulance would be driven onto the battleground to pick up the wounded, she said disapprovingly, "Surely you aren't planning to leave with this wagon. It's too dangerous! You could be injured or killed!"

Her concern for his safety touched him deeply, and smiling tenderly, he replied, "My dear, the fighting is now very heavy and our wounded and fatalities are growing into the hundreds. Some of the dead soldiers might have survived if a doctor had attended to them sooner. So, in an effort to save lives, General Sherman has ordered one doctor to stay close to the battleground at all times. We physicians will take shifts, and I will be relieved in a few hours." He looked about once again, then decided gruffly, "Well, I can't wait any longer for that confounded medic.

276

I'll have to work without an assistant."

"I'll assist you," Leanna replied firmly, disregarding the danger involved.

He shook his head. "I'm sorry, my dear. You are a very courageous young lady, but a battleground is no place for a woman."

Moving to the rear of the wagon, he stepped inside. He had no idea that Leanna was following him until he turned to bid her goodbye, but seeing her lifting the hem of her long skirt and stepping up onto the wagon, he protested, "Miss Weston, I insist you leave this ambulance immediately!"

Ignoring his order, she sat down on the wagon bed, letting her legs hang over the back. Kneeling beside her, Dr. Hamilton argued, "Miss Weston, you cannot accompany me! I told you a battleground is no place for a woman."

"Dr. Hamilton," she scoffed, "I have been your assistant since the day you took it upon yourself to recruit me, and now you're stuck with me." Glancing over her shoulder, she yelled to the driver, "Soldier, let's move out!"

Hesitantly, the man waited for the doctor's consent. Aware of that Dr. Hamilton sat beside Leanna and then told him, "You heard my assistant. Let's move out!"

"Yes, sir," the driver replied, slapping the reins against the team of horses.

The wagon began to roll and Dr. Hamilton said gravely, "Miss Weston, if anything happens to you, I'll never forgive myself."

Reaching over to squeeze his arm affectionately, she replied, "Don't worry. I'll be all right."

She let her hand remain on his arm, and placing his hand over hers, he patted it gently. Chuckling, he teased, "If Major Clayton finds out I agreed to let you accompany me into battle, we may both be on the injured list when he finishes with us."

Leanna laughed lightly. "He does have a short temper, doesn't he?"

"Extremely so," the doctor agreed.

"How long have you known Jeff?" she queried.

Only a few months," he replied. "But I'm well aware of that temper of his." Holding her hand, he said tenderly, "I can tell by the way the major looks at you that he's in love with you."

She nodded, adding dreamily, "Yes, I know he loves me. But I don't think he's aware of it."

"Don't be so sure," Dr. Hamilton advised.

"He hasn't told me that he loves me," she revealed.

"He will," the doctor assured her. "When the time is right, he'll tell you."

Becoming aware of the intensifying sounds of battle, Leanna unconsciously edged closer to the doctor.

"Are you frightened?" he asked gently.

"No, of course not," she whispered shakily, unable to control the trembling in her voice.

"I can have the driver turn the ambulance around and take you back to camp."

She quickly shook her head. "I'm going with you," she said resolutely.

To help ease her fear, the doctor kept their conversation light for the remainder of the trip. As Leanna became more and more conscious of rifle shots and cannon fire, she tried desperately to keep her mood as light as Dr. Hamilton's.

The ambulance came to an abrupt halt, and swerving in the wagon seat, the driver said, "I don't think we should go any farther. We're already so close that the seriously wounded can be brought to you within minutes."

"Very well, soldier," Dr. Hamilton replied briskly, jumping down to the ground. Turning, he placed his hands on Leanna's waist and assisted her from the wagon.

The two soldiers hurried to the rear of the ambulance to help the doctor remove the stretchers. Moving, so she wouldn't be in their way, Leanna walked to the front of the wagon.

In spite of the heat, a cold chill prickled Leanna's neck, and a shiver ran fleetingly through her very soul as she was confronted for the first time by the appalling sight of war. Only a short distance from the actual fighting, she could see the huge mass of soldiers involved in the conflict, and on the far horizon, blanketed beneath a haze of gun smoke, was Atlanta.

Leanna was not aware that tears had come to her eyes, nor did she realize she was walking steadily toward the city that the Confederacy was trying to defend. She had no coherent thought as she continued strolling aimlessly away from the ambulance and toward the line of action. Driven by a natural inclination, Leanna moved instinctively in the direction of Atlanta where she knew she would find her own kind of people.

Dr. Hamilton's hand clutching her arm and spinning her about brought Leanna out of her trance.

"Where in the hell do you think you're going?" he bellowed so loudly that his voice carried above the sounds of guns firing. "Don't you realize how dangerous it is for you to wander toward the fighting?"

Returning to her senses, Leanna cried desperately, "I'm on the wrong side of the battlefield! I should be helping my own people!"

Holding her arm tenaciously, the doctor led her back to the ambulance. When they arrived, he let her go, and she leaned against the side of the wagon. Turning her face to the canvas, she looked away from the raging battle and the city of Atlanta.

Touching her shoulder, Dr. Hamilton advised considerately, "My dear, try not to think about it. You must concentrate on saving lives and close your mind to everything else."

Her first impulse was to cry out that she was helping to save the wrong lives, but the words never passed her lips because she knew they weren't true. Only the lives of her patients mattered, when she worked diligently beside Dr. Hamilton; the color of the soldiers' uniforms was unimportant. "I hate this war!" she groaned intensely. "I hate this war!"

The doctor patted her shoulder consolingly, then said hastily, "Miss Weston, stay here where it's safe. I'm leaving to accompany these two soldiers to where the fighting is taking place. There are medics on the battlefield. I'll give them the order that all seriously wounded are to be brought here, and then I'll return."

Continuing to face the canvas, she mumbled, "But don't they already know that you are here to tend to the injured?"

"The information was supposed to be delivered to them, but I aim to make doubly sure that they received the order. I'll be back very shortly."

Still turned to the wagon, she nodded agreement, but as she heard Dr. Hamilton and the soldiers leaving, she whirled to watch them trudge toward the battle.

A shell from a Confederate cannon soared dangerously close to Dr. Hamilton and the two soldiers. Upon impact, it exploded thunderously, making the ground beneath Leanna's feet vibrate.

Dropping to her knees, Leanna crossed her arms over her head and turned toward the shelter of the wagon. The bursting shell sent a whirlwind of dirt flying through the air, and large particles rained thickly down upon her, falling so heavily that she felt as though she were being buried alive.

As stillness returned, she rose shakily to her feet and brushed at the grime that clung to her. The fidgeting horses neighed nervously, causing the wagon to rock back and forth, but the brake had been secured and the wheels were locked in place.

Rubbing at the stinging particles that had flown into her eyes, Leanna cleared her vision and looked quickly to where she had last seen Dr. Hamilton and the two soldiers. When at first she couldn't make them out, she thought maybe they had managed to escape the explosion. But as her eyes picked out the shapes of three bodies sprawled on the ground, she cried out and willed her trembling legs to move. Running frantically, she screamed, "Oh God, not Dr. Hamilton! . . . Not Dr. Hamilton!"

Reaching the doctor and the two soldiers, she fell

to her knees beside Dr. Hamilton. He was lying face down, and she gently turned him over. Leanna was not aware that Jeff and a medic were rushing toward her. Dr. Hamilton was dead, and she was conscious of nothing except the terrible grief she was feeling.

Standing behind her, Jeff grasped her shoulders and drew her to her feet. Leanna turned numbly to see who was holding her, and finding Jeff, she fell into his arms. She was crying so heavily that deep sobs racked her body. She tried to talk to Jeff, but she could only moan insensibly, "No . . . no! . . . Not Dr. Hamilton!"

Quickly examining the two soldiers and the doctor, the medic reported, "Major, they are all dead."

Catching sight of Jerry and Paul hurrying toward them, Jeff yelled, "Bring my horse!" Then, lifting Leanna, he carried her back to the ambulance and placed her in the back of the wagon. Sitting beside her, he gathered her into his embrace and held her close.

Brushing his fingers through her long hair, he murmured soothingly, "Sweetheart, I'm so sorry. Dr. Hamilton was a fine man."

Clinging to Jeff, she moaned, "Oh, why didn't he stay at home where he was safe? Why did he have to join the army?"

"Honey, he was a dedicated doctor, and he knew he was needed," Jeff whispered.

Slowly, she moved out of his arms so that she could look into his face. "He told me he had a wife, three daughters, and six grandchildren." Feeling a sudden rage consume her, she cried, "Oh God, why didn't he stay home with his family!" Doubling her hands into fists, she yelled, "I hate this war! I hate this war with a vengeance!"

Delivering the major's horse, Jerry and Paul stepped to the wagon to speak to Leanna. They both knew how fond she had been of Dr. Hamilton, and sympathizing with her loss, they gave her their condolences.

Through her tears, she studied her two friends. Would they be next? Today, tomorrow, or the day after, would she be crying because one of them had been killed? She turned her gaze to Jeff. What if Jeff were the next one to die? Oh God, would she be kneeling over his body the way she had knelt over Dr. Hamilton's? The thought was enough to drive her to hysteria, and she had to exert all her will power to remain relatively composed.

Assisting her down from the wagon, Jeff led her to his horse and helped her mount. Then swinging up behind her, he told Jerry and Paul, "I'm taking Miss Weston back to the camp. I'll return shortly."

Picking up the reins, he encircled her with his arms, and leaning back against his chest, Leanna let her tears flow.

Leanna lay on her cot, her back turned to the open tent flap. It had been two hours since Jeff had brought her from the battlefield, and for that entire time, she hadn't moved from the cot. She had kept her face snuggled deeply into her pillow as she lay on her side with her legs drawn up. The shock of Dr. Hamilton's death had hit her severely, and the possibility that Jeff might be the next one to die was so horrifying that she wished she could hide in a place where the war could never touch her.

"Miss Weston?" Recognizing the voice calling her name, she tensed. Why would General Sherman come to her tent? She sat up with a start and, swinging her legs over the side of the cot, was surprised to see the general entering through the open flap.

"Miss Weston, please excuse my intrusion," he said, moving across the small enclosure to stand in front of her. "I came here to tell you how sorry I was to hear about Dr. Hamilton. I know you and he were good friends, and I want to express my deepest condolences."

"You savor this war, General Sherman, and I don't believe for one minute that you care how many men die because of it. So save your false sympathy for Dr. Hamilton's family," she blurted out unfairly, blaming the general for the doctor's death.

He studied her for a moment before replying, "If you feel you must blame someone because Dr. Hamilton died in this war, why must it be me? Why not blame Jefferson Davis or Abraham Lincoln? I am merely a soldier fighting a war I did not start, but which I intend to help finish."

"I blame you because you sent Dr. Hamilton to the battlefield," she said accusingly. "My God, he was a doctor, not a soldier!"

"I didn't send him to the battlefield," General Sherman explained. "I gave him, and all the physicians, explicit orders to stay out of firing range. He should have stayed with the ambulance, instead of taking it upon himself to go to the battleground. But Dr. Hamilton had a way of doing as he pleased and

284

disregarding my orders." He paused for a few moments, then stated with slight amazement, "I can't believe I am actually standing here explaining myself to a rebel spy!"

"Why are you showing me such consideration?" she asked, finding his manners perplexing.

He smiled, and it was the first time he had ever smiled at her with warmth. "You are a courageous young lady, and a very conscientious nurse," he replied, giving his answer considerable thought. "You also have compassion for your fellow man, regardless of the color of his uniform."

"I don't hate Union soldiers," she answered sincerely, "but I despise this war."

"So do I," he admitted. "But if I were to let sentiment get in my way, I would never achieve my goal."

"What is your goal?" she questioned.

"Victory, of course," he replied strongly.

Frowning distastefully, Leanna asked bitterly, "How can you think about victory when men are dying all around you?"

He smiled once again, but Leanna noticed that this time his expression was challenging. "How can you stay enclosed in your tent giving in to grief when these same men are dying all around you? My physicians and medics are working constantly, but they are few and the wounded are great in number. We need every pair of capable hands, so why are you letting yours remain idle? If you truly want to show respect for Dr. Hamilton, you'll put the training he gave you to good use."

Bending over, he grasped her arm and drew her to

her feet. "Come with me," he ordered. She started to pull away, but he merely tightened his hold on her. Without explaining his actions, he ushered her from the tent, and keeping his fingers wrapped about her arm, he led her the short distance to the Union campsite.

Pausing at the edge of the camp, he turned her in the direction of the hospital tent, and the sight that confronted Leanna was devastating. Lying on blankets and stretchers in front of the tent were a multitude of wounded soldiers. She tried to estimate their number, but there were so many that it was impossible to make an adequate count.

Dear God, she thought, General Sherman is right! This isn't the time to give in to grief, or to fear for Jeff's life! Vividly, she recalled the last advice Dr. Hamilton had given her, "You must concentrate on saving lives and close your mind to everything else."

Gingerly, the general released his hold on Leanna's arm, and taking a step away from him, she cleared her mind of all personal thoughts. Straightening her narrow shoulders and moving proudly, she headed toward the wounded soldiers, never imagining that General Sherman's eyes were following her with admiration.

Chapter Nineteen

Walking out of the hospital tent, Leanna made her way past the soldiers busily moving about the camp. She had been working so steadily that she had no idea of the time, except that she was aware it was quite late. The night was exceptionally warm, and she brushed her hand across her perspiring brow as she continued to head in the direction of Jeff's tent. The sounds of soldiers conversing and the constant chirping of crickets permeated the campsite.

Catching sight of Jeff entering his quarters, Leanna started to call to him, but she quickly changed her mind. She had come looking for him only to see if he had returned safely from the battlefield. She hadn't talked to him since he had taken her to her tent earlier in the day following Dr. Hamilton's death. She longed to cross the ground between them and fall into his arms, but she knew he would visit her under more discreet circumstances. So, turning, she headed back through the camp area and hurried to her own tent.

Inside, she hastily shed her clothes, took a thorough

sponge bath, and then slipped into her nightgown. Going to her cot, she lay down and waited patiently for Jeff's arrival. But when an hour had passed and he still hadn't come to see her, she began to worry that he didn't plan to visit her.

Another hour went by before Leanna decided that he wasn't coming. Trying not to cry, she rolled to her side and buried her face in her pillow.

Her back was turned to the tent's opening when Jeff entered so soundlessly that she didn't hear him. He paused for a moment to study the lovely shape of the body that her thin nightgown accentuated. "Leanna?" he called softly.

Startled, she immediately sat up. "Jeff!" she exclaimed. "Why are you so late?"

Smiling tenderly, he went to the cot and sat down beside her. "I had a lot of things to take care of."

Putting her arms around him, and hugging him lovingly, she murmured, "You're here now and that's all that matters."

Her warm welcome touched Jeff deeply, and cuddling her against him, he whispered, "Leanna, you're very sweet."

She could sense there was something troubling him, making him seem a little preoccupied, and she asked, "Jeff, is something wrong?"

He was surprised that she was so perceptive. "No, not exactly," he mumbled.

Moving out of his arms, and looking into his face, she said firmly, "Tell me what is troubling you."

He removed his hat and holster, placing them beside the cot. Reaching into his shirt pocket, he brought out one of his cheroots and lit it. He took a long drag from the small cigar before saying, "When I returned tonight to my quarters, there was a letter waiting for me. It was from Darlene."

For some reason Leanna couldn't completely understand, she was suddenly crestfallen. Why should a letter from Darlene upset him? Had he not been honest with her? Was he in love with the woman he had once asked to marry him? "Oh?" she muttered, hoping she sounded calm.

"From what she said in her letter, she has written to me quite often, but the letters never reached me."

"At times like these, mail delivery is certainly not dependable," Leanna replied hastily, not knowing what else to say.

Standing, Jeff began pacing the restricted enclosure. "She's still waiting for me to come home and marry her," he stated.

Leanna didn't reply, she merely lowered her eyes and stared vacantly down at her lap. He's come here to tell me he's going back to Darlene, she thought dejectedly. Oh, Jeff . . . no! she cried inwardly. Don't leave me! She could never love you as much as I do! No woman will ever love you the way I love you!

"As soon as I have time," he continued, "I must find a way to write to her and let her know I can't marry her."

Instantly, Leanna looked up. "You can't marry her?" she rejoiced.

Stopping his pacing, he faced her. "Of course not. Why do you look so surprised? How can I possibly marry Darlene when my heart belongs to you."

Rising, and throwing herself into his arms, she cried happily, "Jeff, do I truly have your heart?"

"Yes, he confessed. "You will take good care of it, won't you?"

"Always," she promised.

He kissed her cheek before releasing her to step over to the tent's opening. Flipping his cheroot outside, he closed the flap. He kept his back turned for a moment, then whirling to look at Leanna, he said angrily, "I feel like a damned cad!"

"Darling, don't torture yourself," Leanna pleaded. "I'm sure Darlene will accept your decision, and eventually she'll find someone else."

"You don't understand," he groaned. "You don't know what I did to her."

Moving to stand close to him, she asked, "What did you do to her, Jeff?"

He rubbed a hand across his brow; Leanna knew it was a gesture he always made when he was disturbed. Meeting her eyes, he uttered quietly, "I forced myself upon her, it could almost be called rape."

Gaping, Leanna protested, "No! I don't believe you!"

"It's true!" he insisted, raising his voice.

Shaking her head, she replied, "Jeff, you could never do anything like that."

"Couldn't I?" he taunted, his eyes glazed with a rage that was directed at himself. "Have you forgotten about my violent temper?"

"Are you saying that you did this to Darlene in a fit of anger?"

"I don't know," he mumbled with exasperation.

"What do you mean, you don't know?" she demanded.

"I don't remember exactly," he admitted.

Taking his hand and leading him to the cot, Leanna

coaxed firmly, "Let's sit down, and then I want you to tell me what you do remember." Leanna's faith in Jeff remained steadfast. She knew the man she loved, and a man with his integrity was not capable of rape.

Sitting beside her, he began, "I already told you about the night I was drinking with Darrin Spencer and how the liquor made me black out. I woke up the next morning in Darlene's bed. She was lying beside me and her father was standing over us. She said I slipped into her bedroom in the middle of the night. Apparently, I climbed in through the window because there was still a ladder propped against the side of the house. Darlene told her father and me that I was angry because I claimed she had been leading me on. Which was true, I suppose. The last few times I had seen her, she had come very close to making love to me, and then all at once had insisted that I take her home. The last time it happened, I had reacted angrily and told her she was a damned tease."

Pausing, he rested his arms on his legs, and staring down at the ground, he continued, "There were bruises on Darlene's wrists, and her mouth was swollen from where I had struck her. There was also blood on the sheets, she had been a virgin."

"But, Jeff, why didn't she cry out for help?" Leanna asked, finding all this very hard to fathom.

"That's exactly what her father wanted to know. She told him she didn't call for help because she loved me and was afraid he would've killed me. She kept silent to protect me."

"When it was morning, why did her father come into her room?"

"In my sleep I rolled over, and flaying my arms, I

knocked over the bedside lamp. Her father happened to be walking down the hall, and hearing the noise, he entered the room to see what had happened. Apparently, Diane had also been asleep."

"I still don't believe you would stoop to brutal rape," Leanna said inflexibly.

"I was insensibly drunk, and that, combined with my temper, made me become a madman." Sitting up straight, he looked at her. "Anyway," he proceeded calmly, "now you know why I feel so guilty about breaking my engagement to Darlene."

Understanding his dilemma, Leanna nodded. Although she didn't believe he had committed such an act, she knew he believed it.

They were silent for a few moments before Jeff asked, "Do you despise me?"

"Of course not!" she exclaimed.

"You know the kind of violence I am capable of and yet you aren't repulsed?"

"I am repulsed by rape, but I don't think you forced yourself on Darlene."

"But all the evidence was there," he pointed out.

"Evidence can be planted," she said stubbornly.

He chuckled humorlessly. "Don't dramatize what happened, Leanna. There was no conspiracy, and I'm responsible for what I did."

"I can believe whatever I wish, Jeff Clayton, and you will never make me believe otherwise," she answered willfully.

"Do you really have that much faith in me?" he marveled.

"I trust you implicitly," she said sincerely.

"Sweetheart, you are refusing to accept the fact that I

did something so repulsive."

"No," she denied. "That isn't true."

"Well, I think it is true," he murmured. "Leanna, before our relationship can be a strong one, you need to face up to what I did. You can't let yourself love me blindly, you must see me clearly. Obviously, somewhere deep down inside me, I am capable of that kind of violence."

Standing, she planted her feet firmly apart, and pointing her finger at him, she argued, "Jeff Clayton, I have more faith in you than you have in yourself."

Deciding to let the subject drop for now, he reached out and pulled her down onto his lap. "Leanna," he whispered, "I love you."

Sliding her arms about his neck, she answered joyfully, "I love you too, Jeff." Holding him tightly, she added, "Darling, I love you so much."

Bending his head to hers, he kissed her ardently, and when his hand moved to caress her breasts, a contented moan came from deep in her throat. Slowly, he worked his hand down to the hem of her gown, and slipping it beneath, he found the softness between her delicate thighs. His touch was like fire, and Leanna broke their kiss to purr, "Jeff, love me . . . love me."

"Sweetheart, you feel so wonderful," he murmured thickly, before returning his lips to hers.

He placed her on her feet. She quickly removed her nightgown, and as he slipped out of his uniform, she lay down on the cot to await the man she loved.

Her eyes admired his naked physique as he stepped over to turn down the lantern. A warm glow fell across his frame, and his handsomeness caused Leanna's pulse to quicken with desire.

When his body covered hers, she opened her legs so that they could become as one. His lips sought hers and, simultaneously, he entered her inciting warmth.

His penetration was electrifying and sent an exciting chill through her, causing her to wrap her legs about his back.

Leaning his weight on his arms, he positioned himself so he could slide his hard manhood in and out, and matching his movements, Leanna arched her hips back and forth. Her thrilling response made him whisper lovingly, "Oh Leanna . . . you're my sweetheart."

"Jeff," she murmured, her voice tremulous with longing, "I love you . . . Jeff, I love you."

Encircling her in his embrace, he kissed her demandingly, and locking her ankles firmly, she thrust her thighs upward, welcoming his deeper penetration.

Plunging into the depths of ecstasy, they made love passionately, surrendering themselves to the joy of taking and receiving.

As she clung strongly to Jeff, Leanna knew she needed him desperately and she was certain that night was the beginning of forever. Jeff had confessed his love, and she was sure he would soon ask her to marry him. Their future was dawning, and its awakening filled her heart with a mixture of happiness and torment. The war was still raging, and, at any moment, he could be killed. Her fear for his life made her to hold him even tighter, wishing she could become a part of him so that he could never leave her. Cherish these moments with Jeff, her thoughts warned. Lock them in your heart, and guard them closely, for someday your memories may be all you'll have!

"Oh Jeff!" she cried tearfully. "Please don't leave

me!"

Pulling her close, he assured her gently, "Sweetheart, I'm yours forever, don't you realize that?"

Her tears flowing freely, she pleaded, "Love me, Jeff . . . . Love me so powerfully that I can think of nothing else."

"Leanna," he murmured, understanding what she meant. Moving his hands beneath her hips, he pressed her against him, and began thrusting forcefully against her.

Grasping him with all her strength, Leanna equaled his driving force and became rapturously lost in the passionate embrace of the man she loved with all her heart.

Before she was fully awake, the extreme heat inside her tent made Leanna aware that she had slept later than usual. Turning to lie on her side, she placed an arm across the other side of the cot where Jeff had lain. She didn't know when he had left her to return to his quarters. They had fallen asleep in each other's arms, and, as always, Jeff had left during the night, dressing so quietly that Leanna hadn't been disturbed. A faint smile touched the corners of her lips as she remembered Jeff confessing his love. He loves me! she thought happily. She cuddled her pillow to her breasts, hugging it tightly. "Oh Jeff, I love you so much," she whispered intensely. Suddenly she laughed softly. "My goodness, I'm acting like a silly schoolgirl. But I don't care. Jeff loves me, and I'm so happy that I feel like shouting to the whole world that Jeff Clayton loves Leanna Weston."

Sitting up and placing her legs over the side of the

cot, Leanna realized with depressing clarity that the war was not going to disappear just because she and Jeff were in love. As all the wounded soldiers in the hospital tent came to mind, she removed her nightgown and began putting on her clothes. Just thinking about the long work day facing her made Leanna sigh with prospective weariness.

Knowing she was running late, she hurried through her morning preparations and, deciding to skip breakfast, left her tent to walk to the Union campsite.

Becoming aware of disorderly commotion in the camp, Leanna wondered what had happened to cause the confusion. Spotting Paul moving briskly through the soldiers, she called his name as she ran toward him.

Paul halted his rapid steps and, seeing Leanna approaching, waited for her to reach him.

"What's going on?" she asked breathlessly.

"General Hood is retreating," he explained.

"Retreating?" she questioned vaguely.

"He's pulling out of Atlanta," Paul specified.

Leanna sighed heavily. Another victory for Sherman, her loyalty to her own kind made her think bitterly. But, suddenly realizing what this would mean to her and Jeff, Leanna muttered dispiritedly, "I suppose I will be sent back home."

"Yes, ma'am," Paul replied. "Sergeant O'Malley has been ordered to make up an escort for you."

"When will I leave?" she asked, wondering if she would have a chance to see Jeff before she had to depart.

"Probably in the morning," he answered.

Oh Jeff, darling! she moaned inwardly. Tonight will be our last night together!

Tipping his cap, Paul said hastily, "Miss Weston, will you excuse me?"

"Yes, of course," she replied cordially. He started to move away, but she deterred him by asking, "Where is Major Clayton?"

"He's fighting alongside his troops," he answered, before leaving hurriedly.

Turning in the direction of the hospital tent, Leanna tried not to think about the constant danger Jeff was in, not to let her thoughts dwell on their impending separation. Clearing her mind of all personal thoughts, she entered the tent that was lined with cots occupied by convalescing soldiers.

Noticing that John Copeland was sitting up, she walked over to his bed. "Mr. Copeland," she stated, smiling pleasantly. "You are looking very well."

Happily, he announced, "This morning the doctor told me that I am completely out of danger."

She started to respond, but a medic took a step inside the tent and called to her, "Miss Weston, there are three ambulances arriving with wounded. The doctors will be needing your help."

"I'll be right there," she assured him. Three ambulances, she thought, depressed. If General Hood is retreating, then why must the fighting continue?

Telling the young soldier that she'd try to visit him later, Leanna hurried outside. The arriving ambulances were just entering camp, but she started walking to the surgery tent to await the wounded. However, catching sight of Jerry riding Jeff's stallion into the camp, she stopped abruptly.

Racing up to her, Jerry dismounted quickly, and stepping to Leanna, he grasped both her hands.

A feeling of foreboding centered itself in the depths of her soul as she whispered raspingly, "Jeff?"

"He's been shot," Jerry replied gravely. "The doctor on the battlefield sent him here for immediate surgery. He's on the first ambulance."

"Then he's seriously wounded?" she questioned, sounding as though she were in complete control of her faculties, although actually she was fighting the rising panic lurking barely beneath the surface of her air of composure.

"Yes, ma'am," he uttered solemnly.

Her legs weakened, and she fell against him. Supporting her, Jerry slipped his arm around her shoulders and held her against his strong frame. Keeping a firm hold on her, he led her toward the arriving ambulance. It came to a quick halt, and two medics jumped into the wagon. Picking up the first stretcher, they carried the wounded man from the ambulance.

Recognizing Jeff as the injured soldier, Leanna broke free of Jerry's secure hold and followed the medics and Jeff into the tent used for surgery. Placing Jeff on a cot, the medics hurried back outside to bring in more of the wounded.

Moving as though in a trance, Leanna went to Jeff's cot and knelt beside it. As she gazed into his unconscious face, tears streamed from her eyes. His shirt had been removed, and the doctor in the field had wrapped a bandage around his chest. Seeing a spot of blood soaking into the white bandage, Leanna gasped with fright when she saw that the wound was dangerously close to his heart.

Looking for a doctor, she glanced toward the rear of the tent where the operations were performed, but a partition separated it from the rest of the enclosure.

The tent began to fill with wounded and medics, but despite the frantic activity, Leanna continued to kneel beside Jeff's cot. Holding onto his hand, she bowed her head and prayed fervently for Jeff's life.

Feeling a touch on her shoulder, she looked up to see Jerry standing beside her. "Has he regained consciousness?"

"No," she whispered hoarsely.

"Miss Weston, Sergeant O'Malley is outside, and he needs to talk to you."

"I can't leave Jeff!" she cried.

"It'll only take a minute," he assured her.

"All right," she conceded reluctantly. As Jerry walked away, she lifted Jeff's hand, kissing it lightly. Gently, she placed his arm at his side, then hurried out of the tent, stepping back more than once to make room for the wounded soldiers still being carried inside.

Sergeant O'Malley was involved in a discussion with a captain, but seeing Leanna, he motioned for her to wait. Jerry had to report to Lieutenant Buehler, so excusing himself, he left Leanna alone. As she waited for the sergeant, the minutes that passed seemed endless, and she was about to return to Jeff when Sergeant O'Malley was finally dismissed by the captain.

"Miss Weston," the sergeant began, going to her side. "General Sherman has ordered me to take you back home. We will be leaving at dawn."

"No!" she protested sharply.

Confused, he stammered, "But, ma'am, it's the general's orders."

"To hell with his orders!" Leanna retorted angrily. "I'm not leaving here until I know Jeff is all right!"

Tentatively, he answered, "The general is going to insist that you leave."

"Well, you can find General Sherman and give him a message from me. Tell the general that neither he nor his entire army can make me desert Major Clayton. And if he doesn't approve then that's . . . that's just too bad! Because I'm not leaving!"

Whirling brusquely, she marched back into the surgery tent. As she turned in the direction of Jeff's cot, she halted suddenly. The ground beneath her feet felt as if it were rocking, and she swayed precariously when she saw that Dr. Johnson had just finished placing a blanket over Jeff's face.

"No!" Leanna groaned, her hand clutching at her throat.

Noticing her distress, one of the medics stepped to her side. "Miss Weston, are you all right?"

Staring deliriously, she rasped, "Major Clayton!"

Following her gaze, the medic understood why she was so deeply troubled. He knew Major Clayton had been seriously wounded, and as Dr. Johnson walked toward them, he asked, "Did the major die?"

"Yes," the doctor replied abruptly, and spotting two soldiers entering the tent, he gestured toward Jeff's cot. "Carry that body outside."

Her grief hitting her effusively, Leanna screamed heartbrokenly, "No! . . . Oh God! No!" She made an effort to rush to Jeff's cot, but the medic grabbed her.

"Take Miss Weston out of here," Dr. Johnson demanded gruffly, "before she upsets these patients."

"Yes, sir," the medic replied, and grasping her securely, he led her out of the tent. As they stepped outside, she jerked away from him.

"Leave me alone!" she pleaded desperately. "Please, leave me alone!"

Doing as she asked, the medic hurried back inside. Noticing that he had returned, Dr. Johnson walked over to speak to him. "What was wrong with Miss Weston?"

"She was terribly upset over Major Clayton's death," he explained.

"Major Clayton?" the doctor asked. "But he has been taken to surgery. It was Major Stark who died."

"Then why was he on Major Clayton's cot?"

"I suppose he was placed there after Major Clayton was taken to surgery."

The medic wondered if he should try to find Miss Weston and let her know what had happened, but before he could decide, Dr. Johnson put him to work. As he carried out the doctor's orders, he told himself Miss Weston would soon find out that Major Clayton hadn't died, and then he became so busy that the incident completely slipped his mind.

Suffering from shock, Leanna remained standing in the same spot she had been occupying when the medic had left her. As a feeling of numbness spread through her entire being, she moved impassively in the direction of her tent. Vaguely, she noticed that Jeff's stallion was still saddled. Jerry had tethered him to a stake driven into the ground. Slowly, and without coherent thought, she walked over to the horse. Untying him, she held onto his bridle reins and led him out of the camp and to her tent.

Somewhere deep in Leanna's mind she was aware of what she was doing as she stepped inside her tent and packed her few belongings. She was going home! Jeff was gone, and without her beloved, she would not remain in this Union camp one moment longer!

Returning to Jeff's stallion, she attached her bag to the saddle. Then removing the saddle bags, she filled them with canned rations and utensils and swung them across the horse's back. Next she filled the canteen with fresh water. Although her plantation was only about twenty miles from Atlanta, Leanna realized it would be dangerous to take the main road. She would have to travel on back roads and paths so her journey would take at least a day and a half.

Placing a foot in the stirrup, she mounted and, guiding the horse away from the Union camp, headed north. She wanted to cry. She needed to cry! But she couldn't let herself give in to her grief. Not now! Later. She would wait until she was home and then . . . and then? Dear God, what then? How was she going to go on living without Jeff?

Chapter Twenty

David couldn't sleep. He'd tossed and turned for over an hour before he decided a glass of warm milk might help him relax and he left his room to go to the kitchen. As he passed Jennifer's bedroom, he heard a soft muffled sob come from the other side of the door. Realizing Jennifer was crying, he opened her door and stepped quietly into the room.

Lying on her bed, Jennifer was suddenly aware of someone's presence. She sat up, expecting to see Bradley or Matthew. Her lamp was extinguished, but the moon shining through her window silhouetted David's frame as he closed her door.

"David!" she whispered, astounded that he had actually come into her bedroom.

Moving as silently as possible, he crossed the floor to stand beside her bed. "Why were you crying?" he asked tenderly, keeping his voice low.

Wiping at her tears, she murmured evasively, "I wasn't crying."

Sitting on the edge of her bed, he insisted gently,

"Yes, you were. And I think I know why."

She pleaded breathlessly, "David, please leave!"

Ignoring her plea, he clasped her shoulders and held her firmly. "Jennifer, you're falling in love with me, aren't you? That's why you were crying, because you feel guilty."

"David, we must not talk of such things," she replied, flustered.

"Why?" he demanded. "Because Mary Weston has taken it upon herself to run your life as well as mine? Jennifer, I need to talk to you, but you keep avoiding me. You must listen to what I have to say. I'm not in love with Leanna, and I seriously doubt if she's in love with me."

"But you don't know that she doesn't love you," Jennifer cried reasonably.

"That's true," he agreed. "But as soon as she comes home, I intend to tell her that I can't marry her."

"Why?" she asked sharply; her voice tinged with desperation. "Why can't you marry Leanna?"

"Darling, you know why," he replied thickly. "I love you, and I have loved you since I was seventeen years old."

Surprised, she gasped. "Since you were seventeen?"

He smiled warmly. "Brad wasn't the only one who fell in love with you, but he was the one who won your heart, and I never had a chance against him."

"B-but, David, I never knew," she stammered.

"It wouldn't have made any difference, I could never have competed with Bard. But, Jennifer, that is all in the past." Tightening his hold on her shoulders, he drew her closer. "Jennifer," he began intensely, "I

304

love you, and I have never loved any woman but you. As soon as I straighten out everything with Leanna, I want you to marry me."

"Marry you!" she gasped.

"Why should my proposal surprise you?"

"I . . . I don't know why. It's all so sudden," she muttered. "But what about Mary? She's my mother-in-law, and I love her dearly. If we marry, it'll upset her."

"In time, she'll learn to accept our marriage. And if she doesn't, we'll leave."

"But where would we go? Your parents have moved to Savannah, and my parents are dead."

"We'll move to Marietta, and I'll find a way to take care of you and the boys." When she offered no comment, he asked pressingly, "Jennifer, will you marry me?"

She thought for a moment before replying, "I can't give you my answer until Leanna returns."

"I understand," he said considerately. "And I can wait for your answer, but, Jennifer, I must know if you love me."

The soft moonlight fell across his face, and she could see him clearly. Gazing steadily into his hazel eyes, she murmured sincerely, "Yes, David, I love you."

Happily, he took her into his arms and hugged her to his chest. Her full breasts were pressed against him, and his loins responded immediately. He wanted to make love to her so desperately that his entire being seemed to be on fire with his need for her.

Moving Jennifer so that he could look into her face, and finding her lips poised, he bent his head

305

and kissed her. Urgently, his lips savored the sweetness of her mouth, and his tongue darted between her teeth.

Brad had never kissed her so intimately, and at first, Jennifer's response was uncertain. But as a pleasant feeling began spreading through her body, she found herself pressing her mouth to David's.

Easing her back onto the bed and lying beside her, David slipped his hand inside the bodice of her nightgown. As he began to gently caress her breasts, Jennifer experienced an intense longing that became centered between her thighs, and against her own volition, she couldn't help but wonder if David would leave her as unfulfilled as Brad always had.

"Jennifer, I want to make love to you," he whispered hoarsely.

Trembling with the desire he had awakened within her, she murmured seductively, "Oh yes, David . . . yes."

He hastily rose from the bed to discard his clothes, while Jennifer removed her nightgown, letting it drop to the floor. "The lock," she reminded. "Lock the door."

As he hurried across the room, Jennifer studied his naked physique. His weight was almost back to normal, and his frame was solid and strong. When he returned to her side, she lifted her arms to him, and placing his body over hers, he entered her embrace. She parted her legs, expecting swift penetration and believing he would thrust against her a few times then release his seed.

Surprising her, however, he lay at her side and encircled her with one arm. While his lips kissed hers demandingly, one hand traveled from her breasts, to her stomach, and finally to that place where her fiery longing was strongest. At his intimate touch, Jennifer began to moan deeply, arching her hips rhythmically.

"Jennifer," he declared passionately. "I love you." Once again, his lips sought hers, and when she responded by slipping her tongue into his mouth, David became so aroused that he moved his frame over hers. Without interrupting their ardent kiss, he entered her, sliding deeply into her warm depths. At last, he had achieved the heaven he had desired for years, and as her heat consumed him, he whispered tremulously, "Jennifer, my darling. Now you are truly mine."

Stimulated by his confession, she bent her legs, hoping to deepen his penetration. Although she had once been married, and had given birth to two children, Jennifer was totally unenlightened regarding the pleasures of love.

David could sense her inexperience, and he said tenderly, "My innocent darling, if you will do as I tell you, I will take you with me to love's highest peak."

"Yes, David." She replied timidly. "Tell me what to do."

"Place your legs over my back," he instructed urgently.

She did as he directed, and his deeper entry made Jennifer moan sensually.

Encircling her in a demanding embrace, David said huskily, "Thrust against me, darling." Complying, she elevated her hips, pushing herself upward and allowing his throbbing arousal to reach her ultimate depths.

"David, darling," she praised, amazed by the rapturous thrill he was giving her.

He shoved his thighs to hers and, placing his hands beneath her hips, jerked her up against him. Pumping strongly, he drove in and out of her with such sensuous force that Jennifer writhed and moaned with delight.

David continued to make aggressive love until tremors racked Jennifer's body, and then, holding her tightly, he, too, found fulfillment.

Before withdrawing to lie at her side, he gave her a long, loving kiss.

"Oh David," she whispered breathlessly, "for the first time in my life, I feel like a complete woman."

Drawing her into his arms, he murmured, "My woman. Now you belong to me."

"Yes," she complied happily. "My darling, I love you so much."

"I want to make you my wife," he replied, wishing Leanna would return soon.

Jennifer's thoughts coinciding with his, she uttered hopefully, "Maybe Leanna is on her way home." Placing her head on his shoulder, she continued earnestly, "David, I pray nothing has happened to her. She should have returned weeks ago, and I'm so worried about her."

"I know," he agreed. "I'm concerned about her myself. The longer she stays away, the more it looks as if something has happened to her."

"No!" Jennifer cried desperately. "I can't bear to think that she might be . . ."

"Dead?" David concluded. "I'm afraid it's a possibility. A very real possibility."

Although Leanna traveled on the back roads, they were filled with Union invaders and deserters from both armies, which made her journey extremely slow and dangerous. More than once it had been necessary for her to ride the horse off the main road and into the woods to hide from advancing soldiers. She didn't believe the Union soldiers would actually harm her, but she was sure that they would take Jeff's stallion. Furthermore, her gear and the horse's saddle were U.S. Army issue, and if she were captured, Leanna was afraid they would think she had stolen the stallion and would place her under arrest.

Leanna was less than five miles from home when she detected the sounds of approaching horses and, reacting alertly, rode the stallion into a thicket. Dismounting, she held onto his harness as the Union troops began filing slowly past her. The stallion whinnied softly, and for a few tense moments, Leanna froze. But the soldiers didn't hear him, and sighing gratefully, Leanna patted the horse's head, whispering soothingly to him and praying her pacifying gestures would keep him calm.

Finally, the soldiers had passed so Leanna started to lead the stallion back onto the road, but her fatigue was so great that she decided to rest for a few minutes. Tying the bridle reins to a tree, she sat down in the high grass, and raising her knees, she tucked her long skirt about her legs. It was still early, but Leanna had been traveling since the previous morning. She was exhausted, both physically and emotionally, and crossing her arms over her raised knees, she sighed heavily. When she closed her eyes, Jeff's image flashed into her mind so she quickly opened her eyes to stare straight ahead at nothing in particular. I must keep moving, she thought. I must concentrate on nothing but reaching home!

Forcing her tired body into action, she arose lethargically. Dr. Hamilton had trained Leanna to close her mind to anything personal, and now, using his guidance to perfection, she blocked Jeff from her thoughts. She couldn't face his death! Not now! When she was on the plantation she loved so dearly, then she'd make herself accept what had happened. Perhaps her home would give her the strength to carry on without the man she loved.

Moving wearily, she stepped over to the stallion. She was about to untie him when a woman's terrified scream penetrated the woods. Taking Jeff's rifle from its scabbard, she cocked the weapon and hurried cautiously into the dense thicket.

Once again the woman screamed. Moving more quickly, Leanna made her way toward the scene. A saddled horse came into view, and furtively, she moved in the direction of the animal. When Leanna came up to a thick bush, she knelt behind it, and parting the shrubbery to see what was on the other side, she spotted a lone man assaulting a woman. He had thrown her to the ground. Squatting beside her, he was trying to raise her long skirt. His victim screamed piercingly, but he silenced her by slapping her across the face.

Standing and stepping around the bush, Leanna aimed the rifle at the man. "Let her go, or I'll kill you!" she ordered so harshly that for a fleeting

310

instant she was shocked by her own severity.

Bolting to his feet, the man reached for the pistol strapped to his hip, but as his hand touched the butt of the weapon, Leanna fired Jeff's rifle. The attacker sprawled backward, clutching at his bleeding chest. Then he dropped to his knees and fell forward onto the ground.

As Leanna walked over to the man, she was only vaguely aware that the woman had begun to cry convulsively. The shock of Jeff's death was still with her, and her emotions were numb. Checking the man, she saw that he was dead. A deserter, she thought, but this time it's a Yankee deserter instead of a Southerner. She stared down at the man. Dear God, I just killed a man! I should be mortified, but I feel nothing!

Becoming aware of the woman's violent sobs, Leanna turned away from the deserter and stepped over to his victim. The woman was lying face down, but as Leanna paused beside her, she rolled over onto her back.

"Audrey!" Leanna exclaimed, placing the rifle on the ground.

Rising and flinging herself into Leanna's arms, the young woman hugged her eagerly. Then, moving back, she asked astoundedly, "Leanna, what are you doing here?"

Gaping incredulously at David Farnsworth's younger sister, Leanna questioned, "What am I doing here? Why are you here? I thought you and your parents moved to Savannah."

"We didn't get any farther than Atlanta," Audrey explained hastily. "Mama came down with a fever,

311

but she was recovering and we were staying at a hotel. I was doing some shopping for Mama when the hotel was bombarded by one of Sherman's shells. Mama and Papa were killed. I didn't know what to do or where to go. We don't have relatives in Atlanta, and all our friends had already moved on to Savannah. It was rumored that General Hood was planning to retreat and leave Atlanta to Sherman. I was terrified! I didn't want to be in Atlanta when the Yankees arrived. So I decided to try to make it to The Pines. Papa's horses were confiscated by the army so I had to leave on foot. I've been traveling by night and sleeping during the day. I was resting beneath a bush when that horrible man found me." As the attempted rape again became uppermost in her mind, Audrey began to cry again.

Leanna sympathized with Audrey. This cruel war was bringing so much tragedy, not only to herself, but to her friends and family.

Making an attempt to stop her flowing tears, Audrey met Leanna's gaze. Audrey Farnsworth was eighteen. She was tiny and delicate. Long auburn hair fell over her shoulders, and long strands of it streamed across her face. Her hazel eyes were identical to David's, and splashed across her nose and cheeks were a mass of freckles.

Looking steadily into Leanna's eyes and finding them strangely expressionless, Audrey could sense something very different about her. It's almost as though she were a stranger and not herself, she thought. I wonder what has happened to her?

"Leanna," she pried carefully, "what are you doing here?"

"I'm on my way home," Leanna said flatly.

"But where have you been?"

"I was held captive by the Union," Leanna mumbled.

"Sherman?" Audrey exclaimed. Leanna simply nodded. Grasping her arm, and squeezing it, Audrey cried sympathetically, "Oh Leanna, you poor dear! It must've been terrible for you. Did you escape?"

Audrey's grip was uncomfortable, and prying the young woman's fingers from her arm, Leanna replied calmly, "No, I simply rode out of Sherman's camp."

"The soldiers didn't try to stop you?" Audrey asked, astonished.

Briskly, Leanna said, "Let's not waste time talking. We need to keep moving."

"You're right," Audrey agreed. Glancing down at the body of the man who had attacked her, she gasped, "Leanna, are you sure he's dead?"

"Yes," Leanna replied dully, picking up her rifle. Turning, she walked over to the man's horse.

Watching her, Audrey was shocked that Leanna could accept her act of violence with so little emotion. What has happened to Leanna? she again wondered. Good Lord, what did those Yankees do to her?

Leanna was grateful to see that the horse was healthy and strong. Taking the reins, she looked over at Audrey.

"Let's go home," she said, and although she spoke quietly, for the first time Audrey detected emotion in Leanna's voice.

Chapter Twenty-one

Leanna had been home less than an hour when David asked her to take a walk with him so that they could talk privately. Leanna wondered how she was going to tell David she couldn't marry him without hurting his feelings. Now that Jeff was gone forever, she supposed she could marry David to please her mother, but Leanna knew she would never become any man's wife as long as she still loved Jeff with all her heart and soul. It would be terribly wrong for her to force her husband to share her with a memory.

Strolling beside Leanna, David absentmindedly guided their steps toward the wooded path that led to the river. His thoughts were turbulent, for he was trying to figure out a gentle way to break his news to Leanna. If she reacted with anger, he hoped she wouldn't blame Jennifer. He was solely responsible for what had happened between himself and Jennifer; he knew she would never have instigated their relationship.

"David," Leanna began quietly, her tired legs moving slowly down the narrow path, "I'm sorry about your parents."

"Thank you," he mumbled solemnly. The news of his parents' deaths had shocked him severely. Now, he longed to conclude his business with Leanna so that he could go to Jennifer for comfort. When he felt grief for his parents, he needed Jennifer's sympathy, needed her loving arms about him.

They were almost to the river before Leanna asked, "Why did you want to talk to me?"

Swallowing nervously, David replied hesitantly, "I need to talk to you about Jennifer and myself."

Halting, Leanna turned to look at him. "You . . . and Jennifer?" she stammered.

Shifting his weight so that it wasn't resting on his lame leg, he mumbled, "Leanna, I'm in love with Jennifer."

He dropped his gaze and so he missed the tiny smile that flickered across Leanna's lips. "Is she in love with you?"

Raising his eyes to meet hers, he answered, "Yes, she is."

Reaching over and taking his hand, Leanna grasped it firmly. "David, I think that's wonderful."

"You do?" he asked, totally astounded.

"Yes, I do," she assured him, but Jennifer and David's love brought Jeff to mind, forcing her to fight back approaching tears.

"Then you aren't in love with me?"

"David, I've always loved you like a brother."

He smiled joyfully. "And I've always loved you like a sister."

Returning his smile, she pushed thoughts of Jeff

316

from her mind and attempted a bright response. "Now that we have that settled, when do you plan to ask Jennifer to marry you?"

"I already asked her, but she wanted to wait until you returned before giving me her answer." Suddenly, David frowned worriedly.

"What's wrong?" she asked.

"Your mother," he muttered gravely. "She's got her heart set on you and me getting married."

She squeezed his hand encouragingly before releasing it. "Leave mama to me. I'll take care of everything."

"Will you please talk to her now?" David asked urgently. "I want to marry Jennifer as soon as possible."

"All right," Leanna agreed, but she wasn't looking forward to the confrontation, she could imagine how upset her mother would be.

David walked back to the house with Leanna, but when they entered, he went in search of Jennifer, and Leanna headed for her mother's bedroom. Knocking on the closed door, she received permission to enter.

Plastering a pleasant expression on her face, Leanna walked into the room. It was much smaller and was furnished more moderately than Mary's bedroom in the columned home Leanna's grandfather had named The Pines. Her mother was sitting up in bed, leaning back against the oak headboard. Sauntering to the bedside, Leanna pulled up a straight chair and sat down.

Watching her daughter, Mary studied her intently. Although Leanna had sworn to her that Major Clayton and his men had treated her kindly, she wasn't completely convinced that Leanna was telling the truth. There was something drastically different about Leanna, but so far Mary hadn't been able to put her finger on what it was. Her daughter was not herself. She seemed to be moving in some kind of inexplicable trance.

"Mama," Leanna started quietly, "I have something to tell you."

Mary tensed and placed her hand over her heart. She feared those deplorable Yankees had mistreated Leanna and that her daughter had come to confess everything.

Breathing rapidly, Mary groaned, "Leanna, darling, what did those horrible men do to you?"

Confused, Leanna questioned, "What men, Mama?"

"Those horrible Yankees! Major Clayton and his soldiers, did they . . . did they? . . ."

Quickly, Leanna declared, "Mama, I've already told you that they were all perfect gentlemen."

As Mary's breathing returned to normal, she grunted indignantly. No one would ever make her believe that Yankees were gentlemen.

"Mama," Leanna continued, "I'm not going to marry David."

"What?" Mary gasped with surprise.

"I'm not in love with David," Leanna explained. "I was never in love with him, and furthermore, he isn't in love with me."

"Leanna," Mary tried to reason, "sometimes love comes after marriage."

"That myth should have ended with the dark ages," Leanna spat testily. Standing, she proceeded firmly, "I won't marry a man I don't love."

"Leanna Weston," her mother chided impatiently, "you're as hardheaded and as stubborn as your father was."

"Mama, were you and papa in love when you married?"

Mary's expression softened, and sighing dreamily, she murmured, "Yes, we were very much in love."

"Then why should you want less for your daughter?" Leanna retorted. Sitting on the edge of the bed, and holding her mother's hands, she said pleadingly, "Mama, you can remember what it's like to be young and in love so you should understand when I tell you that David and Jennifer are in love. They plan to get married, and they intend to marry soon." When Mary made no response, Leanna asked carefully, "Why aren't you surprised?"

"One night I caught them . . . well, I caught them in a very compromising situation."

"Compromising?" Leanna pondered.

"They were actually kissing," Mary revealed huffily.

Rising, Leanna began pacing the small area beside Mary's bed. When she envisioned Jennifer and David in a lovers' embrace, memories of herself in Jeff's arms flashed before her.

Vaguely, Leanna listened to her mother talk disapprovingly of Jennifer and David. It was extremely difficult for Leanna to retain her composure and try to behave normally. A painful scream deep inside her was longing to be set free. She needed to cry her grief to the heavens and to give in to the torment tearing at her heart. For a moment, she was tempted to fling herself into her mother's arms, to be held like a little girl until her hurt went away. But she knew her mother would show her no sympathy when she found out she was grieving for a Yankee.

Leanna knew Jackson had taken the horses to the woods to keep them safely hidden, and deciding to check on Jeff's stallion, she headed in the direction of the old corral. Her confrontation with her mother had left her emotionally exhausted. Finally, Leanna had pointed out to Mary that if she refused to accept Jennifer and David's marriage they would leave and then she'd lose her grandsons. Sensibly, Mary decided to put her objections to rest.

Reaching the corral where the hogs were penned, Leanna spotted Jackson rubbing down the stallion. He had both horses tethered to trees, but they had enough lead to permit them to nibble at the tall grass. The Westons' old horse had died while Leanna was away.

Hearing her approach, Jackson turned to face her. "Miz Anna, these are two fine horses, especially this chestnut stallion. But don't he belong to that Major Clayton?"

Stopping beside the stallion, and petting his head, she mumbled, "He did, but now he belongs to me." Intensely, she continued, "Jackson, this horse is special. We must take extra good care of him!"

"Yes'm," he replied eagerly. "It'll be a pleasure to take care of such a fine animal."

Sighing dispiritedly, Leanna leaned her face against the stallion's neck. When she did so Jackson was tempted to question her, but knowing it wasn't his place to pry into her life, he kept silent. Audrey and Mary were not the only ones who had noticed a change in Leanna, Jackson was also aware that something was troubling her.

Edging away from the stallion, Leanna looked over the immediate area. Remembering vividly the morning she and Jeff had come here for a shooting lesson, she also recalled that Jeff had asked her if she had ever bothered to find out if Jackson wanted to be free.

Ambling listlessly to a large oak and sitting down in its shade, she queried curiously, "Jackson, do you want to be free?" Then she gave a short and somewhat bitter laugh. "Let me rephrase that question. The Yankees are going to win this war and set all slaves free. But, Jackson, back when you were a younger man, did you long for freedom?"

Jackson was totally shocked by her question. In his wildest dreams, he had never imagined Miss Leanna Weston would ask him if he wanted to be a free man. Taken aback, he stuttered, "Wh-what did you say, Miz Anna?"

"You heard me," she said patiently. "Tell me the truth, Jackson, because as far as I'm concerned you, Matilda, and Louise are already free. You can stay or leave, whichever you want."

"Miz Anna, I could've left right along with them other slaves had I wanted to go," he told her.

"Why didn't you leave? Why did you decide to stay?"

Placing the brush he had been using to groom the stallion on the ground, he walked over to stand in front of her. "I didn't have no place to go," he

321

replied. "Besides, Miz Anna, you needed me and Matilda."

"Yes, I did," she agreed. "And I still need both of you. But, Jackson, we are straying from my original question. Did you want to be free?"

It was a long time before Jackson spoke, and Leanna was beginning to think he wasn't going to answer when he said movingly, "Free? Miz Anna, I don't think there has ever been a slave who didn't want to be free." Once again, he became quiet, and she wondered if he was upset. "Yes'm," he suddenly continued, his voice surprisingly strong. "I wanted to be free. When I was a boy, when I was a young man, and now that I'm a man past my prime, I still longs for freedom."

"Tell me about your life before you came to The Pines," Leanna encouraged.

"Why, Miz Anna?" he asked sharply, his tone surprising her. "Why, after all these years, do you want to know 'bout my life?"

Sighing heavily, she murmured, "I don't blame you for being perturbed with me. I realize it's a little late for me to care about how you have been forced to live, but I'm not the same woman who left here weeks ago. While I was away, I spent the entire time assisting a Union doctor with his patients, and being a nurse made me a more sensitive person."

Stepping over to the tree sheltering Leanna, he leaned up against the trunk. "All right, Miz Anna, I'll tell you 'bout my life 'fore I came here, but it ain't a happy story."

"I was afraid it wouldn't be," she mumbled regretfully. Oh Jeff! Jeff! she cried silently. You were so

322

right! Why did I wait so long to care about Jackson as a fellow human being instead of thinking of him only as a beloved servant?

"I was born on a plantation a few miles outside of Jackson, Mississippi. It was a small plantation, nothin' much more than a farm. My pappy was the white overseer, and my mama was the cook in the big house. It was right after I was born that the masta of the plantation decided there was more money in growin' niggers than in growin' cotton."

"A slave farm!" Leanna gasped.

"Yes'm," he confirmed. "It became one of them slave farms. When the masta made up his mind to raise slaves to sell, he took me away from mama. I must've been 'bout six months old."

"But why did he take you from your mother?" she asked, wondering how the man could have been cruel.

"Well, you see, Miz Anna," he explained, his voice edged with a coldness that startled Leanna, "the masta didn't want any mothers growin' too fond of their babies, 'cause they was bein' born to be sold and for no other reason. He sold most of 'em between the ages of ten and sixteen, and he didn't want no mamas a-grievin' for their children after they was gone. He had a large cabin built where women who had given birth took turns a nursin' the babies. The cabin was called the nursin' house. He had cabins called the toddler house, then the pickaninny house, and then two separate cabins called the prime wench house and the prime buck house. Children never knew who their parents was, they was raised worse than cattle. At least a calf knows his own

323

mama. . . . But I'm gettin' ahead of myself. That all came about when I was a little older. I was the first baby to go into the nursin' house. One of the slave women had just given birth, but her baby was still-born, and the masta ordered her to take care of me. Well, the masta, same as most mastas, didn't think niggers were capable of love like white folks. He thought when I was out of my mama's sight, she'd soon forget all 'bout me. But mama didn't forget. She kept grievin' for me, and goin' down to the nursin' house to see me. The masta had her whipped, but she still kept a-comin' to see me, and he just kept right on havin' her whipped."

Jackson paused, and Leanna asked carefully, "What happened to your mother?"

"She was whipped to death," he mumbled.

"And your father?" she questioned.

"Father?" he spat out, practically choking on the word. "He was a white man, he didn't claim no nigger as his child."

"But you were only a baby at the time. How did you learn all this?"

"When I got older, I heard all kinds of stories, 'bout what happened to the slaves on the masta's land. On a slave farm, prime niggers don't work, they breed, and when they ain't breedin', they ain't got nothin' to do but talk."

"How old were you when you left the farm?"

"I was sixteen when the masta took me and some others to the slave market in New Orleans. I was bought by Masta Gerald Lawrence, whose father owned a plantation close to Savannah. Masta Gerald was only a few years older than me, and he bought me to be his personal manservant. I got along real fine with Masta Gerald, and he as good to me. He even taught me some readin' and writin'. I knew I had to be a slave, but I was sure glad that Masta Gerald owned me. When I was nineteen, the old masta returned from the slave market with two wenches to work in the kitchen. One of them was a little gal named Carrie. Miz Anna, I took one look at Carrie and fell in love. In no time at all, I realized that she cared 'bout me too, and I asked her to be my wife. On the Lawrence plantation, slaves married. It wasn't a legal weddin' like white folks' have, but Masta Lawrence read some words to us from the Bible, then he told us that as long as we was his slaves, we was husband and wife."

Leanna didn't say anything; she knew that her father's slaves were never legally married either. The ceremonies had been performed by a local freed Negro who preached among his people but he was not an ordained minister.

"Carrie and I shared a bedroom off the kitchen." Jackson continued. "I guess that's the only time in my life that I can say I was totally happy. I loved that gal, and she loved me. We had two children, both of them girls. One of my daughters was two years old and the other was four months when Masta Gerald decided to take a short trip to Atlanta. I was his manservant, so I had to go with him."

Jackson stepped away from the tree and turned his back to Leanna. She could see that his strong frame was trembling, and hurrying to her feet, she moved to him and placed her hand on his arm. "Jackson?" she said softly.

325

He whirled to face her, and she was puzzled to see tears streaming down his cheeks.

"It's been over twenty-two years, but I can still see my family as clearly as though it was only yesterday. Carrie was holdin' the baby, and my other daughter was at her side. They was standin' on the front porch, watchin' me leave. Masta Gerald and I was ridin' horseback, and I turned around and waved goodbye to 'em." Suddenly, Jackson's chin quivered, and his deep voice broke as he continued, "Miz Anna, I thought I'd be seein' 'em in a couple of weeks. I didn't know I'd never see Carrie or my babies again!"

He paused a moment before carrying on, "In Atlanta, Masta Gerald got into a card game with your papa. Masta Gerald was losin' heavily, and when he ran out of money, he wagered his prized slave. Masta Gerald lost, and I became Masta Frank's property."

"But, Jackson, if Gerald Lawrence sincerely cared about you, how could he have so unfeelingly bet you in a card game?"

Jackson chuckled coldly. "Masta Gerald was real fond of his huntin' dogs too, but that never stopped him from sellin' one of 'em. And that's all I was to him, just one of his pets like them dogs."

"Did you tell papa about your wife and children? Surely he offered to buy them from the Lawrences."

"Yes'm, I told him, and he wrote a letter to Masta Lawrence askin' if he could purchase Carrie and the girls. After a few weeks went by, your papa finally got an answer to his letter."

"What did Mr. Lawrence say?"

"He sold Carrie and my babies to a slave trader. When Masta Gerald returned home without me, Carrie cried and carried on so much that Mistress Lawrence insisted that her husband get rid of Carrie and her children."

"Did papa try to find them?"

He nodded slowly. "For two long years, he tried to locate my family, but he never even found a trace of 'em."

"Oh Jackson, I'm so sorry!" she sympathized.

"You're sorry," he said, his tone unfairly hard. "How do you think I feel? I don't even know if Carrie and my girls are alive. Somewhere out there, I might have two grown daughters, and if I do, what kind of life have they had? What kind of life did my Carrie have without me?"

"You found Matilda and started a new life for yourself, maybe Carrie found someone too."

"Yes'm, I got Matilda and she's a good woman, but I don't love her like I loved Carrie. I ain't ever gonna get over losin' Carrie. Miz Anna, you don't know what it's like to love someone with your whole heart."

"Yes, I do," she replied somberly.

He looked at her questioningly. "While I was gone," she explained, "I fell in love with Major Jeff Clayton, and now I'm falling . . . I'm falling apart."

"Why, Miz Anna?" Jackson asked gently.

"Because Jeff is dead," she answered. She had meant to reply calmly, but the words had been torn painfully from her throat. It was the first time she had spoken them aloud, and as she did Leanna was overwhelmed by the horrifying fact that she had been blocking from her mind. Jeff was gone, and she would never see him again. She had lost her heart — and her very reason for living! Losing control and trembling violently, she cried piercingly, "I loved him so much, and I can't bear to go on living without him!"

"You'll go on, Miz Anna, just like I went on without Carrie. But you ain't ever gonna get over losin' him. It's been over twenty-two years, and I still grieve when I think 'bout Carrie. But, Miz Anna, you got to accept the fact that he's gone, and let out all that hurt you got bottled up inside you."

"Oh Jackson," she groaned. "If I start crying, I'm afraid I'll never stop."

"Maybe you're right. Maybe you ain't ever goin' to stop your cryin'. If you loved the major the way I loved Carrie, then you ain't gonna ever find an end to the pain."

"I did love him!" she cried piteously. "Oh, I loved him so much!" Placing her hands over her face, Leanna's shoulders began to shake, and deep woeful sobs tore from her throat.

Hesitantly, Jackson took a step toward her and then, suddenly, she was in his arms and he was embracing her compassionately. Holding onto his strength as though it were her life line, Leanna released her tears.

Jackson understood her sorrow only too well. As she wept for the man she loved, he whispered to her soothingly and from the bottom of his heart.

Chapter Twenty-two

Riding in the public carriage, Jeff paid scant attention to the hustle and bustle along the busy streets of St. Louis. The city had changed little during his absence, except that few young men were in evidence. Those he did see wore army uniforms. They were home on leave or were passing through on their way to join their regiments.

Leaning back on the cushioned seat, Jeff pulled his wide-brimmed hat lower down on his forehead to shade his eyes from the sun's harsh rays. He was facing west, and the setting sun was glaring into the open carriage.

The late autumn weather was chilly, and as the sun's warmth faded, cold air seeped through Jeff's uniform, making him wish he hadn't left his jacket at the home he shared with his uncle. Thinking about Walter Clayton, he once again silently cursed himself for not sending a wire to let his uncle know that he was coming back on a medical leave. This morning, when he had unexpectedly arrived home, he had been very disappointed to learn from the family butler that his uncle had gone to Chicago to visit an ailing friend. The butler had not known when the elder Mr Clayton would return, but he'd been quite certain that he'd be away for at least two more weeks.

With his uncle out of town, Jeff now wished he hadn't taken the leave. His wound was healed, and he could have returned to action. Moreover, since he was in St. Louis, he knew he had to visit Darlene. That wasn't a meeting to which he was looking forward. Although he believed Leanna had jilted him, he still planned to break his engagement to Darlene. Leanna's betrayal had so embittered him that he never wanted to marry any woman, and he fervently hoped he'd never see Leanna Weston again for as long as he lived.

Jeff was impatient to get the confrontation with Darlene over so the ride to her house seemed interminable. Since Darlene didn't know that he was in St Louis, he hoped she would be home, but the way his luck was running, he feared she wouldn't be in town either.

Sighing irritably, Jeff wished the driver would make the horse move a little faster, but then he remembered noticing the animal's condition when he'd entered the conveyance. The tired nag was probably moving as well as could be expected. Thought of the horse brought the image of his chestnut stallion to his mind. Everytime he was reminded that Leanna had stolen his prized stallion, his temper became aroused.

After Jeff's surgery, he had not fully regained consciousness for days. When he had come around

Dr. Johnson and the medic who had been with Leanna when she'd thought Jeff had died, had been transferred to another company. Lieutenant Buehler had taken command of Jeff's troops, and they had moved on toward Savannah, including Sergeant O'Malley, Jerry, and Paul. So there had been no one left to help Jeff fit together the jumbled pieces that might have explained Leanna's sudden departure.

Upon regaining consciousness, Jeff had asked immediately for Leanna, only to be told she had stolen his horse and escaped from Sherman's camp.

Fidgeting impatiently, Jeff shifted his weight in the carriage seat. During his convalescence, he had tried to figure out how Leanna could have left him when she didn't even know whether he would live or die. She was a rebel, a very rebellious one. Hadn't she tried to escape the day he had ordered her home burned, and the afternoon at the river? Had her loyalty to the South meant more to her than their love? Or had she never truly loved him? She had once told him she would never forgive him for destroying The Pines, and now he couldn't help but wonder if she had always hoped to find a way to even the score. She had suddenly stopped trying to escape; then she had won his trust, and also his love. Had that been her plan all along, to win his trust and love, then to leave him? She had deserted him the morning after he had confessed his love, which certainly made it look as though that had been her intention. He wondered if she had maliciously taken his stallion to add insult to injury, had that been the last twist of her knife?

Before coming to St. Louis, Jeff had decided to

331

travel back to the Westons' plantation, having convinced himself that his only reason for returning was to take back the stallion that belonged to him. But instead of heading directly to the plantation, he had chosen to ride to Marietta and check into a hotel. Riding into town, he had been astounded to see his stallion and another horse hitched to a buckboard. The wagon had been parked in front of a dry goods store, and going to the other side of the street, Jeff had dismounted. Standing on the sidewalk, he had watched Leanna walk out of the store beside Jennifer and a man he didn't recognize. The sight of Leanna had affected him profoundly, and it had taken all his will power not to call out to her. But this wasn't the time or place to confront her and then demand that she return his stallion. The town was filled with Union soldiers, and although Jeff knew his uniform drew no attention to himself, he still edged his way into the shadow of the building behind him so that there would be little chance of Leanna spotting him. Wondering who the man accompanying Leanna and Jennifer was, Jeff had asked an elderly man standing close to him if he knew the people across the street. When the man had told him they were David Farnsworth with his bride and her sister-in-law, Jeff had quite logically believed that Leanna was the bride and Jennifer the sister-in-law. Thinking Leanna had married David Farnsworth, Jeff had abruptly mounted the horse he had ridden into town and had left Marietta, relieved that Leanna hadn't seen him.

Jeff was sure Leanna had purposely played him for a fool, otherwise she wouldn't have married David Farnsworth. He supposed he could have gone to the

Westons' plantation and waited for them to return with his stallion, and if there had been any way to take back his horse without confronting Leanna, he would have done so. But Jeff feared his own violent temper. He was afraid if he came face to face with Leanna, he might be tempted to break her beautiful, conniving neck.

The carriage pulled up in front of Darlene's house, interrupting Jeff's musings. He paid the driver and stepped down to the sidewalk. The Whitlock home was located in one of the more prominent, residential sections, and the neighborhood was quiet as Jeff climbed the short flight of steps leading up to the front porch. Raising the brass knocker, he rapped it against the door.

Within moments, the door was opened by a maid. She had been in the Whitlock employment for years, and recognizing Jeff, the elderly woman smiled cordially. "Why, Mr. Clayton, what a pleasant surprise." Stepping back, she invited him inside. Showing him into the parlor, she informed him that Miss Whitlock was in her bedchamber and she would go upstairs to announce his presence.

Walking to the liquor cabinet, Jeff helped himself to a glass of brandy as he waited for Darlene. Within minutes, she appeared in the parlor entryway, and her loveliness caused Jeff to catch his breath appreciatively. He had almost forgotten how beautiful Darlene was. She was wearing a white, sheer dressing gown that seductively shadowed her voluptuous curves, making it quite apparent that she had on only the one flimsy garment. Her silken black hair flowed smoothly to her shoulders, and her slanting green

333

eyes sparkled brightly. Moving gracefully, her steps light, she seemed to float across the room and into Jeff's arms.

Placing his glass on the cabinet, he encircled her in his embrace, hugging her warmly.

Stepping back, she gazed up into his face and sighed breathlessly, "Oh Jeff, what a wonderful surprise you are. Why didn't you let me know you were coming home?" Not giving him the opportunity to reply, she continued rapidly, her voice so sweet that it dripped with honey, "Are you on leave, or are you home to stay? Oh, darling, I'm so happy to see you. . . . Are you well? You weren't injured, were you? . . . Why haven't you answered my letters? . . . Jeff, darling, don't you realize how worried I have been about you?"

Picking up his glass, and chuckling lightly, he replied, "Darlene, please, not so many questions at once."

"I'm sorry," she apologized demurely. "But I'm so happy to see you that I can barely control my excitement." She glanced down at her revealing apparel, then she slowly raised her eyes to his, and feigning embarrassment, she murmured, "When my maid told me you were downstairs, I was so beside myself with happiness that I foolishly forgot how I was dressed." Making a half-turn toward the doorway, she continued, "I'll hurry upstairs and change into something more fitting."

As she hoped he would, he grasped her arm and halted her. "That isn't necessary, Darlene."

Her face was turned from his, and Jeff didn't see the brief and calculating smile that curled her sensual

334

lips. She was sure he would try to make love to her, but she hadn't decided yet if she'd pretend to submit to his advances. It might be wiser to make him wait until their wedding night, which Darlene was determined would be very soon.

Releasing his hold on her arm, Jeff downed his drink, then returned the empty glass to the liquor cabinet. "Darlene?" he said softly, and she turned to face him.

"Yes, Jeff?" she replied sweetly, her experienced eyes secretly taking in his masculine physique. Jeff Clayton was indeed a handsome man, and she was anxious to bed him. When it came to male flesh, Darlene was a perfect judge, and she didn't doubt that Jeff would be a virile and expert lover. She hoped after she married Jeff to find a way to get rid of Darrin Spencer. Why would she need him when she had a man like Jeff Clayton to satisfy her sexual desires? And Jeff's excessive wealth was the icing on her cake!

Jeff had no wish to hurt Darlene, and he was beginning to feel like a damned cad. He had once taken cruel advantage of her so he owed her a good deal, but above everything, he owed her honesty. He didn't love her, and if he married her, he knew he'd make a poor specimen of a husband. She deserved better. If he set her free, perhaps she could find a man who would love her and be worthy of her.

"Darlene," he began again, "I came here to see you because I have something I must tell you. I suppose I could have written it in a letter, but I respect you too much to take the coward's way out."

Darlene was no fool. She knew where his words

were leading, and she exerted all her will power to keep her composure. But she longed to leap on him like a tigress, to scratch out his eyes with her long fingernails. How dare he have the gall to break their engagement! Damn it! If she lost him, within a year, she'd be completely destitute!

"I'm not going to marry you, Darlene," he continued gently. "I'm sorry, but I can't help how I feel. I don't want to marry you or anyone else."

Darlene's thoughts raced. What should she do? Should she try to seduce him, or to remind him of the night he had supposedly raped her, or should she pretend her heart was breaking and start crying?

Deciding on the latter, she placed her hands over her face, and sobbing, she cried, "But, Jeff, I love you, and I have waited so long for you! How can you desert me this way?"

"Believe me, Darlene, in time you'll realize I'm right. You don't want to marry a man who isn't in love with you."

Apparently, crying wasn't working, so she quickly stopped her weeping to remind him, "But you are the man who took my virginity, against my will, I might add!"

"I can't undo what has already been done. God knows, I will always despise myself for that night."

Darlene couldn't believe this was actually happening! Jeff had returned home only to break their engagement. She couldn't let him go! She needed his money too desperately!

Taking him by surprise, she threw herself into his embrace, and involuntarily, his arms went about her to steady her.

Standing on tiptoe, she placed a hand behind his neck, and drew his lips down to hers, letting her tongue dart between his teeth. She thrust her soft body to his strong frame, expecting to feel him grow hard as her thighs rubbed against his.

Receiving no response, she moved out of his embrace to look up into his face. She tried to read his thoughts, but his expression was inscrutable. Remembering their dating days, and his passion, she was incredulous to find that he hadn't reacted to her lustful advances.

Mumbling, he said abruptly, "Goodbye, Darlene, and . . . and forgive me."

Leaving Darlene gaping with disbelief, he hurried from the parlor. He grabbed his hat off the rack in the foyer; then opening the door, he darted outside. His sturdy strides quickly carried him from the residential section, and entering the business district, he hailed a passing cab.

Deciding the sooner he left St. Louis the better, he planned to return home, pick up his luggage, and leave the city immediately. There was still a war raging, and he was anxious to return to the battlefields. Perhaps in the midst of exploding shells and rifle shots, he could forget the rebellious little rebel spy who had won his heart only to destroy it.

Recalling Darlene's passionate kiss and her sensual body, Jeff wondered why he hadn't been able to respond. Angrily and reluctantly, he admitted the truth to himself. When Darlene was in his arms, it had been Leanna who was in his thoughts.

Clenching his hand into a fist, he pounded it against the side of the buggy, causing the driver to whirl on the perch seat and stare back at him. "I'll get over her!" Jeff swore furiously. "Somehow, someway, I'll forget Leanna Weston ever existed!"

Part Three

Fort Laramie

Chapter Twenty-three

Riding beside Nathan Hayden, Jeff listened attentively as the scout from Fort Laramie talked about the mountain ranges, rivers, deep gorges, and extensive plains and basins that were all a part of the Wyoming territory. Nathan Hayden had a natural gift for describing scenery, and as he elaborately described the land he considered his home, Jeff could easily envision the Rocky Mountains, the Big Horn, and the Wind River. Nathan Hayden was familiar with the entire territory, and as his horse plodded along steadily beside Jeff's, Nathan talked about the cottonwood, poplar, willow, ash, elm, and box elder that were so plentiful in the Southwest.

But the part of the Wyoming territory that Jeff and his troops were now traveling through was marked by extensive grassy areas, sagebrush flats, pine-clad foothills, and the rolling uplands of the Great Plains. And as they journeyed beside the North Platte River, the vast landscape seemed endless, and the glaring August sun beat down mercilessly upon the weary soldiers.

The scorching heat reminded Jeff of the hot summer he had spent in Georgia, and thoughts of Leanna again crossed his mind. It had now been almost a year since she had left Sherman's camp, and although he had tried to forget her, the memory of Leanna continued to torture him. He supposed she was the main reason why he hadn't returned to St. Louis last spring when the War between the States had finally come to an end. Only when he was in the midst of danger could he seem to keep Leanna from his thoughts. Jeff felt guilty about not returning home to help his uncle with their joint businesses; he knew Walter Clayton had been disappointed to learn that he was going to Fort Laramie instead of St. Louis. But Jeff hoped that after a couple of years in the West, he would lose the restlessness Leanna's betrayal had instilled in him and then he would be ready to return to St. Louis and resume his responsibilities. There was also Darlene to consider; surely after two years she would be married. If not, he supposed he would offer her marriage if she still wanted him, but it would be out of a sense of obligation and not love. Leanna had hurt Jeff so deeply that he was determined to never fall in love with another woman, regardless of how much she might claim to love him and need him.

Jeff became aware that Nathan had begun to talk about Fort Laramie, and he closed his mind to thoughts of Leanna and Darlene to give the scout his full concentration.

Jeff was anxious to reach the fort, and pleased that they were now only a couple of days away from it.

The army had sent Nathan to Kansas City, Missouri, to meet with Jeff and his troops, and to guide them to Fort Laramie. The journey had been a long and demanding one, and Jeff was relieved that it was almost over.

Jeff had had little knowledge of the Western Indians, so Nathan, who had spent most of his life in the West and was familiar with several Indian tribes and their customs, had taught Jeff much of what he knew during their trip from Kansas City. Although Jeff had yet to encounter hostile Indians, he now had some understanding of them.

Jeff liked and respected Nathan Hayden, and as they journeyed toward Fort Laramie, a strong friendship had developed between the two men.

Nathan was thirty-seven years old. He was tall and powerfully built, with sinewy arms and shoulders. He always wore fringed buckskins, and the soft material clung tightly across his wide chest and fit his long, muscular legs snugly. He was an attractive man, with thick flaxen hair trimmed so it barely touched his collar. His clean-shaven face had finely chiseled, prominent cheekbones, and his eyes were as clear blue as the Wyoming sky.

Suddenly, Nathan stopped talking about Fort Laramie, and sitting up straight, he shaded his eyes with his hand as he looked over the landscape.

"What's wrong?" Jeff asked.

"I think I see something, but I can't be sure what it is. We'd better check it out."

Raising one arm, and pulling up his horse, Jeff called, "Company halt!"

There were sixty-five men riding with Jeff, and

upon his command the long procession of soldiers and the five supply wagons came to a stop.

Turning to glance behind him, Jeff ordered, "Privates Rogan and Lammert to the front!"

Many of the men who had ridden with Jeff during the war were still with him, Jerry Rogan and Paul Lammert among them.

Riding out of formation, Jerry and Paul rode up alongside Jeff. "Yes sir!" they snapped in unison.

"You two will come with me," Jeff said, then speaking to Lieutenant Buehler, who was mounted behind him, he continued, "Keep the troops here."

Immediately, the lieutenant passed the order to Sergeant Lewis who relayed the command to the other soldiers, but without the gusto that Sergeant O'Malley would have used. Sergeant O'Malley had been killed in action while Jeff was on medical leave. If the sergeant hadn't died, he would most likely have told Jeff how upset Leanna had been when he was wounded, and that she had flatly refused to ride with Sherman's escort until she knew whether Jeff would survive. His information might have made Jeff have second thoughts, caused him to delve deeper into Leanna's reason for deserting him. Once Jerry had made an attempt to explain to Jeff that Leanna had been gravely worried about him the morning he was shot, but Jeff had told Jerry, with a great deal of bitterness, that she had apparently been feigning concern and he had ordered Jerry never again to mention Leanna Weston in his presence.

Jeff and Nathan broke their horses into a gallop, followed closely by Jerry and Paul. As they rode steadily across the flat plains, the vague form that

Nathan's experienced eyes had picked up in the distance began to take shape, and Jeff saw that it was an Indian boy. He was lying spread-eagle on his back, with his feet and hands tied to four stakes that had been driven into the ground.

Jeff and Nathan dismounted, and stepping to the boy, they knelt beside him. Studying the child, Jeff guessed him to be about twelve years old. He wore only his breechclout, and the scorching rays from the sun had blistered his exposed skin. His lips were cracked and peeling.

The boy stared wide-eyed at the two men kneeling over him. It had been white trappers who had staked him to the ground, and he doubted that these two white men would save him. One of them was even a bluecoat. He wondered if the soldier would decide to order his death.

The boy's name was Black Bear, and he had left the safety of his village to go into the wilderness to earn his manhood and to seek his vision. Six trappers had come upon him. Having captured him, they had decided to stake him to the ground so that he would die slowly before the buzzards feasted on him.

"He's a Sioux," Nathan said, removing his knife from the sheath he kept tied around his waist.

Seeing the white man's knife, Black Bear hoped he intended to kill him swiftly.

"Bring a canteen," Jeff called to Jerry and Paul.

Leaning over the boy, Nathan cut the ropes binding his hands, and as Paul handed Jeff the canteen, Nathan helped Black Bear to sit up. Opening the canteen, Jeff put it to the boy's dry lips.

Black Bear didn't understand why the man and the

345

soldier were giving him a drink, but his thirst was so great that he didn't question their motive. He drank the water they offered.

To Jerry, Jeff ordered, "Tell Lieutenant Buehler to continue, and then bring the medic."

As Jerry left to carry out Jeff's command, Nathan cut the ropes tied to the boy's feet.

Black Bear had been brought up to distrust and hate all whites so he watched Nathan and Jeff with extreme wariness.

Nathan could speak the Sioux language fluently, and he questioned Black Bear, who refused to answer, deciding it would be best not to talk to these white men.

When the medic arrived, Jeff told him to put salve on Black Bear's sunburned skin and on his chafed wrists and ankles where the ropes had dug into his flesh.

Standing beside Jeff, Nathan watched as the medic tended to Black Bear. "What are you going to do with him?" he asked Jeff.

He shrugged. "I don't know. Set him free, I guess."

Nathan smiled skeptically. "He's a Sioux."

"So?" Jeff questioned.

"He's the enemy," Nathan pointed out, his tone light.

"I didn't come west to fight children," Jeff replied inflexibly, before ordering Paul to bring a full canteen, plus a bag of field rations.

When Paul returned with the water and food, Jeff moved over to Black Bear. The medic had finished doctoring him, but the boy was still sitting on the ground. Kneeling, Jeff handed him the canteen and

346

the cloth bag.

"Tell him he's free to leave," Jeff told Nathan.

Without waiting for Nathan to interpret Jeff's message, Black Bear sprang to his feet. He made a quick move to flee, but, pausing, he turned to look at Jeff. "What are you called?" he asked in English.

Shocked that the boy could speak English, Jeff stood slowly as he answered, "Major Jeff Clayton."

"Major Jeff Clay-ton," Black Bear repeated carefully. "I will not forget."

Before Jeff could reply, Black Bear whirled and ran lithely across the plains, heading toward the rolling foothills that lay in the far distance.

The moon was high in the sky and the stars were twinkling brightly as Jeff left the campfire to walk over to his bedroll. It was fairly late, and except for the men on guard duty, most of the soldiers were asleep.

Catching sight of Nathan heading in his direction, Jeff slowed his steps. Nathan had a blanket tucked beneath his arm and was carrying his saddle. He fell into stride beside Jeff, and when they neared Jeff's bedroll, Nathan stopped to spread out his blanket.

Nathan chuckled, causing Jeff to hesitate. "When Colonel Wallace learns you set that Sioux free, he's gonna be madder than hell," he said, placing his saddle at one end of the blanket.

Jeff had never met Colonel Wallace, the commanding officer at Fort Laramie, but he was aware of the colonel's reputation for strict discipline and of his hatred for Indians.

"I wouldn't worry about the colonel though," Nathan continued. "He'll chalk up your decision to let the boy go to inexperience, and this time he'll overlook your behavior. But he'll make a point of reminding you that someday soon that Indian boy will grow into a Sioux warrior, ready and willin' to scalp soldiers and settlers."

"Will he hold you responsible for my actions?"

"He might," Nathan drawled. "But even if he does, he won't say anything to me. I'm not one of his soldiers."

"In my place, what would you have done with the boy?"

"The same thing you did, set him free," replied Nathan casually. Nathan was a good judge of character, and it had become quite apparent to him that Jeff was not the kind of soldier who would enjoy wiping out the Indians. While studying him closely, Nathan asked the questions that had been gnawing at him ever since he had come to know Jeff, "Why did you stay in the army? Why didn't you go home after the war? Was it because of a woman?"

Surprised by the last question, Jeff stammered, "Why would you think it's because of a woman?"

"You've got that look about you," Nathan replied insouciantly. "I can always tell when a man's tryin' like hell to get over a woman." He paused before asking, "Your wife?"

Jeff liked Nathan and didn't resent his prying. "No," he answered quietly, "she wasn't my wife. . . . She was just a girl who came unexpectedly into my life and left the same way."

Turning, Jeff walked over to his bedroll and lay down. Using his saddle as a pillow, he looked up at the dark sky. Recalling his last words to Nathan, Jeff closed his eyes and Leanna's image came to mind. Picturing her as she had been when he'd first seen her, Jeff couldn't stop the smile that touched his lips as he envisioned her in cut-off trousers, sloppy shirt, and tattered fishing hat.

Suddenly, he opened his eyes and her image disappeared. He would never stop loving her if he let himself continue to think about her. Purposely clearing his thoughts, he tried to fall asleep, hoping this time Leanna wouldn't find her way into his dreams.

But that night Leanna did return to haunt Jeff's dreams as she had done many times before and as he would continue to do in the months to come.

Leanna trudged wearily beside the canvas-topped wagon, never imagining that fate had placed her on the same trail that Jeff Clayton had covered only nine months before. It was late spring, but the sun was extremely warm and bright, causing her to pull her wide-brimmed bonnet farther over her eyes to shade them from the glaring rays. The lead wagons were sending clouds of dust swirling through the air, and the grimy particles clung to Leanna's clothes and settled heavily on her face and hands. Longing for a rest, she hoped the wagon train would soon stop for the noon break. She glanced around the area, searching for a good place to camp, but the vast plains beside the Platte River offered no shade or comfort, and Leanna knew it wouldn't make any difference when they stopped. The landscape wasn't going to change with the next mile, but would be identical to the last one and the one before that.

Although she had been traveling westward for over two months, Leanna still found it hard to believe that she was actually moving to California. Never in all her dreams had she imagined herself living so far from home. But now there was no reason to remain in Georgia: her mother had passed away and she had lost her plantation. The Westons had safely hidden much of their silver and jewelry, but that couldn't pay for the excessive taxes Leanna owed on her home. It had been David's idea to move to California. He had an uncle who had lived in San Francisco for years. The man owned more than one business, and David knew he would give him employment so that he could make a home for his family. But Leanna was determined not to become a poor relative living on David Farnsworth's charity. When they reached San Francisco, she intended to find a way to support herself. She hoped there might be a doctor who would hire her as his assistant so she could continue nursing. She could explain to him that she'd had a lot of experience during the war when she'd ridden with Sherman's army.

Soon it would be two years since Leanna had left her plantation with Jeff and his troops. She could still remember the morning as vividly as if it were yesterday. At the time, she had bitterly resented Sherman ordering The Pines burned, but now she was grateful that the columned house had been destroyed. The thought of strangers living on Weston land was depressing, but knowing these same strangers would have occupied the house her grandfather had built for generations of Westons would have been shattering for Leanna, and she was glad that the house no longer existed.

Continuing to walk steadily beside the wagon, Leanna sighed heavily. Dirt particles were constantly flying through the still air, and she felt uncomfortably grimy. There was little opportunity to bathe on a wagon train, and she longed for a bath as much as she longed for a real roof over her head. It seemed to Leanna that she had been living out of a wagon for ages. First there had been the long trip from her home to Independence, Missouri, where they had joined the wagon train bound for the Sacramento Valley. The Westons' silver and jewelry had purchased the covered wagon, mules, and essential supplies, but everything had been so expensive that there had been very little money left so Leanna hoped when they reached San Francisco it wouldn't take long for her to find work.

Slowing her steps, Leanna moved to the rear of the wagon and fell into stride beside Jeff's stallion. The covered wagon was drawn by a team of mules, and the two horses had been tethered to the back.

Walking next to the stallion, Leanna brushed her hand over his sleek neck. She and Jackson had taken special care of him, and he was as healthy and as strong as he had been when he'd belonged to Jeff. Leanna missed Jackson and Matilda and Louise, and she wished they had chosen to move to San Francisco. But Matilda had absolutely refused to travel across the wilderness, believing along the way she would most assuredly be scalped by savage Indians. So Jackson had decided to move his wife and daughter to Marietta, and Leanna prayed they were well and that Jackson had been able to find employment.

The stallion snorted softly and nudged Leanna's shoulder with his nose. She was sure the horse resented being tied to the slow-moving wagon and was probably longing for an exhilarating run. She wished she could saddle him, and climb upon his back so they could race with the wind as they had done back on the plantation. Patting his neck, she said soothingly, "You can't run, it would tire you too much, and we have a long day of traveling ahead of us." Once again, as she had done several times before, she wished she had asked Jeff if the stallion had a name. She could have given him one herself, but for some reason, she only wanted the stallion to have the name Jeff had decided to give him.

Thinking about Jeff caused tears to come to her eyes. Jackson had been right that day when he'd told her the pain of losing Jeff would never completely go away. Her grief was still with her. Leanna knew she would never stop loving Jeff Clayton. He had been her first love, and even if she did learn to care for another man, no future love could possibly compare to the one she had shared with Jeff.

Jennifer was riding on the wagon seat with David, and Audrey was in the back with Bradley and Matthew. The boys had fallen asleep, so Audrey decided to walk with Leanna. David stopped the wagon long enough for Audrey to jump down to the ground. Then as the wagon started to move again, she began strolling beside Leanna.

"I'll be so glad when we finally reach Fort Laramie," Audrey sighed impatiently. Wagon trains always camped at the fort for a few days, and the occasion was one to which the westward travelers

352

looked forward with keen anticipation. The fort had a traders' store where the women could shop, and the enlisted men's bar, which sold wine and beer, was open to the men on the wagon train.

"The wagon master told David that sometimes when the soldiers are on an expedition, and they come upon a wagon train, they escort it to the fort. Wouldn't it be exciting to be escorted by the cavalry?" Audrey asked with enthusiasm.

"I suppose," Leanna mumbled. Unlike the others, she wasn't looking forward to reaching Fort Laramie. It would be filled with soldiers wearing blue uniforms, and she knew the sight of them would bring back too many painful memories. Would there be majors at the fort? How could she possibly look at their uniforms and not think of Jeff? And the troopers, how many of them would remind her of Jerry or Paul?

Leanna's lack of eagerness didn't surprise Audrey who had grown accustomed to her peculiar moods. At times, Leanna would seem like the spirited girl she had been before the war, and then, for no apparent reason, she would suddenly become depressed. Sometimes Leanna's melancholy would last for days. Audrey didn't know why Leanna acted so strangely at times, but she strongly suspected that something traumatic had happened to her when she was Sherman's prisoner and that that was the reason for Leanna's puzzling behavior.

"Oh well," Audrey sighed, "we're still a long way from Fort Laramie." All at once, she smiled a little wickedly, "I'll bet the fort is overflowing with handsome men."

Laughing, Leanna asked, "Are you planning to catch yourself a husband?"

"If he's there," Audrey whispered dreamily.

"If who is there?" Leanna questioned, puzzled.

"The man I will love," Audrey murmured.

"We're only going to be there for a few days, that doesn't give you much time to fall in love."

"When I meet the man who is right for me, I won't need time. I'll know he's the one I've been waiting for, and I'll love him on sight."

Leanna didn't try to discourage Audrey's romantic fantasy. It hadn't taken very long for her to fall in love with Jeff, and if love could overtake her that quickly, then it could very well come about the same way for Audrey.

When Leanna offered no comment, Audrey said hesitantly, "I suppose you think I sound like a silly schoolgirl."

Turning to look at her, Leanna smiled fondly. "No, quite the contrary. I think you should hold onto your dreams. Someday it will come true, and when it does, you'll know the right man was worth waiting for."

Carefully, Audrey pried, "Leanna, are you speaking from experience?"

Leanna hadn't told anyone but Jackson about her love for Jeff. She hadn't kept silent about their relationship because he had been a Yankee or because she was ashamed, she had remained silent only because it hurt too much to talk about him.

"Yes," Leanna admitted sadly. "I'm speaking from my own experience."

"Who did you fall in love with?" she asked curiously.

"A Union major," Leanna whispered.

"A Yankee!" Audrey exclaimed, astounded. "What happened to him? Did he leave you?"

"He died," Leanna murmured.

"Oh, Leanna, I'm so sorry," Audrey sympathized sincerely. "Would you like to tell me about him?"

"No," Leanna replied quickly. "I can't bear to talk about him."

Audrey believed it might help Leanna if she made herself talk about this Union major, and turning to face her, she was about to encourage her to do so, but the vacuous stare that had come into Leanna's eyes dissuaded her. Audrey was familiar with Leanna's present expression, she had seen it many times before, and she was aware that Leanna had become lost in thought. But now she understood the cause of Leanna's moods, and she sensed correctly that Leanna was reliving memories she had once shared with a major in the Union Army.

Chapter Twenty-four

Audrey's steps were buoyant as she headed away from the circled wagons toward the Platte River. She carried an empty water bucket, and as she continued to move along briskly, she swung the bucket back and forth at her side. Audrey's mood was gay. The wagon train was now in Wyoming territory, and they were less than a day's ride from Fort Laramie.

The wagon train had just stopped for the noon break. After that, it would continue until dusk, set up camp for the night, and arrive at Fort Laramie the next morning.

The wagon master had cautioned his people not to wander far from the campsite, but forgetting his warning, Audrey strolled leisurely down to the bank of the Platte River. Jennifer had sent her to fetch water, and Audrey knew she should return promptly, but longing to have some time to herself she continued her careless stroll.

The wagon master had issued the warning to the men on the train, leaving it up to them to pass it on to their women and children. He had not delivered this advice lightly; the wagon train was now traveling across hostile lands where they might encounter the Sioux.

The Sioux Indians, also known as the Dakotas, were first discovered by Europeans when the Indians had lived on the headwaters of the Mississippi. But the neighboring Chippewa had driven them westward onto the Plains, and although their territory was usually in the Dakotas, the nomadic Sioux often wandered into Wyoming territory, attacking whites traveling westward.

David hadn't wanted to frighten Jennifer, Leanna, or Audrey so when he had warned them to stay close to the camp, he hadn't given them the true reason why. He had simply told them this was a precautionary measure and nothing to worry about. If he had told them about the possibility of encountering raiding Sioux, Audrey would not have wandered so far from the safety afforded by the wagons.

Sitting beside the murky river, Audrey placed the bucket at her side. Raising her knees, she tucked her long skirt about her legs and, folding her arms over her knees, gazed dreamily into the distance, taking little notice of the foothills that could be seen on the far horizon.

The two Sioux warriors crept up behind her so soundlessly that Audrey was not aware of their presence until one of them grabbed her arm and jerked her to her feet.

The warriors' faces were hideously painted, and their eyes were ruthless. Staring at them, Audrey screamed piercingly. At the same instant, the sound of gunfire came from the direction of the camp. Only fleetingly did it register with Audrey that Indians were attacking the wagon train; then her knees gave way and she fainted.

Regaining consciousness, Audrey first became aware of a pair of strong, rough hands holding her arms over her head. Opening her eyes, she gasped with fright when she saw that one of the warriors was standing over her. Lying on her back and trying to free herself from the Indian restraining her arms, she arched her body, fighting wildly.

Suddenly the warrior who had been standing beside her dropped to his knees at her feet. Clutching her long skirt and petticoat, he shoved the garments up to her waist, then spreading her legs, he knelt between them.

Audrey knew it was useless for her to fight, and as tears streamed from her eyes, she stopped her futile struggles. Watching the warrior kneeling between her legs, she could see the terrible hate in his eyes, and she was sure when he and the other Indians finished with her, they would kill her. Believing she would soon die, deep sobs tore from her throat as silently she begged God to let them kill her swiftly and mercifully.

The warrior reached for Audrey's underwear, but as his hands grasped the garment, a gush of blood suddenly spurted from the side of his head. As the dead Indian fell to the side, another shot rang out and the warrior who had been holding Audrey's arms collapsed forward, falling on top of her. Panicking, she thrust at his lifeless body, and although she was screaming hysterically, she somehow managed to shove him to the side.

Crossing her arms over her eyes, Audrey began crying uncontrollably. Everything had happened so quickly that she didn't have time to wonder who had killed her attackers, until she heard footsteps approaching swiftly.

The sun was directly overhead, and its glowing rays shone into her eyes as she removed her arms from her face. The man standing beside her was extremely tall. He wore a buckskin shirt that fit snugly across his wide chest and powerful shoulders. He carried a rifle loosely at his side, and his wide-brimmed hat, pushed back from his high forehead revealed locks of hair so blond that they were almost white. The sun's brightness illuminated the man, making him appear phenomenal. In all her dreams of romance, none of Audrey's knights in shining armor could compare to this romantic figure who had just saved her life.

Looking down at Audrey, Nathan Hayden was finding her as attractive as she had found him. Audrey's long, auburn hair was falling radiantly past her shoulders, and her hazel eyes sparkled with tears. The freckles splashed across her cheeks and nose made her resemble a young girl, but the fullness of her breasts left no doubt in Nathan's mind that she was a woman full grown. Audrey's skirt and petticoat were still up around her waist, and Nathan's eyes took in the lovely shape of her slender legs and rounded hips.

Moving unexpectedly, he took her hand and pulled her to a standing position, causing her skirts to fall back down her legs to the tops of her shoes.

"The wagon train?" Audrey suddenly gasped, becoming aware that the sounds of battle were still raging.

Grasping her arm, Nathan began leading her toward his horse as he explained hastily, "I'm a scout from Fort Laramie, and there's a full company of soldiers only a few miles from here. We were on our way back to the fort, but I decided to ride ahead and see if there might be a wagon train close by so that we could offer an escort."

Reaching his horse, he helped her mount; then slipping his rifle into its scabbard, he swung up behind her. Taking the reins, he said, "We've got to get the hell out of here and back to the troops so, little lady, hold on tightly because you're in for one helluva ride."

Audrey grasped the saddle horn, and Nathan's strong arms encircled her, making her feel safe.

He urged the horse into a wild gallop and headed the animal away from the wagon train. The horse's powerful legs stretched out into long strides as his hoofs pounded across the open plains. The fast ride jolted Audrey, and she tightened her hold on the saddle.

Knowing many lives depended on them reaching the soldiers, Nathan pushed the horse to the animal's full potential, and Audrey wondered how long the horse could keep up this rapid gait.

By the time the cavalry came within sight, the horse was foaming at the mouth and sweating profusely.

Seeing Nathan approaching, Jeff raised his arm and ordered his company of soldiers to halt. Lieutenant Buehler was mounted beside him, and watching

Nathan riding toward them, he said with surprise, "He has a woman with him!"

Riding up to Jeff, Nathan reined in the exhausted horse as he hastily described the Sioux attack on the wagon train and its location.

Nathan's horse was so worn out that it was about to drop in its tracks so Jeff said briskly, "Your horse can't make it back to the wagon train, so stay here with the woman."

Nathan agreed. "As soon as the horse is rested, I'll take the lady back to the train."

Looking at Jeff with pleading eyes, Audrey cried, "Oh, please hurry! I'm so afraid for my family!"

"Yes, ma'am," Jeff replied courteously. Then glancing at Nathan, he asked, "Do you want me to leave some men with you?"

"No, we'll be all right. You'll need every man you have, there must be at least a hundred Sioux attacking that train."

Her heart pounding with fear for her family's safety, Audrey watched wide-eyed as the cavalary rode away, the horses' hoofs stirring up loose dirt and sending it swirling about.

Swinging to the ground, Nathan reached up and helped Audrey dismount. "Is it safe here?" she asked.

Unsaddling his horse, Nathan assured her, "We aren't in any danger. When the cavalry reaches the wagon train, the Sioux won't head in this direction."

"But how can you be so sure?" she gasped.

Removing the saddle, he placed it on the ground, then looking at her and smiling charmingly, he answered, "It's my job to know these things."

"Oh, that's right," she remembered. "You said

you're a scout from Fort Laramie."

Taking the horse's blanket, Nathan used it to rub down the sweaty animal. "How many members are in your family?" he asked.

"My brother, his wife Jennifer, their two sons, and Leanna who is Jennifer's sister-in-law." Stepping away from Nathan and the horse, Audrey looked across the plains, but now she could barely see the dusty cloud surrounding the cavalry as they rode farther away. "Oh, God," she prayed raspingly, "please . . . please don't let David or the others be killed!"

Moving to Audrey, Nathan touched her shoulder, and she turned to face him. He was so tall that she had to arch her neck to look up into his blue eyes.

"Ma'am, I hope the soldiers will get there in time save your family."

"Thank you," she murmured.

He patted her shoulder, then stepped back to his horse to continue rubbing him down. Watching Nathan, Audrey noticed the way the muscles in his arms rippled beneath his tight-fitting shirt. She wondered how old he was and decided he must be in his thirties. She was barely past her twentieth birthday. Did their age difference make him think of her as a girl instead of a woman?

Confused, she turned away from him. Why had such a foolish question crossed her mind? Her handsome rescuer probably had a wife and children back at the fort. A man so attractive couldn't possibly be unattached. She was tempted to ask him if he was married but decided the question would be much too forward. But it would not be presumptuous to ask his

363

name.

She moved back to stand at his side. "I want to thank you for rescuing me, Mr. ? . ."

"The name's Nathan Hayden."

She liked his name, it seemed to fit him. "Thank you, Mr. Hayden, for helping me."

Spreading the blanket over the horse's back, he surprised her by mumbling shyly, "You're welcome, ma'am." She found his bashful response charming. It made him seem much younger and somehow vulnerable. Facing her, he asked politely, "What is your name, ma'am?"

"Audrey Farnsworth," she answered.

Smiling, he told her casually, "Miss Farnsworth, you're a very beautiful lady."

His unexpected compliment startled her, causing her to stutter, "Th-thank you."

Continuing his easy manner, he suggested, "While the horse is resting, why don't we become better acquainted?"

"Sir?" she gasped, not sure if she understood what he meant. Surely he wasn't planning to make advances!

Reading her thoughts, Nathan laughed gustily. "Miss Farnsworth, I didn't rescue you so that I could take advantage of you. I was merely suggesting conversation."

Blushing blatantly, she murmured, "Were my thoughts so obvious?" He nodded, and she apologized, "I'm sorry."

"Don't be sorry, Miss Farnsworth, because I'd thoroughly enjoy taking advantage of a lady as pretty as you are."

"You would?" she breathed. She knew she should find his remark in bad taste, but, instead, she was thrilled.

"Yes, I would," he grinned wryly.

Unable to keep her curiosity subdued, she asked in one quick breath, "Mr. Hayden, are you married?"

"No, I'm not married, and why don't you call me Nathan?"

Happy that he wasn't married, she answered with a smile, "I will, if you'll call me Audrey."

Agreeing, he took her hand into his and squeezed it gently before releasing it. Gazing steadily into his friendly eyes, Audrey realized she had been right when she'd told Leanna that she'd know the man who was right for her and love him upon sight. From the very first moment Audrey had seen Nathan Hayden, she had started falling in love.

Chapter Twenty-five

Hiding behind the covered wagon, Bradley kept Matthew between himself and the side of the wagon, sheltering his younger brother with his own body. While firing at the attacking Sioux, David had been shot, and Bradley looked on with fright as Jennifer and Leanna tended to his wound. The threatening sounds of gunshots, the yelping of Sioux, and the pounding of the Indian ponies riding around the circled wagons caused Bradley to place his hands over his ears and to move even closer to Matthew. His brother was crying hysterically, and trying to overcome his own fear, Bradley put his arms around Matthew and held him tightly.

Ripping away part of her petticoat, the distraught Jennifer handed the torn material to Leanna, who placed it over David's gaping wound. The bullet was lodged in his left side, just below the rib cage. Leanna had seen enough injuries during her stay at Sherman's camp to know David's wound was serious.

"Keep the bandage pressed firmly against it,"

Leanna told Jennifer; then she picked up David's rifle. Moving to the edge of the wagon, she cocked the weapon. There were so many Indians that Leanna didn't see how the wagon train could continue to hold them off. She was afraid that they were all doomed, and thinking about Bradley and Matthew tears blinded her eyes, causing her shot to be off target.

Due to the deafening sounds of battle, Leanna did not hear the blaring notes of the bugle, and she did not understand why the Indians suddenly began retreating. But as the cavalry advanced, and the bugler continued to blow "Charge," Leanna and the other settlers began to cheer exultantly.

Looking at Jennifer, Leanna exclaimed thankfully, "It's the cavalry!" Glancing at Bradley and Matthew, she placed her rifle on the wagon seat and held out her arms to them. "It's all over, and we're safe!"

Bounding to their feet, they ran toward her, and kneeling, she gathered them into her embrace, hugging them enthusiastically.

"Dear God," Jennifer prayed intensely, "please let a doctor be with the soldiers! Please!"

Releasing the boys, Leanna stood and watched as the Indians were chased onto the plains. A small group of soldiers left the others to ride toward the circled wagons. They approached at a steady gallop, and the commanding officer was riding in front. They were heading in the direction of Leanna's wagon, so some of the men on the train hastily parted the wagon from the one it was touching, making an opening for the arriving soldiers.

As the horsemen drew nearer, Leanna's eyes turned

368

to the officer riding in the lead. She didn't recognize Jeff at once; recognition came gradually, bringing with it momentary shock. Unable to fully grasp that the man she loved was alive, Leanna responded to Jeff's sudden presence by standing numbly and gaping at him as he rode his horse past her wagon and onto the ground encircled by the covered wagons.

Slowly regaining sensibility, Leanna's breathing deepened, and she placed her hand over her pounding heart. Her eyes were glued to Jeff, and she watched with wondrous disbelief as he reined in his horse alongside the wagon master. She opened her mouth to call him, but she couldn't find her voice. Thank God, he's alive! she thought. But how? How can it be? Doctor Johnson said that he was dead!

"Leanna," Jennifer said urgently, "please find out if there is a doctor with the soldiers." In a daze, Leanna was not aware that Jennifer had spoken to her. "Leanna!" Jennifer repeated loudly.

Startled, Leanna, tore her gaze from Jeff to acknowledge Jennifer. "What?" she uttered weakly.

"Find out if there is a doctor!" the other woman pleaded.

Moving precariously because her knees were trembling, Leanna headed toward Jeff, who was sitting on his horse talking to the wagon master. Her heart was beating so rapidly that she could feel it thumping against her chest. Oh Jeff! she rejoiced inwardly. My darling, you're alive . . . alive!

It was the wagon master who caught sight of her approaching and called out, "Is anyone in your family seriously wounded?"

She tried to answer, but her voice failed her, and

she could only nod.

"Doctor?" the wagon master said hastily, glancing up at the man mounted beside Jeff.

The doctor dismounted, then grabbing his medical bag, he hurried to Leanna and asked, "Where is your wagon?"

Jeff had continued his conversation with the wagon master, not bothering to look over his shoulder at the person to whom the wagon master had spoken.

"Your wagon?" the doctor asked again.

Leanna pointed toward the wagon behind her, where Jennifer was kneeling over David. The doctor left, and Leanna resumed her slow walk toward Jeff. As each step brought her closer to the man she loved, her pulse raced expectantly.

The wagon master walked away to check on his people, and as Jeff started to dismount, he caught sight of Leanna. For a moment he froze, unable to believe that he was actually seeing her. What was she doing on a wagon train bound for California? He had never imagined that she would leave the plantation she loved so dearly.

He tried to look at her indifferently, but against his will, he couldn't help but admire her loveliness. Leanna was wearing only one petticoat, which caused the skirt of her printed dress to cling to her rounded hips, and her low-cut bodice revealed the soft fullness of her breasts. Her blond hair hung loose, and the light breeze drifting over the land blew the long tresses back from her flushed face.

Pausing and standing beside his horse, Leanna looked up into the eyes of the man she had never

370

stopped loving. He's changed very little in two years, she decided, but I do believe he has become more handsome.

She waited breathlessly for Jeff to speak, and when he did, his words shattered Leanna's happiness.

"Well, if it isn't Leanna Weston, the notorious rebel spy, or should I say horse thief?" Jeff took no pleasure in his rudeness, but he'd be damned if he'd let her know how deeply her betrayal had hurt him. Speaking to his troopers, he ordered, "Dismount!"

Swinging down from his horse, Jeff stole a quick look at Leanna's stunned face before glancing away. Her sudden presence had taken him off guard, and he felt uneasy. Not knowing what to say to her, but remembering the doctor had gone to her wagon, he asked politely while trying to keep his voice on a even keel, "Who in your family is injured?"

"David," she replied vaguely, wondering why he was treating her so coldly.

Looking at her with sudden sharpness, he asked brusquely, "David Farnsworth?" Leanna nodded numbly. Jeff's temper was quickly aroused and he said harshly, "Don't you think you should be with your husband, instead of standing here with me where you aren't needed? Or do you make a habit of running out on the men in your life when they are wounded?"

As his accusation slowly registered, Leanna rasped, "Husband?"

Grabbing his horse's reins, Jeff began to lead him away from Leanna. Frantically, she stepped rapidly to his side. Clutching at his arm, she tried to explain, "But, Jeff, I'm not—"

371

Shoving her hand from his arm and raising his voice, he interrupted, "Go to your husband, where you belong!"

Jeff's hot temperament aroused Leanna's own anger, and she shouted furiously, "Jeff Clayton, you are still a hard-headed Yankee!" Tugging at his arm, she tried to deter his long strides. "If only you'd give me a chance to explain!"

Once again, he pushed away her hand. Before she could insist that he listen to her, the rest of the troops arrived. They had successfully driven the marauding Sioux into the plains, and the people on the wagon train welcomed them with vociferous cheers.

Spotting Jerry and Paul riding behind Lieutenant Buehler, Leanna cried happily, "I don't believe it!" Stepping away from Jeff, she called their names. Seeing Leanna, they dismounted hastily and rushed to her side. Hugging Jerry and then Paul, she pronounced, "This is a day filled with miracles!"

Jerry and Paul greeted her excitedly, both of them speaking and laughing at the same time. Her mood as gay as theirs, Leanna smiled and turned to her side, expecting to see Jeff. She was surprised to find he had left, and fleetingly, she looked about, trying to catch sight of him. Failing to locate him, she asked Jerry and Paul, "What is wrong with Major Clayton?"

"Wrong?" Paul questioned, not understanding.

She started to explain, but Jennifer's sudden appearance stopped her. "Leanna," Jennifer began, "the doctor will have to operate on David and remove the bullet." Facing Jerry and Paul, she continued, "The doctor wants me to ask the major or the lieutenant to order the medic to see to the wounded, and as soon as the doctor is finished, he will take care of the others. Could you please tell me where I can find the major or the lieutenant?"

Pointing to Lieutenant Buehler, who was standing only a few feet away, Jerry answered, "There's the lieutenant, ma'am."

Studying Jerry's face, Jennifer asked, "Haven't I seen you before?"

"Yes, ma'am," he replied.

"Of course! Now I remember. You were at The Pines." Recalling how she had cleverly tricked him by pretending to faint, Jennifer blushed noticeably. Turning back to Leanna, she reminded her, "You must report that Audrey is missing."

As Jennifer left to talk to the lieutenant, Leanna remembered regretfully, "Good Lord, how could I have forgotten Audrey!" Excitedly, she told Jerry and Paul, "You must help me find her! Before the wagon train was attacked, she had gone to the river for water."

"Is she a real pretty lady with red hair and freckles?" Paul asked.

"Yes," Leanna replied, astonished.

"She was found by Nathan Hayden, he's a scout from Fort Laramie. She's still with him, but he'll bring her back here."

"Thank God, she's all right," Leanna sighed.

The doctor approached them, and ordered Jerry and Paul to help place his patient in the wagon.

Silently, Leanna uttered a prayer for David's recovery, before once again looking around for Jeff. Where had he gone? She must find him and let him know that she wasn't married to David. Minutes elapsed as she remained where Jerry and Paul had left her, debating whether or not she should go in search of Jeff when they returned.

"Miss Weston," Paul began, "the medic is busy attending to the wounded and can't assist Dr. Douglass. We told the doc that you have some experience in nursing and he was wondering if you'd assist him."

Leanna hesitated momentarily. She was more than willing to help the doctor, but at the same time, she longed desperately to search for Jeff. Her concern for David determined her decision. "Yes, of course I'll assist the doctor," she replied.

But as she followed Jerry and Paul to her covered wagon where Dr. Douglass was waiting, she kept glancing over her shoulder, hoping to catch sight of Jeff.

Dr. Douglass was so impressed with Leanna's nursing ability that he asked her to help him with the rest of the wounded. She complied, although she was terribly anxious to find Jeff. She still found it hard to believe that he was actually alive, and it took all her will power to keep a tight control on her emotions as she assisted Dr. Douglass.

Dusk was falling by the time Leanna and the doctor finished with their last patient. Not giving Dr. Douglass ample time to thank her, Leanna hastily excused herself so she could look for Jeff.

She was walking through the camp when Jerry found her, and falling into stride beside her, he asked, "The man traveling with you, is he going to be all right?"

"Yes, but it'll take awhile before he's completely healed."

"Is he kin to you?"

"He's married to Jennifer." Halting their steps, she asked, "Where is Major Clayton?"

"He left to return to the fort," Jerry replied tentatively, realizing his news would upset her.

"What!" she exclaimed, immediately crestfallen.

"I'm sorry, ma'am, but the major ordered ten troopers to ride with him, and they left for Fort Laramie."

"When?" she cried.

"A couple of hours ago," he answered.

"Miss Weston," the wagon master called, walking toward them, "at dawn we'll be pulling out for Fort Laramie." Pausing at Leanna's side, he proceeded, "Your family will have to remain at the fort until another wagon train passes through. Mr. Farnsworth is too ill to travel."

Leanna was glad to learn that they would be staying at Fort Laramie, Jeff couldn't very well keep avoiding her if they were living at the same fort. Smiling pleasantly, she murmured, "Very well, we'll be ready to leave at dawn."

The wagon master, a large man in his early forties, replied, "Lieutenant Buehler has been left in charge, and he will order one of his men to drive your wagon."

"That won't be necessary. I can manage," she assured him.

"I'm sure you can, but all the same, I think it would be best if you ladies had a man to assist you," he said cordially before bidding her good evening.

As the wagon master was walking away, Nathan and Audrey returned, and guiding his horse close to Jerry and Leanna, Nathan dismounted. Reaching up, his strong hands grasped Audrey's waist, assisting her from the horse.

Quickly bidding Jerry good night, Leanna rushed to Audrey and hugged her vigorously.

"Leanna, is everyone all right?" Audrey asked urgently.

"David was shot, but he's going to recover," she answered.

"Oh Leanna, are you sure?" Audrey pleaded.

Having assuring her that David would be all right, Leanna looked at the tall man standing behind Audrey. He was extremely handsome, ruggedly virile.

"Leanna, this is Nathan Hayden." Audrey made the introduction.

Touching the brim of his hat, Nathan mumbled politely, "Glad to meet you, ma'am. I'm from Fort Laramie."

"Yes, I know. I was told that you rescued Audrey."

Nodding to Leanna, he replied, "Good night, ma'am." Then turning to Audrey, he said warmly, "Good night Audrey."

"Good night, Nathan, and thank you again for saving me."

Leanna waited until he had moved away before teasing Audrey, "Nathan? Are you two already on a first name basis?"

"Leanna!" Audrey breathed. "I am in love!"

"So soon?" Leanna asked merrily.

"Soon?" Audrey repeated. "I've waited my whole

life for Nathan Hayden." Smiling dreamily, she headed toward the wagon to see her brother.

Watching her leave, Leanna hoped Nathan shared her feelings, and that Audrey's heart wouldn't be broken. Then her thoughts turned to Jeff, and tears filled her eyes. Why had he treated her so coldly, and why had he gone back to the fort? Was it because he believed she was now David's wife? And, even more important, why hadn't he come to the plantation to let her know that he was alive and well? Had he never truly loved her? Had he been relieved to find that she had left Sherman's camp? Did he hope she would never learn that he hadn't died that day?

Wiping at her tears, Leanna hurried to where she had tethered Jeff's stallion. Going to the horse and wrapping her arms about his neck, she leaned her face against him and cried until no tears came.

Chapter Twenty-six

Jerry volunteered to drive the Farnsworths' wagon, and sitting on the seat beside him, Leanna strove for patience as the wagon train rolled steadily but slowly toward Fort Laramie. Audrey and the boys were riding in the back of the wagon with Jennifer and David. To Leanna the journey seemed to take forever. She was tempted to saddle Jeff's stallion and ride ahead to the fort. Knowing the horse would have her there in no time, it took all the self-control Leanna possessed to remain on the wagon seat instead of fleeing to the fort on the back of the powerful stallion.

Leanna had recovered from the initial shock of Jeff's presence and could now cope reasonably well with the fact that he was alive. If she hadn't been so overcome yesterday, she would have made him listen to her, would have made it clear that she wasn't married to David. But today she was in complete control of her emotions, and when she saw him again in a couple of hours, she would insist that he talk to her.

Fidgeting uneasily, Leanna wondered how Jeff could have treated her so cruelly. Even if he believed she was married, that was no excuse for his behavior. She had no reason to doubt that Dr. Johnson and the medic had told Jeff that she believed he had died. So she felt that Jeff must have realized seeing him again had been very traumatic for her.

Aware of Leanna's impatience, Jerry told her, "It won't be much longer, Miss Weston. The fort's only about two hours away."

Smiling warmly, she answered, "Jerry, I do wish you and Paul would start calling me Leanna. And speaking of Paul, where is he?"

"He left with the major," he replied.

"Do you know why Major Clayton went back to the fort?"

Jerry shrugged. "I don't know, but he was sure in a foul temper."

"I wish I knew why he treated me the way he did," she mumbled, but she was speaking more to herself than to Jerry.

"Well, Miss Wes—" He stopped, correcting himself. "I mean, Leanna. I might be wrong, but I don't think the major has gotten over you leaving him."

"Leaving him?" she pondered. "What do you mean?"

"At Sherman's camp, when he was in surgery, you left without waiting to see if he'd survive." Shaking his head, Jerry added, "And taking his horse, wasn't that kinda like kicking him after he was already down?"

For a moment Leanna could only stare at Jerry,

trying to make sense out of what he had said. Stammering, she asked, "But didn't Dr. Johnson or the medic tell Jeff that I thought he had died?"

Surprised, Jerry answered, "No, but Dr. Johnson was assigned to another company and pulled out the day after you left. The medic was probably on his staff and left with him. Why did you think the major was dead?"

Sighing, and growing limp, Leanna leaned over and placed her hands over her face, groaning, "Good Lord, no wonder Jeff treated me so coldly! He thinks I deserted him!" Oh, Jeff! she cried inwardly. All this time you believed I ran out on you! My darling, how much it must have hurt you to wake from surgery to find me gone!

Removing her hands from her face and sitting straight, Leanna explained what had happened the day she believed Jeff had died.

"I wonder why Dr. Johnson told you the major was dead." Turning and facing her, he asked, "Did the doc say Major Clayton died, or did he only say the major died?"

Thinking back, Leanna answered, "Neither one. The medic asked him if the major had died, and the doctor simply said yes."

Snapping his fingers, Jerry decided, "That must be it! Major Stark died that day. While you were outside talking to Sergeant O'Malley, Major Clayton was probably taken to surgery, and Major Stark was given his cot. Naturally, Dr. Johnson thought the medic was asking about Major Stark."

"Oh Jerry!" moaned Leanna. "You're probably right! If only I hadn't left the camp! But I was so distraught and also in shock."

Consolingly, he told her, "You can't change the past; but, thank God, you and the major have found each other again."

Tears swimming in her eyes, Leanna sobbed, "Jeff believes I left him without caring if he lived or died! He probably hates me!"

"No, I don't think he hates you," Jerry assured her gently.

"I'm sure he does!" she argued desperately.

"Well, even if he does, he won't after you explain everything to him."

Impulsively, Leanna clutched Jerry's arm, her fingers digging into his flesh. Intensely, she murmured, "These next two hours are going to seem like an eternity!" Deciding she couldn't wait that long to see Jeff, she asked rashly, "Will you please stop the wagon so I can saddle Jeff's horse and ride to the fort? I can be there in half the time."

Apologetically, he replied, "No, ma'am, I can't let you ride alone to Fort Laramie. This ain't Georgia, but Wyoming territory. If you want to see the major again, you'll stay with the wagon train where you're safe. The Sioux would love to see your pretty blond hair hanging from one of their lances."

Admitting reluctantly that Jerry was right, Leanna said no more about riding the stallion to the fort. She resigned herself to getting through the next two hours, but she knew they would be the longest two hours of her life.

Leanna paid little notice to Fort Laramie as Jerry guided the wagon through the gates and into the yard. The fort was built in the shape of a square, with a fortified blockhouse at each corner. The compound was filled with soldiers, trappers, and trading Indians, but the constant hubbub barely attracted Leanna's attention. Sitting on the edge of the wagon seat, and arching her neck, she hoped to spot Jeff somewhere in the midst of all the commotion.

"Is the fort always this busy?" she asked, still looking about for Jeff.

"Usually," Jerry replied. He headed the wagon to the location reserved for covered wagons remaining at the fort until another wagon train passed through.

David had been the only traveler severely wounded so the other wagons would camp outside the fort walls, then move on within two or three days.

The moment Jerry pulled the mule team to a stop, Leanna jumped to the ground. "Where is Jeff's office?" she asked.

Leaving the wagon, and going to her side, Jerry offered, "I'll take you to see him."

Leanna's excitement was so great that she completely forgot to tell her family where she was going, and with explaining her abrupt departure, she strolled away with Jerry.

Totally unaware of all the appreciative glances she was receiving from the soldiers and trappers, Leanna kept up with Jerry's long strides. They walked across the congested courtyard, toward a group of stone buildings that resembled barracks.

As they neared the wooden sidewalk, Jerry touched Leanna's arm, and guiding her in the right direction, he said, "Here's the major's quarters."

Seeing Paul standing in front of Jeff's office, Leanna smiled at him and said hello as she walked up the short flight of steps and onto the sidewalk. Tipping his cap, Paul returned her greeting with a large grin.

"Is the major inside?" Jerry asked.

"No, he left this morning with Captain Taylor and his troops," Paul replied.

Her heart sinking, Leanna moaned, "Oh no!"

"How long will he be gone?" Jerry queried.

"A week, maybe two," he answered.

"Why did he leave with Captain Taylor?" Jerry questioned, wondering why the major would choose to ride with another company.

Looking quickly from Leanna to Jerry, Paul answered hesitantly, "Well . . . from what I understand he asked Colonel Wallace if he could ride with the captain. He said for a personal reason he didn't want to be here when the wagon train arrived and he prefers to be away until after it leaves."

"And I'm the personal reason," Leanna sighed, disheartened.

To cheer her up, Jerry said brightly, "But your wagon won't be gone when the major returns. You'll still have your chance to explain everything."

"Did you say he'll be gone a week or two?" she asked Paul, hoping she hadn't heard him correctly.

"Yes, ma'am," he answered.

"So long!" Leanna cried. Dear God, she must wait at least a week before seeing Jeff! She had just spent the longest two hours of her life; now she was destined to spend an endless week or two!

* * *

384

Jeff was gone ten days in all, each day dragging by interminably for Leanna. She was in the fort hospital, doing voluntary work, when Jerry rushed inside to inform her that Major Clayton had returned with Captain Taylor and his troops.

Leanna had been folding bandages, and leaving the chore, she followed Jerry outside where she saw the returning soldiers entering the fort. Jeff was riding beside the captain, and the mere sight of him took Leanna's breath away.

She was quite a distance from him so he didn't see her, but he did notice that one of the covered wagons had remained. Cutting his horse from the orderly formation, he rode over to where the wagon was parked.

Recognizing his stallion tethered close to the wagon, Jeff dismounted swiftly, and going to the animal, he patted the horse's head. The stallion responded with a friendly whinny. Running his hand over the horse, Jeff was pleased to find him in perfect condition. It was apparent that Leanna had taken care of her stolen goods. But realizing the stallion's presence meant the remaining wagon belonged to Leanna and her husband, Jeff stepped back from the horse. He could hear low voices coming from inside the wagon, and not wanting to know if Leanna was one of the people talking, he walked to his mount. Irritated that his plan to elude Leanna had faltered, he took long, angry strides. Obviously her husband had been seriously wounded, and it had been necessary for them to stay at the fort. Now he could only hope that David Farnsworth would heal quickly and another wagon train would soon arrive. To be in the same fort with Leanna, with her married to another man, was almost more than he could cope with.

Leanna had seen Jeff ride in the direction of her wagon and had followed him. "Jeff!" she called, hoping he wouldn't ride away without waiting to hear what she had to say.

Mounting his horse, and taking the reins in his hands, he turned in the saddle to look back at her. She hurried her footsteps, and when she reached him, she paused at his horse's side. Gazing down into her upturned face, he was drawn to her loveliness. Her eyes were as blue as a clear morning sky, and the flush that had come to her face had turned her cheeks rosy. Finding her desirable, Jeff had to fight the urge to dismount and take her into his arms. But he'd be damned if he'd hold another man's wife!

"Jeff, you must listen to me," she began breathlessly. "There has been a terrible misunderstanding."

"A misunderstanding?" he questioned, his tone mocking.

But before Leanna could explain, a trooper on horseback rode close to them and called, "Excuse me, sir, but Colonel Wallace wants to see you immediately."

"Very well!" Jeff yelled back.

He started to turn his horse, but Leanna deterred him by crying, "But, Jeff, you must listen to what I have to say!"

"Leanna," he said curtly, "I seriously doubt if you have anything to say that I would be interested in hearing." Slapping the reins against the horse's neck, he rode away.

Watching him leave, Leanna's temper exploded, and placing her hands on her hips, she yelled at his departing back, "Jeff Clayton, you won't get away from me that easily!"

Her mind made up, Leanna marched determinedly to Jeff's quarters. There was a sentry stationed outside the door that led into the major's office, and when he tried to refuse her entry, she angrily defied him. Barging into the office and purposely slamming the door behind her, she sat heavily on a chair placed in front of Jeff's desk.

Surely when Jeff completed his business with the colonel, he would come to his office and she would be here waiting for him.

Folding her arms beneath her breasts, and frowning obstinately, she swore, "This time, Major Clayton, you won't get away from me, and you will hear what I have to say!"

Upon leaving the colonel's quarters, Jeff had joined some officers for a game of cards and it was dusk before he decided to go to his office. Greeting him, the sentry told him about Leanna's intrusion. Dismissing the soldier, Jeff stepped quietly into his office before slamming the door closed.

Leanna hadn't heard him enter, but the thunderous bang made her leap from the chair. Whirling, and seeing Jeff, she started to smile but the stern set of his jaw dissuaded her.

Removing his hat and hanging it on the rack beside the door, he said severely, "Hereafter, when you are refused permission to enter my quarters, you will do as you are told!"

"And if I don't?" she taunted. "Will you place me under arrest? If I remember correctly, it wouldn't be the first time."

Stalking across the room to his desk, he sat down in the chair placed behind it. Eying her warily, he gestured for her to be seated. As she complied, he asked coldly, "What can I do for you, Mrs. Farnsworth?"

"Well, you can start by not calling me Mrs. Farnsworth!" she snapped.

Cocking an eyebrow, he quipped, "Do you have something against the name?"

"No," she replied casually, deciding to be nonchalant. "But if we are going to be formal, then I prefer to be called by my own name and not someone else's. And my name, in case you have forgotten, is Miss Weston."

Puzzled, he stammered, "What are you trying to say?"

Smiling at his baffled expression, she answered, "I'm not David's wife. He's married to Jennifer." Dumbfounded, he stared at her with amazement. Unable to continue pretending aloofness, she asked excitedly, "Oh Jeff, why did you think I was married to David?"

Regaining his composure, he explained about the day he had ridden to Marietta. When he finished his explanation, it was Leanna's turn to stare at him with astonishment.

Her voice coming to her in a gush, she exclaimed, "You mean to tell me that you were actually in Marietta, across the street from me, and you didn't even bother to talk to me!" Thinking of all the grief he could have spared her, she bounded to her feet and yelled angrily, "Jeff Clayton, how could you?"

Finding himself suddenly on the defensive, he uttered hesitantly, "I . . . I thought you were married."

Leaning over and placing her hands on the desktop, she demanded, "Why must you always jump to conclusions? You have been that way ever since the day I met you when you presumed that I was a boy. And the day you ordered my home burned, you just took it for granted that I was attempting to escape when I was merely trying to put a little distance between the house and myself. Then that day down at the river, you once again assumed I was escaping when I waded into deep water looking for the bar of soap."

His own anger rising to the surface, Jeff stood to meet her unyielding gaze with one of his own. "Miss Weston, I don't give a damn whether or not you believe I draw my own conclusions!" he roared. "As far as I'm concerned, when you rode out of Sherman's camp without waiting to see if I would live or die, you proved that you are a conniving, resentful little rebel!"

"And once again you jumped to your own conclusions, proving you are a hard-headed Yankee!" she retorted.

"Damn it, Leanna!" he raved furiously, anger making him forget his resolution not to let her know how deeply she had hurt him. "After the love we shared, how could you have deserted me? Why in the hell did you leave me when I needed you most?"

"Because Dr. Johnson told me you were dead!" she

yelled.

It took a moment for Jeff to fully digest her words, and at first he responded with silence. Startled, he whispered hoarsely, "Dead?"

Suddenly, Leanna's anger was replaced with tears, and covering her face with her hands, she began crying.

Moving out from behind his desk, and hurrying to Leanna, Jeff grasped her trembling shoulders. "Why would Dr. Johnson tell you that I was dead?" he asked gently.

Calming herself, Leanna explained everything that had happened the day she left Sherman's camp, and she also told him the conclusion that she and Jerry had come up with.

Remembering, Jeff mumbled, "Major Stark did die that day. Of course I didn't know it at the time, but I was told later about his death." Leanna's eyes were lowered, and placing his hand under her chin, he tilted her face upward. "All this time," he marveled tenderly, "you thought I was dead. Sweetheart, I'm so sorry."

With fresh tears stinging her eyes, she studied his features, which she had never forgotten. She could see that he had aged a little in the past two years, but he had become more handsome with maturity. His dark mustache still curled downward, framing his full lips. Raising her gaze, she saw that there was more gray on his temples, but the premature streaks mingling through his black curly hair were extremely attractive.

"Leanna," he whispered intensely, "do you still love me?"

"Yes!" she cried, tears now streaming down her cheeks. "Jeff, you are the only man I have ever loved!"

Drawing her into his embrace and pinning her tightly against his lean frame, he murmured thickly, "Leanna, I love you. I tried to stop loving you, but I couldn't."

Clinging to him, she sobbed joyously, "Being in your arms again is like a miracle."

"Sweetheart, don't cry," he crooned.

"Jeff, you know I always cry when I'm happy," she reminded him.

Holding her so that he could gaze down into her face, he replied, "Yes, I know." Bending his head, his lips sought hers.

Initially, their kiss was tender, both merely content to feel the other's touch, but as their passion began to build, Jeff pressed her body closer to his. As her lips parted, his tongue entered to taste her sweetness.

Moving his warm lips to her ear, he said ardently, "Leanna, I want to make love to you."

"Oh yes, Jeff!" she breathed, holding her thighs flush to his so she could feel his wonderful hardness.

Sweeping her into his arms, he carried her to the open door at the back of his office. It led into a small bedroom. Taking her inside, he placed her on the bed, and then turned to close and lock the door.

The plain room was furnished with only the bare necessities, a bed, a night table, and a wardrobe. And as the long shadows of dusk were falling over the fort, it was quite dark.

Going to Leanna and lying beside her, Jeff took her back into his arms and kissed her desperately as he fondled her full breasts.

His nearness awakened the passion that had lain dormant in Leanna since the last time they had made love. Moaning with desire, she wrapped her arms about his neck, pressing his lips ever closer to hers.

"Jeff . . . Jeff," she pleaded raspingly. "I need you . . . my darling, I need you so much."

Standing, he helped her to her feet. "Leanna," he groaned, wanting her so badly that his strong frame trembled with his need. "Please get undressed."

Sharing his intense feelings, she slipped hastily out of her clothes as he removed his uniform. Still standing beside the bed, he drew her into his arms, and as their bare flesh touched, he kissed her, then moved his hands to her rounded buttocks and eagerly pressed her thighs to his.

Feeling his hardness throbbing against her, Leanna's knees weakened with anticipation.

"Leanna . . . Leanna," he moaned huskily, before kissing her forehead, her cheeks, and then her waiting lips.

Placing his strong hands on her narrow shoulders, he bent his head to run fleeting kisses over her neck and her breasts. Then kneeling, his lips touched her flat stomach, his tongue teasing her navel. Lowering his mouth, and grasping her hips, he kissed her delectable mound.

Entwining her fingers in his dark hair, Leanna urged him closer, and when his tongue flickered against her, she moaned aloud with ecstatic pleasure. Losing herself in their intimacy, she responded passionately to the glorious and heated thrill of his mouth.

Standing and easing her onto the bed, Jeff's frame covered hers. Her legs went about his back, and his hard arousal slid easily into her moist depths.

His exciting entry made her cry tremulously, "Jeff . . . darling!"

"Leanna," he rasped as her heat consumed him, sending waves of desire flowing through his entire being.

Sliding his hands beneath her hips, he elevated her thighs and, delving deeper into her warmth, pounded vigorously against her.

Equaling his demanding thrusts, Leanna arched her hips back and forth, and his manhood gliding in and out of her was so exciting that she purred provocatively, "Yes, my darling. . . . yes. . . ."

"Sweetheart, I love you," he moaned hoarsely.

"Oh, Jeff, I love you too," he murmured, thrusting upward and welcoming his thrilling penetration.

As their passion began to build feverishly, he moved strongly against her time and time again, and clinging tightly to each other, they reached the peak of pleasure simultaneously.

He kissed her lovingly before moving to sit on the edge of the bed. Reaching over, he lit the kerosene lamp on the night table and then bent to pick up his shirt from the floor. He took a cheroot from the pocket before he dropped the garment. Placing his pillow against the headboard, he leaned back and, stretching leisurely lit the small cigar. Then he put an arm around Leanna's shoulders and drew her to his side.

"Jeff," she began as an idea occurred to her, "would it be all right if I spent the night here?"

"Won't your family miss you?" he asked.

"Audrey and I are staying at the hotel, but we have separate rooms, so no one will know that I'm not there."

Not wanting her to leave, he agreed. "Of course you can stay." Pulling her closer, he murmured, "It's still so hard for me to believe you are a part of my life again. Oh God, I love you so much!"

"When I thought you had died, I wanted to die too," Leanna confessed intensely.

"Sweetheart, don't think about that time," he said soothingly, as as she snuggled her head against his shoulder. Bending down, he kissed her forehead, murmuring, "We're together now, and nothing or no one will ever separate us again."

Chapter Twenty-seven

Leanna dressed hastily, Jeff was waiting for her in his office. He was determined to take her to the hotel dining room for breakfast, but she was not sure if they should be seen together so early in the day. Jeff had told her that Colonel Wallace was very strict, and if he should suspect they had spent the night together, she felt that Jeff might get into trouble with his commanding officer.

Sitting on the edge of the bed, Leanna slipped into her shoes. She recalled the night she had just spent with Jeff, and she sighed. It had been the most beautiful night of her life. Not only had they made love several times but they had long talks. She and Jeff had spoken of their innermost feelings and had related to each other what had happened in their lives while they were separated.

"Leanna," Jeff called from the other room, "are you about ready?"

Apparently the man she adored was still an impatient one, and smiling tolerantly, she answered, "I'll be right there."

Realizing she was quite hungry, Leanna hurried from the bedroom, and entering the office, she saw Jeff sitting behind his desk. "I'm ravenous," she said eagerly. "Making love all night has certainly given me an appetite."

Getting out of his chair and moving to Leanna, Jeff took both her hands in his. For a moment he studied her face before murmuring sensually, "Leanna Weston, I love you."

"Jeff," she whispered, her eyes worshipping him, "I love you too."

He drew her into his embrace bringing his lips down to hers, and sliding her arms about his neck, she returned his kiss with all her heart.

As he released her, she asked carefully, "Aren't you worried that Colonel Wallace might see us going to breakfast together and suspect I spent the night with you?"

"I do not care what the colonel thinks," he replied, showing no concern. He longed to tell her that soon he wouldn't be a major and would owe Colonel Wallace no explanations. Jeff had taken the Fort Laramie assignment without signing on for a full term. His reenlistment papers were at this very moment lying on his desk unsigned. He had decided not to sign them, but to marry Leanna and leave the army. He was a wealthy man, and he certainly didn't expect his wife to endure all the hardships connected with army life when he could offer her so much more. But he would wait until tonight before asking Leanna to marry him and informing her of his plans. He wanted it to be a special and romantic evening.

He would take her to dinner, then they would go for a buggy ride, park beside the river, and there beneath the moon and the stars, he'd ask her to be his wife.

Suddenly, a solid rap sounded on the office door, and Jeff called out, "Who is it?"

"Trooper Rogan," they heard Jerry reply.

Striding to the door, and opening it, Jeff asked, "What is it?"

Saluting, Jerry answered, "Sir, Captain Rhodes and his troops are arriving."

Returning Jerry's salute, Jeff grumbled, "I didn't expect the captain for another day or two." Sighing heavily, he continued, "Very well, trooper. When Captain Rhodes arrives, show him into my office."

Closing the door, and returning to Leanna, he explained, "Captain Taylor and his company are to be transferred to Fort Casper; Captain Rhodes and his troops are their replacements. They are arriving from Independence, Missouri."

"My goodness," Leanna marveled, "there are so many soldiers being transferred to the West."

"Yes, and it won't be very long before these lands are tamed and the Indians who survive are placed on reservations."

"In a way, I feel sorry for the Indians," Leanna uttered sadly. "They were here first, and we are the intruders."

He wanted to tell her not to worry, they wouldn't be involved with civilizing the West, but he still wished to wait until tonight before revealing his plans for their future. "I'm sorry, Leanna," he apologized, "but I'll be a little late for breakfast. I must welcome Captain Rhodes, so why don't you wait for me at the hotel?"

"I'll meet you in the dining room," she replied.

Hearing the troops arriving, Jeff took her arm to escort her to the door, but he paused to embrace her and give her a lingering love-filled kiss.

A loud knock on the door broke them apart, and Jeff said firmly, "Come in."

Opening the door and standing beside it, Jerry announced, "Sir, you have a visitor."

"A visitor?" Jeff responded, puzzled.

Making her entrance grandly, Darlene Whitlock swept into the office, her long skirts flowing gracefully with her light steps. She moved so elegantly that she appeared to glide across the floor, and taking Jeff by surprise, she embraced him as though he belonged to her. As she hugged him, Darlene caught sight of Leanna and was instantly filled with jealousy.

Hesitantly, Jeff returned her greeting before moving away from her.

Leanna looked on with amazement. She had never seen a woman so beautiful, and she knew without being told that this was Darlene Whitlock. Enviously, Leanna's eyes examined Darlene's olive green riding habit. She hadn't seen a garment so grand since before the war. It had been made to fit Darlene's voluptuous curves perfectly, accentuating her ample breasts and full hips. A matching green bonnet with a plume was perched atop Darlene's raven black curls which were pinned up so that tiny ringlets framed her face and slender neck. She wore tight-fitting leather gloves, and in one hand she carried a braided quirt. Glancing down at her own mended gown, Leanna felt terribly unattractive by comparison.

"Darlene!" Jeff said, astounded, "What are you doing here?"

Pretending surprise, Darlene looked up at him innocently, her enticing green eyes sparkling. "What do you mean, darling?" she asked in her husky, provocative voice.

Hearing another woman call Jeff darling was more than Leanna could take, and holding back her tears, she hurried past Jerry who was still standing at the open door. As she rushed outside, she heard Jeff call her name, but she couldn't bear to be in the same room with Darlene so she hurried on.

Looking at Jerry, Jeff ordered, "Tell Captain Rhodes I have a personal matter to attend to with Miss Whitlock, and I'll talk to him shortly."

"Yes, sir," Jerry answered, leaving and closing the door behind him.

"Darlene," Jeff began, his voice edged with impatience, "why did you come here? And how in the hell did you talk Captain Rhodes into bringing you with him?"

Feigning sincerity, she answered, "Jeff, I don't understand why you are so surprised to see me." Trying to appear perplexed she furrowed her brow. "Didn't you receive my letter?" she asked, knowing he couldn't very well have received a letter that had never been written.

"What letter?" he demanded irritably. "And how did you know I was at Fort Laramie?"

"Your uncle has told everyone where you are. And, darling, I wrote you and told you how much I still love you. In my letter, I said if you don't want me to join you to write back and let me know. I said if I

399

didn't hear from you, I would sell my house and my father's business, and come to you."

"Good God!" Jeff said, astonished. "Darlene, I can't believe you acted so irrationally! Didn't you realize how easily a letter could get lost between St. Louis and here?"

"But, Jeff," she began, pouting now, "when I met Captain Rhodes in St. Louis and explained to him about my letter, he said it was very unlikely that it didn't reach you."

"How in the hell would he know?" Jeff remarked testily. "He's probably never been farther west than Missouri!"

Darlene had prepared herself thoroughly for this meeting. She had suspected that Jeff might be upset so she had rehearsed this scene over and over again in her mind. She knew it was now time for her to start crying.

Turning away from Jeff, she covered her face with her hands, and sobbing with the expertise of a professional actress, she cried, "Oh Jeff, I'm so dreadfully sorry! Please forgive me! But when I didn't get a letter from you, I thought you wanted me to come to Fort Laramie. I asked Captain Rhodes to let me accompany him and he agreed."

"Did you meet Captain Rhodes by chance?" he asked.

Making a believable attempt to stop the tears that she had forced to materialize, Darlene answered quietly, "While Captain Rhodes was visiting St. Louis, he played cards with Darrin Spencer, and it was Darrin who informed me that the captain was being transferred to Fort Laramie." Facing him and brushing away the last of her tears, she sniffled, "Darrin knew that I had written to you. He and I are very good friends, and he has always known how much I love you."

His anger mellowing, Jeff moved to Darlene, and placing his hands on her shoulders, he gazed down into her beautiful face. It seemed he was always causing her heartache, and feeling guilty, he murmured compassionately, "Darlene, I'm so sorry about this unfortunate incident."

"Jeff, my darling," she intruded, not allowing him time to continue, "if you'll only give me a chance, I know I can make you fall in love with me!"

"That would be impossible," he explained tenderly, "because I'm already in love with someone else."

"The woman who was here when I arrived?" she wasked, her expression kind, although inwardly she as immediately consumed with jealousy.

"Yes," he answered. "I plan to ask her to marry me."

"When?" she asked breathlessly.

"Tonight," he replied. Removing his hands from her shoulders, he stepped back. "Darlene, you will have to return to St. Louis at the first opportunity."

Darlene had calculated her plans carefully, but she hadn't counted on another woman. She had been certain that fort life would have rendered Jeff so hungry for female companionship that she would have no problem manipulating him into marriage. That Jeff might be in love with a woman who was actually living at the fort had never entered Darlene's thoughts. Darlene knew Jeff was not the kind of man to fall in love lightly, and if she tried to compete with

401

this other woman, she would most likely lose. To win Jeff, it would be necessary for her to find a way to get rid of her rival, but she would need time to make her plans.

"Darlene?" Jeff repeated gently. "You must go back to St. Louis."

"How long will it take to make arrangements for me to leave?"

"There will be a company of soldiers arriving within two or three weeks from Fort Casper."

"Will they let me accompany them?" she asked.

"Yes, of course," he replied. Jeff had planned that he and Leanna would leave with these soldiers, but Darlene's presence would create an awkward situation for the three of them. He wondered if he should postpone his and Leanna's trip.

Darlene realized that two or three weeks would give her time to think of a way to dispose of the woman Jeff planned to marry. Hopefully, she could do so before they married, but if not, then if it was within her power, Jeff would soon find himself a widower.

"Jeff," she began sweetly, "I want you to know that I am very happy for you. I hope this woman you intend to marry realizes how fortunate she is to have a man like you."

Smiling, Jeff answered, "I am the fortunate one. Leanna Weston is a very lovely and compassionate woman."

"I'm sure she is," Darlene agreed generously. "Otherwise, you wouldn't have fallen in love with her. Although it is breaking my heart to lose you, I wish you both the very best."

Studying her with admiration, he replied, "Thank you, Darlene." Taking hold of her arm and leading her to the door, he said, "I'll walk you to the hotel and help you check in."

As she faced him, she displayed a smile she knew he would interpret as one of noble defeat; then she murmured, "Jeff, please don't let my presence put a damper on your happiness. I have always loved you unselfishly, and when I said I wish you the best, I meant it with all my heart."

Chapter Twenty-eight

As soon as Jeff had helped Darlene check into the Fort Laramie hotel, he had gone to the dining room, hoping to find Leanna, but she hadn't been there. Although he had wanted to continue to search for her, he had military business to carry out so it was past noon before Jeff finally found time to try to locate her.

He decided to check the covered wagon first, and he saw Leanna behind it, grooming the stallion. Walking toward her, he moved quietly and she didn't hear his approach.

"Leanna?" he said softly, pausing to stand behind her.

Startled, she dropped the brush she had been using to groom the stallion and whirled about. "Jeff!" she breathed.

Taking her by surprise, he drew her against him, and swiftly, his lips came down on hers. He kissed her with deep longing before murmuring in her ear, "Leanna, I love you very much."

Embracing him, she replied intensely, "I love you, Jeff."

Releasing her slowly, he asked, "Why did you run out of my office? If you had stayed, I would have introduced you and Darlene."

"Oh, Jeff," she blurted out, "I just couldn't stay in the same room with Darlene! She's so beautiful!"

Grinning tenderly, he queried, "You left because Darlene is beautiful?"

"She called you darling," Leanna mumbled, wishing she weren't so jealous of Jeff.

Chuckling heartily, Jeff pulled her back into his arms to hug her tightly. "My little rebel spy, you have nothing to worry about. I told you a long time ago that you have my heart . . . and my horse," he added teasingly, cocking an eyebrow as he glanced at the stallion.

"I intend to give him back to you," she quickly explained.

Kissing the tip of her nose, he replied, "You keep him."

"Oh, I couldn't!" she objected. "I know how fond you are of him!"

"Leanna," he began, using his military voice of authority, "never look a gift horse in the mouth."

She laughed gaily. "Jeff, what is his name?"

"I never gave him one," he answered.

"How could you have been so neglectful?'

"He didn't seem to mind," Jeff replied with a wry smile.

"We must give him a name," she decided, turning to rub her hand down the horse's neck. "Do you have any suggestions?"

406

He thought a moment before replying, "Why don't we call him Rebel? After all, he was born in Kentucky."

"He was?" she asked.

"When he was a two-year-old, he was brought to St. Louis, and I bought him at a horse auction."

"All right," she agreed. "His name will be Rebel." Facing Jeff, she paused and then asked the question that had been weighing heavily on her mind, "Why did Darlene come to Fort Laramie?"

Hastily he explained everything to Leanna, then finished by saying, "The troops from Fort Casper will arrive within two or three weeks and she'll leave with them."

"I don't trust her," Leanna stated impulsively.

"How can you distrust Darlene when you don't even know her?"

"Female intuition, I suppose. But I've had my doubts about her ever since you told me she claimed you slipped into her bedroom and forced yourself on her."

Sighing, Jeff said impatiently, "Leanna, there was no conspiracy that night. I'm fully responsible for what I did." Holding onto her shoulders and gazing deep into her eyes, he continued gently, "Sweetheart, we discussed all this once before, and I told you then that you must admit to yourself that I could be capable of that kind of violence."

"I'll never believe Darlene's accusations. She lied!" Leanna said firmly.

Before Jeff could try to convince her otherwise, Jennifer stepped down from the wagon, and seeing Leanna and Jeff together, she stammered, "Major

Clayton."

Standing at Leanna's side, Jeff nodded cordially to Jennifer. "Good afternoon, Mrs. Farnsworth."

Jennifer didn't know why she had been so surprised to see Major Clayton. She should have known when she recognized Jerry Rogan at the wagon train that he would have the same commanding officer he'd had during the war. Jennifer still felt a lot of bitterness toward Yankees, but looking closely at Leanna and Jeff, she sensed their relationship was not a casual one. "Major Clayton," she said ill-manneredly, "I realize we are camping in your fort, but, all the same, you are not welcome at this wagon."

"Jennifer!" Leanna exclaimed.

Releasing her resentment, Jennifer turned to Leanna. "This Yankee burned The Pines, the home Brad loved, and the house that was supposed to be inherited by Bradley junior!"

"I don't believe you!" Leanna cried incredulously. "Even if The Pines hadn't burned, Bradley would never have inherited it! Have you forgotten that none of us could pay the taxes owed?"

"Of course, I haven't forgotten," Jennifer said irritably. "But that is beside the point. When Major Clayton destroyed the house, he didn't know the North was going to win the war."

"Of course he knew the North would win," David said suddenly, as he moved to the rear of the wagon to look out at the others. He had a bandage wrapped around his chest, and his shirt was draped over his shoulders. "Jennifer, the South had already lost the war. We should have surrendered and saved all the lives, on both sides, that were lost during those last, blood-spilling months." Glancing at Jeff, he continued, "Major, I wish to apologize for my wife's rudeness. I would also like to thank you for running off the Sioux and saving my family from being massacred."

"You're welcome, but I was merely doing my job," Jeff replied. "And you needn't apologize for your wife. The lady is honest and speaks her mind. For that, I respect her." Turning toward Jennifer, Jeff removed his hat, and bowing gallantly, he said, "Good day, madam."

Coldly, she replied, "Good day, Major Clayton."

Jeff whispered to Leanna, "Meet me in the hotel dining room at seven o'clock. We'll have dinner, then take a buggy ride."

She gladly consented, and not caring what Jennifer thought, she stood on tiptoe and kissed him affectionately before he left to return to his office.

Audrey descended the hotel stairway and walked swiftly through the small lobby, intending to go to the wagon and spend the rest of the afternoon with Jennifer and David. As she stepped outside, she was happy to see Nathan Hayden strolling across the compound. Calling to him, she hurried past soldiers and trappers.

Waiting for her to reach him, Nathan smiled as his eyes took in Audrey's beauty. Her long auburn hair was tied back from her face with a pink ribbon that matched the roses in her colorful dress.

"You look very lovely," Nathan complimented. "Is that a new dress?"

Standing in front of him and glancing down at the garment she was wearing, Audrey replied, "No, I've had this dress for years. It's been mended time and time again." Slowly, she raised her eyes to his. She knew the question she was getting ready to ask was much too forward, but she had been staying at the fort for almost two weeks and, to her dismay, Nathan hadn't bothered to call on her. She decided she must take it upon herself to make the first move; if she waited for Nathan to start a relationship between them, it might never come about.

"Nathan," she asked apprehensively, "why have you been avoiding me?"

She noticed he looked a trifle surprised. "I haven't been trying to avoid you, little lady."

"Don't call me that!" she spouted, frowning.

"Why not?" he asked, grinning charmingly.

"When you call me little lady, it sounds as though you think of me as a girl instead of a woman," she answered rashly, immediately embarrassing herself.

Guffawing loudly, Nathan's broad shoulders shook with deep laughter. Gazing down into Audrey's blushing face, he replied mirthfully, "You don't beat around the bush, do you? You come right out and say what's on your mind."

His masculinity was overwhelming Audrey, and his handsome good looks accelerated her pulse. The difference in their ages only made her love him more, and not caring if he thought she was chasing him, she explained breathlessly, "I am not a flirt, Nathan Hayden. But I find you . . . well, I find you very attractive, and I was hoping you would ask my brother if you could call on me."

"Call on you?" he questioned, his blue eyes twinkling amusedly.

Raising her chin proudly, she answered while keeping her tears in check, "Apparently, you had no such intention, and I have behaved much too forwardly. Please forgive my imprudent conduct."

She turned brusquely to leave, but Nathan stopped her retreat by grasping her arm. "Not so fast, little lady."

Perturbed because he obviously did not plan to abide by her wish to quit referring to her as little lady, she jerked away from his hold.

"In the first place," he said clearly, "I will not ask your brother's permission to see you. I don't ask any man what I may or may not do. I have always done as I damned well please, and I will continue to do so. In the second place, I haven't been avoiding you. I couldn't very well call on you when I have been away from the fort."

"Why didn't you tell me you were leaving?" she asked impetuously.

Raising his eyebrows questioningly, he answered with a half-grin, "I didn't know I was supposed to report my whereabouts to you."

Sighing, she apologized sincerely, "Nathan, I am sorry. Once again I behaved too impulsively. I wouldn't blame you if you never spoke to me again."

Placing his hand beneath her chin, he tilted up her face so that he could see into her eyes. "How old are you?"

"Twenty," she answered.

Continuing to cup her chin, he said gently, "Audrey, this fort is filled with young, handsome soldiers, so why are you wasting your time on a man seventeen years older than you?"

"Am I wasting my time, Nathan?" she pleaded.

Stepping back, he answered, "I'm not the right man for you. Find yourself a well-bred gentleman."

"But you're obviously well bred and also a gentleman," she argued.

"Am I?" he challenged. "How can you be so sure?"

"Are you telling me that looks can be deceiving?"

"In my case, yes," he replied. Touching the brim of his weather-worn hat, he said politely, "Good day, Audrey."

Watching him as he strolled away, Audrey felt terribly disillusioned.

Audrey was not the only woman whose eyes were on Nathan Hayden as he walked across the compound. Standing at her hotel window, Darlene had seen Nathan leave Audrey, and she found him fascinating. She wondered who he was and considered making a play for him, but afraid Jeff might find out, she immediately rejected the idea.

A knock sounded, and although she was wearing nothing but a dressing gown so sheer that it was transparent, she nonetheless crossed the room and opened the door.

"Captain Rhodes!" she exclaimed.

Admiring her full breasts and the dark vee between her thighs that the wrap merely silhouetted, the captain stepped uninvited into the room. "Captain Rhodes?" he questioned. "Why so formal? In St. Louis, and during the journey here, you were only too willing to call me Larry."

Closing the door and locking it, she replied, "I told you when we reached Fort Laramie we would no longer be lovers."

"Yes, I remember," he answered, taking off his hat and pitching it onto a nearby chair.

Captain Rhodes was a good-looking man in his early thirties, and Darlene had thoroughly enjoyed him as a lover, but she certainly had no intention of continuing their affair.

"Why did you come to my room?" she asked.

"I had a talk this morning with Major Clayton, and he told me he never received your letter. He also informed me that he has every intention of sending you back to St. Louis. I understand you will be leaving with the troops from Fort Casper."

"So?" she huffed.

Pulling his shirt out of his trousers and unbuttoning it, he answered calmly, "Apparently, Major Clayton has no plans to take care of your sexual needs. So I am here to offer you my services, and I will continue to do so until it's time for you to leave."

"I don't need your services," she spat, but her voice lacked conviction.

"Of course you do," he insisted tolerantly, removing his shirt. "You are the kind of woman who will always need stud service." Smiling slyly, he added, "If you still have your cap set for the major, I'll never tell him about us. You can trust me, Darlene."

Captain Rhodes' physique was solid and muscular, and as he continued to disrobe, Darlene couldn't stop the tingling sensation that suddenly pinpointed itself between her legs.

Sitting on the edge of the bed, he took off his

413

boots; then he unbuckled his belt and slipped his pants and undershorts over his hips and down his legs. Without getting up, he stepped out of the clothes, kicking them to the side.

Aroused, Darlene licked her lips as she looked hungrily at his hard erection. Unable to refuse him, she was out of her dressing gown in one swift move. Lithe as a cat, she stalked to the side of the bed. Kneeling in front of him, she parted his legs, and a contented purr sounded deep in her throat as she took him into her mouth.

Chapter Twenty-nine

Stopping the buggy at a secluded area beside the river, Jeff assisted Leanna from the carriage and walked her to the water's edge. There, he spread out the blanket they had brought and then they sat upon it. Placing his arm around her shoulders, he drew her close.

Admiring the romantic setting, Leanna sighed with deep contentment. The night was clear, and the golden moon, surrounded by thousands of twinkling stars, shone down on the two lovers.

"This land is so beautiful," Leanna murmured. "No wonder the Indians are fighting so desperately to hold onto it."

Jeff agreed, but he hadn't brought her here to discuss the Indians, he was anxious to ask her to marry him so they could set a date for their wedding. "Leanna," he began gently, "there's something I want to ask you."

Facing him and gazing into his brown eyes, she replied, "Yes, Jeff?"

Leaning over, he kissed her deeply, and sliding her arms about his neck, she pressed her lips ever closer to his.

"Leanna," he whispered, "will you marry me?"

She smiled, and her smile was filled with such joy that even in the darkness of night, Jeff could see her radiant happiness.

Flinging herself into his arms and holding him tightly, she answered ecstatically, "Yes, darling, I'll marry you!"

"When?" he asked at once.

She thought a moment, then replied, "I'd like to wait until David is well enough to attend the service. Perhaps he'll agree to give me away."

"How long will that be?" he queried urgently.

"David should be well within a week," she answered.

"In the morning I'll talk to the chaplain, and we can be married in the fort chapel."

"I have my mother's wedding gown. It was one of the few possessions my mother remembered to move to the overseer's house. It's too formal for a fort wedding, but I've always planned to get married in her wedding dress."

"You'll be very lovely," he mumbled vaguely, his thoughts elsewhere.

His vagueness didn't escape Leanna, and she asked anxiously, "Jeff, is something wrong?"

Sighing, he said heavily, "I was thinking about the morning I ordered your home burned." Holding her hand, he proceeded somberly, "Sweetheart, that day you told me you'd never forgive me for destroying The Pines."

"But, Jeff, I have forgiven you," she said hastily. "I forgave you a long time ago. Besides, you weren't to blame. You were merely carrying out Sherman's orders."

He nodded his agreement. "All the same, I've always felt bad about it."

Taking him into her embrace, she murmured, "Darling, I love you."

He eased her down onto the blanket and leaned over her, his lips seeking hers. Leanna clung to him as she responded ardently.

"Sweetheart," he uttered thickly, his fingers probing the bodice of her gown to feel the fullness of her breasts.

Moaning sensually, she pleaded, "Jeff, I want you. Make love to me, darling."

Rising to his knees, he shoved her long skirt and petticoats up to her waist. Removing her panties, he parted her slender legs so that he could then kneel between them.

Leanna's eyes shone with passion as she watched Jeff unbuckle his belt, then push his trousers past his hips. She wanted him desperately, and when she felt his manhood touch her, she grasped his thighs, pressing him inside her.

"Jeff!" she cried, as his penetration sent glorious chills up her spine.

Sliding one arm under her hips, he lifted her and entered her even more deeply. "Leanna, I love you," he whispered huskily.

"Jeff, I need you," she confessed. "I never knew it was possible to need someone as much as I need you."

Pulling her closer, he molded her body to his. "Leanna," he groaned. "Love me, sweetheart . . . love me."

She brought his lips down to hers, and as her tongue entered his mouth, she wrapped her legs across his back. Locking her ankles firmly, she began arching her hips, relishing the feel of him within her.

Jeff gathered her into his strong embrace, and they were soon lost in love's wonderful bliss.

Jeff halted the buggy in front of the hotel, and after giving Leanna a lingering kiss, he waited until she entered the lobby before heading in the direction of the stables.

Leanna hurried up the flight of stairs and moved down the hallway toward her room. Removing the key from the cloth purse she carried, she unlocked the door and was about to step inside when Darlene suddenly called her name. Turning around, Leanna saw Darlene standing across the hall in the open doorway to her own room.

"Yes?" Leanna asked, trying to keep her composure, but she couldn't help admiring Darlene's negligee. It was the palest blue, with soft ruffles sewn to the long sleeves and the flowing hemline. It had been such a long time since Leanna had owned beautiful clothes that, for a moment, she wished her closet could be filled with an expensive wardrobe, but she quickly decided she didn't need fine clothes. Material possessions could not bring her happiness. She had Jeff, and he was her happiness.

Darlene had seen Jeff and Leanna return from their buggy ride. Watching from her bedroom window, she had witnessed the way in which Jeff had kissed Leanna good-night. His tender, but clinging, embrace had left no doubt in Darlene's mind that Jeff was head over heels in love with this . . . skinny blonde.

Smiling, Darlene stated her request, "May we talk a moment?"

Studying her with wariness, Leanna inquired tentatively, "What do you want to talk about?"

"My dear," Darlene began as though she were speaking to a child, "we really shouldn't converse in the hallway and disturb the other guests."

Agreeing, Leanna invited Darlene into her room, and as soon as the door was closed, Darlene asked expectantly, "Are congratulations in order?"

"Wh . . . what do you mean?" Leanna stuttered.

Cattily, Darlene continued her questioning. "Didn't Jeff propose? He told me he was going to ask you to marry him."

Leanna turned her face away from Darlene so that the other woman couldn't see her deep hurt. Why had Jeff confided in her? It seemed that Darlene had known of Jeff's wish to marry her before he had asked Leanna.

Attempting to keep her expression impassive, Leanna turned back to look at Darlene who was smiling invidiously. Leanna sensed that Darlene had set a spiteful trap into which she had foolishly fallen. Deciding Jeff probably had a very good reason for confiding in Darlene, Leanna answered evenly, "Yes, congratulations are in order. Jeff and I are getting married next week."

"You're a very lucky woman," Darlene murmured

smoothly. "Jeff is such a virile and exciting lover."

"How well I know," Leanna made a point of replying.

"I can see the telltale evidence of how well you know." Reaching over and removing a blade of grass from Leanna's hair, she taunted with exaggerated sweetness, "Jeff has always been an outdoors man."

"Darlene," Leanna said curtly, "if you don't mind, it's quite late, and I'd like to go to bed."

"Of course, you must be very fatigued. I'm sure it's been a tiring night for you. I remember very well how Jeff can leave a woman completely exhausted." Darlene continued to provoke Leanna.

"Exhausted?" Leanna quipped. "Quite the contrary. It's been an exhilarating night, and I'm not the least tired."

"You aren't tired?" Darlene said as though she were surprised. "Well, maybe you are the kind of woman who mellows a man's passion."

Through playing Darlene's vindictive game, Leanna replied, "I think we should be honest and straightforward with each other, don't you?"

"By all means," Darlene responded, her green eyes suddenly flashing daggers.

"Let me start by telling you that when I said I'd like to go to bed, I was merely being polite. I really want you to leave my room because I don't like you, nor do I trust you. Furthermore, I think you are catty, conniving, and a liar. You may have pulled the wool over Jeff's eyes, but, Darlene, if you think for one minute that you can get him back, then you are badly mistaken. Because to get to Jeff, you're going to have to go through me."

Darlene itched to rake her fingernails down Leanna's face, but she knew she must play her cards very carefully. It would be foolish to give Leanna just cause to turn Jeff against her. When the time was right, she would savor the sweet taste of revenge.

Looking quite offended, Darlene replied as if she had been greatly insulted. "Apparently, you are insanely jealous of Jeff, and I regret that I came to you hoping we could become friends."

"Does that mean you're finally going to leave my room?" Leanna spat testily.

Darlene gasped. Moving quickly to the door and opening it, she threatened. "Don't think I won't tell Jeff about this!"

"I'm sure you will!" Leanna replied as Darlene stepped out of the room, slamming the door behind her.

The next morning Leanna was enjoying a late breakfast. She was the only patron in the hotel dining room when Jeff appeared and with long, sturdy strides headed for her table. Leanna knew the man she loved, and she could tell by the set of his handsome jaw and the way he moved that he was disturbed. As he pulled out a chair, she dropped her gaze to her plate, her appetite suddenly gone. Sitting down, Jeff folded his arms across his chest, and feeling his eyes on her, Leanna looked up into his reproachful face.

"I see by your expression that Darlene didn't waste any time running to you and tattling," she mumbled, knowing full well that Darlene had made her sound like a jealous shrew.

421

"Leanna," she said firmly, "you must learn to control that temper of yours."

"Look who's talking," she retorted.

"My temper is not the one we are discussing," he pointed out.

Stubbornly, she replied, "I won't apologize to Darlene, so don't suggest that I do!"

"I had no such intention," he revealed.

"You didn't?" she asked, happy that he hadn't taken Darlene's side. "Then you aren't upset with me?"

"No," he smiled. "I know you're a hotheaded little rebel. But, Leanna, Darlene will be leaving soon. All I ask is that you try to be civil to her. I have enough to worry about with the Sioux. I don't need you and Darlene starting a war."

"Jeff, I don't like her," Leanna stated. "And I wish you didn't trust her."

"Sweetheart, she's never given me a reason to distrust her," he said tolerantly. Reaching across the table, he took her hand in his. "For some reason, she makes you feel insecure, but you needn't feel that way. I love you, and there isn't a woman on the face of the earth who could take me away from you. Believe me, Leanna, Darlene is no threat to us."

Deciding to let the topic of Darlene rest, Leanna didn't speak her thoughts. But she sensed that Darlene was indeed a threat, and a dangerous one.

Chapter Thirty

The last rays of sun were fading over the horizon, and Audrey's room was becoming dark; but she didn't bother to light the lamp on the night table. She was lying across her bed, with her head pillowed on her folded arms. She had never felt so depressed. She had been such a fool to believe in her romantic fantasy. Hold on to your dream, Leanna had once told her. Someday you'll know the right man was worth waiting for. Well that might be true in Leanna's case, Audrey thought glumly, but it certainly isn't true in mine.

Less than a hour before, Leanna had come to Audrey's room to tell her that Jeff was the major she had believed to be dead. Audrey was happy that Leanna and the man she loved had been reunited, but at the same time, Leanna's joy made her feel her own unhappiness more acutely.

David was making an exceptionally fast recovery, and they would be leaving with the next wagon train to arrive. She was destined to ride away from Fort

Laramie and never see Nathan Hayden again, but she knew she'd never forget him. She was sure he thought she was still too young to know her own mind, and perhaps he was right. Hadn't she been acting like a silly schoolgirl? Falling in love with him at first sight was definitely immature. Recalling her forward behavior when she'd talked to Nathan in the fort's compound, Audrey felt flushed. Her behavior had certainly been juvenile, and he had most assuredly put her in her place.

A knock sounded on her door, and moving listlessly, Audrey sat up and lit the lamp before answering it. When she opened the door and saw Nathan Hayden, her heart suddenly began to race and her knees weakened. He had actually come to see her! She couldn't believe it!

Audrey's face reflected her thoughts, and grinning tenderly, Nathan asked, "May I come in?"

Flustered, she stammered, "Yes, of course."

He stepped into the room, and closing the door, she leaned back against it. Standing next to her, he removed his hat, holding it in his hands. As always he was wearing buckskins, and Audrey's eyes roamed boldly over his manly frame, noticing how the soft material clung skin-tight across his wide chest and down his muscular legs. Oh, he is such a powerful figure of a man, she marveled, how could I have thought for one minute that he could fall in love with me? It'll take a very beautiful and exciting woman to win his heart, not a plain little nobody like me!

"Have you had dinner yet?" he inquired.

"No," she answered, her voice barely above a whisper. Was he planning to ask her to have dinner with him? What should she wear? Did he intend to eat now? She supposed the dress she was wearing would be perfectly all right. It wasn't her nicest gown but then it wasn't her worst either.

"May I take you to dinner?" he asked, his blue eyes studying her with such intensity that Audrey felt intimidated.

She meant to appear quite composed, but against her will, her voice quivered, "I'd love to have dinner with you."

"Before we leave, I'd like to talk to you," he said casually, and when he tossed his hat onto her bed, Audrey swallowed nervously. He moved closer to her, and placing his hands on her shoulders, he gazed down into her eyes. "I wish to apologize for the way I treated you yesterday afternoon. I was quite rude, and I hope you'll forgive me."

Watching him, wide-eyed, and wishing his nearness wasn't making her tremble, she answered breathlessly, "I am the one who should apologize. I was much too forward."

He chuckled pleasantly, and she wondered why he thought her answer humorous. "You are not forward, little lady," he explained. "You are merely very honest."

"Little lady," she repeated distastefully. "Why must you call me that?"

"Why not? You're a lady, and you're not much bigger than a minute."

Audrey giggled. "I've never heard such an expression."

His hold on her shoulders tightened, and as he drew her closer, she hoped he planned to kiss her.

But, instead, he advised her gently, "Don't let your romantic notions turn this dinner date into something it isn't. It's simply two friends sharing a meal together and nothing more."

Intuitively, she questioned, "Are you trying to convince me or yourself?"

For a moment he stared at her with an expression that was inscrutable; then releasing her and stepping back, he grinned, "I can assure you, I wasn't trying to convince myself."

"Nathan," she began impulsively, "why did you tell me to find a well-bred gentleman? You are apparently an educated—"

Interrupting, he said, "I also pointed out that looks can be deceiving."

Experiencing insight, she answered, "You are deceiving no one, Nathan Hayden, but yourself."

Her response caught him off guard, and he suddenly found himself on the defensive. Surprised that a mere girl could so easily confuse him, he stammered, "Are you ready to go to dinner?"

Understanding why he had called on her, she answered, "No." Raising her chin with pride, she continued, "You apparently asked me to dinner because you feel sorry for me. You believe I have a silly schoolgirl crush on you, and out of the kindness of your heart, you have decided to be nice to me so my feelings won't be hurt. Well, Mr. Hayden, I think I'll have dinner with my brother and his wife." Opening the door, she proceeded through it and said with dignity, "Good evening, sir."

Moving to the bed, Nathan retrieved his hat. Turning to face Audrey, he started to speak, but realizing

426

she was right, he simply left her room. Walking swiftly down the hallway, he contemplated returning to tell Audrey his actions hadn't been intentional. But intentional or not, he was guilty, and she had seen right through him. As Nathan hurried down the stairs and across the lobby, he began to think of Audrey as a mature woman instead of a lovely girl blooming into womanhood.

Leaving the hotel, Nathan headed straight for the officers' club, where he forgot all about eating dinner and drank bourbon instead. The potent liquor hit his empty stomach like a rock, and when he finally left the club, he was on the verge of a good drunk.

As he strolled unsteadily toward the Farnsworths' wagon, he told himself he wasn't hoping to find Audrey there, he was merely trying to walk off his drinks. And when he caught sight of Audrey leaving the wagon and heading in his direction to return to the hotel, he tried to convince himself that their meeting was simply one of chance.

Seeing Nathan approaching, Audrey halted. Aware of his wavering gait, she guessed he had been drinking quite heavily. The wagon was parked in a fairly secluded area, and there was no one about except the two of them.

Reaching her, Nathan tipped his hat. "Good evening, Miss Farnsworth," he said, and in spite of his condition, his words didn't slur.

Folding her arms beneath her breasts, and raising her eyebrows, she asked, "Have you been drinking?"

"I had a couple," he admitted.

"A couple, Nathan?" she challenged.

"Well, a man needs to relax every once in a while," he drawled, wondering why he felt he had to answer to a girl seventeen years younger than himself.

"Why did you feel a need to relax? Or are you still trying to deceive yourself? You haven't been drinking because you need to relax. I'm the reason why you are tipsy."

"You?" he roared, as though incredulous.

"You can't get me out of your mind, can you, Nathan?" she taunted as everything suddenly became clear. "First, you tried to run away from your feelings for me, so you left the fort. Then when you returned, you convinced yourself that I'm still a child so you treated me accordingly. When that didn't get me out of your thoughts, you decided to take me to dinner, making a point to yourself as well as to me that the date was only one of friendship. When I turned you down, I forced you to start seeing me as a woman with a certain degree of maturity. That really scared you, didn't it, Nathan? You were so scared that you had to run out and get drunk!" Seeing the truth on his face, she cried desperately, "Why, Nathan? Why are you afraid to fall in love?"

"I can't love a decent woman," he groaned. "I'm not worthy of one."

"Why?" she pleaded.

Brusquely he whirled about, intending to walk away. Moving alertly, Audrey stepped in front of him, blocking his path. "Answer me, Nathan!" she insisted.

"Damn it, Audrey!" he yelled, his eyes flickering with rage. "Don't you understand, you are too good for me!"

"You mean I'm too decent?" she snapped.

"Yes, damn it! You're too decent!" he uttered thickly.

"Very well, Nathan," she responded casually. "Then I shall go to the enlisted men's bar, wait outside the door, pick up the first soldier who comes outside and take him to my bed. When I finish with him, I shall pick up another and then another until I finally become indecent."

Turning sharply, she started to leave, but instantly, he had a hold of her arm. "You can't be serious!"

"Can't I?" she retorted.

Relinquishing his grip on her arms, he said irritably, "I know you won't actually go through with your threat."

"For twenty years I have valued my virtue, saving myself for the right man. Well, now I have found him, only to learn that a decent woman is not what he wants. What other choice do I have except to become indecent?"

"Audrey," he mumbled testily, "you are trying my patience!"

"And you are trying mine, Nathan Hayden! It's quite apparent that this conversation is a waste of time. So good night, sir."

Walking away rapidly, she could feel his eyes on her as she headed toward the compound. He's actually wondering if I'll go to the bar, she thought. She was tempted to do just that, but afraid Nathan would be too angry to come to her rescue, she decided that game was too dangerous for her to play.

As she entered the busy compound, she glanced over her shoulder, wondering if Nathan was still watching, but she couldn't see him. Unaware that he was safely hidden in the shadows and eyeing her every move, Audrey had no ulterior motive when she spotted Jerry Rogan and asked him to walk her to the hotel. Some of the trappers visiting the fort made her feel uncomfortable, and Jerry's presence provided her with some protection. Audrey liked Jerry, and she knew he was a good friend of Leanna's, so when he casually placed his arm around her shoulders as he escorted her to the hotel, she accepted his friendly closeness.

As they walked together, Jerry made a funny remark that caused Audrey to laugh gaily, and her laughter carried across the compound to where Nathan was standing. He hadn't believed she was serious when she'd threatened to pick up a soldier, and seething inwardly, his eyes filled with a murderous rage.

Jerry left Audrey in the lobby, and spotting Leanna and Jeff in the dining room, he decided to join them and pay his respects.

Nathan waited a couple of minutes for Jerry to come out of the hotel, and when he didn't appear, Nathan knew there was only one course of action for him to take. His gait was no longer unsteady as he crossed the compound with fast, strong strides. Barging into the lobby, and taking no notice of the people in the dining room, he headed straight up the stairs. By the time he reached Audrey's room, he was breathing angrily, and his powerful hands were clenched into tight fists. Banging on the closed door, he shouted furiously, "Open this door!"

It was opened immediately, and storming inside,

Nathan looked around the room, demanding, "Where is he?"

"Where is who?" Audrey asked, closing the door.

Infuriated, he yelled, "Trooper Rogan!"

Suddenly understanding, Audrey began laughing, and doubling over, she said between giggles, "You think . . . you think . . . Jerry and I . . . he only walked me to the lobby."

Realizing he had behaved like a complete fool, Nathan raved, "So you think it's funny, do you?"

Making a futile attempt to stop her laughter, she replied, "Nathan Hayden, you're jealous."

"Jealous?" he said as though her accusation was outrageous. "Jealousy had nothing to do with it. I was merely trying to keep you from making a big mistake."

Finding his blunder concerning Audrey and Trooper Rogan embarrassing as well as frustrating, Nathan suddenly moved to the door. Opening it, he stepped into the hall.

"Nathan!" she cried, rushing to the doorway. "Please don't leave!"

Unexpectedly, the door down the hall opened, and dressed in one of her seductive dressing gowns, Darlene left her room to stand in front of Nathan, obstructing his retreat. She gave Audrey only a passing glance, it was Nathan Hayden who received her full concentration. As her eyes openly took in his masculine physique and handsome face, she said in a sensual tone, "You two are making quite a disturbance."

Nathan was very aware of Darlene's striking beauty, but it didn't have the effect on him that

Darlene was hoping it would, and moving past her, he mumbled, "Excuse me, ma'am."

Catching his arm, she said so softly that Audrey couldn't hear, "I want to talk to you. Come to my room later." She wanted this handsome stranger in her bed so badly that she could already feel a longing spreading through her body.

"Miss Whitlock, I don't think we have anything to talk about," he replied quietly.

"You know who I am?" she whispered.

"I'm good friends with Major Clayton."

Oh damn! Darlene thought. How was I to know this man is one of Jeff's close friends? Now he'll probably run and tell Jeff that I propositioned him. Covering her behavior, she lied smoothly, "Well, I knew you and Jeff were friends, but I wasn't aware that you knew who I was. I hope you didn't get the wrong impression when I invited you to my room. I only wanted to talk to you about Jeff."

Nathan glanced down the hall to see if Audrey was standing in her doorway, but she had returned to her room and closed the door.

Abruptly, Nathan said, "Good night, Miss Whitlock."

Perusing him as he walked away, Darlene mumbled to herself disappointedly, "Such a shame, I'll bet he's quite a man."

Pacing her room, Audrey wished she knew what the woman in the hall had been discussing with Nathan. She had never seen anyone so sensually beautiful, and she wondered who this woman was. My goodness, if she decided she wanted Nathan,

Audrey was sure she could never compete with her. Audrey suddenly had a sickening feeling that the woman was not a decent one, which would make her even more appealing to Nathan.

Hearing Nathan calling her name from outside, Audrey hurried to the open window, and glancing down, she saw him standing in front of the hotel.

"Will you please have dinner with me tomorrow night?" he yelled up. "And I'm not asking you for a date because I feel sorry for you."

"Then why are you asking me?" she replied loudly, smiling.

"Have dinner with me, and you'll find out why," he invited, his grin cocky.

"Mr. Hayden, how can I refuse such an intriguing challenge?"

"I'll see you tomorrow night at eight," he answered; then sweeping off his hat, he bowed in a gentlemanly way before strolling away from her window.

Hugging herself, Audrey danced across her room. She had never been happier in her life!

Chapter Thirty-one

"I'll never accept a marriage between you and a Yankee!" Jennifer screeched, her eyes blazing angrily into Leanna's.

Upon Leanna's request, Audrey had taken Bradley and Matthew for a walk. Leanna hadn't wanted the boys present when she told Jennifer that she planned to marry Jeff. She had known the news would infuriate Jennifer.

David was lying on a mattress placed in the back of the wagon, and Jennifer was sitting at his side while Leanna sat across from them. Propping himself up by placing a stack of blankets beneath his head and shoulders, David ordered sharply, "Jennifer, calm down!"

"No!" she refused. "I won't calm down!" Her eyes still staring into Leanna's, she continued scathingly, "I'm almost glad that Brad and your parents aren't alive to see this day! Leanna, if you marry that Yankee, you will never be welcome in my home, and I will forbid you to see your nephews!"

Before Leanna could reply, David spoke up firmly, "Not your home, Jennifer, but our home. And Leanna will most assuredly be welcome. I may not be Bradley's and Matthew's natural father, but I am their stepfather, which gives me certain rights, and you will not keep Leanna from seeing them."

"David!" Jennifer cried with disbelief. "How can you be so treacherous as to take Leanna's side? You are a Confederate and she's marrying a Yankee!"

"There are no more Confederates or Yankees," he argued. "Now we are all Americans. And the sooner you can accept that fact, the better off you're going to be."

"David," Leanna pleaded, "please don't argue with Jennifer. I don't want to cause trouble between the two of you." Facing Jennifer, she continued earnestly, "I understand how you feel, honestly I do. I had hoped you would attend my wedding, and I was going to ask David to give me away. I should have known that you'd force me to choose between Jeff and my family." Standing, and stepping down from the wagon, she turned back to say, "I love Jeff with all my heart, and I intend to marry him. But, Jennifer, I also love you, and I hope someday you will lose all that bitterness and resentment you have inside you."

"How can you expect me to forgive the Yankees who killed Brad and destroyed my homeland?" she shrieked.

"It's not a question of forgiving, it's a question of forgetting. You keep looking backward, when you should be looking forward."

As Leanna walked away, David took Jennifer's

436

hand in his, and at his touch, she turned to look at him. "She's right," he murmured.

Jerking her hand away, she snapped impatiently, "Even when you were a boy, you always tried to see both sides of an argument."

"Aren't there always two sides to one?" he queried.

"But what about my side?" she implored.

"I understand how you feel, and so does Leanna. We suffered and lost loved ones during the war, the same as you did. But Major Clayton didn't start the war, he was merely a soldier who happened to fight for the North." Reaching back over, he clasped her hand. "You can't alienate yourself from Leanna. My God, you owe her so much! Have you already forgotten how she once worked from sunup to sundown so you and your sons could survive?"

Tears came to Jennifer's eyes as she admitted, "No, I haven't forgotten."

"Will you accept her marriage?"

"I don't know if I can," she answered honestly. "I'll have to think about it."

"Don't take too long, you never know what tomorrow might bring."

"What do you mean?" Jennifer asked.

David shrugged. "I don't know exactly. But during the war, I quickly realized that sometimes tomorrow is too late."

"Well this isn't wartime, and Leanna certainly isn't in any danger."

"Tonight, I want Leanna Weston dead!" Darlene said to the two trappers in her hotel room.

The men nodded agreeably as their ruthless eyes

437

devoured Darlene's curves. Her crimson gown had a sweeping neckline which revealed the deep cleavage between her voluptuous breasts. Darlene was aware of their hungry stares, and their lustful scrutiny sent a chill of loathing up her spine. She had never seen two men so unkempt and odious. The offensive odor of their unwashed bodies caused Darlene to wave her perfumed handkerchief in front of her nose.

Although she thought these men disgusting, she was pleased that she had found them. Earlier in the day, she had stepped out of the hotel, and while pausing on the sidewalk to look around the compound, she had happened to overhear a conversation between two soldiers. They were discussing two trappers who were parking their buckboard in front of the enlisted men's bar. When it became clear that those trappers were men capable of extreme brutality, Darlene knew at once that she could use them to get rid of Leanna. She had gone to the bar and, standing close to the entrance, had waited impatiently for the trappers to come back outside. When they had finally emerged, she had inconspicuously caught their attention and had hastily told them that she wanted them to come to her hotel room. She had specified that they should use the rear stairway. Then she had quickly returned to the hotel. Within minutes they were at her room, knocking on the door.

When she explained to them that she wanted to pay them to kidnap Leanna and kill her, they listened to her without revealing any emotion. They had no qualms about killing Leanna. Human life meant nothing to them, but money was important; and the larger of the two trappers asked gruffly, "How much you aimin' to pay us?"

Raising her left hand, she showed them the diamond engagement ring that Jeff had given her years before. "This ring is worth more money than you two can make in ten years. When I see that you have abducted Leanna Weston, this ring will be yours."

As one trapper eyed the sparkling diamond, the other asked, "Well, what do you think, Dub?"

Grinning at his companion, he drawled, "I think the lady just made herself a deal, Stan."

"Good!" Darlene said briskly. "Now we must make our plans."

Captain Rhodes had informed Darlene that Colonel Wallace had called a conference of the officers at the fort. Those attending would be in the colonel's quarters until late that night. Darlene was sure that Jeff had also told Leanna about this scheduled meeting, so she wrote a note to Leanna, carefully copying the handwriting from one of Jeff's old letters. Then smiling with satisfaction, Darlene signed Jeff's name at the bottom of the note.

Leaving her room quietly, Darlene stepped across the hall and slipped the note beneath Leanna's door, then she rapped twice on the door before hurrying back into her own room.

Leanna was lying on her bed resting when she heard the knocks. Going to the door, she opened it, and finding no one on the other side, she frowned, bewildered. As she was closing the door, she spotted the note on the floor. Bending over, she picked it up, unfolded it, and read it.

Dearest Leanna,

The Conference with Colonel Wallace was canceled. It is vitally important that I talk to you privately. Meet me behind the stables at seven o'clock and I will explain everything.

Trust me,
Jeff

Folding the note, Leanna walked over and placed it on the dresser. Why did Jeff need to talk to her privately? Why didn't he simply come to her room? Glancing at the clock on the night table, she saw that it was now six-thirty. She slipped off her dressing gown and, opening her closet, selected one of her dresses. Putting on the simple calico gown, she stepped into her slippers and returned to the dresser to brush her long hair, then tie it back from her face with a silk ribbon.

Her thoughts centered on Jeff's strange note, Leanna didn't hear Darlene's door open and close, nor was she aware of Darlene's steps rushing down the hallway.

Smiling spitefully, Darlene hurried through the lobby. Outside, she walked swiftly toward the stables. If everything went as planned, she would soon be rid of Leanna and then Jeff would be hers. Oh, he'd probably be heartbroken for a while, but she'd pretend to be a true and consoling friend. She'd refuse to leave with the troops from Fort Casper, telling Jeff she couldn't possibly leave him when he was so distraught. She had told the trappers to be sure to place Leanna's body where it could be easily found;

she certainly didn't want Jeff searching endlessly for her.

Reaching the stables, Darlene glanced cautiously about, and seeing no one nearby, she moved steathily to the back of the building. The trappers' wagon was parked where it was supposed to be so she called softly, "Dub and Stan, where are you?"

The trappers had been obscured by the shadows, and when they suddenly stepped forward, they caught Darlene by surprise, causing her to gasp.

"You'd better hide with me, so you won't be seen," Dub said while leering at her ample breasts.

"All right," Darlene agreed shakily.

He grasped her arm, and his touch made Darlene's skin crawl. But holding her firmly, he led her to the stable where they pressed their backs against the solid foundation. The building cast a huge shadow, and Darlene knew Leanna wouldn't be able to see them.

"Where is Stan?" she asked.

Moving so close to her side that their bodies touched, he answered, "He's crouched behind the wagon. When the woman passes by, he'll grab her."

His nearness was repulsive, and feeling slightly nauseated, Darlene wished Leanna would hurry. Fighting back the sickening bile rising in her throat, Darlene swallowed heavily. But when she heard Leanna call Jeff, she quickly forgot her queasiness and smiled victoriously.

"Jeff? . . . Jeff?" Leanna repeated, walking slowly past the buckboard. Where was he? Had she arrived too soon?

Stan sprang to his feet. Grabbing Leanna from behind, he circled her waist with one arm and jerked her roughly against his brawny frame. She attempted to scream, but he had clasped his hand over her mouth.

Her eyes wide with fright, Leanna saw Darlene and Dub materialize from the shadows. Dub removed his knife from its sheath, and seeing the deadly weapon, Leanna's knees grew so weak that only Stan's hold kept her from collapsing.

Placing the sharp blade against Leanna's side, Dub snarled, "If you scream, I'm gonna stick this here knife right through your rib cage. Do you understand me, girlie?"

Leanna nodded feebly, and cautiously, Stan removed his hand from her mouth.

"Tie and gag her," Dub ordered.

As Stan reached into the wagon for the strips of rope, Leanna looked at Darlene. The woman's smug expression made Leanna long to hit her.

Darlene's green eyes sparkled triumphantly as she said venomously, "Don't worry about Jeff, he'll find solace in my loving arms."

"Go to hell!" Leanna spat furiously. She had every intention of saying more, but Stan quickly stuffed a gag into her mouth, tying it so tightly that Leanna winced. Pulling her arms behind her, he bound her hands before taking her to the wagon and lifting her onto the wagon bed. As he was tying a strip of rope about her feet, Leanna watched Darlene remove the diamond ring from her finger.

Smiling, Darlene handed the ring to Dub and reminded him, "I want her dead!"

Taking the ring and dropping it into his pocket, the trapper answered, "I'll kill her, but not 'til Stan and

442

me get to enjoy a little pokin'."

Laughing huskily, Darlene replied, "Poke her all you want, just make sure when you finish with her that she's quite dead!" Turning to Leanna, she continued vindictively, "You little bitch! I only wish I could be there to watch you spread your legs for these two . . . gentlemen."

Moving with sudden speed, Dub captured Darlene, and as his hand went over her mouth, he sneered, "You'll be there to watch, in fact you're gonna be participatin'. Did you think Stan and me would be satisfied with one good-lookin' woman, when we could just as easily have two?"

Wildly, Darlene fought against the powerful arms restraining her. Unexpectedly Dub turned her loose, and hoping he had decided to let her go, Darlene took a step forward to flee, but the man's strong fist caught her flush on the jaw. The solid blow knocked Darlene to the ground, and she was engulfed in total darkness.

Chapter Thirty-two

During dinner, Nathan asked Audrey about her life, and because he seemed to be genuinely interested, she talked about the Farnsworths' plantation. Letting her thoughts drift back into the past, she relived the peaceful and bountiful days before the war. Speaking of her parents brought tears to her eyes, and Nathan considerately reached across the table to hold her hand. His touch made Audrey's pulse quicken, and as she gazed into his face, her eyes reflected her mood. He responded by gently squeezing her hand before releasing it. Hoping to become close to him emotionally, Audrey asked Nathan to please talk about his life, but he firmly refused, although he did promise to confide in her later when they were alone.

Alone! Audrey's heart pounded rapidly. She was confused by her own feelings. She longed desperately to be alone with him, but at the same time, she was apprehensive. She adored him so much that she knew she'd never have the will power to refuse him if he should decide to make love to her. But then what would happen? Would he ask her to marry him, or would he allow her to leave Fort Laramie with her family and ride out of his life forever?

When they finished their dessert and coffee, Nathan asked, "May I take you to my quarters? I need to talk to you, and there we can be alone and undisturbed."

Audrey gulped, she couldn't help it; then, believing she was acting quite immaturely, she blushed noticeably.

Smiling at her embarrassment, Nathan said tenderly, "Little lady, if you're afraid to be alone with me, then we can end the evening by taking a leisurely stroll through the most crowded part of the compound."

Piqued because she was sure he was teasing her, she looked steadily into his twinkling blue eyes and said calmly, "Of course I'm not afraid to be alone with you. I don't know where you got such a foolish idea."

Standing and dropping some money onto the table, he grinned, "Shall we leave, Miss Farnsworth?" Stepping to her chair, he pulled it out as she got to her feet.

The prospect of being alone with Nathan made Audrey feel weak, and as she walked at his side, she hoped her wobbly legs would not reveal her insecurity.

Taking her to his quarters, he opened the door and ushered her inside. He had left a lamp burning, and its light cast a soft glow over the room, which consisted primarily of a large bed and a sitting area in front of the unlit fireplace.

Leading her to the sofa, he asked her to be seated. Then he removed his hat and holster before joining her. Sitting casually, he stretched out his long legs and folded his arms across his chest.

Studying him, Audrey could tell his thoughts were running deep. Hesitantly, she placed her hand on his, and getting his attention, she asked quietly, "Nathan, why did you bring me here?"

"I already told you why," he mumbled.

"Because you want to talk to me?" she questioned.

"Audrey," he began, his eyes looking steadfastly into hers, "I'm going to tell you things I have never told anyone. What I have to say is not pretty, and you will most likely be repulsed."

"Then why must you tell me?"

He grasped her hand, and lowering her gaze, Audrey could see the strength in the hand that was now holding hers so tenderly. "I'm not sure why I've decided to confide in you."

Raising her eyes to his, she murmured, "Maybe it's because you're falling in love with me."

He smiled vacuously. "Maybe. But it's been so long since I've been in love that I'm not sure I would recognize the emotion again."

"Who did you love?" she whispered.

"My wife," he replied solemnly.

"Did she die?"

He was silent for so long that Audrey had begun to believe he wasn't going to answer, when he replied finally, "Yes, she died."

Standing, he stepped to the fireplace, and sighing heavily, he leaned his arm against the mantel. He made a half-turn so that he could see her face. "My wife's name was Melanie. We were both raised in Memphis, Tennessee. I was the son of a wealthy lawyer, and my family was considered to be aristocrats. Melanie came from the wrong side of town, and her family was what is commonly referred to as poor white trash. Well, to make a long story short, she and I fell in love. I knew my father would never accept Melanie, so I asked her to run away with me. We traveled into southern Texas, where we married. I wrote to my father and told him that Melanie was my wife. He disowned me, and cut me out of my inheritance. After two years of hard work, I was able to buy a small piece of land. I built a cabin. It wasn't much but I had hopes of building Melanie a fine house someday. I raised horses and sold them to the Texas Rangers and the U.S. Army. After a couple of years, I began to make a good profit, and I even had men working for me. By this time, Melanie and I had two children. My son was three years old, and my daughter was two months old when I made a trip into central Texas to round up wild horses. At that time we weren't having any problems with the Indians in the vicinity, and I didn't think my family would be in any danger, so I left only two ranch hands behind."

Nathan paused for a moment before continuing bitterly, "I was so goddamned wrapped up in finding herds of wild horses that I didn't even think about Mexican bandits, who can be more cold-blooded than an Indian ever thought to be!"

Getting to her feet, and moving to stand at his side, she asked softly, "Did Mexican bandits kill your

448

family?"

Suddenly, Nathan's fist struck the mantel so severely that it partially broke loose from its foundation. "Yes!" he groaned. "They killed my family! My wife, son, and daughter!" Grasping the unsteady mantel with both hands, he bowed his head between his outstretched arms, and his wide shoulders shook as he cried hoarsely, "My son and daughter's throats were slit, and Melanie's nude body was mutilated."

"Oh, my God!" Audrey gasped. "Nathan, did you see them this way?"

"My men and I arrived home a few hours after it happened. We were the first ones to find them."

Turning away from him, Audrey placed her hand over her mouth to hold back her sobs. Thinking about Nathan entering his home and finding his family so grotesquely murdered caused cold chills to creep up her spine. Her voice breaking, she asked, "The two men you left behind, were they also killed?"

"One of them survived. Jake's recovery was slow, and as I waited for him to heal, I plotted my revenge. Jake had seen the Mexicans and could identify them. There were six of them, and as soon as Jake was well, we rode into Mexico. It took a year before we located all of them."

"Did you kill these men?" she asked, facing him. The delirious rage she saw in his eyes, shocked her.

"Kill them?" he repeated gruffly, sneering. "Yes, I killed them, and I made sure they died slowly and painfully!"

"Dear God!" she moaned.

"I was crazy!" he shouted. "I was totally insane! It wasn't until I killed the last man, that my sanity

449

returned. Then I had to live with what I had done."
Groaning, he continued, "I had become as cold-
blooded and as ruthless as the men I killed."

"No!" she cried. "You had a reason to kill, they
killed without cause!"

"Sometimes, even after all these years, I'll wake up
in the middle of the night in a cold sweat because I've
been dreaming about those days."

"After you killed the last man, what did you do?"

"Jake and I parted company, and I roamed into
Wyoming territory. I've been here ever since."

"How long has it been since your family was
murdered?"

"Eleven years," he murmured.

"And all this time, you have been punishing yourself," she replied gently.

"Punishing myself?" he repeated. "I don't think
so. I'm merely existing."

"Refusing to let a woman love you, refusing to love
her is your way of punishing yourself. You should
want to live again and love again, not merely exist!"

"I'm not worthy of a good woman. My God, how
can I expect a woman to love me after what I did to
those men?" Moving suddenly, he clutched her shoulders, and jerking her against his strong frame, he
stared wildly into her eyes. "Shall I tell you how I
killed them? Do you think you could hear the vivid
details and still love me?"

Pushing away from his painful grip, she said
firmly, "No. I don't want to hear what you did to
them, but if you insist on telling me, I'll listen
because Nathan, it won't stop me from loving you."

"How can you be so sure?" he demanded.

"Because I understand," she murmured.

"Do you?" he questioned harshly. "Well, I'm glad you understand how an ordinary husband and father can turn into a raving killer because I don't!"

"Nathan," she pleaded, "you must learn to put that time in your life behind you. The man who killed those bandits only existed temporarily."

"But he'll live on my conscience forever," Nathan answered gravely.

"Let me help you!" she implored. "I know I can help you forget!"

He smiled cynically. "Do you believe love can move mountains, Audrey?" he mocked.

"No, but I do believe love can heal wounds better than time."

Controlling his emotions, Nathan said abruptly, "It's late, I'll walk you back to the hotel."

He stepped to the side, expecting her to walk past him toward the door. Instead, she flung herself into his arms and pleaded, "Nathan, make love to me."

Holding her carefully, he asked as though he hadn't heard correctly, "What did you say?"

"Make love to me," she repeated.

Moving her so that he could look down into her face, he asked, "Why?"

"Because I want the first time to be with the man I love."

"You'll fall in love again," he assured her.

"Perhaps," she agreed. "But I won't love him the way I love you." Standing on tiptoe, she placed one hand behind his neck and drew his lips down to hers.

Tightening his arm around her waist, he pulled her thighs against his, and as her lips parted, his tongue

451

probed between her teeth.

"Audrey," he murmured in her ear, "if we don't leave right now, I won't be able to control myself. So I'm giving you one last chance to change your mind. Which will it be? Do I walk you to the hotel, or do I carry you to my bed?"

"Your bed," she whispered, although she was a little frightened.

"Are you hoping if I take your virginity, I'll ask you to marry me?"

"If that was your reason for asking, I would refuse. I want to be your love, Nathan Hayden, not your obligation."

Intensely, he told her, "I can't make any promises."

"I'm not asking for any, I'm only asking you to make love to me."

Groaning with passion, he lifted her into his arms and carried her to the bed. Placing her on her feet, he turned her around so that he could undo the buttons at the back of her dress. He helped her out of the garment and then draped it across a nearby chair. Slowly, he began to take off the rest of her clothes, and shyly, Audrey closed her eyes. When he had her completely undressed, he said tenderly, "Open your eyes, honey." She did as he asked, and gazing into her flushed face, he murmured, "You're very beautiful."

Placing his hands on her shoulders, he eased her to the bed, and lying beside her, his mouth sought hers as he caressed her breasts. He whispered her name while his lips traveled to her neck, then down to the hollow of her throat, making Audrey moan with awakened passion. His hand moved from her breasts down to the softness between her thighs. She was lying stiffly, and he murmured, "Part your legs, Audrey."

She complied and then gasped at the delicious rapture of his intimate touch. "My innocent darling," he moaned before once again relishing her lips, and as he deepened their kiss, he stroked her until her hips were moving in perfect rhythm with his hand.

Wonderfully aroused, Audrey moaned rapturously, "Oh Nathan . . . I feel so strange."

"Strange?" he questioned, grinning tenderly.

"Yes, but gloriously strange," she mumbled breathlessly.

Leaving the bed, Nathan hastily discarded his buckskins as Audrey watched with fascination. He was such a handsome man, and his physique was solid and muscular. When he was totally unclothed, Audrey's scrutiny fixed on his manhood. It seemed so large she inhaled deeply.

"Don't be afraid," he whispered, lying beside her. "Man and woman were made for each other, and you can accommodate me."

"Will it be very painful?" she asked.

"A little, but the discomfort will be gone quickly."

"And then?" she pressed.

"Then, little lady, you will feel a pleasure so wonderful that there are no words to describe it."

Whispering in his ear, she replied, "Don't tell me how wonderful it will be, prove it to me."

He moved over her, and she opened her legs for him. As the tip of his manhood touched her, Audrey grasped his shoulders, and determined not to cry out, she clenched her jaw tightly.

He penetrated her with one quick movement, and

the sharp pain that shot through her was gone almost instantly.

Kissing her passionately, he moved his hips circularly, and, as her heat engulfed him, he trembled with desire.

A thrilling sensation washed over her, and she murmured ecstatically, "Oh, Nathan, you were so right. There are no words to describe how wonderful it feels to have you inside me."

Boldly, she pressed her lips to his, and when he began thrusting against her, Audrey responded to Nathan's love with fiery abandoment.

Nathan was getting ready to walk Audrey back to the hotel when a firm knock sounded on his door. "Who is it?" he called.

"Jeff," came the reply from outside.

Going to the door, Nathan opened it, and Jeff stepped briskly into the room.

"Is something wrong?" Nathan asked.

Jeff handed him the note he had found in Leanna's room, and after reading it, Nathan questioned, "Did you write this?"

"No," Jeff answered. "But I think I know who did. She did a good job of copying my handwriting, but I can still recognize it as hers."

"Miss Whitlock?" Nathan guessed.

"Yes, Darlene!" replied Jeff angrily.

"Has something happened?" Audrey suddenly asked.

Audrey couldn't tell by his expression whether Jeff was surprised to find her in Nathan's quarters.

He looked at her and asked, "When did you last see Leanna?"

"This afternoon when she came to the wagon to

speak to Jennifer and David. Why? Did something happen to her?"

"She's disappeared," Jeff answered.

"Disappeared!" Audrey exclaimed.

Hastily, Jeff explained that it had been quite late before the conference with Colonel Wallace had ended. He had gone straight to Leanna's room, expecting her to be there. When she hadn't answered his knock, he had tried the doorknob, and finding it unlocked, he had stepped inside, where he'd seen the note on her dresser. Recognizing the handwriting, he had hurried across the hall to Darlene's room, only to find her gone.

"Have you searched the fort?" Nathan asked.

"Not yet," Jeff replied. "But I did go behind the stables. I found wagon tracks and footprints. It looks as though there were two men and two women."

"When we report this to the colonel, he'll still insist that the fort be searched. You'd better go see the colonel, and I'll take Audrey back to the hotel."

"No," Audrey spoke up. "I must let Jennifer and David know what has happened."

"Nathan," Jeff began, "you start the search, and I'll take Audrey to the wagon. I need to question the Farnsworths. Maybe they saw Leanna tonight, or God willing, maybe she's with them." Taking Audrey's arm, Jeff led her to the door, but before they left, he told Nathan, "If we don't find Leanna and Darlene in the fort, we'll ride out at dawn. Tell my troops to be ready to move."

Standing alongside the wagon between David and Audrey, Jennifer watched Jeff as he walked away swiftly to join in the search for Leanna and Darlene. She and David had explained to Jeff that they hadn't seen Leanna since she'd come to their wagon during the afternoon.

Suddenly, Jennifer rushed forward, and her long skirt flayed about her ankles as she chased after Jeff. "Major Clayton! . . . Major Clayton!" she called.

He halted brusquely, and she caught up to him. Breathing rapidly, she said between deep breaths, "I'm so afraid something has happened to Leanna!"

"So am I, Mrs. Farnsworth," he replied impatiently, wondering why she had stopped him.

"But, Major Clayton, you don't understand!" she cried piteously. "This afternoon when she came to see David and me, she told us she was going to marry you. I treated her terribly! But I didn't mean all the cruel things I said." Covering her face with her hands, Jennifer sobbed, "I love Leanna! . . . Oh God, how could I have been so mean to her!"

"At a time like this, the color of a uniform doesn't seem very important, does it?"

"No!" she moaned wretchedly. "All that is important is that Leanna be alive and well! Major Clayton, is there anything I can do?"

"You can try praying," he answered, before leaving abruptly.

Chapter Thirty-three

Dub and Stan encountered no problems in taking Leanna and Darlene from the fort. Stan gagged and tied the unconscious Darlene; then he put her in the wagon beside Leanna. Ordering Leanna to lie down, Stan then placed himself between the two women. He held his knife to Leanna's throat as Dub spread a blanket over the three of them. To help camouflage the shapes of their bodies, Dub piled several pieces of his and Stan's gear on top of them. Although it was a clumsy coverup, Dub was sure in the darkness it would probably work, and besides, the soldiers at the gate had no reason to look closely at his wagon.

Leanna felt the springs of the wagon give under Dub's heavy frame as he climbed up into the seat. Darlene still lay unconscious, but sticking the blade of his knife closer to Leanna's throat, Stan warned threateningly, "Make a noise or a move and you're dead!" Leanna was sure the man would have no qualms about killing her, so she remained silent and lay perfectly still as the wagon rolled past the compound and through the fort gates.

When they had traveled a good distance from the fort, Stan left the back of the wagon to join Dub. The blanket remained over their captives, and the wool covering blocked off the evening air, making it difficult for Leanna to breathe.

They had journeyed for almost an hour before Darlene finally came to. Leanna had already begun to wonder if Dub's violent blow had caused her severe injury.

Moaning, Darlene opened her eyes, and finding herself beneath a blanket, she was frightened. It took a moment for her thoughts to clear, and when she realized she was being abducted, she turned her head to see if Leanna was beside her. It was too dark for her to make out Leanna's face, but she could hear her even breathing. Darlene wanted to speak to her, but the gag Stan had rammed into her mouth made that impossible.

Suddenly, the men's voices carried beneath the blanket to Leanna and Darlene, and tensing, they listened closely to the conversation.

Rubbing his crotch, Stan complained, "Damn it, Dub! When are we goin' to stop and get us some of that good stuff we got in the back of the wagon?"

"Don't be so goddamned anxious," Dub replied impatiently. "We gotta get farther away from the fort."

"How long have I gotta wait?" Stan asked urgently.

" 'Bout dawn. We should be far enough away then, and we can stop and give them gals a little of the ol' in-and-out treatment."

"Hot damn!" Stan rejoined, slapping his knee.

"What a way to start off the day. Come sunrise, the roosters ain't the only ones that are gonna be cock-a-doodle-dooin'!"

Guffawing loudly, Dub threw back his head and roared with laughter, and finding his own remark very humorous, Stan's laughter mingled with Dub's.

Leanna felt sick, but she knew if she didn't control her nausea, the gag in her mouth would cause her to strangle to death on her own bile. She preferred death to being molested by Dub and Stan, but she must hold onto the hope that Jeff would find her in time.

Darlene was also feeling extremely ill, the thought of Dub and Stan using her body made her shudder. Nonetheless, she decide to pretend to respond to their sexual advances. She knew her only chance for survival was to be so agreeable that they would decide to keep her with them. And then? Well, she'd find a means for escape!

Neither Leanna nor Darlene slept through the long, frightening night, and as the sun began to rise over the horizon, they were both aware of daylight seeping through the blanket.

"Well, Stan," they heard Dub say as he pulled up the wagon. "I reckon it's time for us to do a little pokin'."

Leaping to the ground, Stan called with enthusiasm, "Are you gals ready for a little fun?"

Snickering, the men moved to the sides of the buckboard and jerked off the blanket. Stan was standing at Leanna's side of the wagon, and smiling down into her face, he said excitedly, "I've always been kinda partial to blondes, so I reckon I'll stick it to you 'fore I pleasure your girl friend."

"I ain't partial," Dub laughed. "So Stan, my boy, if you want that blonde filly first, go ahead and jump into the saddle. I'll ride this here dark filly."

Knowing now that Jeff wouldn't find her in time, Leanna closed her eyes and wished for merciful death.

"What the hell!" Dub suddenly said fearfully, and wondering what had happened to frighten him, Leanna's eyes flew open. Lying in the back of the wagon, she couldn't see her surroundings, and was only aware of Stan and Dub's pale faces as they stared at something or someone. With her hands and feet tied, it was difficult for Leanna to sit up, but awkwardly, she managed. The terrifying sight that confronted Leanna, caused her to gasp.

Clumsily, Darlene also managed to sit, and as she looked around, her eyes widened with terror.

Advancing from four different directions, painted Sioux warriors were heading steadily toward the wagon. Leanna wondered where they had come from; it seemed that the Indians had materialized out of thin air. They were riding war ponies, and the few who weren't carrying rifles, held pointed lances.

Leanna estimated there must be close to a hundred of them, and a new fear surged through her whole body, causing her to tremble. Suddenly, Dub and Stan had become the lesser of two evils, and her heart pounded rapidly as she recalled fleetingly all the rumors she had heard at the fort concerning the horrible ways in which the Sioux tortured their captives.

Staring at the Indians, Leanna became aware of

460

the two warriors riding in the lead. She noticed that one of them wore a headband with one white feather attached to it. He didn't appear to be carrying a weapon, but the man riding at his side had a rifle cradled in his arms. Her eyes fastening on the two warriors, she studied them intently as they drew closer. The brave with the white feather had a streak of black war paint across each cheek, but the other warrior's face was painted with several streaks of different colors. The heavily painted warrior was a threatening figure of a man, and the mere sight of him sent cold chills up Leanna's spine.

"We gotta make a run for it!" Stan rasped, his eyes bulging.

"Stan, you jackass, we can't run! They got us surrounded!" Dub said, and those were the last words he ever spoke.

The warrior Leanna had found threatening, raised his rifle, and taking perfect aim, he fired. The bullet hit Dub in the middle of the forehead, transforming his face into a bloody mass before he fell. Reacting, Stan whirled to grab the rifle he had left on the wagon seat. The painted warrior shot again, and because Stan had turned around, the bullet stuck him in the back of the head, causing him to sprawl down onto the ground.

A scream rose to Leanna's throat, but the confining gag pushed it back. She watched with terror as the two leading warriors pulled up their horses beside the wagon.

They spoke to each other in their own language, but Leanna could tell by their sharp tones that they were disagreeing. Apparently, the man with the white feather won the argument because the other one shrugged as though he were indifferent, and dismounting, he pulled his knife from its sheath. He stepped over to Dub's body, and when Leanna realized he was taking Dub's scalp, she quickly dropped her gaze. Feeling the wagon suddenly bounce from Darlene's fallen weight, Leanna knew she had foolishly watched what the warrior was doing and had fainted. Serves her right! Leanna thought resentfully.

The warrior who wore the white feather began speaking authoritatively, and Leanna raised her eyes to look at him. Obeying his order, two braves dismounted and, going to the wagon, leaped onto the seat. One of them picked up the reins and slapped them against the two horses so unexpectedly that the animals bounded forward, causing the wagon to lurch abruptly. The sudden jolt sent Leanna falling back onto the bed of the buckboard, and the rough ride across the plains tossed her repeatedly against Darlene and the hard sides of the wagon.

Hours later, Jeff accompanied by his troops and Nathan, reached the area where the Sioux had abducted the women. Knowing Leanna had now been taken by the Sioux, Jeff's fears for her life grew. Time was of the utmost importance, and Jeff knew he couldn't waste it lingering long enough to bury the trappers, nor could he afford to leave any men behind to take care of the chore. He had no choice but to leave the corpses to the hot sun and the vultures.

Moving onward, the troops followed the wagon tracks, and Jeff prayed the trail wouldn't end with them coming upon Leanna's mutilated body.

Nathan's thoughts coincided with Jeff's, and riding beside him, he suggested, "Maybe I'd better check ahead."

"That isn't necessary," Jeff mumbled.

Nathan's murdered family flashed across his mind. "If Leanna's dead, you shouldn't be the one to find her. Good God, man, you'll carry the picture in your mind for the rest of your life!" Jeff made no reply, so Nathan stated flatly, "I'm riding ahead."

"I'll go with you," Jeff replied firmly. Glancing over his shoulder, he called to Lieutenant Buehler, "We're going to have a look around."

Urgently, Nathan pleaded, "Jeff, for your own sake, stay behind!"

"I can't," Jeff moaned, then he broke his horse into a fast canter. Within minutes, Nathan caught up to him.

The Sioux had unhitched the wagon, and their captives were now riding face down across the backs of the two horses that had belonged to Dub and Stan. The Indians had left the gags on the women, and their hands and feet were still tied.

Stopping their ponies within the shelter of boulders and cottonwoods, the Indians dismounted. The heavily painted warrior stepped to Leanna as she lay across her horse's back. Slinging her over his shoulders, he carried her to a shady spot beneath one of the trees and flung her to the ground.

Shaken from the hard fall, Leanna watched fearfully as he walked back for Darlene. Once again he slung his captive over his shoulder and, returning, threw her down. As she hit the solid ground, Darlene moaned with pain.

Suddenly, the warrior with the white feather knelt between the two women. First he removed Leanna's gag and then Darlene's.

Leanna's mouth was so dry, it was painful for her to swallow. "Water," she pleaded raspingly, massaging her throat.

The warrior kneeling at her side, beckoned to one of his braves, who quickly brought over a canteen of water. Taking it, the warrior helped Leanna sit up and then tilted the canteen to her parched lips. Her thirst made her try to drink greedily, but the warrior knew she shouldn't have too much water all at once so he took the canteen from her mouth. Turning to Darlene, he gave her a drink in the same manner as he had Leanna.

Assuming that this wild savage hadn't mastered the English language, Darlene said bitterly to Leanna, "I suppose you're hoping we'll be saved by the cavalry with Major Jeff Clayton riding gallantly to the rescue!"

Clutching Darlene's arm, the warrior bounded to his feet, drawing her with him. Taking his knife, he cut the ropes tied about her hands and ankles. Holding onto Darlene's arm, he forced her to walk with him until they were a good distance from the others?

"Are you Major Clayton's woman?" he asked gruffly.

Shocked that he could speak English so well, Darlene responded by stuttering, "Wh-what?"

He gripped her shoulders, and his strong fingers

464

dug painfully into her flesh. "Are you Major Clayton's woman?" he repeated, his tone hard and brusque.

Looking into his wild black eyes, Darlene shivered with fear. My God, did this savage have a personal vendetta against Jeff? Was that why he wanted to know if she belonged to him, so he could kill her in revenge? Hoping she had guessed correctly, she answered hastily, "No, I'm not Major Clayton's wife, but the woman with me belongs to him. They plan to get married next week."

"You speak truth?" the warrior demanded.

"Yes," she assured him breathlessly. "If you don't believe me, ask her yourself." Darlene's curiosity got the better of her, and she asked with barely controlled enthusiasm, "Why? Do you plan to kill her because she belongs to Major Clayton?" She knew even if Leanna suspected that this Indian would murder her because of Jeff, she still wouldn't deny her love.

Refusing to explain himself, the Indian grabbed her arm and led her back to Leanna. Allowing Darlene to stand at his side, he glared down at Leanna and asked, "Are you Major Clayton's woman?"

The warrior's question startled her, but she still managed a firm reply, "Yes, I am."

Leanna watched, puzzled as the warrior then turned to his heavily painted comrade and spoke to him in their own language. Their discussion lasted only a few moments. Returning his attention to Leanna, the brave harshly informed her, "You belong to me!" Shoving Darlene toward his comrade, he told her, "You belong to Crazy Wolf!"

Kneeling beside Leanna, he used his knife to cut away her ropes. "I am called White Feather," he explained. "When ponies are rested, we leave."

She wanted to speak to him, but he moved away swiftly, brushing past Darlene as Crazy Wolf stood by, looking on with interest.

Stepping lithely, Crazy Wolf suddenly grabbed Darlene, sweeping her into his strong arms. Imprisoning her against his powerful chest, he carried her away from the others. Taking her behind a large boulder, he roughly dropped her to the ground. The solid fall jolted Darlene's entire body and she yelped sharply.

"You take off clothes!" Crazy Wolf ordered, his dark eyes roaming over her tantalizing curves.

"I . . . I wasn't aware that you could speak my language," Darlene stammered as her thoughts began to race. If she pleasured this disgusting brute, he'd probably decide to keep her alive so she could continue to satisfy his savage desires. Studying his bulky frame, and ghastly painted face, she wished Crazy Wolf were the one who hated Jeff instead of White Feather. She would have enjoyed giving herself to White Feather; unlike Crazy Wolf, he was a handsome figure of a man.

"Take off clothes!" Crazy Wolf demanded again.

Believing her life depended on whether or not she pleased Crazy Wolf, Darlene displayed a seductive smile as she rose gracefully to her feet. Her jaw was discolored from Dub's violent blow, but the bruise didn't mar Darlene's beauty. Her long black hair had come partially loose from its pins, and reaching up,

466

she removed all the hair pins, dropping them at her feet. She brushed her fingertips through her long, full tresses, causing her hair to fall provocatively past her shoulders. .

Her crimson gown buttoned in front, and while looking sensually into Crazy Wolf's eyes, she undid the tiny buttons slowly, almost teasingly. Then she stepped out of the dress and stood before Crazy Wolf in her ruffled petticoat. She tried frantically to read the man's thoughts, but his stony face was inscrutable.

Good Lord! Darlene thought. What is wrong with this barbarian? Is he too much of a savage to appreciate a white woman's beauty? She removed her dainty slippers, then in a desperate effort to arouse him, she parted her lips and ran her tongue across them, making her mouth moist and inviting. While gazing lewdly into his expressionless face, she unlaced the strings on her petticoat, slipping slowly out of the undergarment. Deepening her breathing, purposely she stripped off her lace panties and revealed her dark mound to Crazy Wolf's staring eyes.

"Crazy Wolf," she purred, caressing her voluptuous breasts, "I can make love to you as no woman ever has. I know all the little and delightful secrets that pleasure a man."

Impatiently, Crazy Wolf discarded his buckskin leggings and breechclout. Darlene was very relieved to see that his manhood was erect and throbbing. Oh yes, he wanted her, and she would make damned sure that he continued to desire her!

Feeling confident, Darlene moved to Crazy Wolf, letting her hips sway with her light steps. She was now sure everything would work out to her advantage. White Feather would kill Leanna, and eventually, she'd be saved by Jeff and his troops. As soon as she finished seducing Crazy Wolf, she must conjure up a believable lie to tell Jeff, one that would explain why she and Leanna had been abducted by Dub and Stan. But she would think about that later, now she must concentrate wholly on pleasuring Crazy Wolf.

Sliding her arms about his neck, she pressed her bare thighs to Crazy Wolf's hard erection. She was expecting him to take her into his embrace, but, instead, he ordered brusquely, "Lay down on ground, then turn over and get on knees!"

"Crazy Wolf," she objected sweetly, although she found his request so boorish she wished she could tell him that he was not only disgusting, but also had about as much sex appeal as a filthy animal. Continuing, she murmured, "There is much more to making love than . . . what you have in mind."

"What white woman mean?" he barked.

"Let me show you what I mean," she tempted.

"You show Crazy Wolf," he agreed, and she was happy to see him suddenly smile.

Doing what she knew how to do best, Darlene knelt in front of Crazy Wolf, and taking his firm erection into her hand, she lowered her mouth.

Chapter Thirty-four

Walking beside Crazy Wolf as they headed back to where they had left the others, Darlene was almost certain that she had managed successfully to insure her life. To please Crazy Wolf, she had used her talents to their fullest, and to her relief, he had responded passionately.

"Crazy Wolf," she began, using her husky, sensual tone, "did I please you?"

"You give me much pleasure," he replied without emotion.

"Does that mean you won't kill me?" she asked, holding her breath expectantly as she waited for his reply.

He thought for a moment, then answered, "Crazy Wolf show thanks and be merciful."

Releasing her breath, Darlene smiled victoriously as she continued her questions, "Will White Feather kill the woman who travels with me?"

Crazy Wolf nodded stiffly. "White Feather say he take her to his village, and then she burn at stake."

"He intends to burn her?" she asked, astounded.

"White woman ask too many questions!" Crazy Wolf snapped.

Pretending submissiveness, Darlene murmured, "I'm sorry, Crazy Wolf." She was sure these savages thought women inferior to men and expected them to behave meekly as well as obediently. Darlene considered herself a survivor. She would play by Crazy Wolf's rules, but she hoped when she was rescued by the cavalry that he would be the first Indian to die.

Returning to Leanna, who was still sitting within the shade of the large cottonwood, Darlene smiled smugly as she sat down beside her. "Leanna, dear, I hope you weren't too worried about me while I was gone," she purred.

"Darlene, to be perfectly honest, I was a little worried, but I was concerned about Crazy Wolf. I'm sure no man is safe in your presence."

Darlene's green eyes flashed vindictively, as she hissed, "Do you know what White Feather intends to do with you?"

"No, but I have a feeling you're going to tell me," Leanna replied, wishing her heart wasn't pounding so heavily. Dear God, if White Feather planned to kill her, why must Darlene be the one to tell her? Leanna could only imagine how much this malicious woman must be gloating.

"He plans to take you to his village and burn you at the stake," Darlene informed her very willingly.

"But why?" Leanna gasped, trying not to think about her terrifying fate.

"I think it's because he hates Jeff. Why he despises him, I don't know. But when I told him that you and

470

Jeff are engaged, he quickly made his choice. He gave me to Crazy Wolf and took you for himself."

"How do you know he plans to kill me?" she asked intensely.

"He told Crazy Wolf, and Crazy Wolf told me," Darlene replied calmly.

"And what happens to you?" Leanna asked, although she was quite sure Darlene had used her feminine wiles to secure her safety.

"Crazy Wolf likes the way I please him, so he will keep me as his woman." Darlene was obviously very proud of herself.

"Darlene, I can't quite picture you as an Indian squaw."

"Oh, I don't intend to be his squaw for very long," was the nonchalant reply. "I'm sure Jeff will soon rescue me." Reaching over, Darlene patted Leanna's hand. "Don't worry about Jeff, my dear. I will take good care of him, and I'll console him as he grieves over your death. I'll be so kind and understanding that eventually he'll ask me to marry him."

"Why does it mean so much to you to marry Jeff?" Leanna demanded, pushing away Darlene's hand. "It's very apparent that you don't love him!"

Darlene stared at Leanna incredulously. Was it possible that this virtuous Southern belle didn't know that Jeff was extremely wealthy? Why hadn't Jeff told her? Had he planned to surprise her after they were married? Deciding to bait Leanna, Darlene replied with an insidious smile, "Maybe I want to marry him because he's the only man who can satisfy me in bed."

"How would you know?" Leanna spat. "Jeff has never made love to you!"

"He was the man who took my virginity," Darlene lied haughtily.

"Are you referring to that night when he supposedly slipped into your bedroom and forced himself on you?" Leanna asked irritably.

"He told you about that night?" she asked, not upset by the knowledge.

"Yes, he did," Leanna answered firmly. "How did you do it, Darlene?"

"Do what?" she inquired innocently.

"Deceive him," Leanna came back. "We both know Jeff never raped you!"

Darlene laughed huskily. "I don't suppose there's any harm in confessing the truth to you. After all, you won't be alive to tell Jeff." Smiling, Darlene continued, "While I was dating Jeff, I was also having an affair with Darrin Spencer. Naturally, Jeff didn't know about my relationship with Darrin, but Darrin knew I wanted to marry Jeff, and he was more than willing to help me get Jeff to the altar."

"But why did Darrin want you to marry Jeff?" Leanna asked.

Smirking, Darlene replied, "Apparently, you don't know as much about Jeff as you think you do. I gather he hasn't bothered to inform you that he is very wealthy."

"Jeff is rich!" Leanna exclaimed.

"Filthy rich," Darlene specified greedily. "I promised Darrin that if he helped me trap Jeff, I would share my fortune with him. Don't think I was poverty stricken, because I wasn't. My father had a substantial business, and I believed we were quite well off. But I knew my father's wealth was meager when compared to Jeff's."

Trying to ease her tired body, Darlene braced her back against the tree trunk, and settling herself comfortably, she explained, "In the beginning, I thought I could get Jeff to marry me by pretending to be virtuous. Many times I would almost give in to his advances, then I'd seem to suddenly come to my senses and I would demand that he take me home. I hoped that he'd soon desire me so badly that he'd decide to marry me, but it finally became quite apparent that teasing Jeff was not working. In fact, he started seeing less of me, and that was when Darrin and I decided to trick him into marriage. Darrin invited Jeff out for a night on the town, and he encouraged Jeff to drink heavily. When they were having their last drink of the evening, Darrin laced Jeff's brandy with a potent sedative. They had scarcely entered Darrin's carriage when Jeff passed out. Darrin brought him to my house. My father wasn't expected to return until late that night, and so the servants had the night off. So Darrin used the front door to carry Jeff into the house and up the stairs to my bedroom. We stripped Jeff of his clothes, and so it would appear that Jeff had attacked me, Darrin put bruises on my wrists and even slapped me a couple of times. We also planted a ladder at my open bedroom window. Jeff believed he used that to slip into my room."

"You weren't a virgin so how did blood get on the sheets?" Leanna asked, barely controlling her rage toward this malevolent woman.

"I used chicken blood," Darlene answered with a sly smile. She paused, then proceeded with her story,

"My father was always a very accurate man, I could've set my watch by him. I knew exactly what time he'd leave his bedroom the next morning to go downstairs."

Interrupting, Leanna concluded, "So you knocked over the lamp, knowing he'd come into your room and find Jeff."

Darlene's green eyes narrowed resentfully. "Everything worked out just as I'd planned, and then the day before my wedding, father died from a stroke. I had no choice but to postpone the wedding, and Jeff, damn him, used the war as an excuse to run out on me. Oh, he promised he'd come home on leave and we'd be married. I wasn't too upset because I believed father's inheritance would be more than substantial. I planned to live in relative luxury until Jeff returned."

"But your father didn't leave you well off?" Leanna guessed.

"No," Darlene replied sullenly. "We weren't nearly as wealthy as I thought we were. In no time at all, Darrin and I gambled away my inheritance. Finally, I had to mortgage the house. When Jeff came home on leave, I thought he would marry me, but he only came to see me to break our engagement."

"You never wrote a letter to Jeff at Fort Laramie, did you?" Leanna asked.

"Of course not. I knew he would've written back and told me not to come. But luck was with me and Darrin happened to meet Captain Rhodes who was on his way to Fort Laramie. The bank had foreclosed on my house, and father's business went bankrupt. I had no choice but to try to get Jeff to marry me." Frowning hatefully, she added, "Of course, I hadn't counted on your presence."

"Good Lord!" Leanna moaned, finding Darlene's immoral character hard to believe. "You want Jeff's money so desperately that you'll even stoop to murder. You ordered those two trappers to kill me, only your little scheme didn't turn out the way you planned."

Raising her chin smugly, Darlene replied, "Everything will still work out to my advantage. White Feather will get rid of you for me free of charge." Suddenly, Darlene paled as she exclaimed, "Damn! My diamond ring was left on Dub's body!"

Sickened by Darlene, Leanna got hastily to her feet.

"Where are you going?" Darlene asked.

"Away from you!" Leanna replied distastefully. She turned sharply, intending to put some distance between herself and Darlene, but White Feather's sudden presence stopped her.

"It now time to leave," White Feather informed Leanna, his tone firm.

Standing, Darlene said with as much sweetness as she could muster, "Goodbye, Leanna. I'll be sure to tell Jeff, reluctantly of course, that you tried to buy your life by offering White Feather your body. And when White Feather took you, I will say I was totally abashed by your wanton response."

Lurching toward Darlene, Leanna raged, "Why you lying . . ."

But White Feather's strong arm encircled Leanna's waist, halting her in midstride. Effortlessly, he lifted her, and as she fought against him, he carried her to her horse. Placing her upright on the animal's bare back, he said so quietly that Leanna barely heard him, "Trust me."

He walked away to mount his own horse, and Leanna watched him, puzzled. "Trust me," he had said. Why would he lie to her? Apparently, he didn't realize that she knew he planned to kill her.

Guiding his mount next to Leanna's, White Feather took hold of the rope that he had tied to her horse's harness, and sitting his war pony proudly, he said a few words to Crazy Wolf in their own language. Then, with no forewarning, he sent his pony into a fast canter, and Leanna's horse started off so suddenly that she came very close to falling off the animal's back. Regaining her balance, and glancing over her shoulder, she saw that many of the warriors were leaving with them while others remained behind with Crazy Wolf.

Darlene walked to Crazy Wolf and stood confidently at his side. She waited until Leanna had ridden out of sight before turning and placing her hand on Crazy Wolf's arm. She was sure Jeff and his troops were not too far behind, and if she could tempt Crazy Wolf into lingering, maybe that would give the cavalry time to catch up to them.

Brushing her fingertips over the warrior's arm and up his shoulder, Darlene murmured provocatively, "Crazy Wolf, let's take a walk so we can be alone. I want to pleasure you again."

Eluding her touch, he said brusquely, "It time to leave and return to village."

"What is your village like, and will your people accept me?" Darlene asked, stalling for time.

Crazy Wolf smiled, an unmistakably sardonic smile that sent terror surging through Darlene's body.

Reaching over and caressing her raven black hair, he said smoothly, "White woman have pretty hair. I will carry it on my lance with much pride."

Her knees weakening, Darlene gasped deeply, "Crazy Wolf, please don't tease me!"

"Crazy Wolf never tease," he replied strongly. He motioned to one of his braves, who quickly brought Crazy Wolf his rifle.

Panic-strucken, Darlene screeched, "But you told me I would live!"

"I not say you live, I say Crazy Wolf be merciful. I kill you swiftly so there will be little pain," he answered, his black eyes boring unyieldingly into hers.

Clutching at her throat while backing away from him, Darlene begged, "Crazy Wolf, please don't kill me . . . please! . . . I'll do anything you say, only please let me live!" When Crazy Wolf did not respond to her pleas, hysteria overcame Darlene, making her body tremble violently. She had never felt such fear. Terror gripped her chest like a vise, causing her to gasp convulsively.

Filled with panic, Darlene turned and began to run wildly, but pointing his rifle, Crazy Wolf took careful aim. He pulled the trigger, and the deadly bullet hit its intended target. Darlene plunged to the ground, and as life ebbed from her body, the exploding gunshot rumbled ominously across the vast landscape.

Crazy Wolf stepped to Darlene's lifeless body and clutched her long black hair. Pleased with the scalp he was about to take, a large and primitive smile spread across his painted face.

Leanna felt as if every muscle in her body was sore.

477

The rough ride in the trappers' wagon had continuously tossed her against the hard sides of the buckboard. Then, later, when the Indians had forced her to ride face down across her horse's back, she had been jounced continually, and her stomach had pained her as the animal's pounding hoofs sped across the vast terrain. Now, she was sitting on the horse's bare back, and her hiked skirt left her legs uncovered, causing her mount's prickly hair to chafe her delicate thighs.

The sun was directly overhead, and Leanna found it hard to believe that it was only midday. So much had happened to her within the past few hours that she felt as though she had been living this present nightmare for days.

White Feather was riding beside Leanna, and she turned her head slightly to study him. He was a handsome man, probably about Jeff's age. Unlike Crazy Wolf's, White Feather's looks were not intimidating. But Leanna felt that his outward appearance must be deceptive and inwardly he was capable of extreme violence.

Taking a deep breath, she decided to ask White Feather the question that had been plaguing her since they'd left Darlene and the others, but she dreaded hearing his answer. "When will we reach your village?"

"We not ride to village," he answered.

Leanna looked at him dubiously. "Then where are we going?"

"We ride toward fort." White Feather had been staring straight ahead, but shifting his gaze to Leanna, he asked, "Is Major Clayton searching for you and the other woman?"

"I'm sure he is," she mumbled vaguely, finding this

conversation confusing.

"Then we should find him very soon," he stated.

"But why are you looking for Major Clayton?" Leanna continued to pry.

"I give you back to him," White Feather revealed.

"What!" Leanna exclaimed, her heart accelerating with sudden joy. "But I thought you were taking me to your village to kill me!"

He smiled briefly. "Why you think that?"

"Darlene, the woman who was traveling with me, said Crazy Wolf told her you were planning to kill me."

White Feather nodded. "Yes, I tell Crazy Wolf that I will kill you."

"But why?" Leanna gasped.

"Crazy Wolf and me not from same village, but we decide to go on raiding party together. When I ride with Crazy Wolf, we make pact to kill all whites. But when I learn you Major Clayton's woman, I know I cannot kill you. But I not tell Crazy Wolf because it would cause much trouble. Crazy Wolf give me many problems, and I ride with him no more. I not want him for an enemy. All Sioux must stay together so we can be strong and fight to keep our land. So there be no trouble between us, I tell Crazy Wolf that you will die."

"What does Major Clayton have to do with all this?"

"I owe Major Clayton much, but when I give you back to him, we be even."

"You owe him?" she questioned, totally perplexed.

"Later, you understand," he replied.

"But, White Feather, why did you feel you had to lie to Crazy Wolf about killing me? He plans to let Darlene live.

"Crazy Wolf kill all whites. Men, women, children, it

479

make no difference to Crazy Wolf."

"You're wrong," Leanna argued. "He intends to keep Darlene with him."

"Crazy Wolf kill white woman," he answered flatly.

"But, Darlene said—"

Interrupting, he told her, "The white woman you call Darlene is a fool. She hear only what she want to hear. After she pleasure Crazy Wolf, he tell her he be merciful, and she think that mean he not kill her."

In spite of the warm temperature, Leanna felt a sudden chill. "Do you mean he intends to kill her mercifully because she . . . she was nice to him?"

White Feather shrugged uncaringly. "That she pleasure him have little to do with Crazy Wolf's decision to kill her swiftly. If he had time, he would torture white woman, but Crazy Wolf must hurry back to village before bluecoats find him. He not take Darlene as captive because he not want to be bothered with a woman on journey back to his people." Leanna started to speak, but White Feather said gruffly, "We talk no more." Digging his knees into his pony's side, he rode ahead of her.

Leanna's first impulse was to call him back and ask him to save Darlene, but she knew her plea would be useless. Suddenly, remembering the distant gunshot she had heard shortly after she and White Feather had ridden out of the camp, she wondered if Crazy Wolf had already killed Darlene. She had never disliked anyone as much as Darlene, but all the same, the thought of the woman's fate made Leanna feel sick inside.

* * *

Jeff and Nathan were riding in front of their troops when they spotted the group of Sioux warriors in the distance. Pulling up their horses, they waited for the soldiers to catch up to them, then Jeff gave the command to halt.

As the Indians drew nearer, Jeff suddenly caught sight of Leanna. "Thank God, she's alive!" he sighed gratefully. The Indians stopped their horses, and Jeff looked on with amazement as one of the warriors and Leanna continued to ride toward them.

"What in the hell is going on?" he asked Nathan.

"I don't know, but it looks like White Feather is returning Leanna," Nathan answered, recognizing the warrior.

"So that's White Feather," Jeff mumbled aloud, although he was speaking mostly to himself. Jeff had heard of White Feather, whose father was Chief Wild Horse. Their tribe was extremely hostile toward whites, and that Leanna was alive seemed a miracle.

White Feather and Leanna halted their horses alongside Jeff and Nathan. Leanna started to jump down to the ground and rush to Jeff, but White Feather placed a hand on her arm, stopping her.

"First, I talk to Major Clayton; then you may leave White Feather," he said. Looking into his face, Leanna detected a deep tenderness in his dark eyes that made her decide to be agreeable.

Turning his attention to Jeff, White Feather asked, "Are you called Major Jeff Clayton?"

"Yes, I am," Jeff answered, exerting all his self-control to sound calm and to remain on his horse instead of going to Leanna and sweeping her into his arms.

481

"You save my son's life. I save your woman and bring her back to you. Now we even," White Feather stated firmly.

"Your son?" Jeff questioned, confused.

"Black Bear caught by white men. They leave him to die in sun, but you find Black Bear, give him food and water, then set him free. He tell me bluecoat's name Major Jeff Clayton."

Remembering the Indian boy he had found staked to the ground, Jeff marveled, "He is your son?"

White Feather nodded stiffly. "You save my son, now I save your woman. We even, and I not owe debt to bluecoat. If we meet in battle, I now free to kill you."

"We won't be meeting in battle, White Feather," Jeff explained. "I'm leaving this land to return to my home in the East."

White Feather smiled. "That good. It would not give me pleasure to kill the man who saved my son."

"Nor would it have given me pleasure to kill the warrior who rescued the woman I love."

Jeff offered White Feather his hand, and familiar with the white man's handshake, White Feather accepted Jeff's token of friendship. Then without further words, he turned his horse and rode back to join his warriors.

Dismounting quickly, Jeff went to Leanna and helped her dismount. Taking her into his arms, he hugged her tightly. "Thank God, you're all right!"

Holding onto him desperately, she cried, "Oh Jeff, I thought I'd never see you again!"

Separating himself from her with reluctance, he asked, "Where is Darlene?"

Hastily, she explained that Darlene had been left

behind with Crazy Wolf, who planned to kill her.

Turning to his soldiers, Jeff ordered, "Troopers Rogan and Lammert to the front!"

Getting down from their horses, Jerry and Paul reported promptly to Jeff. "Yes, sir!" they snapped in unison.

"I want you to pick ten men to ride with you and escort Miss Weston back to the fort," Jeff commanded.

Jerry and Paul left to carry out their orders, and Nathan said to Jeff, "I'll ride ahead."

"All right," Jeff agreed. "My men and I will move out in a few minutes, and we'll be close behind you." As Nathan was riding away, Jeff again drew Leanna into his embrace. "I must search for Darlene. Later, you can explain everything to me, but I already know that Darlene was behind it all."

She told Jeff about the gunshot she had heard when she was riding away from the camp. "Do you think it's too late to save Darlene?" she asked intensely.

"I don't know," he answered somberly. "But I'm afraid that's a grave possibility."

Chapter Thirty-five

It was the middle of the night when Jeff and his troops returned to the fort. The procession passed slowly through the gates, but once inside the compound the weary horses perked up as they sensed that rest and bags of oats were awaited them in the nearby stables. The soldiers, as fatigued as the horses they rode, sat lethargically atop their mounts. Their mission had taken almost twenty-four hours, and the troopers, tired as well as depressed by Miss Whitlock's death, rode with bowed heads. The horse bringing up the rear of the procession carried Darlene's body, which had been tied across the animal's back and covered with a blanket. Although Darlene had brought her own demise upon herself, the soldiers had no way of knowing this and if they had it wouldn't have changed the way they felt. A white woman had been killed by the Sioux, and the tragic incident made them more determined than ever to civilize the West.

Of all the troopers, none was more dispirited than

their commanding officer, Major Clayton. Jeff didn't know if Darlene had decided to leave with the trappers and had tricked Leanna into leaving with them, or if somehow her plans had gone wrong and the trappers had taken Darlene against her will. In either case, he felt as though he were to blame for her death. Since the night he had slipped into Darlene's bedroom and forced himself upon her, he had continued to treat her unfairly. Apparently, as a last resort, she had become a scheming and desperate woman, and he was starting to convince himself that in the final analysis he was at fault.

After filing his report with Colonel Wallace, Jeff went to the hotel. He was sure Leanna would be asleep, but the questions he needed to ask her were too pressing to wait until morning. Reaching her door, he rapped on it lightly.

Leanna was not sleeping soundly, and she awakened instantly. Sitting up in bed, she called out, "Who's there?"

"Jeff," he replied.

Leanna lit the bedside lamp. Rising hastily, she didn't bother to cover her nightgown with a robe as she hurried to the door and opened it. Flinging herself into Jeff's arms, she exclaimed, "Oh darling, I'm so glad you're back!"

He held her close for a moment, needing to feel her warm body clinging to his. Gently, he relinquished her, and entering the room, he closed and locked the door.

Standing in front of him, Leanna gazed up into his troubled face. "Darlene?" she whispered.

"We were too late," Jeff mumbled despondently.

Moving past her, he took off his hat and placed it on a chair; then, ambling to the open window, he stared out at the night. "We brought her body back to the fort," he continued somberly. He grimaced, remembering that Darlene's beauty had been grotesquely marred by Crazy Wolf's scalping. Swallowing slowly, Jeff proceeded quietly, "Darlene will be buried tomorrow morning in the fort's cemetery." All at once, his strong frame stiffened, and whirling to face Leanna, he groaned hoarsely, "My God, I feel as though Darlene's death is all my fault!"

Going quickly to his side, Leanna asked urgently, "Why do you think you are to blame?"

"I made her the kind of woman she became!" he raged, inwardly despising himself. "I raped her, took her virginity, than ran out on her! She loved me, and in return I gave her nothing but heartache and one disappointment after another!"

Clutching his arm, Leanna cried, "Oh Jeff, my darling, you never raped her! And you didn't make her a malicious and conniving woman, Darlene was always that way!"

His brow furrowing with confusion, he asked, "Leanna, what are you saying?"

Taking his hand in hers, she coaxed, "Come sit on the bed with me, and I'll explain everything."

Agreeing, he replied, "We need to talk, I have so many questions to ask."

As they sat on the edge of the bed, Leanna said firmly, "There is no need for questions, just be quiet and let me explain everything, starting with the note Darlene sent me, a note I believed was from you."

Jeff started to tell her that he already knew about

the forged note, but she had asked him to remain silent, so he didn't say anything.

As Leanna's story began to unfold, Jeff listened closely, and although he was shocked by Darlene's vindictiveness, he still believed he had caused her to become that kind of woman. It wasn't until Leanna described the conversation in which Darlene had confessed that she and Darrin Spencer had tricked him that Jeff's guilt began to dissolve.

"So you see, darling, you aren't to blame for Darlene's actions," Leanna finished. "She was always a malevolent woman."

"All these years," Jeff sighed, "I believed I forced myself on her." Impatient with himself, he uttered angrily, "How could I have been such a fool!"

Placing her hand over his, and patting it gently, Leanna replied, "Don't be so hard on yourself. You thought Darlene and Darrin Spencer were your friends so, naturally, you trusted them."

"Darrin Spencer!" Jeff seethed. "When I return to St. Louis, he'd better hope he isn't there, because I have a score to even with him!"

It was on the tip of Leanna's tongue to ask Jeff to forget the past and not confront Darrin Spencer, but she knew her plea would be useless. Jeff had his pride, and she sensed that Darrin Spencer would pay dearly for deceiving Jeff while pretending to be his friend.

Wishing to turn the conversation away from Darlene and Darrin Spencer, Leanna asked curiously, "Jeff, why didn't you tell me that you were wealthy?"

"When we first met, there was no reason to bring up my wealth. Later, I wanted to tell you, but because of the war you were almost destitute, and I was afraid if I talked about my money, it would have sounded as thought I was gloating."

"But why didn't you tell me when you asked me to marry you?"

Studying her, Jeff smiled lovingly. "I was planning to tell you on our wedding night. I thought it would be a pleasant surprise."

Returning his smile, she inquired pertly, "Just how wealthy are you?"

His brown eyes twinkling merrily, he replied, "Rich enough to buy you anything you want." Chuckling, he added, "Well, almost anything."

Leanna's gaiety mysteriously vanished, and as a look of sadness crossed her face, Jeff asked pressingly, "Sweetheart, what's wrong?"

"Oh, Jeff," she sighed disconsolately, "all the money in the world couldn't buy what I want. You can't purchase what no longer exists."

"You mean The Pines," he muttered, depressed.

"Darling, I don't blame you because it was burned," she said intensely. "The war destroyed my home."

Comforting her, he placed an arm around her and drew her close. Snuggling against him, she continued, "But The Pines was my home, where I was born and raised. Now my house is gone, and I lost my land because I couldn't pay the taxes. I'm sure my land has been bought by a distasteful carpetbagger or . . ." Catching herself, Leanna's voice faltered.

"Or a Yankee soldier?" Jeff concluded lightly.

A little embarrassed, Leanna mumbled, "I'm sorry. I didn't mean to sound bitter."

He responded tenderly. "You have a right to feel a certain bitterness."

"Perhaps," she agreed, but thinking about Jackson, she admitted, "The abolitionists were right. We should have freed our slaves."

"Why do you think that?" he asked, and although he was genuinely interested, he couldn't stop from yawning with fatigue.

She moved out of his arms, and was about to elaborate on Jackson's life as a slave, but becoming aware of Jeff's weariness, she decided, "I'll tell you some other time. Now I think you should get some rest."

Jeff agreed. He was so exhausted that he was finding it difficult to concentrate. "Do you mind if I sleep here?" he asked. "I need to be close to you."

Leaning over, she brushed her lips across his. "I want to be with you too."

Jeff unbuckled his holster and placed it on the night table. He slipped off his boots, then stretched out on the bed. Turning off the lamp, Leanna laid down beside him. Entering his embrace, she nestled her head on his shoulder.

"Leanna," he whispered, "I love you very much."

"I love you, Jeff," she responded softly.

Needing only to be close, each feeling safe and secure in the other's love, they both drifted into sleep.

When Leanna was awakened by Jeff's fitful tossing, she sat up, and shook his shoulders, saying firmly, "Jeff! Jeff, darling, wake up!"

His eyes opened suddenly, and seeing Leanna leaning over him, he apologized, "I was having a nightmare. I'm sorry if I disturbed you."

"Were you dreaming about Darlene?" she asked quietly.

"Yes," he moaned, wondering if he'd ever fully recover from finding her mutilated body.

"Jeff," Leanna asked hesitantly, not sure if she really wanted to know the answer, "How did Crazy Wolf kill Darlene? I thought he shot her."

"He did," Jeff replied; then, not wanting Leanna to know any more about Darlene's tragic death, he said in a light tone, "Let's talk of more pleasant things, shall we?"

Lying beside him and snuggling close, she queried, "For instance?"

"Like how much I love you," he suggested.

"That sounds like a marvelous topic of conversation," she agreed happily.

Smiling, he began, "I love you more than life itself. How's that for a start?"

Pertly, she asked, "Does this confession get better as it progresses?"

"Naturally," he replied.

"I can hardly wait to hear the rest," she murmured.

"I love you so much that my whole world revolves around you."

Nuzzling his neck, she encouraged him to continue. "Don't stop now."

"You're in my heart as well as my soul," he said softly, drawing her even closer.

Kissing, and blowing teasingly into his ear, she purred, "Go on."

"I love you so deeply that you're a part of me."

Raising her head so she could gaze down into his

face, she responded gaily, "It sounds as though you love me almost as much as I love you."

"Almost?" he chuckled. "Leanna Weston, you do not love me more than I love you because it would be impossible for anyone to love someone more than I love you."

"Very well, Major Clayton, I will settle for a compromise. We love each other equally."

"And passionately," Jeff added, sliding one hand to her rounded buttocks, kneading her soft flesh.

"And wantonly," she continued, moving her body over his, pressing her hips against him.

"And urgently," he groaned, feeling his aroused manhood pushing uncomfortably against his confining trousers.

Leanna giggled, "Urgently, Jeff?"

"Sweetheart," he explained tolerantly, "in case you haven't noticed, a problem has arisen."

"I can take care of that problem," she offered, and kneeling at his side, she unbuckled his belt. Quickly she undid his trousers, and as he lifted his hips, she slid his pants and undershorts past his thighs. Then removing them completely, she dropped the garment onto the floor.

Wanting to love him as she never had before, Leanna bent over him and her warm mouth found his aroused manhood.

Groaning with passion, and loving the pleasure she was giving him, Jeff entwined his fingers into her long, blond hair. Leanna's lips and tongue brought him to such an ecstatic peak that he had to pull away to delay his fulfillment.

Urging Leanna onto her back and lifting her

gown, Jeff moved over her. His arousal sought her womanhood, and as she clung tightly to him, he entered her velvety depths.

She wrapped her legs about his waist, wanting and loving his deeper penetration. As she surrendered herself to her passion, Leanna was amazed by how dearly she loved Jeff Clayton. She had never dreamed that she could adore a man as she did Jeff. He was her world, her life, and the center of her very soul!

Finding total ecstasy in Leanna's loving embrace, Jeff's thoughts coincided with hers. He, too, was astounded by his deep love for Leanna Weston. She was the perfect woman for him, and he'd never let her go.

"I love you," she cried desperately.

"I need you, Leanna," he moaned, gathering her ever closer. "And, sweetheart, I love you with all my heart."

Cleaving only to one another, they drifted together into love's supreme paradise.

Late the next day, when Leanna was alone in her hotel room, a knock sounded on her door. "Who is it?" she asked, hoping to hear Jeff's deep voice announcing his presence.

"Jennifer," came the reply.

"Come in, the door isn't locked," Leanna invited.

Jennifer entered, carrying a bundle wrapped in plain paper, and sat down on the bed next to Leanna.

Yesterday, when Leanna had returned to the fort with her escort, Jennifer and David and Audrey had welcomed her. But Jennifer hadn't had an opportunity to be alone with Leanna who had been so tired that she had told her family she needed rest more than company. Abiding by her wishes, they had let her go to her hotel room and had not disturbed her.

Placing the bundle on her lap, Jennifer began hesitantly, "Leanna, I'm very sorry about all the cruel things I said to you the other day." Tears brimming in her eyes, she pleaded, "I hope you'll forgive me!"

Patting Jennifer's hand, Leanna said tenderly, "Of course I forgive you." Smiling at her sister-in-law, she asked, "Does this mean you've decided to accept my marriage?"

"I'm not merely accepting your marriage, I'm giving you my blessings, and I pray you will be very happy with Major Clayton." Squeezing Leanna's hand, Jennifer explained, "David had a long talk with me, and he made me realize that during the war I never personally knew any Yankees the way you did. I never had a reason to see beyond the color of their uniform. They were the enemy, and I naturally presumed that one is supposed to despise one's enemy."

"Jennifer," Leanna intruded, "you don't need to explain all this to me. I once felt the same way. I also hated Yankees, but that was before I came to know men like Doctor Hamilton, Jerry, Paul, and . . . and, of course, Jeff." Glancing down at the wrapped bundle on Jennifer's lap, she asked curiously, "What's in the package?"

Standing, Jennifer placed it on the bed, and while unwrapping it, she answered evasively, "Early this morning, I took a very special gown to one of the fort's laundresses and had it washed and pressed."

Jennifer removed all the paper, and looking at the uncovered gown, Leanna inhaled deeply. "Rising to her feet, she exclaimed, "Mama's wedding dress!"

Anxiously, both women unfolded the white gown and spread it out over the bed. "It's so elegant!" Jennifer praised, admiring the graceful garment.

Leanna couldn't hold back the sentimental tears that filled her eyes as she closely examined the dress her mother had worn the day she'd married the dashing plantation owner, Frank Weston.

The beautiful gown was made with layers of white silk, and its tight-fitting sleeves were adorned with tiny pearl buttons sewn to the forearms and all the way down to the wrists. The sweeping neckline was heart shaped, and the fitted bodice was followed by a soft pleated front. The flowing train began at the waist and was then attached to the back of the gown.

"You should try it on," Jennifer suggested. "We might need to do some altering."

"It'll fit perfectly," Leanna assured her. "Mama was always so sure that David and I would marry that years ago she had it altered to fit me."

Going to Leanna's closet, Jennifer removed a clothes hanger. Returning, she said, "We'd better hang it up so it won't get wrinkled."

After the wedding gown had been hung safely in the closet, Jennifer sat beside Leanna on the edge of the bed and asked, "When are you getting married?"

"Saturday night in the chapel."

"That's only four days away."

"Yes, I know, and I'm so anxious that I've already started counting the hours."

"What do you and Major Clayton plan to do? Will

you stay here at the fort?" Jennifer asked.

"No," Leanna answered. "We plan to move to Jeff's home in St. Louis."

"When will you leave?"

"A company of soldiers is expected from Fort Casper. They are returning to the states, and Jeff said we'll travel with them. They should be here within a week or two."

"Do you think you'll be happy living in St. Louis?"

"Oh, Jennifer." Leanna sighed heavily. "I'll never love any home as much as I loved The Pines!" Standing, she looked down at Jennifer and added sincerely, "But I'll be happy living anywhere as long as I'm with Jeff!"

Rising to stand beside her, Jennifer asked, "Do you love him very much?"

"Yes, I love him with all my heart," Leanna revealed.

"And he loves you," replied Jennifer. "When you were missing, and he came to the wagon to speak with David and me, he was so terribly worried. I could see on his face how strongly he loves you. I found myself feeling so sorry for him that I was tempted to hold him in my arms and comfort him the way I console Bradley and Matthew."

Her blue eyes shining, Leanna smiled, "You were actually tempted to embrace a Yankee?"

Jennifer responded pertly, "Well, when a Yankee is as handsome as Major Clayton, a lady could very easily forget that during the war he fought for the wrong side."

"But the winning side," Jeff's voice suddenly rang out. Having found Leanna's door ajar, he had stepped undetected into the room and had overheard part of their conversation.

Whirling to face him, Jennifer's cheeks darkened to a scarlet shade.

Jeff moved to Leanna, and placing an arm over her shoulders, he studied the blushing Jennifer. He'd heard her say that she had been tempted to hold him so, grinning, he told her gallantly, "Mrs. Farnsworth, if a Southern lady as beautiful as yourself were to embrace a Yankee, for whatever reason, he would most assuredly forget that there had ever been a war."

Jeff's generous tribute put Jennifer at ease, and smiling amiably, she replied, "Since we are to be family, I wish you would call me Jennifer."

Stepping to her, Jeff lifted her hand and placed a light kiss on it. "I'll consider it an honor to call you Jennifer, and I hope you'll be so kind as to address me as Jeff."

Emphasizing her Southern accent, Jennifer teased, "Suh, I am impressed with your impeccable chivalry. Could it be possible that you might have a touch of Southern blood in your veins?"

Laughing good-humoredly, Jeff replied, "If the South had allowed their women to go to war instead of their men, not one shot would have been fired. Southern ladies could've won the war hands down with their innate diplomacy."

Chapter Thirty-six

Nathan had purposely avoided Audrey, but hoping he'd eventually come to her, she didn't seek him out. Forcing herself to hold on to her pride, she waited until the night of Leanna's wedding before deciding to throw pride to the winds and go to Nathan.

Arriving at his quarters, she knocked firmly on his door. It was opened almost immediately, and seeing Audrey, Nathan asked curtly, "What are you doing here? Shouldn't you be getting ready for the wedding?"

Brushing past him and entering his quarters, she answered, "I still have time to prepare myself for the wedding, and I shouldn't think it necessary to explain why I am here."

Closing the door, he said apologetically, "Audrey, the other night when we were together, I told you I wasn't making any promises."

"And I didn't ask for any, did I?" Audrey snapped irritably.

"Then why are you here?" he questioned.

Sighing, she replied, "I don't really know why. Maybe

I was hoping you had changed your mind."

Moving to stand closer to her, he mumbled, "Audrey, I'm sorry."

Lifting her chin proudly, she remarked, "Nathan Hayden, don't you dare pity me!" She pivoted away and took a few steps before once again facing him. "Do you know that a wagon train arrived this morning?"

"Yes, I know," he answered.

"Do you also know that it'll be leaving in three days and that my family and I will be traveling with it?"

"Jeff told me you'd be leaving," he admitted.

Noticing a packed bag on top of his bed, she asked with surprise, "Are you going somewhere?"

"I'm taking off for a few days," he explained. "I want some time alone."

"Where will you go?"

He shrugged. "Find myself a secluded place in the mountains, I suppose."

It was only a wild guess on Audrey's part but she lashed out anyway. "You're running away because you don't want to be here when I leave!" But seeing the naked truth on Nathan's face, she realized her rash accusation had been right. Suddenly, everything became crystal clear to Audrey, causing her to race on. "Nathan Hayden, you're afraid! You're not turning me away because you believe you aren't worth a decent woman's love. It's because you're afraid to be in love with me!"

"Afraid?" he mocked, his expression cynical.

"Yes!" she exclaimed excitedly. "You're afraid if you fall in love with me, you might someday lose me, and you'll have to once again suffer all the pain you felt when you lost your wife."

"That's ridiculous!" he denied, short-temperedly.

Going to him, and grasping his arm, she replied firmly, "Yes, it is ridiculous! It's ridiculous for you to feel that way!" Her fingers gripping him, she continued imploringly, "Oh Nathan, you can't run away from life! Tragedy is a part of living, but there is also happiness. You can't have all of one and none of the other. You must learn to accept whatever life brings, and if it's so tragic that it almost destroys you, then you have to rise above it, put the pieces of your life back together, and start over!"

Prying her fingers from his arm, he replied without emotion. "That's a lot of wisdom coming from one so young." Heading abruptly for the door, he opened it. "Audrey, I think it'd be best if you were to leave."

She longed to continue pleading with him, but Audrey valued her dignity, which was all she had left. She'd already given him her heart and her body; by coming here, she had now given him her pride. She walked to the door with her head held high. As she was about to brush past him and step outside, unexpectedly, he touched her arm.

"Audrey, you are a very beautiful and compassionate lady. You might think your heart will never mend, but in time—"

Interrupting, she said testily, "Nathan Hayden, I don't need, nor do I want your advice!" She stepped through the open doorway, but impetuously, she turned back and faced him. "If you should decide to stop running from life, you'll find me in San Francisco, but don't take too long making up your mind, because I'm too young to wait forever."

"And what makes you think my mind isn't already made up?"

"This is why," she whispered. Wrapping her arms about his neck, she brought his lips down to hers. He hesitated for only a moment; then, responding, he drew her closer. Her thighs flush to his, she could feel him grow hard against her.

Breaking their kiss abruptly, she looked steadfastly into his eyes, saying shrewdly, "Actions speak louder than words, Nathan Hayden."

She left and hurried across the compound, and standing in the doorway, Nathan watched her for a little while before closing the door. While he finished packing and changed his clothes for the wedding, he decided to simply wipe Audrey's visit from his mind. But as hard as he tried, Nathan couldn't stop thinking about what she had said, nor could he forget how good it had felt to have her in his arms, her sweet lips pressed so lovingly to his.

Although Leanna's wedding wasn't elaborate or lavish—that would have been impossible at a military fort—it was nonetheless done in good taste. Leanna was a beautiful bride, her mother's wedding gown fitting her to perfection, and Jeff made a dashing groom in his dress uniform. The newlyweds' reception was given by Colonel Wallace and his wife, the function taking place in the colonel's home in the compound.

Because Jeff was resigning his commission, he and his bride didn't move into one of the houses for married officers. Instead, they had decided to stay at the hotel, since Leanna's room was much larger than the confining one off Jeff's office.

Mrs. Wallace, with Jennifer's help, had baked a three-tier wedding cake. Although anxious to be alone with

Leanna, Jeff knew the bride and groom couldn't leave until the cake had been cut, and he was greatly relieved when, at last, Mrs. Wallace announced it was time to carry out the tradition. Shortly thereafter, Jeff, with his bride close to his side, thanked the colonel and his wife for the nice reception. Jeff knew it wasn't necessary to make excuses for their sudden departure, the early departure of the bride and groom was also a tradition, and one Jeff intended to observe.

Escorting Leanna to the hotel and up to their room, Jeff carried her over the threshold, then kissed her passionately before placing her on her feet.

"I've been wanting to kiss you like that all evening," Jeff confessed. "I was beginning to think Mrs. Wallace was never going to suggest that we cut the cake."

"Why so anxious, darling?" she questioned saucily. "It's not as though we haven't made love before."

"Yes, but I've never made love to my wife," he pointed out.

"Do you think it'll be different?" she smiled.

"I don't know, but let's find out," he said, reaching for her. Hugging her enthusiastically, he suddenly noticed that a table, set with a bottle of brandy and two glasses, had been moved into the room. "What is this?" Jeff asked, releasing her.

Leanna turned and followed his gaze. "I wonder who sent us brandy?" she pondered.

Seeing a slip of paper beside the bottle, Jeff went over, picked it up and read aloud, "For Major Clayton and his beautiful bride, with our very best wishes, Jerry and Paul." Putting the note back on the table, Jeff commented admirably, "It's a good brandy and cost them nearly a month's wages. If the fort stored champagne, they probably would've sent the best brand in stock."

Thinking about her two dear friends, Leanna's eyes dampened with tears. "They are so sweet. I'm going to miss them."

"So will I," Jeff realized. "Those men have been with me for a long time."

Going to her handsome husband, Leanna turned her back to him as she suggested, "If you'll unbutton me, I'll take off my gown. Then while you pour the brandy, I'll slip into something very seductive and revealing."

"Seductive and revealing?" he repeated with anticipation.

"Jennifer loaned me a very pretty dressing gown. If you'll remember, except for what I had packed in my reticule, all my clothes were destroyed in the fire."

Jeff grimaced, recalling again that he had been the one who had ordered The Pines burned. Finishing with the tiny buttons, he promised, "When we get to St. Louis, I'll take you on a shopping spree. You will be the best-dressed lady in town."

Although Leanna knew material possessions couldn't bring happiness, the thought of a new wardrobe thrilled her, and walking to the closet, she said gaily, "I can hardly wait. It's been so long since I had new clothes." Stopping and facing Jeff, she continued, "There is no privacy in this room, so I want you to turn your back and remain that way until I tell you otherwise."

Cocking an eyebrow, he answered with a wry smile, "I'm not to be allowed to watch my wife undress?"

"Not tonight," she objected. "I don't want you to see me until I'm out of this wedding dress and into my negligee."

"You will be a vision of loveliness. But I find you most beautiful when you are wearing nothing at all."

"Jeff, turn around," she said sternly. "Flattery will not change my mind."

Complying, he did as she asked, and while Leanna readied herself, Jeff opened the bottle of brandy. He filled the two glasses, then waited impatiently for Leanna to finish.

"Jeff?" she called softly.

He turned, and seeing Leanna in a pink satin peignoir that seductively shadowed her feminine contours, he was struck speechless. Finding his voice, he whispered huskily, "Mrs. Clayton, you're more beautiful than words can express."

Leanna twirled gracefully, and the voluminous folds of the peignoir flared about her. "Oh Jeff!" she cried, her voice as excited as a young girl's. "It's so marvelous to wear lovely clothes again! First my mother's wedding dress and now this splendid negligee!"

Drawing her into his arms, he reminded her, "Soon you'll have all the fine clothes you could possibly want." Suddenly, he held her against him in an embrace so strong it was almost painful. "Leanna, I promise you that I'll make up for everything you lost. I don't know how I'll do it, but I'll find a way!"

Leanna had to use pressure to free herself from his firm hold. Looking up into his face, she asked confusedly, "Jeff, what do you mean? You talk as if you were to blame for my destitution."

"Indirectly, I was to blame," he uttered.

Putting her arms about his neck, she told him firmly, "I refuse to listen to such nonsense." Her mouth sought his with a fierce passion, and as Jeff brought her

505

yielding body ever closer, all his thoughts of the past were quickly forgotten.

He began removing her peignoir and Leanna reminded him, "But, Jeff, what about the brandy?"

"We'll drink it later," he murmured. Her gown dropped about her feet, and lifting her, he carried her to the bed where he gently laid her down. Anxiously, he removed his boots and uniform, and dropping his clothes on the floor in a disorderly heap, he entered Leanna's embrace.

"I love you, Mrs. Clayton," he uttered thickly, before relishing her mouth with his lips.

"Jeff, my darling," she murmured happily. "I can hardly believe that we're actually married."

"Believe it, Leanna," he whispered, his hand traveling familiarly over the lovely body he knew so well and loved so passionately.

Her entire being on fire with her need for him, Leanna pleaded desperately, "Darling, make me truly your wife."

"Ah yes, sweetheart," he groaned hoarsely, as his body covered hers.

She opened her legs, and when Jeff's manhood plunged deeply into her warm depths, she cried ecstatically, "Oh, my husband, I love you so much!"

Gathering his bride into his strong embrace, Jeff took her with him to love's wondrous paradise.

Walking between her two escorts, Jerry and Paul, Leanna crossed the fort's compound. She was on her way back to the hotel from Jeff's office, where he had informed her that Colonel Wallace had received a wire from Fort Casper. The expected troops were on their way to Fort Laramie. Soon now, she and Jeff would start their journey back to the states. Leanna was especially elated about leaving because Jeff had promised her that before going to St. Louis, they'd travel to Marietta and find Jackson and his family. Jeff planned to offer Jackson and Matilda employment in his home in St. Louis, and Leanna hoped desperately that the couple would accept.

The sudden pounding of a horse's hoofs caused Leanna and her two escorts to pause and look toward the fort's gate. Seeing Nathan entering the compound at a fairly fast speed, Leanna was puzzled as to why he was in such a hurry. She knew he had left the fort the morning after her wedding, saying he wouldn't be back for at least two weeks. She wondered why he had returned so soon.

Catching sight of Leanna, Nathan rode over to her, reining in his mount so roughly that loose dirt swirled through the air. Dismounting from the fatigued horse and dropping the reins hastily, Nathan stepped to Leanna and demanded, "Where is the wagon train? It wasn't supposed to leave until tomorrow."

"The wagon master decided to leave a day early," she explained. Had Nathan returned hoping to find Audrey? Knowing how much Audrey loved him, Leanna crossed her fingers behind her back and pleaded silently. Let it be true . . . please, let it be true!

"Did the Farnsworths leave with it?"

"Yes, they did," she replied.

"When?" he questioned.

"A couple of hours ago."

"Leanna, would you please find the chaplain and tell him that this afternoon I'll need him to perform a

507

marriage ceremony?"

Smiling happily, she answered, "I'll be only too glad to tell him."

Looking at Jerry, Nathan ordered briskly, "Trooper Rogan, saddle me a fresh horse! I have a wagon train to catch!"

Feeling depressed, Audrey walked beside the covered wagon, trying not to think that each step was taking her farther away from Nathan Hayden. Should she dare hope he might come to San Francisco to search for her? No! Audrey told herself angrily. I must not allow myself to wish for something that will never come about. I lost him, and although losing him is breaking my heart, I must take my own advice: pick up the pieces of my life and start over. But, Nathan . . . Nathan, I love you so much, and it's going to take a long, long time before I can get over you!

Audrey heard a horse galloping in her direction, but thinking it was one of the men on the wagon train, she didn't bother to turn around to see who was approaching. As the horse's hoofs drew near enough for her to actually feel them vibrating the ground beneath her feet, she whirled. She turned just in time to catch a quick glimpse of a horse and his rider so close to her that she could reach out and touch them. The man's strong arm encircled her waist, lifting her off her feet and onto the front of his saddle.

"Nathan!" she cried joyfully as he pulled up his horse.

Looking out the back of the wagon, Bradley had seen the scout from Fort Laramie sweep Audrey onto his horse, and he called excitedly, "Stop the wagon, David!

Stop the wagon!"

Sitting on the seat beside Jennifer, David brought the mule team to a halt, and he and Jennifer glanced back to see why Bradley had yelled. Seeing his sister mounted on a horse with Nathan Hayden, David started to leap down, but Jennifer grasped his arm. "Let them be," she said.

"Wh . . . what's going on?" David sputtered.

Smiling romantically, Jennifer replied, "I don't think Audrey will be moving to San Francisco with us."

"Of course she will!"

"She's in love with Nathan Hayden, and it looks as though he also loves her."

"What!" David barked incredulously. "Why doesn't anyone ever bother to tell me what's happening with my own family? Audrey's in love with the Fort Laramie scout, you knew this, and you didn't tell me?"

Scooting to the far side of the seat so that she could better see Audrey and Nathan, Jennifer fussed, "David, hush! I want to hear what he's telling her."

"Audrey," Nathan was explaining, as he and Audrey sat his horse, "everything you said to me the other day was true. These last couple of days, I've given my life serious thought. Alone, in the wilderness, I had a lot of time to think. You were right, I've been running away because I'm afraid to love again." Looking deep into her eyes, he continued sincerely, "And I'm still afraid, but, honey, I can't let you disappear from my life. I need you, Audrey."

"Do you love me, Nathan?" she asked intensely.

Pulling her against his wide chest, he held her tightly as he confessed, "Yes, I love you. Maybe I'll always be afraid of losing you. I don't know, I only know that I

509

can't let you go. Will you marry me, Audrey? Will you return to Fort Laramie with me and be my wife?"

"Oh yes, Nathan," she sighed happily before lifting her face to his so that he could kiss her to seal the beginning of their life together.

Becoming aware that Audrey's brother had stopped his wagon and the others on the train were passing it by, Nathan guided his horse over to Jennifer and David.

"Mr. Farnsworth, I apologize for holding you up and causing you to lose your place in line. I won't detain you any longer. I'm taking your sister back to Fort Laramie. She has agreed to be my wife, and we'll be married this afternoon."

Staring at Nathan with disbelief, David objected, "Mr. Hayden, I can't possibly agree to this marriage. It's nothing personal, sir, but I must insist that you pay proper court to my sister before—"

Interrupting, Jennifer scoffed, "David, don't talk such foolishness. How can he court Audrey when she's in San Francisco and he's at Fort Laramie?"

David had a distinct feeling that he was about to lose his sister to Nathan Hayden; just the same, he mumbled, "Well, they could write to each other."

"I don't aim to sleep with letters, I intend to sleep with my wife," Nathan told him inflexibly. Looking at Jennifer, he continued, "Mrs. Farnsworth, when you reach the next military post, leave Audrey's belongings with the army, and I'll have her things sent to Fort Laramie."

"But what will she do for clothes until then?" Jennifer queried practically.

"I'll buy her some more at the Traders' Store," Nathan explained. To Audrey, he whispered secretly, "But I plan for us to spend most of our time in bed, where you certainly won't be needing clothes." Audrey responded by taking his hand into hers and squeezing it agreeably.

Exercising his right as Audrey's older brother, and guardian, David opposed him. "Mr. Hayden, you are taking too much for granted. I have not given my permission —"

This time it was Audrey who intruded, "David, I love Nathan. Please try to understand and give me your blessings."

"Of course you have David's blessings," Jennifer answered for him. "And you also have mine."

"David?" Audrey pleaded, wanting her brother's approval.

"But, Audrey . . ." he stammered, his protest fading on his lips. After a slight pause, he proceeded tenderly. "Honey, I hope you'll be happy. And as soon as we're settled in San Francisco, we'll write to you." Standing, he offered Nathan his hand. "Take good care of my sister."

Accepting the handshake, Nathan promised to protect and love Audrey who quickly said her goodbyes to her family.

As David whipped the mule team, and the wagon wheels once again began to roll, Jennifer remained on the far side of the seat so she could watch Audrey and Nathan ride back toward Fort Laramie. When they had finally ridden out of sight, she moved closer to her husband. Holding his hand, she pressed it reassuringly. "Don't worry, darling. Audrey will be happy." Sighing dreamily, she murmured, "It was so romantic the way Nathan Hayden came riding after her. It's quite apparent that he loves her a great deal."

511

"Jennifer, you're a hopeless romantic," David replied with a half-smile.

"Yes, I know," she agreed. "But you made me a romantic."

"I did?" he asked, pleased.

"I never knew love's passion until the night you came into my bedroom in the overseer's house and seduced me." Placing her other hand on his arm, Jennifer's face glowed as she gazed into his hazel eyes. "Oh, David, don't you see? If I didn't love you so much, I wouldn't be a romantic!"

Still adoring the woman he had loved since he'd been a young man of seventeen, David bent his head and pressed his lips against Jennifer's.

Epilogue

Return To The Pines

Impatient for Jeff to return, Leanna paced her hotel room. She and Jeff had now been in Marietta for over a week, but to Leanna's dismay, they had been unable to locate Jackson. Jeff had left this morning, telling Leanna that he would once again make inquiries in the town to see if he could find a lead to Jackson's whereabouts. Extremely worried about Jackson and his family, Leanna had insisted that this time Jeff let her accompany him, but he had firmly refused. Although she had pleaded with him, he had remained adamant. But Leanna's mind was made up, and if, today, Jeff failed in his mission, tomorrow she'd search for Jackson herself.

The door opened, and Leanna watched Jeff expectantly as he entered the room. She was anxious to know whether he had heard any news concerning Jackson, nonetheless, she took time to admire her husband. Jeff had always been very dashing in his uniform, but he was just as handsome as a civilian. His well-tailored jacket was made of white linen, and he wore it over a dark brown shirt, which he had left unbuttoned at the neck. His fawn-colored trousers fit snugly across his slim hips and down his long, muscular legs.

Hurrying to his side, Leanna asked with bated breath, "Any news about Jackson?"

Shaking his head, Jeff mumbled, "No, I'm sorry."

"Oh Jeff!" she cried disconsolately. "Where could he and Matilda be? I'm so afraid we'll never find them!"

"Leanna, I rented a carriage. I thought you might like to take a ride in the country. It'll help take your mind off your worries."

An outing sounded marvelous to Leanna. Since they had arrived in Marietta, Jeff had barely allowed her out of the hotel. He had taken her shopping a couple of times, and once they had taken an evening stroll. But each time she ventured outside, Jeff had stayed close to her side and had refused to let her ask anyone about Jackson.

"A buggy ride is a wonderful idea," Leanna remarked, her spirits lifting.

"I stopped at the hotel dining room and ordered a picnic basket. Once we're in the country, we'll find a good place to stop and enjoy a leisurely lunch."

Studying her, Jeff suddenly smiled secretively, and noting his subtle grin, she asked, "What are you thinking about?"

Drawing her into his arms, and still smiling, he replied, "I was remembering you the way you were when I first saw you. Today, I'm feeling very nostalgic."

Leanna giggled, recalling, "I was quite a sight then

day. Not only was I shamefully barefooted, but I was wearing cut-off trousers, a sloppy shirt, and Jackson's old fishing hat."

"But you were beautiful," Jeff put in. "In spite of your bedraggled appearance and dirty face."

Leanna laughed, and hugging him close, she replied, "When you very calmly informed me that my face was dirty, I thought I would die of embarrassment."

Chuckling, Jeff told her happily, "My little rebel spy, I love you." His lips sought hers, and sliding her arms about his neck Leanna returned his kiss.

When Leanna entered the buggy, she noticed a long rolled-up piece of paper on the floorboards. Curious, she asked Jeff about it. He told her that it wasn't anything important and he'd explain later. Believing him, she quickly dismissed it from her mind, never imagining that it had anything to do with The Pines.

As Jeff drove the carriage out of Marietta and headed south, Leanna did not connect the southerly direction to her former plantation. She just naturally presumed that Jeff was taking this particular route because he would be familiar with the countryside.

It wasn't until after their picnic, when Jeff didn't turn the buggy back toward town, but continued traveling southward that Leanna realized where he was headed. She couldn't understand why Jeff was taking her to the plantation. Before arriving in Marietta, she had made it perfectly clear to him that she did not want to visit her former home. Even though her parents were buried in the Weston cemetery and she knew, out of respect, she should visit their graves, she still couldn't bear the thought of seeing her beloved home in the hands of strangers.

"Jeff, please turn the buggy around!" she pleaded, her voice tinged with desperation.

"I told you at the hotel that I'm feeling very nostalgic. I think a visit to The Pines would be pleasant."

"The home called The Pines no longer exists, and the land has probably been taken over by weeds and brambles. There's nothing left to see!"

Cocking an eyebrow, Jeff smiled slyly, "We won't know that until we get there, will we?"

Grasping his arm, she cried piteously, "Jeff, why are you doing this to me? I don't want to see my land! Seeing it again will only break my heart!"

Placing his hand over hers, he replied gently, "Sweetheart, be patient with me. I don't often get attacks of nostalgia."

"But, Jeff—" she began.

"No buts," he broke in firmly. "Just pamper me, will you?"

She nodded reluctantly. She loved Jeff and would do anything to please him, but she wondered if he had any inkling how much he was asking of her.

Leanna retreated into silence, and Jeff didn't try to draw her into conversation. Sitting rigidly, she said nothing as Jeff turned the carriage onto the winding lane that had once led up to the six-columned mansion. Leanna was surprised to see that the burned ruins had not been cleared away. Apparently, the new owner was not overly anxious to clean up the rubbish. As she had guessed, the property was overrun with weeds and the land was desolate, although the tall pine trees were still abundant. Looking about, she saw that the slave cabins and the overseer's house was still standing.

Jeff stopped the buggy at the crumpling steps in front of the charred remains of the former mansion. Stepping down to the ground, he reached for Leanna's hand, and hesitantly, she accepted his assistance.

Standing beside the carriage, she studied the ruins of the elegant home that had once so proudly overlooked acres upon acres of budding cotton. Three chimneys were still partially intact. Their brick flues, looming upward, appeared portentous by comparison to the scattered remains that lay below them.

"I wonder who owns my property," Leanna mumbled vaguely.

"We do," Jeff announced calmly.

Looking at him wide-eyed, she gasped, "What did you say?"

Smiling broadly, he repeated, "We own this property."

Her excitement overflowing, Leanna stammered incoherently, "You mean . . . it belongs . . . We own . . . This land is ours!"

He laughed joyously, before explaining, "The day after we arrived in Marietta, I checked on this property and learned it hadn't been purchased. But even if it had, that would not have deterred me. I was willing to offer the owner such an outlandish price that he'd have been only too glad to sell. I would've told you about all this sooner, but I wanted to wait until everything was final and official."

"You bought my home?" she gasped, her mouth agape.

"We . . . bought your home," he specified. "I paid the back taxes and now this land belongs to Mr. and Mrs. Jeff Clayton."

Flinging herself into his arms, she cried, "Oh thank you, Jeff . . . thank you!"

Releasing her gently, he reached into the buggy to withdraw the rolled-up paper. Showing it to her, he asked, "Do you have any idea what this is?"

"No. Should I?" she questioned.

His deep voice filled with excitement, he revealed, "This, my dear, is The Pines. It seems your father's lawyer had the drawings of the interior and exterior of the house. From this detailed diagram, I intend to have a perfect replica of The Pines built." His face suddenly sober, he continued, "Sweetheart, I can't give you back your original home, it's gone forever. To build you a reproduction is the best I can do."

Shading her eyes with her hands to block out the glaring sun, Leanna's gaze followed the heights of the towering chimneys. "Jeff," she asked, "will these chimneys have to be torn down?"

"I imagine they could be strengthened and reused," he replied. "They don't appear to be in bad condition."

Turning to Jeff, Leanna's eyes sparkled. "If these chimneys can remain, then, Jeff, our new home will truly be a part of The Pines!" She whirled, and looking at the ruins, she envisioned the home that would be as grand as its namesakes. "When did you plan all this?" she asked, facing him.

"It didn't occur to me until a few days after we left Fort Laramie; then I was bound and determined to make it work, one way or another."

Once again, she threw herself into his arms, and with tears of joy streaming down her cheeks, she sobbed, "Oh Jeff, I couldn't possibly be happier than I am at this very moment!"

"I wouldn't be so sure about that," Jeff told her as he tenderly relinquished her. "I think it's quite possible for you to be even happier." Placing his hands on her shoulders, he turned her in the direction of the overseer's house.

The sight of Jackson, Matilda, and Louise walking toward them caused Leanna's tears to flow even stronger.

"I also found Jackson the day after we came to Marietta. He was out of work, and Matilda was taking in washing. Because they were living under very poor conditions, I brought them out here to the overseer's house. I wanted you to be reunited with Jackson and his family on the same day your home was returned to you. That's why I've tried to keep you in our hotel room. I was afraid that somehow you might find out about everything."

Jackson and his family drew closer, and raising their hands, they waved to Leanna, welcoming her with large smiles on their faces.

Lifting her hem so she could move more freely, Leanna ran to greet them. First she hugged Matilda, then Louise, who was no longer a child but a lovely young girl blooming into womanhood. When she turned to Jackson, and she was surprised to see a trace of tears in his eyes.

"Miz Anna, welcome home!" he said, emotion causing his voice to quiver.

Leanna wiped at her own tears, but to no avail; she

was crying so hard that a solid stream rolled down her cheeks. "Jackson," she whispered, her chin trembling. She had so much she wanted to say to him, but her feelings were so great that her voice faltered and gave way to uncontrollable, but happy, sobs.

Jackson took a tentative step toward Leanna, uncertain if he should offer her his embrace. Leanna understood his hesitation, and going to him, she placed herself in his gentle arms.

It was dark before Leanna and Jeff decided to head back to Marietta. Excited about the future, Jeff had spent the entire afternoon making plans. In a couple of days, he and Leanna would leave for St. Louis, where they'd visit Walter Clayton. Real estate and construction were once again Jeff's livelihood, and he planned to send one of his crews from St. Louis to Marietta to build the replica of The Pines. If the sawmills around Atlanta couldn't handle the supply of lumber, then he'd have it delivered from St. Louis. Knowing he could trust his own crew, Jeff decided he would take Leanna on an extended honeymoon in Europe while their home was being built. During their trip, they would shop in England and France for imported pieces of furniture and for accessories for their new home. Jackson and his family would continue to reside in the overseer's house, with Jackson now employed as a groundskeeper. Upon Jeff's and Leanna's return, Jackson would become the butler in the new house and Matilda the cook.

"Jeff," Leanna began as the carriage rolled slowly down the road to Marietta, "how do you intend to make a living when we move back here?"

"There will still be a lot of freed slaves needing employment. I'll offer them substantial wages, and with their labor, the Weston land will once again be prosperous."

"You're going to be a planter!" Leanna exclaimed.

"Partly," he answered. "I also intend to open a real estate and construction business in Atlanta. Sherman destroyed a lot of the city, so it will have to be rebuilt and expanded. While we're in Europe, I'll have one of my lawyers in St. Louis travel to Atlanta and buy up property."

"One . . . of your lawyers?" she questioned, amazed.

"My uncle and I employ a whole firm."

"Why do I get the feeling that I have yet to fully grasp how wealthy you are?"

"How wealthy we are," he declared.

As an idea occurred to Leanna, she said with growing excitement, "Jeff, let's ask David and Jennifer to come home."

"Come home?" he pondered. "But they just moved to San Francisco."

"Yes, I know," she replied hastily. "But, darling, they never really wanted to leave there. We all left because we had no other choice. Jeff, if you're going to be a planter, then you'll need a man with experience to run your plantation. Also, you must realize that in this part of the country most people are still very hostile toward Yankees, and it would be to your advantage to have a respected Southerner as a partner."

"A Southerner like David Farnsworth," he concluded.

"I'll write to Jennifer and tell her that as soon as we return from Europe, we'll send for them. Jackson and Matilda will be living in the servants' quarters in the new house, so David and Jennifer can move into the overseer's house."

Smiling, Jeff replied, "If David and Jennifer agree, it's perfectly all right with me."

"Oh, they'll agree," Leanna said definitely. "They are Georgians, and Georgia is where they want to live."

Continuing his plans for their future, Jeff said, "I also want to raise thoroughbred horses, which means I'll need to hire a couple of men who know how to take proper care of them."

"I know just the men!" Leanna exclaimed.

"A couple of your father's ex-slaves?" he asked.

"No, I was thinking of Jerry and Paul," she announced.

Snapping his fingers, he replied, "You're right. They'd be ideal for the job. And I'm sure they'll accept my offer."

"Except for Audrey and Nathan, I'll have all my friends and family with me once again," she declared happily.

Jeff chuckled. "Well, who knows, maybe we can think of a way to convince Nathan to leave his wilderness and return to civilization."

He pulled up the carriage and Leanna asked, "Why are we stopping?"

"I told you, sweetheart, I'm in a nostalgic mood. Do you recognize this place?"

Although night had descended, the full moon illuminated her surroundings, and looking about

524

Leanna answered, "Of course, I do. After I overheard General Sherman's military tactics, I slipped out of my bedroom to ride to Marietta, and this is the place where you caught up to me."

Holding her hand, he helped her down from the buggy. Slipping out of his linen jacket, Jeff placed it on the carriage seat. Then taking the blanket they had used on their picnic, he led Leanna off the main road. As they strolled hand in hand, Jeff reminisced, "You threw dirt into my face, then took off, running." He waited until they had reached a specific place before continuing, "I chased after you, and this is the spot where I finally caught you."

As he spread out the blanket, Leanna said pertly, "Caught me? Don't you mean you tackled me?"

Smiling, he once again took her hand in his. They stood side by side, and looked dreamily down at the blanket, both of them remembering the night they had found each other in wonderful, reckless passion.

Moving her gaze to her husband's face, Leanna studied him with adoration. Slowly Jeff turned and his eyes met hers.

"I love you, Mrs. Clayton," he whispered, his voice deep with longing.

Sharing his thoughts, and feeling an urgent need for him, Leanna murmured throatily, "I love you, Mr. Clayton." Undoing the miniature buttons on the front of her dress, she smiled invitingly, "Darling, suddenly I am also feeling very nostalgic."

Jeff had never desired her more than he did at that moment. His hands trembled slightly as he helped her undress and let her gown fall to the blanket. He took her in his arms, and his lips came down on hers with demanding force. Gently, he released her, and she lowered herself onto the spread blanket. Because they were outdoors, Leanna decided not to remove her petticoat, but reaching up beneath her undergarment, she slipped her lace panties past her soft thighs and down her slender legs.

Kneeling beside her, Jeff undid his trousers, releasing his throbbing manhood. Then easing Leanna down onto the blanket, he moved over her. He raised her petticoat, and his arousal found her womanhood, penetrating her swiftly. Her heat encircled him, and her legs went about his back, pressing him ever farther inside her.

Sliding his hands beneath her hips, he pulled her thighs up to his. Clinging tightly, they came to each other time and time again, until their passion rose to its crescendo.

Lying at her side, Jeff took Leanna into his arms, and she nestled her head on his shoulder. Grinning wryly, he commented, "I like it when you're feeling nostalgic."

Once again, Leanna's thoughts turned to the night she'd tried to flee to Marietta and Jeff had stopped her. Remembering the reckless passion they'd shared, she knew that she would always be sentimental about this particular place, and struck by a sudden idea, she sat up abruptly. Smiling contemplatively, she asked a little breathlessly, "I wonder if this land is for sale?"

"Why?" he asked.

"It would be nice to own it, because in a special way, I'll always feel as though it belongs to us."

"Well, it isn't for sale," he told her.

"How do you know?" she inquired, surprised.

"I just happen to know," he answered calmly and uninformatively.

"Do you have any idea who owns it?"

"Yes, I do," he said evasively.

"Who?" she asked, but detecting a certain twinkle in his eyes, she suddenly knew the answer.

"It belongs to Mr. and Mrs. Jeff Clayton," he replied. "And I know for a fact that they will never sell it."

"Jeff, did you really? . . ."

"Yes, I really did buy it. Besides it borders on your plantation."

Leanna's voice rang with gaiety as she exclaimed, "Jeff Clayton, because of you I'm so happy that I feel like shouting!"

"Then why don't you?" he coaxed, smiling broadly. "After all, you're on your own property."

RAPTUROUS ROMANCE
by Wanda Owen